# THE COLOR OF MURDER

*A Veronica Shade Thriller*

## Book 1

## Patrick Logan

For my dad.
You continue to inspire creativity even
after you're gone.

# Prologue

A HAND SLID OVER LUCY Davis' mouth and her eyes snapped open. She tried to scream but couldn't generate a single sound.

That's when she saw him.

Her father.

Like her, Trevor Davis' eyes were also wide, and as she watched, he brought the index finger of his free hand to his lips, indicating for her to be quiet.

She opened her mouth to answer, but he squeezed his hand against her lips even tighter. Lucy nodded instead.

Apparently satisfied, he finally released his hold on her and pulled back her blankets. As Lucy swung her legs over the side of the bed, she looked toward the window, wondering if she'd somehow slept in, or if she was going to be late for school. But then why did she have to be quiet? Was mommy sick?

The curtain was closed, but they were a light color, and if it had been early in the morning, the sun would have shone right through them.

Her mind began to race.

Was this a game? Her father playing a silly trick on her?

Trevor, or Papa to Lucy and her brother Benny, was always playing games. One time, he'd pretended to cut his finger while chopping onions, squirting ketchup all over the place. Lucy and Benny had screamed, and their mother had nearly fainted. On Lucy's fourth birthday, he'd treated her, and just her, to a special ice cream dessert—his homemade creation: strawberries and whipped cream. She'd looked at her father, looked at his bright eyes, just before taking her first bite.

She should have stopped then. Seeing that look, that half-smile—even four-year-old Lucy should have known to stop and listen to her gut. But, in this case, even if she had, her gut was telling her to eat.

One bite and she desperately reached for a glass of water. Her father had slipped some hot peppers into her dessert, disguising them as strawberries. Mom was angry, called him cruel, but Papa just laughed. He never meant any harm and was always a good sport when it came to pranking him. And if Lucy paid attention, close attention, she could pick up the signs that something wasn't quite as it seemed. Her dad's eyes were always big and sparkling, his mouth not quite a straight line but not a full smile, either.

Now, with her back against the wall and Papa's hand gently holding her back as he peered out the crack in the door, she saw no twinkle in his eyes.

And he definitely wasn't smiling.

He was breathing fast, however, as if he'd just gotten back from a run. But that didn't make sense. Papa was wearing his pajamas and it was still dark out.

Forgetting Papa's warning not to speak, she opened her mouth to ask him what was going on.

But Lucy didn't say anything—she stopped when her brother's voice reached her.

"Papa? Papa!" it wasn't a scream, but close. A pained whine.

Lucy instinctively started to move, but her father shoved her backward so hard that she nearly fell.

"Papa!" and now it was a scream. Papa peered out the door one final time then turned to face her.

"Run," he whispered, looking directly into her eyes. "Run downstairs and out the door. Just keep going—run to... the

Johnsons. Or the Whitneys. Just knock until they answer. Whatever you do, Lucy, don't look back. Just *run.*"

If she was scared before, Lucy was absolutely terrified now.

Once more, Lucy started to speak but her father grabbed her shoulders and squeezed hard.

"I'm going to open this door and you *run.*"

He gave her no chance to ask questions — Papa just released her and pulled the door all the way open.

"*Run!*"

Lucy bolted from her bedroom, going straight to the stairs.

"Papa! *Help!*"

She wanted to listen to Papa, to keep going. But her brother...

Lucy didn't stop, but she did glance over her shoulder.

And what she saw, didn't make sense. Benny was fighting with a shadow. He was punching and kicking a dark figure that was holding him by the waist. Then the shadow slapped a piece of gray duct tape over her brother's mouth and his shouts became muffled cries.

It wasn't a shadow, but a man wearing dark clothes.

"Run! Lucy, Run!"

But she couldn't. She couldn't do anything except stand there, frozen, staring at the stranger who was holding Benny.

"Lucy!"

There was a flurry of movement from behind her and then Papa was suddenly scooping her up in his arms.

Lucy had a moment to register that she was being carried just like her brother, and then they were flying down the stairs. Angling her head and neck, she could still see Benny, his mouth covered, tears soaking his cheeks and the duct tape.

They made it to the bottom of the stairs and were nearly at the front door when panic gripped her.

They were leaving—Papa was taking her out of the house and Benny was being attacked. And Mommy? Where's Mommy?

*We can't leave… we can't.*

"Papa?"

They were within ten feet of the door when something happened. Papa tripped. He grunted and it was all he could do to not land on top of Lucy as he crumpled to the ground. As it was, the air was knocked out of Lucy when her backside and then upper back struck the cold tile floor.

"Papa! Get up!"

But he wasn't getting up. And he hadn't tripped either.

She knew this the second someone grabbed her around the waist and wrenched her off the floor. Someone had hit Papa, hit him hard enough to make him go to sleep, just like in the movies. Hard enough to make blood pool around his head.

*Wait, maybe this is a game,* she thought. *Maybe that's just ketchup.*

But deep down, Lucy knew that this wasn't the case.

As tape was roughly slapped across her mouth and, like Benny, she started to kick, scratch, claw, do anything and everything to try and escape, she knew that this was anything but a game.

# PART ONE:
# A SONG

## Chapter 1

"WHAT IF—" DETECTIVE VERONICA SHADE began, but as she knew he would, her partner quickly interrupted.

"I hate *what ifs*, Veronica, you know that."

"I know, I know, but hear me out, Freddie."

Detective Fred Furlow grunted in disapproval. In addition to despising *what-if* games, Veronica's partner also hated being called Freddie, which was precisely why she insisted on doing both.

"What if you *had* to run? I mean, you absolutely *had* to." Veronica paused as she tried to come up with the right motivation for the big man. During this interval, Freddie grabbed a hand full of fries and jammed them into his mouth. "You're being chased," Veronica finally settled on. "A demon, or something, is after you. If you don't run, it's all over."

"Demon?" Freddie asked, eyebrows raised.

"Whatever—proctologist, then. The point is you *have* to run."

"I'm fifty-eight—many people have died younger than that. Better people than me," Freddie said nonchalantly as he chewed his fries.

"Okay, okay," Veronica said impatiently. "Fine, you're not being chased. You're running towards something. You're running towards—" she scanned the interior of Freddie's car. It was filthy, of course. The police radio embedded in the dash glistened with greasy fingerprints — the volume dial in particular was nearly translucent. The seemingly never-ending carton of fries — supersize? Yes, please — from which Freddie ate was wedged between the gearshift and the coin tray. A large Coke jutted from the cupholder closest to the driver's seat, while Veronica's held a Styrofoam cup of black coffee. Her side of the car was clean-*ish*. This hadn't been the case less than six months ago when they'd first been teamed up. Veronica had had to wade through the fast-food refuse to just find a comfortable place for her feet. To his credit, this had only lasted a day or two. Noticing her displeasure, and perhaps disgust, Freddie had promptly tidied the passenger seat. But with every winner, there was an inevitable loser. In this case: the backseat. It was littered with bags, candy wrappers, old cups, and soda cans — if a product contained some sort of hydrogenated oil or refined sugar, most likely a combination of both, then its sheath was present in the diabetes-inducing mausoleum that was the Sebring's backseat. Detective Freddie Furlow might have been a fifty-eight-year-old man, but he had the diet of a college kid living on trust funds who played video games all day, every day. The only thing the car was missing, was a thin layer of Cheetos dust, and that was only because the big man was allergic. "I've got it, I've got it," Veronica continued, snapping her fingers. "You're running towards your favorite fast-food joint — McDonald's—" she paused and shook her head. "No, *Wendy's*. And if you don't get to Wendy's in thirty seconds, you can never eat there again. It closes its doors forever. That's it, no more Wendy's."

"That's stupid." Freddie swallowed the bolus of French fries.

"I know, this whole thing is stupid. But humor me."

To his credit, Freddie appeared to contemplate Veronica's asinine scenario. Eventually, however, he shook his head.

"Forget it, Wendy's is good, but so is McDonald's, Burger King, and Carl's Jr. No, I'm not running for Wendy's."

Veronica looked skyward for inspiration.

"The Yankees then. You *love* the Yankees. And—and they have a giveaway. Yeah, the first person there, gets to meet the team, in their dressing room. Would you run for that?"

"I love the Yankees, but I'm no fan boy."

Veronica finally gave up.

"One of these days, I'm gonna find something that you'll run for." She gestured towards his massive gut that wrestled against both the buttons on his XXL shirt and the seatbelt. "And you're not going to be able to do it because you eat that shit every day."

To show his disdain, Freddie grabbed an immensely large quantity of fries and gnashed them obnoxiously.

"Why," he began, spraying the steering wheel with flecks of fries, "would *I* need to run? You think that this partnership was an accident? No—it was by design. You're here to do the running, rookie. But I'll tell you what, Veronica, if there's ever any sort of famine, I'll do whatever you do during a famine."

This made no sense, but Veronica, good-natured as her ribbing was, had pushed the man quite hard this afternoon, and she let the comment go without challenge.

"Now, can we please focus on this case?" Freddie asked.

Veronica, a smirk creeping onto her lips, finally relented. She brushed salt from her lap, and then reached into her pocket and pulled out her cell phone.

"Maggie Cernak, twenty-seven," she said, reading the text message out loud. "Found two hours ago hanging from the rafters of her neighbor's barn. Apparent suicide."

"Barn?" Freddie asked as he wiped the grease from his hands on a beige napkin, before balling it up and tossing it into the backseat.

Veronica knew what the man was getting at. Farms were a dime a dozen in Oregon, but not so much in the City of Greenham, the second most populous city in the state. The city they were employed by.

"The barn's not in Greenham, it's in Matheson."

Both of Freddie's dark eyebrows migrated up his forehead.

"Go on."

Veronica chuckled. Freddie was well over three-hundred pounds, and for some reason, the extra meat on his cheeks, chin, and neck, the boundaries of which were significantly blurred, added a level of comedy to common facial expressions. It was disarming, to say the least.

"Yeah, it's Bear County jurisdiction," she confirmed.

"Foul play?"

"Not based on the text I received while you were loading up at McDonald's."

"*Uhhh…* Veronica, is this another of your *what-if* scenarios? What if Maggie whatever-her-name-is was murdered? Why are we going to a Bear County crime scene? For a suicide, no less?"

"Because get this: the man who owns the barn?"

"Yeah?"

"Well, he just happens to be the newly elected sheriff."

"*Ohhhhh,*" Freddie said, drawing out the word and cocking his head to one side.

Veronica laughed again.

"You ever met him? Sheriff—" Veronica looked down at her phone again, searching for the name of the person who had sent the text. "Steve Burns?"

Freddie shook his head and then started the car.

"Nope. All I know is that he used to be high up in the State Police before coming to Bear County."

"A Statie, huh," Veronica mused.

The City of Greenham was part of Bear County, which also included Matheson, Sullivan, and East Argham, as well as dozens of unincorporated areas, the Hilltona Forest, and the Casnet River. But business in Greenham was usually taken care of by the local PD. Even though Veronica hadn't as of yet been involved in a case that required the collaboration or cooperation of the sheriff's Department, she was, as Freddie never failed to point out, a rookie. She had heard of crimes that required multiple departments to work together—usually when places with a third or less of Greenham's 100,000 population, like Sullivan and East Argham, were running low on resources. Generally, cities, and counties, liked to keep things simple and in-house.

They were heading East and had already left the City of Greenham's borders. The drab gray apartment buildings for which Greenham was infamous, were gone, replaced by immature corn stalks and yellow wheat fields. As March bled into April, the corn would quickly outgrow the wheat, making visibility from the road a problem. But for now, at least, Veronica could see for miles in almost every direction.

"Probably wants a second set of eyes," Freddie offered, breaking the silence. "Just to be sure—conflict of interest and all that."

Veronica shrugged.

She didn't mind getting out of Greenham. It was one of those places that, while it had its unique charm, exuded a staleness that became oppressing over time. Veronica was in no way in love with the city that signed her paychecks. She'd just never grown attached to it.

Fifteen minutes later, she spotted a typical middle-American two-story house—which she noted, wasn't quite in Matheson, but on the outskirts. It had a pretty wraparound porch, with an obligatory American flag hanging over the door. Roughly twenty yards to the left of the home was the barn. The massive wooden doors were open wide, but her view of the interior was blocked by two sheriff vehicles and a black, CSU cube van.

Freddie turned down the long dirt laneway, and then parked a respectable distance from the crime scene just in case they determined that this wasn't a suicide and evidence needed to be preserved. Veronica put her phone away and quickly got out of the vehicle, grateful to fill her nostrils and lungs with fresh air instead of aerosolized saturated fats. She adjusted her slacks and her blouse, and then strode with determination toward the man with a wide-brimmed hat who stepped from the barn. She'd taken a dozen or more strides before realizing that Freddie wasn't beside her.

She looked over her shoulder, saw the man struggling to hoist his girth out of the car, and grinned.

"You... you want to run for this, Freddie?"

# Chapter 2

SHERIFF STEVE BURNS WAS YOUNGER than Veronica expected. As she approached, she put him in his mid-forties, but then he tipped the brim of his hat up, and she saw young eyes flanked by only a smattering of crow's feet, and a handsome face. The sheriff had an intentional, sand-colored five o'clock shadow, and he nodded politely as she approached.

"Sheriff Steve Burns," the man proclaimed in an even tone. He held his hand out and Veronica shook it.

"Detective Veronica Shade."

Red in the face and slightly out of breath from walking from his car to the barn, Freddie introduced himself next.

"I got back from my morning run and found the barn door ajar—didn't notice before I left. Peeked inside and found her." Succinct, to the point. No hint of an ego, either.

"Did you check her pulse? Try to get her down?" Freddie asked.

Veronica was surprised by her partner's questions. It was common to ask the person who had discovered the body if they'd touched it in case prints or fibers had transferred from them to the corpse. And while not specifically designed to trip a person up, if they said no and this turned out to be a lie? Well, that would spur a host of additional questions. Ones that were intended to ascertain guilt.

But for a sheriff? A man who has gone above and beyond to make sure everything was done by the book?

Sheriff Burns pushed his hat even higher and shook his head.

"No. She was long gone. Pale, unmoving. Her bowels had let go and she'd soiled her pants."

As they spoke, Veronica tried to look behind the sheriff and into the barn but couldn't make anything out. It was still early, but the sun was unusually bright, illuminating the barn's peaked roof from behind.

"You said you didn't notice anything before you went on your run? Anything different about the barn?"

"I didn't look, to be honest. But judging by her appearance, I suspect that she's been dead pretty much all night. I didn't hear anything last night, either."

Veronica peeked around the back of the CSU van.

"The Medical Examiner on their way?" she asked absently, wondering why the ME hadn't arrived yet. According to the text, the body had been discovered nearly two hours ago. Wind back the clock and that meant that Maggie Cernak had been hanging since at least 7:30 AM. And if the sheriff's observations were accurate, long before that. And yet, they were still waiting for the cause and manner of death to be declared.

"Not Medical Examiner—coroner. Not yet, but she had a trial this morning, which is why she's running late."

"A case we might be familiar with?" Freddie asked.

The sheriff's dark blue eyes widened.

"Oh, right—no, nothing criminal," he clarified. "The coroner, Kristin Newberry, is an elected official. A lawyer by trade. She should be here soon, though."

Veronica nodded. She was still getting used to the idea of the sheriff's office and associated people being elected, while she and all other police officers were hired.

"She's good," Sheriff Burns continued. "After you guys are done here, she'll take the body back to Matheson, get liver temp and a more accurate time of death. But, as I said, I'm pretty sure Maggie died hours ago. I'd say around midnight or even earlier."

All Veronica wanted to do was get inside, see the scene for herself, but Freddie wasn't done with his Dan Rather's routine yet.

"How did you ID her so quickly?"

"Wallet, back pocket," the sheriff replied. "Deputy McVeigh retrieved it—like I said, I didn't touch anything. As soon as I found the body, I called my chief deputy in. But," the man looked off to one side as he spoke, "we didn't need the wallet— I recognized her. Maggie Cernak is the local librarian."

As Veronica internalized this information, she found herself breathing in slowly through her nostrils. This had become a habit of hers but was particularly appropriate given the fact that she was less than thirty feet from a barn. She smelled no horse manure, no chicken coop, no animals of any kind. She was thinking about how strange this was when a man stepped from the shadows.

He appeared to materialize out of nowhere, surprising Veronica, who took several steps backwards only to bump into something large: Freddie's massive belly. The man barely budged, and she didn't think anyone noticed.

"This is Chief Deputy Marcus McVeigh," Sheriff Burns said.

Unlike the sheriff, Deputy McVeigh didn't offer his hand. He did tip his hat, however, to both she and Freddie, and Veronica thought about how strange this custom was. She was reminded of English Bobbies, what with their silly, impractical hats and outfits, serving only tradition and nothing else. In her experience, tradition was just a less offensive synonym for oppression.

The Stetson-hatted Chief Deputy Marcus McVeigh's appearance was in stark contrast to the sheriff's. He was younger, in his late twenties or early thirties, with wide, dark eyes, and an even darker shock of black hair visible beneath his hat. There were fading, but not faded, acne scars on his cheeks, and he had thick lips along with a propensity to lick them.

"Suicide," the man said bluntly. Then he waved his hand, gesturing for them to make their way to the barn, even though it was clear that he was annoyed that his assertion needed vetting.

The sheriff went first, walking around the CSU van, and Freddie followed. Veronica sucked in a deep breath, straightened her spine, and then started to walk. She was forced to squint almost immediately, as the shadow of the barn blocked the sunlight.

Freddie was saying something about the lack of animals within, but she paid him no heed. The sheriff and his deputy might have claimed that Maggie Cernak's death had been a suicide, but Veronica needed to see the body to be sure.

After stepping around Freddie's girth, her vision cleared, and Veronica allowed her eyes to drift upward. Even though the peaked roof was a good twenty-plus feet high, flat support beams ran across the width of the barn at only maybe twelve to fourteen feet above the ground. A yellow rope was looped across one of them, the cheap kind that you might pick up at either the hardware store or perhaps even the dollar store. Hanging from the end of this rope was Maggie Cernak.

The woman's face was pale, her jaw slack. A thick tongue hung from her mouth, the color of which matched the bruising on her chin and jaw. Her eyes were open and blank, and she was wearing a plain black T-shirt and jeans. There was a dark stain that ran from her crotch to nearly her knees. Beneath her, a wooden stool lay on its side.

At first blush, Veronica agreed with the Bear County Sheriff's Department: this was a clear suicide.

But that was before the colors.

Veronica thought she was prepared for them, but they came out of nowhere and with shocking intensity. It started as a slight glowing around Maggie's edges as if she were being back lit by the sun, illuminated as the barn roof had been when they'd approached by car. But these tendrils of light quickly expanded, and the yellowish hue was now interspersed with splashes of orange and red. As Veronica stared, struck by the absurd beauty of this hallucination, the pigments continued to bleed. The watercolor halo spreading from Maggie's corpse reminded her of dipping a paint-laden brush into a glass of water.

This alone was startling, but when Veronica began to hear that dreaded song, it all became too much for her.

The sound was muted at first, as if someone, a child, was standing outside the barn and humming to themselves. Then, like Maggie's aura, the singing grew stronger, more distinct.

A child, taunting.

*La, la, la, la, laaaaa, laaa.*

It grew louder and louder and unlike the glowing reds, oranges, and yellows that nearly filled the entire barn now, and if not the barn, most definitely all of Veronica's vision, she couldn't make it stop by shutting her eyes.

"This was no suicide," she whispered. Veronica squeezed her eyes closed and covered her ears with both hands. "It was murder."

# Chapter 3

VERONICA WASN'T SURE EXACTLY WHEN it had started. The earliest instance she could fully recall was way back when she'd been in grade three, but occasionally she saw flashes or portions of memories from when she was even younger. But grade three… she remembered the incident as if it had been yesterday. It had been lunch hour, and after Veronica had finished eating—a cream cheese and cucumber sandwich on white bread, crusts removed, half a bag of Sun chips (she'd eaten the other half during first break), and some baby carrots —everyone was heading outside for recess. Veronica had chased her lunch with a whole carton of milk, and that, coupled with the bottle of water that she'd consumed earlier in the day, had made for a dire situation.

Veronica hurried into the bathroom, only to immediately stop short. A girl she didn't recognize, but who appeared to be in a higher grade, fifth or six, perhaps, was leaning her head over the sink and staring at her face in the mirror.

Blood trickled from both nostrils, and tears leaked from her eyes. The two liquids combined somewhere near her chin and formed a thin pink mixture that had already dripped onto the girl's white blouse.

Being much younger, Veronica knew better than to say anything. She just bowed her head and hurried into a bathroom stall where she did her business. Veronica was startled a second time when she opened the door and saw the girl standing right *there*, hands on hips, face still moist.

The stranger opened her mouth to say something, and indeed sounds came out, but what Veronica heard wasn't words. Instead, she heard singing of all things.

Not a song, not really. More of a creepy lullaby, something kids in the schoolyard sang when they were teasing one another.

*La, la, la, la, laaaaa, laaa.*

It was close to Ring Around the Rosie, but somehow less endearing and whimsical, which was saying something, considering the fact that the song was describing a death sentence from the Great Plague.

Veronica's first instinct was that she was being pranked, set-up for the amusement of others. But a glance at the bathroom's sole, heavily frosted window, revealed no shadows, no cadre of children holding hands outside and singing. A look back at the empty bathroom stalls confirmed that they were alone.

But despite being unable to locate the source, the song continued to get louder until it grated on Veronica, vibrated her molars, made her squint. She tried to block it out by pushing her palms against her ears, but that's when the girl slapped her hands away.

This time when she spoke, Veronica was relieved to hear actual words.

"Did you hear what I said?" she spat angrily.

*Do you... do you hear that singing?* Was what Veronica wanted to reply, but she was so confused that nothing came forth.

"I said," the girl repeated, her face turning red now with anger instead of pain, "I walked into the door. That's why my nose was bleeding."

Veronica, on the verge of tears herself, began nodding vigorously and inhaled with a shuddering breath. They were in a bathroom, and while Edinburgh Elementary did its best to keep the place clean, there was a limit to what miracles the staff could perform. However, the smell that inundated Veronica's nostrils wasn't that of antiseptic solution masking urine, but inexplicably, of gasoline. The scent was strong, powerful enough to make the muscles in her neck stand out, and it reminded her of sitting in her father's truck with the window open as he filled the tank.

Like the singing, which had faded but was still present, the odor was out of place here. Veronica had no idea where either was coming from nor why this was happening—was it only happening to her? Was she the only one who could hear that song and smell the gas? The teary-eyed girl didn't seem to notice the smell or the singing. And where was it coming from?

Veronica shook her head, trying to clear her mind of the confusing stimuli that threatened to overwhelm her.

The girl was lying, that much was obvious.

Walked into a door? Unlikely. And even if you managed to walk into a door hard enough to give yourself a nosebleed, would you lash out? Maybe. Would you get angry and explain something that wasn't even asked? Perhaps. But would you be so adamant to try and convince a stranger that this was all an accident?

No, Veronica concluded, the girl was lying—this was no accident.

"Don't shake your head at me." The girl had clearly misinterpreted Veronica's gesture. "I walked into a door, okay? That's what happened."

Veronica moved her head up and down, the only response she could muster, fearful that if she tried to speak, she'd gag from the stench of gasoline.

"Good." The girl wiped the tears from her face, then reached out and gripped Veronica tightly by the shoulders. "But you're not gonna tell anybody about this, right?"

Head shaking again.

"Don't," the girl warned, and Veronica didn't.

She didn't tell anybody about the girl and the bloody nose, the tears. She didn't tell anybody about the music or the gas.

Children's memories were fickle, malleable things, and over time, Veronica simply forgot about both, allowing them to fade into the murky milieu that was navigating elementary school.

Days went by, and if she never saw that girl again, the undeniably strange encounter would have been completely erased from her memory.

But she did, and everything came flooding back.

It was a month before school let out, and Veronica was excited, mainly because her father had enrolled her in summer camp this year. A summer *sports* camp, and she loved sports. Adding to the excitement was the fact that her best friend, Mark Wills, was going with her.

But Veronica never got to go to sports camp that summer.

It happened before the third and final recess of the day. Veronica was at her locker, slipping her outside shoes on, preparing to play soccer against the boys and beat them *again*, when she heard someone scream.

This wasn't uncommon at Edinburgh—kids were always shouting and hollering, especially before recess. But this was different.

This wasn't a screech of surprise, shock, or even anger. This was a shriek of sheer terror. Veronica's eyes were drawn to the bathroom, perhaps because that was where she thought the sound had come from, or maybe it was her subconscious reminding her of the long-forgotten incident.

As Veronica watched, a wide-eyed girl rushed out of the girl's bathroom, bumping into several other students, but not appearing to notice. For a second, Veronica thought that the girl was coming for her, and she forgot all about her shoes and stood. But the girl stopped three lockers down, placed both hands against them, and vomited on the floor.

The scene had drawn the attention of a hall monitor and Mr. Gregory, the science teacher who just happened to be walking by, and they both quickly came to the girl's aid.

The shriek had faded and was replaced by uncomfortable murmurs.

And something else.

Something that Veronica heard in the back of her head.

*La, la, la, la, laaaaa, laaa.*

To this day, Veronica wasn't sure why she didn't go back into her classroom like her teacher, Mme. Cloutier, had instructed. But she didn't. Instead, Veronica moved against the crowd and approached the bathroom. The closer she got, the louder the song that nobody else seemed to hear became.

And then Veronica remembered.

When she pushed the door open and peered into the bathroom, seconds before somebody, most likely Mr. Gregory, grabbed her beneath her armpits and guided her away, Veronica expected to smell the gasoline.

Only she didn't.

But she did see something.

There was the girl, of course, the one with the bloody nose. Only now, her face was clean — the blood was coming from her wrists instead and had pooled below her slumped body. But there was also the fire. There was no other way to describe what Veronica saw. Yellow, orange, and red, but it wasn't a real fire. There was no smoke, no heat, no destruction. Only colors that seemed to swim and dance, spreading outward from the girl's body. It reminded Veronica of touching a wet paintbrush to a sheet of paper and watching the colors bloom.

And then Mr. Gregory pulled her away, and someone else blocked the bathroom door.

Veronica Shade didn't get to go to sports camp that summer.

Instead, she stayed local and, like many of the Edinburgh Elementary School students, spent her summer speaking with counselors and psychiatrists. The difference was, Veronica wasn't struggling to deal with the death of a girl whom she'd only met once and never really knew.

She was trying to deal with herself.

Trying to understand what was wrong with her, why she saw those colors, heard that song, and smelled gasoline when none of it was real.

# Chapter 4

"**VERONICA?**"

She shook free of Freddie's hold and stumbled out of the barn. She made it to the CSU van and was tempted to place her palms against it, but this reminded her of the girl who had discovered the body in the bathroom. And the last thing she wanted to do was vomit in front of... well, anyone.

"Sorry," she grumbled to herself. No longer in the vicinity of the body, the phantom sights and sounds quickly diminished and Veronica recovered.

"First suicide?" Deputy McVeigh had a tiny smirk on his pockmarked riddled face, whereas Sheriff Burns looked genuinely concerned.

"N—" *No, not my first. Third,* Veronica wanted to say, but Freddie, last out of the barn, answered for her.

"Yes," he lied. Veronica's eyes darted to her partner, but Freddie was focusing all of his attention on Sheriff Burns. "It's also been a long coupla days." Another lie. "Back-to-back doubles."

With each additional lie that came out of Freddie's mouth, the smell of gasoline intensified. Veronica knew from experience that if Freddie continued down this path, the fumes would become strong enough to make her head swim.

*Again.*

This was the last thing Veronica wanted to happen. She was already embarrassed by how she'd acted. Being a woman and the youngest detective in all of Greenham meant that people, people like Deputy McVeigh, looked at you a certain way. And feeding stereotypes wasn't part of her job description.

"Yeah, I get it—I'm really sorry for dragging you guys out here," Sheriff Burns said, his eyes moving from Freddie to Veronica. Unlike McVeigh, the man appeared genuinely concerned for her wellbeing. "It's just—I'm new," he proclaimed with almost childlike innocence, "and this—well, this isn't the first big case I envisioned as Bear County Sheriff, if you catch my drift. Thought it best to keep everything above board."

Even though Maggie's body had sent Veronica reeling, the fact that someone had committed suicide twenty to thirty feet from where he slept had affected the sheriff, no matter how much of a front he put on.

"I completely understand." Freddie peered over the sheriff's shoulder. "I just want to take another look."

"Of course."

"You can stay outside, if you want," Deputy McVeigh offered, leaning into Veronica.

"Thank you, but I'm fine."

Freddie shot her a concerned look, but she nodded. Yet, despite her silent reassurances, Veronica was wary of stepping back into the barn. Having been in law enforcement for the better part of six years, she'd grown accustomed to her auditory, visual, and olfactory hallucinations. Not only that, but they'd come in handy during several investigations. But they'd never reached the height that they had that day in elementary school when she saw the girl's body.

Until now.

Until she'd seen Maggie Cernak hanging in Sheriff Steve Burns' barn.

"No evidence of foul play. No visible bruising," the sheriff explained as the four of them walked toward the barn. "Other than around her throat, of course. The ground is soft dirt. Not sure we'll be able to get any usable footprints, but I didn't note an indication of a struggle."

"I found only two sets of footprints —yours and hers." The voice came from a fifth person and if it hadn't been smooth and even, it would have startled all of them. Coming toward them was a man in all black, with CSU in white, capital letters across the right breast.

"This is Holland Toler," Sheriff Burns said, "CSU."

Holland was a tall man, six foot three, and despite looking like he was in his late twenties, his hair was thinning at the sides and back. He also had unusually dark eyes.

"Detectives Shade and Furlow."

They shook hands.

"No evidence of anyone else?" the sheriff asked the CSU tech. "A third party?"

"No, sir. Got two distinct prints. I'm guessing you didn't go in there much?"

The sheriff shook his head.

"Just moved in."

"Any idea who lived here before you?" Veronica asked.

Again, the sheriff's head moved back and forth.

"Never met them."

"And you said that you knew the woman, Maggie, from the library?" Veronica followed up.

"Yeah. I mean, I've only gone once or twice. New to this area, not much time to read."

The gasoline smell returned with its sweet vengeance, and Veronica observed the man closely. He caught her stare and then immediately looked away.

*He's lying. Why is the sheriff lying?*

Before she could even consider challenging him on this, Freddie spoke up.

"Any idea where Maggie lives? I didn't see a car."

"Her car's not here," the sheriff stated matter-of-factly. "As for where she live—"

"Maggie lives in town, 'bout four or five miles from here. Sixty Lester St.," the tech cut in.

Veronica eyed him suspiciously, and the man shrugged.

"It was on her driver's license."

This was troubling.

"Did you guys reach out to any of the cab companies in Matheson? See if any of them dropped Maggie off here?"

McVeigh stepped in front of Veronica and answered.

"Called all cab companies in Matheson and Sullivan. No fare to the sheriff's house yesterday or at all over the last week." The Deputy's tone suggested that he was annoyed that she'd asked such an obvious and basic question.

"What about Uber? Lyft?"

McVeigh shook his head.

"They don't service out here."

Veronica exchanged a look with Freddie, and she knew that they were both thinking the same thing.

This wasn't just a random spot Maggie had stumbled across on the way to ending her life. It was in the middle of nowhere, and a good two hours from where the woman lived on foot.

"There are fresh blisters on both heels and the outside of her big toes," the tech offered.

No, this wasn't happenstance. This place meant something to Maggie.

Veronica thought about the sheriff's lie.

Or maybe the sheriff meant something to her.

"Where's the library?" Freddie asked.

The four men entered the barn and Veronica took a moment before following. She didn't look directly at the corpse this time but instead glanced around. The song returned, as did the colors, but they were muted now.

The one thing that Sheriff Burns hadn't lied about was not being in the barn often. It was impeccable—even the dirt on the ground was mostly undisturbed everywhere but at the entrance and near the body.

"Also in town," McVeigh said, not bothering to hide his annoyance this time.

"Then why here?" Veronica asked. The words just came out—an internal query accidentally verbalized.

But just like inside her head, there was no answer forthcoming.

"I'm guessing you don't have any cameras in here or outside?" Freddie asked, raising a chubby finger in the air.

The sheriff shook his head.

"I moved in about a month ago. Didn't install any." He paused, appearing introspective. "Until now, I didn't think I needed any, either."

The men continued to speak, but Veronica distanced herself from a conversation that she suspected was going nowhere.

She took two steps forward, then three. One more sharp inhalation and Veronica looked up at Maggie Cernak once more.

The colors grew more vibrant and while not as intense as before, the idea—the *certainty* that Maggie hadn't committed suicide persisted just as strongly.

"Can we cut down the body now?" Deputy McVeigh asked.

Freddie gave an approving nod and the deputy moved to retrieve a ladder from deeper in the barn.

"There is one more thing," CSU Toler said. "Something I found in her pocket. Not sure if it means anything, but I figured I'd bag it just in case."

The tech was holding a plastic evidence bag in one hand. Veronica, being the closest to the man, got the first look. Inside the bag was a torn piece of paper, only slightly larger than a business card. And written in black ink on the paper, in all block letters was a single word: *EENIE*.

# Chapter 5

"**ARE WE GONNA TALK ABOUT** what happened?" Freddie asked as they pulled away from the sheriff's home.

Veronica, whose eyes were trained out the window, watching as the deputy and CSU carefully lowered Maggie's body onto plastic sheeting, said nothing.

"Ah, I get it. We can talk about my addiction to saturated fats, you can make fun of my weight, but I can't talk about your... whatever the hell that was?"

Veronica kept her eyes locked on the barn until it faded out of sight.

"I wasn't making fun of you, Freddie."

"Sure as hell sounded like it. Anyways, are you okay?"

Now Veronica looked at Freddie and saw concern plastered over his features, from his dark green eyes to the jowls that hung below his cheeks.

Back when she'd been a beat cop, Veronica had heard stories about detectives, especially detectives who had been on the job for years, of which Freddie, as a twenty-two-year City of Greenham veteran detective, most definitely qualified.

Curmudgeonly alcoholics who had lost hope in humanity. Clichés, certainly, but those were the stories that were told and sold.

Freddie was an outlier, one of the good ones. Not only did he care, but he still seemed human. And while he enjoyed the occasional drink, it wasn't the bottle that would kill him. It was diabetes and heart disease.

A less sexy villain, but a villain none-the-less.

"I'm all right," Veronica assured the man. She sniffed, trying to rid herself of the scent of gasoline inspired by her own lie. "I was just shocked, that's all."

Freddie had kind eyes, which was one of the first things she'd noticed when they'd been partnered up. That and his immense size, of course.

*Kind eyes.*

Veronica knew firsthand that these impressions could be deceiving, even manipulated. Back when she'd been just a Greenham police officer, she met someone named Max Featherstone. That man had the brightest, kindest eyes she'd ever seen. They almost exuded hope if that were possible. Max was an upstanding member of the community, a philanthropist who donated large sums of money acquired in the textile industry to both the church and the school.

But altruism was an elusive beast.

Max made these donations so that he could have keys to both institutions, mainly to allow him to come and go as he pleased, without anybody batting an inquisitive eye. And he did.

He also did horrible things to children in both locations.

But Freddie Furlow was no philanthropist, he didn't have large sums of money, and Veronica was almost a hundred percent certain that his taste was in women of age.

And fried foods.

"It just doesn't make sense. The sheriff said it wasn't his rope, meaning that Maggie brought it with her. She walked five miles to the sheriff's house in the middle of the night to hang herself? Why? And that suicide note? *EENIE*? What the hell is that all about?"

Freddie shrugged.

"Probably not a suicide note. Something from the library, maybe. Unrelated."

"Perhaps. But why the sheriff's place? I'm telling you—" *she was murdered*, "—there's something off about this. It doesn't make sense."

Freddie's eyes drifted back to the road.

"Sure," he admitted. The man reached for his Coke, rattled it to see if there was ice left, then took a sip. "But the McLachlan suicide didn't make sense, either, and that was caught on video."

Veronica rubbed the back of her neck and gazed out the window as she considered her partner's words.

The McLachlan suicide had been one of the stranger cases that she'd worked, then just a beat cop. Collin McLachlan had been a young tech entrepreneur who had made around three million dollars designing software to help organize your day. It integrated everything from your morning alarm, to scheduling your email, telephone meetings, that sort of thing.

He was married to a beautiful wife and had a six-year-old daughter. By all accounts, he was a model citizen, what Max Featherstone pretended to be. Then, on a seemingly random Tuesday, a rare, sunny, beautiful Tuesday in early March, Collin McLachlan, woke up at his regular time—thanks to his app—and dressed in his running gear. The man kissed his wife and daughter, told them he loved them, and then went on his run.

Halfway between miles two and three, Collin reached a bridge that crossed the Casnet River, one that he'd traversed dozens, if not hundreds of times before.

He didn't cross it this time, however. Something happened and a week later his body was discovered by a man who was trolling with a large magnet—it pinged his expensive watch.

Collin McLachlan had drowned. His pants, with a tight waistband and ankles, had been loaded down with rocks. More than twenty pounds of them.

Veronica had been the first cop on the scene and immediately thought that Collin's fate had been the result of an elaborate murder, despite the lack of glowing colors. She'd called in homicide, and Detective Freddie Furlow just happened to be on duty. They discussed the case, and both agreed that something was amiss.

But that was before they saw the video. A couple of years back, a man had been assaulted on the same bridge and Bear County had succumbed to public pressure, repurposing one of their wildlife cameras to cover the area.

Collin McLachlan wasn't murdered. He'd committed suicide. The video clearly showed him reaching the bridge, stopping, and then proceeding to load his pants with rocks from the riverbed. Then he waded into the water and never reemerged.

There was no note, no reason behind the suicide that could be uncovered despite Veronica digging deep into both the man's financial and personal background.

To this day, it was one of the strangest cases Veronica had ever been involved in.

But the fundamental difference between Collin McLachlan and Maggie Cernak?

The song and the colors.

Veronica had meant what she said when she'd first stepped inside the barn.

Maggie Cernak had been murdered.

But she couldn't rightly say this to Freddie. She'd already blurted it once and that hadn't gone over too well. As close as they were, and as nice as Freddie was, as kind as his eyes were, there were only two people who knew about her condition.

And for her sanity, as well as theirs, Veronica wanted to keep it that way. She couldn't imagine what her colleagues would think of her—not only was she a woman, but she was also the youngest detective on the force... and now she had psychedelic superpowers?

She'd be tossed into the Loony Bin. Shit, Freddie might even be the one who had her committed, kind eyes or not.

"I know, I know," Veronica said, eventually. "But I think we should look into it. I mean, you do too, right? Otherwise, you would have signed off on it being a suicide back at the barn."

Freddie shifted his weight and the springs beneath his seat groaned miserably.

"I didn't sign off on it because I want to wait until the ME gives a definitive time of death."

Veronica smelled gas but would've spotted this lie even if her nostrils had been plugged with smelling salts.

"You think the sheriff's lying?" she asked after a prolonged pause.

"Why do you say that? Wait, it's because *you* think he's lying."

"Hey, I asked you first."

Freddie rubbed his nose before answering.

"Just a hunch but I'm thinking that Sheriff Burns knew Maggie a little more than he let on."

Veronica's eyes widened. That was exactly the same impression she'd gotten.

"You think it's a murder, too," she exclaimed. Again, the words had just slipped out and, like back in the barn, she wished she could take them back.

Freddie laughed.

"I never said that. I just think... I dunno, I have this gut feeling," he tapped his massive belly as he spoke, "that maybe the sheriff was familiar with Maggie. Maybe he was sleeping with her, I don't know."

"Well, if *you* have a gut feeling, then that's saying something," Veronica teased.

"Ha, ha."

"No, seriously, we should go to the morgue, check with the ME. See if—"

"Relax, relax. Easy with the hunt for America's next serial killer. We'll follow up. But right now? Right now, we have something else to do, somewhere else to be."

Veronica felt her upper lip curling. She'd made this face to show her displeasure since she'd been a little girl, and her dad hated it. He said it made a beautiful girl look mean and told her to stop. She couldn't break the habit, however, and the few times she'd looked in the mirror while doing it, Veronica didn't think she appeared mean. It wasn't pretty by any stretch, but it was something of a hidden talent that someone would appreciate one day.

Maybe.

"Where? The captain said—"

"The captain said to go meet the new sheriff and witness the suicide, not take over the case—it's still a Bear County case. And, last time I checked, we're City of Greenham Detectives. We have our own cases."

Veronica sat up in her seat and glanced out the window. She instantly knew where she was headed.

"No," she begged, curling her lip to the point that it nearly flipped over completely. "Freddie, please, not this again. Anything but this."

# Chapter 6

SHERIFF STEVE BURNS HAD TOLD Veronica that his farm
didn't have cameras and that he didn't think he needed any on
the outskirts of Matheson before last night. But the City of
Greenham was a different animal. Hit hard by first the opioid
epidemic that transitioned into a meth outbreak, the entire
lower west side, which was just under an hour from Portland,
had one of the highest crime rates in the State of Oregon.

Most incidents were of the non-violent variety, or moderately violent with drug involvement, including break-ins, mug-
gings, theft, soliciting, and, of course, drug use, abuse, and *dis-
tribuse*, as the saying amongst cops went.

But stalking? That was rare. Rarer still, was the stalking of a
nineteen-year-old senior who lived in an upscale part of town
and whose father just happened to be a city councilor.

The kicker? Everyone was convinced they knew who the
stalker was: Dylan Hall.

Dylan grew up in the system, Renaissance Home, an orphanage in Matheson, and when he wasn't there, he was in and
out of foster care forever. But unlike most young boys, he was
lucky enough to have been hosted by not one, but three foster
families. Veronica was familiar with both the man and his file.
Dylan's history read something like a real-life Goldilocks and
the Three Bears. The first family who adopted him, a couple in
their mid-fifties, were horrible people. They beat him, rented
him out, burned him, treated him as a slave. They were arrested
and Dylan was returned to foster care. His second family, the
Rosemears, were completely the opposite. They already had
three biological children plus one adopted child before Dylan
came into the picture. Mr. and Mrs. Rosemear loved their family, but they both worked full-time jobs, and five unsupervised

boys between eight and fourteen didn't always make the best decisions. One of the older boys convinced Dylan to throw a rock through a jewelry store window in the middle of the night. It was unclear whether stealing a watch worth nearly five grand was his decision or if he was put up to that, too.

Either way, boom — Dylan was shipped back to foster care, but, thankfully, he was too young to face any charges. Still, it marred his reputation, and he became the type of teenager who simply never got adopted. But for some reason, an affluent husband and wife took a liking to him, and he integrated seamlessly into their family. By all accounts, they were a good family and worked well together.

And then there was the accident. Just sheer, dumb, bad luck. The three of them had been coming back from dinner on the town when their car hit a patch of black ice. The vehicle flipped twice and then struck a tree. Both parents died at the scene, but by some miracle, Dylan came out unscathed.

He kept their surname, although Veronica wasn't sure if this was to pay homage, or if it was just the last name he had.

Dylan Hall.

At fifteen, the now lanky young man voluntarily left the foster home, opting for a life on the streets instead of one in the orphanage. It wasn't long after that he was picked up and shipped to another institution: prison.

It started with larceny, then extortion, misdemeanor assault, drug possession, and possession with intent.

These and the litany of other crimes were almost all related to the man's drug addiction, which, by all accounts, began in juvenile hall following his first arrest.

But now, stalking?

In Veronica's opinion, Dylan Hall was motivated by only one thing: feeding his addiction.

So, while almost everyone in Greenham pegged Dylan as the stalker, Veronica was of a different mind, despite the evidence to the contrary.

"You don't think it's him, do you?" Veronica asked. There was a fine line between exploring all aspects of a crime and denying facts in search of grandiosity. The latter happened, of course—it was human nature to seek a higher motivation or reason behind terrible accidents, for instance. People wanted—*needed*—someone or something to blame. It was near impossible to accept that someone's child was murdered by a sociopath whose only motivation was to 'see how it felt'. They blamed the parents of serial killers, comic books, Stephen King, pornography, and Marilyn Manson. The President, too. It's just the way our minds work. But this isn't a desirable trait for a detective. And twice in one day? Veronica knew that she was on the verge of developing a reputation, of becoming a type, but she couldn't help it.

Besides, she felt safe with Freddie. If you couldn't shoot the shit, discuss ideas or scenarios no matter how out there they might be, with your detective partner, with whom could you?

They were cruising the streets, driving slowly in Freddie's unmarked Sebring, moving up and down alleys that they or others had arrested Dylan in previously. They encountered the usual riffraff, addicts, junkies, homeless people with funny signs that they believed would net them greater pity and even greater generosity.

"Doesn't really fit his MO," Freddie admitted. "But you know Dylan..."

And, unfortunately, Veronica did. During one arrest for cocaine possession that turned out to be greater than 90% baby laxative, Dylan had responded not with violence, or even by trying to break free.

He was so high that the man had grabbed her ass.

This was something that Dylan immediately regretted. Veronica had given him such a strong kick to the groin, that rumor had it one of his testicles had to be surgically lowered from inside of his body cavity.

"Do I ever."

But copping a feel while blasted on fentanyl and who knew what else was a far cry from a sophisticated and prolonged stalking operation.

"I mean, how many six foot seven, hundred-and-seventy-pound bald men with a forearm crow tattoo are there? Even in Greenham?"

"Good point."

Freddie turned down a side street barely wide enough for the Sebring, which ended in a T-intersection. To Veronica, the hard right angles looked impossible to navigate, but Freddie wasn't about to give up yet. As he attempted to circumvent the laws of physics in a mid-sized automobile, she leaned forward, looking first to her right down an alley that was mostly populated by garbage bins and other refuse. When she looked left, past Freddie, who was starting to mumble a series of curses as his car, rather predictably, became stuck, she noticed a blue tarp affixed to a fire escape on one side and a wire fence on the other, forming a makeshift covering.

Beneath this, she noticed two sleeping bags. The bottom of one of them had been slit and two skinny feet poked out.

"Shit, that's him!" Veronica said. It had to be Dylan—his bald head poked a foot out of the top, and his ankles twice as far out of the bottom.

She fiddled with the door and the man stirred. She wasn't sure how Dylan could hear her, but apparently, the man did as he started to rise.

The car door opened only partway before banging against a wall, which really got Dylan moving. The man sat up and their eyes met. He looked high and hungover, but the man's hastened movements indicated that he was lucid enough to recognize her.

"Shit."

Veronica tried to push the door wider but the way that Freddie had wedged the Sebring meant that she only had about eighteen inches to work with. As Dylan struggled to extricate himself from his sleeping bag, Veronica saw her only way out— up. She managed to raise her arms out of the car, and then her head. Using her elbows, Veronica hoisted her entire upper half onto the roof.

"Veronica?" Freddie said.

She ignored her partner and slithered completely onto the roof and then down the hood. When her feet struck solid ground, she looked up.

Dylan was free of his sleeping bag now and, sporting only a pair of either dark or dirty boxers, he glared at her.

"Don't even think about it," Veronica warned. Her hand went to the pistol on her hip, but she didn't draw her weapon.

Evidently, Dylan had thought about it. And a moment later, he did it.

Veronica looked back at Freddie, who had since opened his window but had the same chance of getting out of the car that a goldfish had of taking flight.

"I can't run," he proclaimed in desperation. "I can't run."

But thankfully for both of them, Veronica could.

And that's exactly what she did.

# Chapter 7

DYLAN HALL HAD THE BENEFIT of a lengthy stride on his side. He also had intimate knowledge of the layout of these back alleys. But Veronica was an avid runner and had athleticism on her side.

Not to be understated was Dylan's chronic drug abuse. Yet, the man took off like a shot, slapping the blue tarp up and out of his way as he sped down the alley in the opposite direction of Veronica and Freddie's car. Veronica didn't even have to duck to slip beneath the tarp, but the sunlight passing through the thick material made it glow an aqua blue. Given her history with colors, this was particularly disorienting, and she nearly lost her footing.

But then she was free and clear of the tarp and her stride became steady again. She saw a flash of white—Dylan's bare heel, maybe—moving right at another of those tight junctions. Veronica pumped her arms and legs and made a deliberate attempt to keep her breathing in check.

Dylan was closer now, and with each one of Veronica's strides, the distance between them shrunk. Part of this was due to Veronica pushing her body even harder, the rest because Dylan's gait had changed. Instead of being coordinated, with his heels flicking toward his boxers, they splayed outward in an almost circular motion. It was as if his quads were completely taxed and other less used, and less practiced, muscles were trying to take over.

"Stop!" Veronica yelled, but the blood was pumping so loud in her ears that she barely heard it and doubted Dylan had picked up any more than a whisper.

He wasn't going to stop, anyway.

They made one more turn and, once again, Dylan's elongated form was an advantage. Instead of the large, dumpster-style garbage bins, this alley was riddled with the round, personal kind. And someone—Dylan, in preparation for this moment, perhaps?—had decided to knock them all over.

Even in his fatigued state, Dylan had no problem leaping over the barrels. Veronica, on the other hand, was forced to weave between them. She banged her shin on the only one made of metal and not cheap plastic and cried out.

*"Fucking* stop!"

Veronica hobbled for a few paces, nursing her bruised shin, then regained her composure. They made one more turn, a left this time, and she thought that Dylan had finally made his first tactical error, that meth had made him forget the intricate rat-like maze that was Greenham's alley system.

There was no intersection here, just a nine or ten-foot wall. There was a fire escape on one of the adjacent buildings, but Dylan had no interest in this—he and his sloppy gait blew right by it without a single glance.

And that's when Veronica realized that coming down this alley was no mistake. This had been by design.

Dylan was six foot seven. Veronica, five-five. No matter how athletic she was, there was no way she was going to be able to scale the wall. But it wouldn't pose much of a problem for Dylan, even as exhausted and high as he probably was.

If he got over that wall, he'd be gone.

Veronica pushed her body even harder, ignoring her screaming thighs, her burning lungs, and her biceps, which ached from pumping so hard.

Dylan barely slowed when he reached the wall. He tried to run up the side, putting one foot on the wall itself and the other on the building that formed the left-hand corner. His fingers scrambled for the upper edge and eventually grabbed hold.

Veronica was close enough to smell the man's sweat now — his translucent skin was glistening with it. Cartoon-like lines radiated from Dylan's body, more concentrated on his head, armpits, and crotch, only these were blue instead of green or yellow as they were often depicted on-screen.

*Not now,* she begged, *please not now.*

The last thing she needed was another distraction, but her condition was beyond her control. Dylan had pulled himself up to his elbows, and Veronica did her best to ignore the blue plumage. The man's bare thighs and knees scraped against the rough concrete wall as he finagled himself to his waist.

Veronica caught up a second later. She leaped, planting her foot against the wall for additional leverage. While she had no chance of making it to the top, she got high enough to grab one of Dylan Hall's ankles.

And grab it she did. Veronica wrapped both of her small hands around the bony appendage and hung from Dylan's leg. The man's strength was surprising, and he didn't come tumbling down as she thought he would — he was still rising. Veronica was on her tiptoes and began bouncing on his leg like a bungee cord. Dylan finally started to slip, and he let out a string of obscenities as the flesh on his forearms began to shred.

Veronica's strength waned and Dylan, perhaps sensing this or maybe just starting to panic, kicked at her with his free foot. His first attempt missed as Veronica somehow managed to spin out of the way like Tarzan on a vine. The second struck her in the shoulder. But instead of dislodging her, it served to infuriate Veronica. She ground her teeth and gave the man's leg a final, violent yank.

"No!" Dylan screamed as the flesh from elbows to wrists turned red.

Veronica's feet hit the ground moments before Dylan's did, and she was ready. She wrapped her arms around the man's narrow waist and spun him around, throwing an off-balance Dylan against the wall. He shouted again as he struck his shoulder and then slumped to his ass. It looked like the fight was all out of the man, but Veronica was taking no chances.

She drew her gun and stepped forward, deliberately planting her right foot between Dylan's outstretched legs.

"Stay down," Veronica warned.

Dylan's eyes fell on the gun first and he snarled. But when he saw her foot being reared back in anticipation of another hardy kick to his injured scrotum, he eventually gave up.

# Chapter 8

AFTER DYLAN WAS IN HANDCUFFS and had calmed down some, Veronica leaned up against the wall and allowed herself to relax, just a little. Her breathing was heavy, but it quickly regulated after just a minute or two.

"I didn't do nothing," Dylan claimed.

Veronica didn't even justify this comment with a reply. She did, however, smell the reek of gasoline. This, combined with the blue manifestation of the man's sweat, made it look like Dylan was some sort of Urban Fantasy demon engulfed in blue flames.

"This is harassment. *Fucking* harassment."

Veronica sighed, and she looked to the mouth of the alley, waiting for Freddie to appear. She didn't know exactly where she was, what with all the twists and turns that Dylan had taken her on, but she didn't think they'd gone that far in terms of total distance. She could have called Freddie and dropped a pin, but what her partner lacked in physical ability, he made up for in directional awareness.

It was savant-like the way Freddie could navigate his way around the city, even a city like Greenham.

He would find her; she had no doubt about it.

"You know what's harassment?" Veronica began. She was bored, otherwise, she wouldn't even have bothered wasting her breath. "You stalking Chloe Dolan."

"I didn't—" when he abruptly stopped speaking, Veronica glanced down. Dylan's forearms were scratched and leaking blood, as were his knees, but none of these injuries looked at all serious. "Chloe Dolan?" Dylan said. The name came out of his mouth like putty. "You fucking serious?"

Veronica just stared.

"Have you *seen* Chloe Dolan?"

Veronica hadn't but decided to leave this open-ended and just listened to Dylan ramble. His pupils were pinprick small, and his shoulders kept twitching awkwardly with his hands cuffed behind his back.

"Ha." The sound came out like a goat bleat. "Clearly you haven't. Chloe got teeth like a fucking horse—a big old horse and she's prolly heavier than even your partner. Why the fuck would I be stalking her?"

This came as a surprise to Veronica.

"So, you know her?"

Dylan snarled, realizing that he'd tripped up.

Veronica had never seen or met Chloe—the case had simply been passed onto them, likely because the nineteen-year-old high school senior's well-connected father had decided that this whodunnit was best suited for detectives. But like the suicide in Sheriff Burns' barn, Freddie and Veronica were just lending a hand. This case still technically belonged to the responding officer, Officer Ken Cameron. And all Veronica knew about it was what the man had jotted down. It started with an inappropriate note in the girl's locker, then reports of someone standing outside her window, and notes at home. It culminated with a used condom being flung at her window. Chloe reported seeing a tall bald man with a tattoo on his forearm in the vicinity following both incidents at her house.

"The bitch just made it up. You wanna know the real story?"

*No, but I suspect you're going to tell me anyway.*

"Chloe and her two horse-faced friends wanted something to party with, you know what I mean?"

"Something to party with?" Veronica said, playing dumb.

"Yeah, okay, you know what I mean. But I ain't gonna say it. They wanted something to party with and I gave it to them.

Get this, Seabiscuit says she forgot her wallet or some bullshit. Says she gotta go get it from her car. I don't know where the fuck she goes, but she doesn't come back to pay me. I look for her, but this is in December and it's fucking cold. So, the next day, I follow her home from school. Knock on her door, but she doesn't answer. That's it. I didn't stalk her. C'mon."

Veronica raised an eyebrow.

"Did you just admit to selling an illicit substance?"

Dylan frowned.

"Nah, I didn't say that. You're—y-you're missing the point. I'm not stalking her. I just wanted her to pay me back."

Veronica had heard enough and was about to tell the man to be quiet when she realized something.

She could no longer smell gasoline. Veronica could smell the man's sweat, see the blue hue coming off him, but there was no odor of gasoline.

It was March and the man was wearing next to nothing. He was also high. Veronica's ability to determine if someone was lying was good bordering on great, but not perfect by any stretch. Hell, she didn't even know how it worked. Still...

"So, you're telling me that when we compare your DNA to what was left in the condom, there won't be a match?" Veronica pressed.

This was a bluff of course; the likelihood of any DNA analysis being done in this case was next to zero, even with Chloe Dolan's father being a city councilor.

"What condom?"

"The one you threw at Chloe's window."

Dylan bleated again.

"Wait, you're telling me that I nutted in a dome and threw it at her window? Why the fuck would I do that?"

Veronica couldn't honestly say. She supposed that, deep down, it was a control thing. The culprit couldn't have the girl, so they intimidated and frightened them, tried to show them who's boss.

Or something like that.

Thankfully, Veronica didn't have to answer because Freddie appeared. She expected him to be huffing and puffing and red-faced, but he didn't arrive on foot. The man somehow managed to get his Sebring halfway down the alley and then stopped before it became too narrow to open the door. The detective got out of his car and walked over to them.

Now he was red-faced and out of breath.

"You really don't run, do you?" Veronica said with a smirk.

Freddie just looked at her, shrugged, and then glanced down at Dylan, who suddenly wasn't interested in talking anymore. Freddie' eyes drifted from the man's face to his soiled briefs.

"How's the old twig and berries, Dylan?"

Dylan sucked his teeth but said nothing.

"All right, on your feet," Freddie ordered. Dylan was so tall and his legs so long, that they both had to help him up. They put him in the back of the car and reversed out of the alley.

As they drove to the station, Veronica kept sneaking peeks at the man in the backseat. It was all she could do to resist sniffing him.

*He's telling the truth,* she thought with sudden clarity. *Dylan Hall isn't stalking Chloe Dolan.*

This realization was quickly followed by a question: *Then who the hell is?*

# Chapter 9

THEY DROPPED DYLAN OFF AT booking, with both Freddie and Veronica deciding that it would be best to let the man stew for a few hours before conducting an interview. After Freddie paid an ungodly sum to purchase a cream-filled pastry from one of the many vending machines, they refilled their coffees and made their way upstairs. The City of Greenham had roughly a hundred police officers, of which sixteen were detectives, all of whom were spread evenly over two campuses: the main campus, located in the heart of downtown; and a smaller office near the southern tip of the city.

Freddie and Veronica had offices on the main campus on the same floor as the captain, most likely because of the former's experience and the latter's lack thereof. 'Office' was used loosely here—they each had a chair and a computer and were separated by a lightweight partition that offered the illusion of privacy. Including themselves and the captain, there were eighteen officers on their floor, with double that number on the two floors below, and half as many manning the holding cells or evidence lockers in the basement.

Veronica didn't mind the proximity to her coworkers, or her boss, or the traffic that she had to contend with both coming and going. It was just one particular coworker that she had an issue with. Even that wasn't exactly true—it was more like the other way around.

And it all stemmed from a single incident, which all Veronica wanted to do was forget, while the other party seemed to want the complete opposite. It wasn't as if what had happened was a secret to their coworkers, either. In fact, when Randy Dolan had called the captain directly to suggest that his daughter's stalking case required detective involvement, the first person

that he'd volunteered was Veronica. As if her and the responding officer working together would help mend the perceived
slight.

As if Veronica cared. All she wanted to do was come in, get
her work done, and go home.

Or stay later and work longer, as the case often was.

"Ken," Freddie licked frosting from his lips as he addressed
the officer who approached their desks, "we brought Dylan
Hall in. He's in holding, thinking of letting him stew for an
hour."

Veronica didn't say a word. She just sat behind her desk and
logged into her computer. On several occasions, she'd tried to
speak to Officer Cameron about what had happened, but this
just served to make the stubborn cop angry.

"Make it five or six hours," Ken said, with a chuckle. "I'll
wait until whatever's in his system wears off and he's jonesing
for more. Then he'll cop to stalking a goddamn Billy goat, am I
right?"

Veronica bit her tongue.

*Except he didn't do it,* she thought.

Arguing with Ken Cameron, however, would get her nowhere. Instead, Veronica turned her focus to the other case.

She'd hoped to find Maggie Cernak in the system, but the
woman had no priors to speak of. A search for the woman's
social media profiles proved equally as fruitless. Maggie was
on Facebook, but her account was set to private. The only thing
Veronica could access was the woman's profile picture. It was
a simple head shot that showed a pretty, smiling young
woman. A stark contrast to the thick-tongued corpse in the
barn. The dichotomy was so extreme that Veronica shivered.

Suicide… everything about the scene suggested Maggie had
committed suicide. Sure, there were some oddities, a handful

of inconsistencies, but nothing to definitively suggest it wasn't a suicide.

But this didn't matter. What mattered were the colors, the swashes of yellow, orange, and red that Veronica had seen. These were indicators of a violent crime, not suicide.

Recalling what Sheriff Burns had told her, Veronica pulled up the Matheson Public Library website next. Sure enough, she found Maggie Cernak listed as one of two librarians. The woman's picture was different from her Facebook profile, but it showed the same smiling face. Here, however, Veronica detected a sadness in her digital eyes. Or maybe she was just imagining this, given the fact that she knew the ending to Maggie's story.

Veronica scrolled down to the text in the *About* section.

*Maggie has always loved books, ever since she was a little girl. She's a big fan of historical romances and her favorite book is* A Regrettable Reputation *by Lynn Bryant.*

*No help here, either,* Veronica thought glumly.

"Veronica?"

She shook her head and raised her gaze from her computer. Freddie was staring at her with a strange expression on his face.

"Sorry," she mumbled. "Say that again?"

"Ken was wondering if Dylan said anything after you chased him down?"

"He denied everything," Veronica said. "Had some choice words about Chloe Dolan, as well."

She was about to recount Dylan's story about the whole 'Chloe and her friends wanted to party' but Officer Cameron interrupted.

"I bet he did," Ken snapped. "Fucking guy threw a condom at her window."

Veronica's eyes drifted from Freddie to Ken.

He was two years older than her and had a modern, frat boy look about him. Great hair, square jaw, and a decent physique, which he showed off by ordering his uniform shirts one size too small. Both of them had applied for detective at the same time, but budget restrictions had limited hiring to just one spot. It was no secret that Ken was pissed she'd gotten the job over him, but that wasn't what had put the dagger in their relationship.

That had come when both of them had been drunk at the annual work Christmas party. Veronica had left early, and Ken had followed. He'd asked her out, but Veronica wasn't interested and politely let him know that she wanted to keep her work and private life separate. The man had laughed at that, then had turned cold and had been that way ever since.

Shit, Veronica was surprised that it wasn't Ken throwing used condoms at *her* window.

"To be honest," Veronica said, still looking at Ken, "I'm not sure that Dylan is behind this."

Ken, whose expression had been closer to a leer than a smile at this point, suddenly scowled.

"What do you mean?" The man's words came out more as an accusation than a question and Veronica felt Freddie stiffen beside her. Before he could come to her defense, she clarified her comment.

"Just doesn't fit his MO," she said simply. She left out the part about the lack of gasoline smell when Dylan insisted he wasn't behind the stalking.

"His *MO*?" Ken repeated, thickly. "Dylan Hall is a Grade A scumbag. Fuck his *MO*."

Veronica nodded.

"Oh, I know. He is a scumbag. But I don't think he's a stalker."

"You know any other six-foot-seven bald men with a Raven tattoo on his forearm?" Ken asked.

"That's the thing—Chloe said she saw him outside her window? At night?"

Ken grunted.

"And have you seen his tattoo?" Veronica asked.

"We all have," Freddie said, trying to keep the conversation from escalating.

"Right. It's about five inches tall, three inches wide. One thing I learned about Dylan Hall is that for some reason he doesn't like to wear clothes, and I doubt the man is big on sunscreen. I saw that tattoo today—it's faded, gray, blurry. And you're telling me that Chloe Dolan looked through her jizz-streaked window, at night, terrified, and noticed... his tattoo?"

"Then how would she know about it?" Ken demanded, crossing his arms over his chest. The buttons on his shirt looked about to pop.

Once again, Veronica was tempted to mention the drug deal gone wrong, but for some reason, she was inclined to keep this information to herself. For now, at least.

"I never said they haven't met, all I said is that I'm not so sure Dylan is stalking her."

Prior to asking her out and before being overlooked for the detective position, Ken respected Veronica's opinions. They even joked with one another.

Not now.

Now, the man took everything personally.

"Yeah, we'll see," Ken grumbled as he trudged back to his desk. "We'll see if the bald canary sings a different tune after a six-hour sweat."

*Six hours...*

Something suddenly occurred to Veronica.

"Maybe we don't have to wait that long," she said under her breath. When she rose to her feet, Freddie made a move to join her. Veronica discouraged her partner with a head shake and a look that said, *I'll be fine.* "Back in ten. Let me know if the Bear County coroner reaches out, would you?"

# Chapter 10

THE LETTERS THAT CHLOE HAD received both at home and in her locker were truly vile. There were four of them in total, each sealed in their separate clear evidence bag. Veronica chose the one that was the least offensive, put all the others back, and then proceeded to holding.

In Greenham, it was the junior police officers who manned the holding cells. Veronica had done it years ago, when she'd been a rookie, a 'boot', and it had been an eye-opening experience, to say the least. Most violent offenders were held in County until their arraignment, meaning that their holding cells were usually full of either drunks or addicts. Most of them just needed a cool-down period and actually appreciated the safe and relatively clean place to rest for the night. On weekends, there was the occasional need to hold people who had gotten into a bar fight. They eventually came to their senses, too, but sometimes their anger persisted for an hour or more. But Veronica knew how to deal with hotheads.

It was the junkies who were coming down that slung the worst insults. Veronica was by no means a prude, but some of the words that came out of their mouths were absolutely repugnant. Once, she'd even had human feces launched at her through the bars.

Often used as a litmus test for boots, Veronica's time in the basement had nearly broken her. It wasn't the obscenities or the flying shit, but her condition.

Sweat, lies, and violence were all triggers for her, and just being in a crowd was borderline unbearable. Having to oversee a handful of junkies coming down from a week-long meth binge? That was a different animal altogether.

But Veronica persisted and got through it, and she was a better person for it. A better cop, too. She was stronger, able to deal with the Dylan Halls of the world grabbing her ass without batting an eye.

Today, the officer in charge was Court Furnelli, a baby-faced man with curly black hair and soft, round features.

"Detective Shade, I thought you were going to leave him alone for a bit," Court said when he saw her approaching.

"Changed my mind—I want to have a little chat." Veronica scooped a piece of paper and a pencil off Court's desk. "And to ask for an autograph."

Officer Furnelli offered her a confused grin, but he didn't ask for clarification. Boots rarely challenged their superiors.

Court unlocked the outer door and held it open for her. He remained a respectable distance behind her as she walked to the last of the four cells. Someone, probably Furnelli, had given Dylan a gray tracksuit to wear. It was, of course, too large in the midsection and waist, and far too short on the ankles and wrists. Veronica could tell this even though the man was curled up on the concrete bench with his back to her.

He didn't stir as she approached.

"Dylan," she said. No response, so Veronica raised her voice. "Dylan!"

The man grunted and rolled over and Veronica realized that she'd been right about one thing.

Dylan was definitely on his way down.

The man was perpetually pale, but the dark circles around his eyes now, accentuated by the poor yellow lighting, made his face look like a skull. His skin was stretched taut over high cheekbones, and it glistened slightly, reinforcing this image.

Dylan said nothing, just sat there, shivering on the bench, staring blankly at her.

"I want you to write something for me." Veronica extended her hand with the paper and pencil through the bars, but the man made no move to sit up or budge at all. "Take it."

Dylan still didn't budge.

"Why would I do anything for you?" His voice was dry, his words almost sandy.

"Just do it. If you want to get out of here, just write down what I say."

The prospect of leaving this place and getting another fix, no matter how minute, was too tempting to ignore. With a Herculean effort, Dylan made it to a seated position, then standing, before staggering to the front of the cell. Under normal circumstances, Veronica would have been prepared for Dylan to do something unpredictable, but the man could barely stand. The idea of him lashing out, maybe grabbing her through the bars, was incomprehensible.

With a trembling hand, he took the paper and pencil and then backed away like a frightened zoo animal.

"Alright, here's what I want you to write," Veronica told him, and he immediately tried to give the paper back.

"I'm not writing that."

Veronica frowned.

"I literally just pulled you off the wall in your underwear. Don't act coy now."

Dylan remained hesitant.

"Th-this is a trick. I write this, and you're gonna claim its harassment or some shit."

"Harassment? Do you remember grabbing my ass, Dylan?"

It was difficult to tell, but Veronica thought his skull of a face reddened a little.

"What? No, I—"

"Yeah, you did. And I didn't charge you, did I? Now write down what I told you."

Blue waves were coming off Dylan as he reluctantly lowered the paper to the concrete bench and scribbled down the phrase. When he was done, he thrust it back at her.

"Satisfied?"

Veronica took one look at the paper then slid it into her pocket and grinned.

*Satisfied and vindicated.*

Dylan might have deliberately altered his handwriting, but that gave a junkie in his state too much credit. And judging by the growing blue aura that surrounded his body? He was getting worse.

Dylan went back to the concrete bench and was about to sit.

"No, don't do that—come over here."

Dylan scowled.

"I knew this was a trick. I didn't—"

Veronica looked over her shoulder at Court, who had been watching this interplay with interest.

"Let him go."

Court's dark eyes widened.

"Excuse me?"

Veronica glanced back at Dylan, who had a similar expression of disbelief on his face as Officer Furnelli.

"Let him go," Veronica instructed.

"Are you—are you sure? Because it's Officer Cameron's—"

"Open the door, Furnelli."

Her tone left nothing to interpretation and the junior officer immediately stepped up and unlocked the cell. Veronica expected Dylan to bolt, but he just stood there.

"This, *uhh*, this some sort of trick?" Dylan asked, wiping the sweat from his brow with the sleeve of the sweatshirt that barely made it past his elbow. His blue aura was more like a hard outline now.

"No trick, but if you don't leave now, I might change my mind."

*And arrest you for dealing drugs to Chloe and her friends.*

Dylan's eyes darted back and forth as he slowly left the cell. It was almost comical the way the man expected to be grabbed and thrown back in at any moment.

*Where the fuck do you think you're going? Get back in there!*

"What about the sweatsuit?" Court asked, still very confused as to what had just happened. "Should I go get it from him?"

Veronica thought about the thick, dark sweat stains that marred the fabric, and the blue aura that extended nearly a foot from Dylan Hall's body.

"Yeah, I don't think we want that back."

# Chapter 11

"YOU *WHAT?*" THE WORDS CAME out of Officer Ken Cameron's mouth as if he were vomiting them. "You let him go?"

Ken took a step toward Veronica, and Freddie tensed.

Veronica didn't back down.

"He didn't do it. I told you; Dylan isn't stalking Chloe."

Ken's face contorted into a mask of fury.

"This is my case—I never asked for your help. You know what? You know what I think? I think you and this Dylan guy have something—"

"Easy now, Ken," Freddie warned.

Veronica wasn't a big fan of her partner coming to her rescue like this, and she'd told him as much on several occasions. It made her seem weak. But, like her teasing, 'what ifs', and calling him Freddie, it was a part of their nature.

"No, it's not because he grabbed my ass, and it's not because my foot drove his balls into his stomach," Veronica snapped. Normally, she kept a cool head, even around Ken. But today was different, her emotions were heightened, her patience frayed. She pulled out the piece of paper that Dylan had just written on and slammed it, along with the note in the evidence bag, down on her desk. "It's because he didn't write this."

This was Veronica's gotcha moment, but it didn't pan out the way she'd hoped. Ken barely even looked at the notes, let alone compare the handwriting.

"He could've faked it. Hell, he could've written this with his wrong hand for all I know."

"And spell the word swallow with one 'l'?" Freddie offered.

At least her partner was trying.

Ken had said his piece and didn't justify this with a response.

"Look," Veronica said, her tone softening, "you said it your-self, it's hard to mistake someone who looks like Dylan Hall. But that first note was found in Chloe's locker. If he was lurking around their school, someone would have noticed."

Ken's face reddened.

"He could have paid someone to put it there. A student."

The man was embarrassing himself now and sounded like a petulant child.

*Give the baby his goddamn rattle already.*

"You're grasping, now. You're—"

"Grasping or not, that was my prisoner. You had no right to let him go."

"I brought him in!"

Freddie grabbed her arm. While she'd been arguing with Ken, her partner's phone had evidently rung because he was holding it in the palm of his hand.

"We gotta go." Veronica, grateful for the intrusion, didn't ask why, but Freddie elaborated anyway. "Sheriff Burns just texted. They're getting started on Maggie Cernak."

\*\*\*

"There are more diplomatic ways of getting your point across," Freddie remarked as they drove toward the Bear County coroner's office.

Veronica shrugged.

She didn't want to talk about Ken. And, truthfully, Veronica was a little ashamed by how she'd acted. Disagreeing with a fellow officer was one thing, outright embarrassment, espe-cially when dealing with a wannabe Alpha like Ken Cameron, was taboo. And it wasn't her.

"I'm thinking this isn't all about Ken, though."

This got Veronica's attention.

"What do you mean?"

Freddie bit his upper lip and chose his words carefully.

"Well, you were so adamant that Maggie had been murdered, and the sheriff and his deputy challenged you on that. And then Dylan…" He let his sentence trail off and Veronica grimaced.

"What do you want me to do? Just rubber stamp everything?" She put on a baby voice. "Oh, Detective Furlow, sir, you're *sooo* right about everything."

Freddie didn't reply and kept his eyes locked on the road.

"Shit, I'm sorry." Veronica sighed. "I'm a dick."

"Not always."

They continued in silence for several minutes before Veronica spoke up again.

"What do you think, Freddie? Did I fuck up? Is Dylan stalking Chloe Dolan?"

"I don't think so. But the risk-reward ratio of letting him go? Not worth it. Not when Chloe's dad is a Greenham city councilor."

That had been rash. They could have kept Dylan for a minimum of twenty-four hours without charging him. And because he was high when they brought him in, they might have been able to push that to thirty-six.

"Shit."

Freddie waved her concerns away.

"I'd be more worried about pissing off Ken Cameron. It's a small office, and you don't want to be making enemies. Especially with that hothead Ken."

"I can handle Ken," she said a little too defensively.

"I've seen your kick—I'm pretty sure you can." Freddie laughed, but it felt forced. "I'm just not sure *I* can."

Making enemies in the office when you were a cop wasn't the same thing as if you worked as a data entry specialist. What's the worst that could happen at IBM? Someone deletes your spreadsheet? Veronica had heard horror stories of actual deaths during a shootout because one cop had a weapon 'malfunction' while providing backup for a despised colleague.

Reprehensible, but true.

Freddie, Veronica knew she could count on matter what. Ken? Not a chance.

Trying to clear her mind of Ken Cameron, she found herself thinking of Sheriff Burns again and the fact that he'd lied to her.

Why lie about knowing Maggie Cernak?

"Freddie, do you know if Sheriff Burns is married?"

Freddie slowly looked over at her, a sly grin on his face.

"Whatever." Veronica rolled her eyes. "It's about Maggie."

"Ah, yes. To be honest, I don't know. I don't think so, though. I imagine if his wife was home, he would have sent her away real quick after he found the body. But it probably would have come up. So, no, I don't think so."

Freddie pulled into the parking lot of a squat building that had Bear County Medical written in embossed letters above a set of tinted windows.

"You can always ask him," he offered. "But be prepared to accept a drink date, if he's single."

"What?"

Freddie raised a pudgy finger and pointed out the window.

Sheriff Steve Burns was standing by the front door, one foot against the wall. As their car pulled up, he tipped his hat back with one finger, smiled, and waved.

# Chapter 12

BEAR COUNTY'S MORGUE WAS LOCATED in the basement of the medical building and wasn't much larger than a walk-in freezer of a large restaurant. There were two gurneys, one of which was occupied, a sink, a table of tools, a weighing station, and a small mobile cart with a computer on top, which was covered with a plastic coating to protect it from biological material. Off to one side there appeared to be two cooling lockers.

The coroner, a woman in her mid-sixties named Kristin Newberry, was short, with gray hair pulled up into a bun, and wire glasses that matched her figure.

Sheriff Burns introduced them, and the no-nonsense woman promptly led them to the occupied gurney and pulled the sheet back.

Maggie Cernak had been stripped of her clothes and was lying on her back, arms at her sides. Her face was more relaxed now that gravity wasn't working on it, and her tongue, while still thick, was mostly inside her mouth. Veronica was once again struck by just how young the woman looked.

Young and healthy.

"Other than the bruising around her neck," Kristin indicated the purple and red streak beneath Maggie's chin with a gloved hand, "I found Ms. Cernak to be in excellent condition. No sign of broken bones, bruises, or trauma." She slid a finger into the woman's mouth, pulling back her lips to reveal healthy gums and teeth. "No signs of excessive drug use, either. Liver temp indicated that she died between eight and ten hours ago. So, just after midnight."

It wasn't what Veronica saw, but what she *didn't* see that raised concern.

"I thought you were doing an autopsy?"

The coroner looked at her strangely, and then her eyes drifted to Sheriff Burns.

"I don't do autopsies. I'm not a doctor—I'm an elected official."

"Kristin is a lawyer by trade," Sheriff Burns reminded her.

"Right," Veronica said, trying to hide her annoyance. She had to remember that the county worked much differently than the City of Greenham. It was one of those quintessential American oddities, given that Greenham was part of Bear County. And then there was the State Police to consider, which meant that at any given time, a crime could be in three law enforcement jurisdictions at once. And each agency had its different rules and procedures.

"For most cases, I try to get out to the crime scene—that just wasn't possible today. But based on the photos that Deputy McVeigh and Sheriff Burns provided me, I'm confident in making a manner and cause of death assessment. No autopsy necessary."

"Which is?" Veronica said a little more forcefully than intended. Her eyes darted to Maggie Cernak's corpse.

The sound was faint, and growing less audible by the moment, but she could hear that song, the children taunting.

*La, la, la, la, laaaaa, laaa.*

"Suicide," Kristin stated flatly. Her brow knitted as she looked at the sheriff. "Am I missing something?"

"No," Freddie interjected, trying to keep the conversation civil. "Just want to be thorough. Did you do blood work?"

Kristin's eyebrows lowered.

"Yes." Kristin backed away from the body and walked over to the table of tools. In addition to various metal instruments, there was also a single sheet of paper. "Nothing in her system other than trace amounts of ibuprofen. No alcohol, no drugs."

She held the paper out for Veronica and Freddie to look at, but they just glanced it over quickly. "I only ran a general tox-screen. If you want me to order a more detailed report that covers exotic drugs, then I have to ship a sample to another lab."

The way the coroner and the sheriff continued to exchange glances made it clear that they'd had a discussion before Freddie and Veronica's arrival. Which, Veronica surmised, was probably protocol. Only, this case wasn't normal because— *Maggie didn't commit suicide, she was murdered* —the body was found in the sheriff's barn.

"What happens during criminal cases? If there's evidence of foul play?" Veronica asked.

"Evidence of foul play? There is no evidence of foul play," Kristin said sharply. "Like I said, no bruising, no—"

Sheriff Burns silenced the coroner by raising his hand.

"It's okay, we're on the same side here."

"It's just, *uhhh*, it's been a while since we've been out of Greenham," Freddie said, trying to keep the peace.

"I understand," Sheriff Burns replied. To his credit, despite what some might consider an obvious challenge, he remained inexplicably calm. "The coroner," he tipped his chin to Kristin, "is responsible for the initial investigation. If she deems that no foul play is involved, then she'll contact the next of kin and let them know. Pretty much ends there. If, however, there is even an inkling of a crime having been committed? Then Kristin will put in a request for a Medical Examiner or pathologist to come in and perform an autopsy. Usually, takes about a day —sometimes we get someone from your city, from Greenham, but if they're busy, we'll get someone from Portland. Am I missing anything?" The query was directed at Kristin, and Veronica reminded herself that the sheriff was also new at this, that he used to be part of the State Police.

Kristin pressed her lips together.

"Pretty much it."

"Right. Well, I get that this is a strange case, and I brought you guys in to make sure that everything was done according to the book. Now, if either of you," the sheriff's eyes stayed on Veronica just slightly longer than Freddie, "think that something's not right, I'm more than happy to—"

"No, that's fine. If it walks like a duck, that sort of thing," Freddie said. He moved to shake the sheriff's hand and Veronica spoke up.

"What about the note?"

"Note?" Kristin asked.

"It's not much of a note," the sheriff said. This time, there was a hint of defensiveness in his voice and Veronica wondered why he hadn't mentioned it to the coroner.

"The CSU tech—what's his name?"

"Holland."

"Sure, Holland. He found a note in Maggie's pocket. It said *EENIE*."

"Eenie?" Kristin asked.

"Yeah," Veronica confirmed. "Like the song, you know? *Eenie, Meenie, Miney, Mo?*"

The sheriff cleared his throat.

"It was more of a scrap of paper than a note, though. I thought it was from the library—forgot to mention it."

Veronica inhaled deeply, trying to detect if Sheriff Burns was lying. But the harsh mixture of antiseptic cleaning solution and formalin that was prevalent in the morgue made it impossible to pick up even the recognizable odor of gasoline.

"Do you have a picture of it?" Kristin asked.

"Even better," the sheriff replied, tapping first his pant pockets and then the breast of his khaki shirt. He pulled the scrap of paper, still in the evidence bag, from the latter and handed it to Kristin. To her credit, the coroner inspected the note thoroughly before handing it back.

"I don't know what it means, but it's not like any suicide note I've ever seen. I'm tempted to side with the sheriff, though—it's probably unrelated. Either way, it won't change my decision here. That being said, if you detectives think that—"

"*Quack, quack,*" Freddie said. "We're on board with—"

"Can I see that?" Veronica interrupted, reaching for the sheet of paper. *EENIE* was written in block letters, and she immediately thought of Dylan Hall and Chloe Dolan. "Did you check this against Maggie's handwriting?"

No one answered.

"I can," Sheriff Burns offered. "But, like I said, even if it's not her writing, it could've just come from the library."

"You mean the library that you told us you haven't been to more than a couple of times?" Veronica challenged. She knew she was on the verge of making enemies here, but the sheriff called them in for a reason. And Veronica couldn't shake the feeling that there was more to this case, much more than a simple suicide.

Sheriff Burns' face reddened.

"No, I meant—"

Freddie gave her a stern look and Veronica knew that she'd gone too far.

"I'm sorry," she blurted. "Mind if I take a picture of this?"

"Go right ahead."

Veronica used her cell phone to snap a picture of the note, then gave it back to the sheriff.

"Look, I'm new here," the sheriff admitted, "and if I said, or did something, or—"

"Sheriff, c'mon, same side here," Freddie said. He slapped the man on the shoulder. "Mark it off as a suicide."

"You sure?"

Freddie rarely pulled the seniority card on Veronica, but in this instance, it was probably the right call. After all, making an enemy of a man who you might have to work closely with for at least four years wasn't a smart decision. And based on what? Phantom colors and smells?

Veronica recalled what Freddie had said about not making enemies with officers who you might rely on to have your back. What about an entire county?

"Absolutely," Freddie confirmed. The sheriff looked at her, but Veronica just couldn't bring herself to say it. She did, however, manage an unconvincing nod.

"Well, thanks for your help on this one. If you ever need anything, I owe you one."

They all shook hands and, on the way out, Veronica turned back to address Kristin.

"The sheriff said that you're responsible for notifying next of kin?"

"Yes. So far, no luck, though. No siblings, no parents, that I can find. I'll keep looking though."

"Good."

*And so will I,* Veronica thought, but didn't say.

# Chapter 13

FREDDIE DIDN'T SAY IT—HE didn't have to. Veronica asked herself the question that was on both of their minds.

*What's wrong with me?*

This wasn't her. She was calm, detail-oriented, methodical.

Self-doubt slowly started to creep in. It was amazing that no matter how many cases you solved, you failed one and that's what stuck in your brain, that's what held you back. You could be 99/100 and the one you can't figure out gnaws at you constantly and eats your soul like a cow chewing cud. Veronica had earned her spot as the youngest detective in Greenham, but...

Ken Cameron's angry face suddenly appeared in her mind.

*Maybe he's right, maybe I only got this job because—*

"Why are you looking at me like that?" Veronica said. "I know I was a little harsh back there but—"

"It's not that."

"What then? We both said it: the sheriff is lying about something."

"I'm not so sure."

"What do you mean? You said it before."

Freddie had a strange smirk on his face that was starting to bother her.

"Freddie, I'm not in the mood for—"

"Maybe he's not lying, maybe he's just nervous."

Veronica squinted at her partner.

"Nervous? Why? 'Cuz he's a new sheriff?"

"No, Veronica. Nervous around *you*."

Veronica rolled her eyes.

"Fuck off."

Freddie laughed, sending a ripple of fat from the bottom of his mouth to the waddle beneath his chin.

"I'm serious. Every time he looks at you, he gets this like —
yeah! Like that face you're making right now. Blushing or
whatever."

"I'm not blushing."

Freddie just gave her a knowing look.

"Okay, okay, sorry." He held up his hands. "I'm just saying
that maybe you're picking up on his nervousness and not a lie."

Veronica pursed her lips and remained quiet.

*Then how do you explain the smell of gas, huh?*

As much as she wanted to ignore her partner's words, she
couldn't quite do it. If someone else had said what Freddie had,
Veronica would have passed it off as sexist bullshit. But not
Freddie. Coming up, she'd had to deal with a lot of bullshit,
from perps like Dylan, to colleagues, and even occasionally her
superiors. Even though in a lot of ways, Freddie Furlow was
old school, he'd always treated her as an equal.

Ken Cameron, on the other hand... Sheriff Steve Burns was
everything the man wasn't. Handsome in a conventional way,
without effort, polite, and respectful.

Also, a liar. Maybe a murderer.

They pulled into the precinct parking lot, and Veronica, who
was feeling drained, looked at her phone. It was nearly 5:30.

"You coming up?" Freddie asked.

The last thing that Veronica wanted right now was another
confrontation with Ken Cameron.

"I think I'm just gonna take off," she said. "If that's okay
with you, boss."

"Well, let's put it this way." Freddie tapped his considerable
gut. "If you run, I can't stop you."

Veronica laughed and Freddie smiled.

"I'll see you tomorrow."

"Early day," Freddie said with a nod.

"Yeah?"

"Yeah. You did let our prime suspect in the Chloe Dolan case loose, remember?"

"Right. Okay, early day."

*And late night.*

Because Veronica had no intention of heading home. Freddie may have agreed with Bear County's coroner that Maggie had committed suicide, but she remained unconvinced.

*I'm just doing my due diligence,* she told herself as she drove to the Matheson Public Library. *That's all I'm doing.*

The faint smell of gasoline began to permeate the inside of her car, and Veronica quickly opened the window.

\*\*\*

Gina Braden looked nothing like a librarian. Broad shoulders, thick arms, and even though Veronica couldn't see her legs from this side of the desk, she suspected that buying regular pants to fit her quads would prove difficult. She looked like a professional CrossFitter.

"I'm Detective Shade." Veronica produced her badge and flashed it.

Instantly, she knew that she'd made a mistake. Gina's expression revealed that Kristin hadn't come here yet. And why would she? The coroner was still searching for next of kin; informing friends and colleagues wasn't high on the priority list.

Now, burdened with the task of telling this woman that Maggie was dead, Veronica wished that she'd taken Freddie's advice and just let the case go.

But she was here now and leaving would make things even worse.

"Yes? Is everything okay? Is Toby fine?"

Veronica had no idea who Toby was—Gina's son? Boyfriend?—but it didn't matter.

"I'm not here about Toby," Veronica said, shifting into her professional voice. "I'm here about Maggie. I have some very unfortunate news to tell you."

The woman's eyes instantly welled with tears.

"Is she... is she all right?"

"I'm afraid not." The library was mostly empty, yet she lowered her voice anyway, out of respect. "Maggie died early this morning."

Gina gasped, and tears spilled down her cheeks. Veronica looked for tissues on the desk, but when she saw none, she offered an apology instead.

"I'm sorry for your loss."

"How—" Gina sobbed. "How did she die?"

Having not anticipated this conversation, Veronica was unsure of how to answer. If she suggested something that directly contradicted the coroner's report, which she and Freddie had signed off on, there was the potential for real repercussions.

Veronica decided that the best course of action was straddling the truth.

"Apparent suicide, but we're still investigating some details."

"Suicide?" Gina's voice was high and tight, nothing like what one would expect from a woman as muscular as her.

"Like I said, we're still investigating. Were you guys close?"

Gina started to nod, but at the last second, changed her mind.

"I wouldn't say we were close, not really. We went out for drinks a couple times. Maggie—well, she is a pretty private person."

Veronica nodded, noting Gina's use of 'she is' instead of 'she was'. It could take a long time to refer to some in the past tense after they were gone.

"How long have you worked together?"

"A couple of years. Maggie works the day shift, while I work nights. Usually, a place this size wouldn't require two employees, but I'm phasing out—putting more time into CrossFit. Anyway, we often see each other during shift change, but not always. I didn't—I didn't see her today."

This intrigued Veronica.

"Nobody reported that she didn't turn up for work this morning?"

Gina shook her head.

"No. We mostly use self-checkout here. Our job is to help people find what they're looking for, register new cards, pay fines, put books on the shelves, that sort of thing. If someone came looking for the librarian and she wasn't around, they probably just thought Maggie was using the bathroom. To be honest, we really aren't that busy."

"I'm guessing you guys don't have security cameras?"

Gina suddenly appeared nervous, which was also out of place given her immense muscularity.

"You think that something—"

"No, no, I don't think anything happened here. I'm just asking."

Gina licked her lips.

"No cameras. We've barely enough money for new releases. Libraries just aren't as popular as they used to be."

"Over the past few days, or even weeks, did you notice any changes in Maggie's behavior? Like, was she more withdrawn or nervous, maybe? Anything like that?"

"I didn't notice. But like I told you already, Maggie's a private person. Even when we went for drinks, she didn't say much. Just that she loved to read. Oh, and that she has a cat."

Veronica chewed her bottom lip. She wasn't sure what she was hoping to learn coming here—someone harassing her at work? An abusive boyfriend?—but a revelation didn't seem to be forthcoming.

Unless...

"Do you know Sheriff Burns?"

The sudden change in the line of questioning took Gina by surprise.

"Steve? Y-yes, of course. He comes in often."

Veronica suppressed a smile.

*Gotcha.*

"And Maggie? Did Maggie know him?"

"Why are you—"

"Just curious. I don't spend much time in Matheson, trying to get a better understanding of how things work around here, that's all."

Gina tensed.

"You're not from Matheson?" she asked hesitantly.

Veronica replayed her introduction in her mind. She'd said she was a detective, just not from where. It indicated Greenham on her badge, but no one looked at the details. They were usually too nervous, which was one of the reasons why it was so easy to trick someone into believing you were a cop when you just bought a shitty Halloween costume and fake badge over the Internet.

"No, Greenham. Just helping out on this case."

Veronica was treading water here, and her legs were beginning to tire. Gina didn't strike her as a stupid person and the next logical conclusion would be that if Veronica was just helping out, there was a high probability that she was working with the sheriff. And if so, why not just ask him?

"You know what? Forget I asked — it's not important." *I already caught Sheriff Burns in his lie.* "Again, I'm very sorry for your loss."

Gina wiped the tears away.

"What about — what about her cat?"

Veronica raised an eyebrow.

"If she's gone — if Maggie's gone, what's going to happen to her cat?"

Veronica thought about this for a moment. She'd gotten nothing from coming here, but perhaps there were clues at Maggie's house.

Two birds, one cat, that sort of thing.

"You wouldn't happen to have a key to her place, would you?"

Gina sniffed and opened one of the drawers and started rooting around.

"She went on vacation once, and I think — yeah." Gina produced a single key and held it out to Veronica. "She asked me to feed the cat once a day. I can't really keep it — I'm terribly allergic."

Veronica took the key.

"I'll make sure the cat is okay. Thanks."

Gina looked like she was on the verge of breaking down, and Veronica hurried out of the library and back to her car.

She was staring into space, tapping Maggie's house key against the wheel when a familiar vehicle passed directly in front of her.

"Shit."

It was Sheriff Burns' squad car, and the man was behind the wheel, hat and all. He started to turn in her direction, and she ducked.

*Please don't see me. And please don't go into the library.*

Veronica waited for a ten count and then slowly raised her eyes to peek through the windshield. The sheriff's taillights were receding down Matheson's main artery. If the man had seen her, there was no acknowledgment.

Her heart rate began to slow.

*What are you doing, Veronica?*

The answer came quickly and unexpectedly. It also smelled like a gasoline-drenched lie.

*Just looking after a poor, lonely cat, that's all.*

# Chapter 14

MAGGIE CERNAK LIVED IN A SMALL, two-story house about ten minutes from the library, which meant she probably walked to work. The fact that there was no car in the driveway suggested one of two things: she didn't own one, or it was parked somewhere else. Maybe she drove somewhere—a restaurant? Not a bar because Maggie didn't have alcohol in her system—and Veronica made a mental note to see if there was any video footage of her downtown last night.

It felt strange walking up to the woman's front door, knowing that Maggie would never open it and walk inside again. Everything was exactly the same as when she'd left, and it would remain that way. The house and everything in it would be undisturbed as if waiting for the woman to return. If her next of kin was found, they'd take possession and begin moving her things out. If there were no parents, siblings, or offspring, Maggie's items would be auctioned off. In six months, maybe a year, another family would move in, the library website would take down her photo, and it would be as if she never existed.

Out of habit, Veronica knocked on the front door. She didn't expect an answer and didn't get one. Before trying the key, she looked around. Maggie didn't appear to have any security cameras—neither the fancy doorbell kind nor the more traditional kind—and the street itself remained quiet. If something had happened here, something that had preceded Maggie's death, it was unlikely to have been noticed or recorded.

Without further hesitation, Veronica slipped the key into the lock, and it turned easily. She opened the door and was surprised to be greeted by the sound of a bell ringing. Her first thought was that Maggie had installed one over the door, like at a retail shop to signify to the employees that someone was entering, but that didn't make sense.

Veronica shut the door behind her, smiled, and dropped onto her haunches.

A gray cat sauntered forward, the bell around its neck chiming with every step.

"Hi," Veronica said. The cat, sensing that something was different, stopped a few feet from her. "It's okay, I'm not going to hurt you."

The cat purred, and Veronica beckoned at it. The animal was probably hungry because it quickly got over the inherent stranger danger and continued forward. Veronica scratched the soft fur beneath the cat's neck and discovered a heart-shaped name tag beside the bell.

"Lucy," Veronica read out loud. "Well, hi, Lucy, my name's Veronica."

The cat purred again, louder this time, as if understanding her.

"I bet you're hungry. Let's get you some food."

Veronica scooped the cat up in one hand and looked around. The kitchen was off to the right, and she headed there first, resisting the temptation to tell Lucy what had happened to Maggie. Not only would this feel strange, but she was taxed from her encounter with Gina.

Would the cat even understand that Maggie wasn't coming back? Probably. Would she understand that Veronica was here because everyone thought that Maggie committed suicide, while she was convinced that the poor woman had been murdered? Definitely not.

One thing soon became obvious. If Maggie had been a tormented soul, the state of her house did not reflect this fact. It was clean, tidy, perfectly normal, and average in every way. No evidence of violence, abuse, addiction... nothing.

There were piles of books on the table near the couch —everything from Dean Koontz to Margaret Atwood—and no TV to be found, but this seemed normal for someone whose main passion was reading and who was a librarian by profession.

Although Veronica had little to no experience with cats, a woman like Maggie who lived alone struck her as someone who would treat her pet to quality food. And she figured that the wet, perishable kind, was probably more expensive than kibble.

She set Lucy down and was about to open the fridge door when her eyes fell on the calendar attached to the freezer. A calendar that had several handwritten messages on it. With Lucy purring and nestling up to her leg, Veronica compared the writing on the freezer to the photograph of *EENIE* on her phone.

Not even close to a match. The difference between the two was even more dramatic than the note in Chloe Dolan's locker and Dylan Hall's chicken scratching. Maggie had pretty, looping letters while the note found in her pocket was written in jagged, aggressive text.

"I knew it," she whispered, feeling vindicated. Once more, she reached for the fridge handle, only to stop a second time.

Something else had caught her eye.

Maggie's work schedule was written on the calendar, but there was more.

*Online book club, 9 PM.*

This didn't make sense. Who planned a book club when—

A noise, footsteps, put Veronica on high alert. She put a hand on her gun and even Lucy stiffened.

The footsteps persisted, but they weren't coming from inside the house as she'd first thought—they were coming from outside. They were approaching—two people, and they were chatting.

It took her a moment to place both voices.

The first, a female, was the coroner, Kristin Newberry. The second, Veronica was fairly certain belonged to CSU Tech Holland Toler.

There was a light knock on the door and Veronica grimaced. She wasn't sure what to do—she wasn't supposed to be here. The case was closed, a suicide. The coroner was here to break the terrible news to Maggie's roommate or a live-in boyfriend. Would they come in? And if they did, what would they do when they found Veronica here? She knew that it would be worse if she didn't answer and they discovered her standing in the kitchen, but Veronica was frozen with indecision, something else that wasn't like her.

*Just go away*, she silently pleaded. *Go away.*

Another knock.

Did I lock the door? Did I lock it behind me?

Veronica couldn't remember.

In response to the new visitor, Lucy began moving and her tiny bell tinkled. Veronica quickly grabbed the cat and the bell. Then she held her breath and waited.

The voices were muffled, but she thought she could make out what they were saying.

"You're new here, too?" *Kristin.*

"Yeah, just moved to the area a couple of weeks ago." *Holland.*

*Is everyone new here?* Veronica wondered. *The sheriff, the tech, what about the goddamn mayor?* She shook her head. *Does Bear County even have a mayor?*

"Ah, nice. It's quiet, but Matheson's a good place to live. Greenham, on the other hand? Well, let's just say that I wouldn't want to raise my children there." *Kristin.*

"Right." *Holland.*

There was a pause.

"Should we—should we go in?" *Holland.*

"Legally, we have to wait for the sheriff." *Kristin.*

*Please don't be on his way.*

"Is he on his way?" *Holland.*

"Knowing Sheriff Burns, he's getting his evening coffee at Daphne's." *Kristin.*

*Please don't wait here.*

"Should we wait?" *Holland.*

"Naw. We can come back tomorrow. Actually, I could do a coffee." *Kristin.*

"Me too." *Holland.*

Veronica finally exhaled when she heard footsteps receding. After a few moments, she went to the nearest window and teased back the curtain in time to see a black Mercedes pulling away, with Kristin behind the wheel.

*Thank God I parked on the street.*

Veronica waited until she could no longer see the Mercedes before grabbing some cat food from the fridge—indeed, the fancy kind—and leaving Maggie's home. She locked the door, double-checked, then got behind the wheel of her car.

As Veronica started to drive away, Lucy purred loudly from the passenger seat. The cat placed its paws on the door and stared out the window.

For some reason, this nearly broke Veronica's heart. She wasn't even sure why she'd taken the cat—after all, it wasn't her responsibility. And then there was the added fact that when

Kristin returned, this time with the sheriff, they'd wonder where the animal was.

But there was something about the cat just being left alone that Veronica couldn't bring herself to ignore.

"I'm sorry, sweetie, but you can't go back."

*And neither can I. That was too close.*

# Chapter 15

FREDDIE INTERCEPTED VERONICA BEFORE SHE entered the precinct. The man was wearing his typical uniform: an over-sized golf shirt, and khaki slacks. A little light for the cool weather, but he had plenty of insulation to work with. What was different about her partner today, was his expression. Normally, Freddie was grinning, at least in the morning before she had a chance to annoy him.

Not today.

Veronica's first thoughts went to her break-in last night.

"What's up?" she prodded.

"Captain wants to see you. Does not seem happy."

"Ken," she hissed.

Freddie nodded.

"You want to go for a coffee first?"

"No, let's just get this over with."

Freddie held the door open for her and as she passed, he sneezed.

"You get a cat?"

Veronica hesitated before saying, "Just pet a stray."

Even before they got out of the elevator on the third floor, Veronica sensed Ken's eyes on her. She refused to even acknowledge him as she strode, chin high, through the maze of cardboard partitions to the captain's office. She knocked and a gruff voice instructed her to enter.

In many ways, the man behind the desk was like Freddie. He was large, but whereas Freddie was all fat, the captain had more of an athletic build. He looked like a retired football player, who used to be all muscle but now, while he'd retained most of it, it had been smoothed by a layer of adipose tissue. He didn't smile as much as Freddie, but the captain was a loyal, caring man.

The first thing that Veronica picked up on after entering the office wasn't the smell of gasoline, but stale cigarette smoke.

"You smoking again?" she asked.

The captain's lips twisted into a frown. He was clean-shaven with bushy eyebrows and hazel eyes. His hair, a medium brown, was cut short, probably to hide the fact that it was thinning at the crown and temples.

"You released Officer Cameron's prisoner?" the captain said, ignoring her comment about smoking.

"It wasn't him," Veronica replied defensively. "It wasn't Dylan. I know everyone wants it to be Dylan, but it's not. He didn't write the notes—he's not the one stalking Chloe."

"Dylan's got a rap sheet longer than my arm," the captain shot back.

"I know, I know. I'm not defending him, it's just—"

The captain waved his hand, silencing her.

"Not the point, V. Not the point. That's Officer Cameron's prisoner and you shouldn't have released him."

V—the captain was the only one who called her that.

"He asked us to be on the lookout for Dylan. Freddie and I were just—"

"I know you guys don't get along. Everyone knows. But you have to work together. You have to communicate, V."

"Ken's a royal asshole. I hurt his feelings by rejecting him, now he's looking for any excuse to report me. And by the way, he doesn't care about who's actually stalking Chloe. He's got a hard-on for Dylan. And if we arrest Dylan and Chloe keeps getting harassed? What do you think her city councilor father is going to—"

"That's not your job!" the captain nearly shouted. Taken aback by this, Veronica immediately shut up. When he spoke again a second later, the captain's voice was calm as if the outburst had never happened. "Look, I don't want you worrying about the politics, that's my domain. Just focus on your work. This is Officer Cameron's case, you're just here to lend a helping hand. And that doesn't mean taking it over, nor does it mean going against his wishes. If you have a problem, just put it in the report, *V.*"

"Why can't you just give the case to me and Freddie?"

The captain shook his head.

"No, it's his case and it will remain that way. You and Detective Furlow are to offer support in any way that Officer Cameron sees fit."

Veronica's eyes bulged.

"What? No way. I don't want to have anything to do with him."

"Precisely. That's why I'm making you work with him on this case."

"No, I—"

"That's an order."

This was one of those teachable moments, something about working with, or for, people whom you didn't like. Veronica just hated that it had to be Ken Cameron.

She knew better than to push back, however. And after a few seconds, the captain spoke again.

"When was the last time you saw Jane?"

This about-face caught Veronica by surprise, which was probably why she answered even though she preferred not to discuss her personal life at work, even with the captain.

"Nearly two weeks," she admitted with a shrug. "But I'm fine. Really, I'm fine."

There was that gasoline smell again. The captain might not have been able to smell it, but he could read her in a way that no one else could.

"You need to see Jane, V."

"Is that an order, too?" Veronica asked, her bitterness returning. When she saw the captain's caring eyes widen, she immediately regretted the comment. "Sorry." Veronica sighed, realizing that she'd just proven the man's point: she wasn't fine. "I'll make an appointment."

The captain looked at the clock on the wall.

"Why don't you see if Jane can fit you in this morning?"

"Now?"

"Sure. I'll let Freddie know."

Veronica was hesitant but a session with Jane would postpone any interaction with Ken, which was a definite bonus.

"Okay, sure."

"And try to get along with Officer Cameron, V."

"Will do—as long as you quit smoking, Dad."

With that, Veronica left the captain's office. Avoiding Ken's eyes was impossible now—he'd sought her out and was looking at her with a smug expression, like Veronica knew he would.

Veronica wanted to say something, wanted to tell Ken to wipe that grin off his face or she'd do it for him. But Captain Peter Shade had just reamed her out and if she knew her father, getting into a fight with Ken now would result in a more severe reprimand, perhaps even a suspension—despite being the man's only daughter, or maybe because of it.

There were positives to your dad being the police captain, no doubt about it, but there were negatives, too. Often, Veronica thought he punished her more severely than others for mis-steps or mistakes, likely to avoid looking like he was playing favorites.

So, Veronica remained mum, which worked.

Ken stopped smiling.

"I want Dylan Hall arrested. *Again.*"

"How about," Veronica began, "you look for Dylan while Freddie and I go speak to Chloe."

Ken shook his head.

"No—you let him out, you bring him back in."

Veronica set her jaw.

The man knew how to push her buttons, and right now Officer Ken Cameron was mashing them like an erratic game of Whack-a-Mole.

"Sure, no problem," Freddie interceded. Veronica hadn't even noticed the man standing beside her, which was saying something—it was hard not to notice Detective Furlow. Her partner wrapped his hand around her waist and together they moved to the elevator before Veronica could say, or do, something that she'd regret.

Forget reprimand or suspension, she was thinking jail time.

"Fucking asshole," Veronica muttered when they were out of earshot.

"Let it go."

They made it all the way downstairs and nearly to Freddie's car before Veronica remembered her promise to her father.

"Freddie, there's something I have to do first—Captain's orders. Meet you back here in an hour or so?"

The man looked concerned, but he nodded.

"Be safe."

"I will."

It took a minute longer for Veronica to realize just how mad she was. It would be days before she realized exactly why.

*Dad was right, I really need to see Jane.*

# Chapter 16

DR. JANE BERNARD WAS THE only person who knew about Veronica's synesthesia. She was her first psychiatrist, the very one who had treated Veronica for PTSD after the suicide she'd witnessed at Edinburgh Elementary. She knew about the smells, the colors, and the song.

Dr. Bernard, then in her late forties, had a wealth of experience when it came to psychiatric care, with a specialty in dealing with childhood trauma. The doctor's first thought had been that what Veronica was experiencing was a complicated coping mechanism, but when these hallucinations reoccurred, and with such consistency—the smell of gasoline when someone was lying, the blue aura associated with sweating, and the reddish plumes in the vicinity of violence—Dr. Bernard began to suspect that something deeper was at play.

They'd run a gamut of tests, tests that scared the shit out of Veronica—everything from MRIs to eye exams. But everything came back normal. By all accounts, Veronica was a well-adjusted young girl, someone who had seen something tragic and horrible and had dealt with it rather formidably.

What had started as a three-session mandate by the school, had quickly become a weekly, hour-long meeting. But even with her vast experience, Jane still couldn't figure out where these visions were coming from.

That was until they saw the video.

Testing out a theory, Dr. Bernard had asked then twelve-year-old Veronica Shade to watch a video about lying. It was an instructional video, commonly used by law enforcement to train their officers, and outlined some of the common tells that a person was being deceitful. Looking up and to the right while recounting a story, for instance, suggested that what was being said was fabricated instead of recalled. There were many, including shifting your feet or body away from the authority figure, clammy hands, shifty eyes, repeating questions, speaking in sentence fragments, and even self-grooming. This wasn't foolproof and was something that could, in fact, be used by a liar to deceive more convincingly. But it was a good, general gage of whether or not someone was telling the truth.

Toward the end of the video was a test component, in which the viewer was asked to guess which of a variety of subjects were lying.

Veronica got them all correct. This, in and of itself, was impressive for a twelve-year-old, especially because some of the clues were subtle in nature. But what was downright amazing, was when the show deliberately deceived the viewer, in part, to illustrate how lie detection wasn't an exact science, Veronica still got every one right.

When Dr. Bernard asked her how she knew, Veronica's answer was confusing.

"I smell gasoline. It's like... it's like someone is opening a can of gas right in front of my nose. I don't—I don't know how to explain it better than that."

It was another two sessions, and many calls to experts around the world before Dr. Bernard thought she'd figured it out.

"Veronica, I think you have something called synesthesia," she'd said at last. "Multimodal synesthesia, to be more precise."

These words meant nothing to Veronica and, young as she was, the doctor's elaboration was also difficult to understand. To her credit, however, Dr. Bernard stayed true to her doctrine: explaining as simply as she could without dumbing things down or patronizing.

"When you see something, light hits your eyes and special cells send a message to your brain. Your brain interprets this signal, and this is how we visualize the world around us. The key here is that your brain is what turns these signals into an image. And every one of us has a different brain so the world is always just a little different. Consider a person who is color blind... they believe that the world is black, white, and gray, and to them, it is. Same thing when we hear music — our brain interprets what we hear. But some people have more sensitive ears than others, and they can hear things we can't — certain pitches, for example. Now, occasionally, these signals can get crossed on their way from your ear or your eyes or your nose to your brain. For instance, when someone hears a type of music, they might smell a very specific odor, like vanilla. But that odor... it's not there. Think of it this way: if you hear the sound of a car crash, you might be inclined to cringe. You didn't think of it, didn't plan it, didn't have the time to consider the consequences of the crash, you just cringed. That's what I think you're experiencing, Veronica. The signals from your eyes are getting mixed up along the way to your brain and you're interpreting what you see as an odor."

"But I don't just smell things, I see them, too — the colors. And hear them."

Dr. Bernard nodded.

"I know. And you see things outside of your head, right? I mean, when you see the colors it's almost as if they exist in the real world, like you can touch them?"

Veronica agreed.

"What you're experiencing, Veronica, is *multimodal* synesthesia — meaning more than one type. Not only that, but you're a projector. No, don't be scared. This isn't a disease, and it isn't dangerous. It's very rare, but you're not sick. You're just very special."

"I don't... I don't understand. How can I tell if someone is lying?"

Dr. Bernard scratched her head.

"What did I say when we first met? That's right—I'm not afraid to tell you when I don't know something. And, to be honest, I'm not a hundred percent certain how this all works."

Feeling let down, Veronica bowed her head.

"But if I had to guess?" Dr. Bernard continued quickly. "I think it's your subconscious working overtime."

"Subconscious?"

"It sounds like a complicated word, but it isn't. You know what it means to be conscious, right? Awake, aware, that sort of thing? And unconscious? Zonked out. No feeling, no thinking. Well, the subconscious is like, between conscious and unconscious. Things are happening all around us, all the time. But it would be impossible to process everything at once. Think of when you're looking at, I don't know, at a bird, let's say. You see the bird; you see it flying through the air. But you also see the sky, the clouds, maybe the bird is flying over water, and you see that, too. There could be boats in the water, people swimming, a buoy, and so on. Your subconscious is picking up these things and they're affecting how you feel as you watch the bird. But you're not thinking about them. In fact, the moment you think about them, they move from the subconscious to the conscious. Remember the police video we watched? The police video on lying? Well, I think that your subconscious is looking for hints like the ones we saw on that tape all the time, and when it notices them, it pushes them into your consciousness. That's when the signals get crossed and instead of a eureka moment, you smell gasoline."

"Why—why gasoline?" Veronica asked.

Jane smiled.

"I don't know if we'll ever have the answer to that. But it's a cool trick, Veronica. And you're a smart girl—I bet you're going to find a way to use this trick to help you in life."

Over nearly two decades together, Dr. Jane Bernard and Veronica had learned a lot about synesthesia. They'd also grown close, partly because, at Veronica's request, Jane was the only one who was aware of her condition—not even her dad knew of it. Also, because Veronica's synesthesia meant that being in crowds was difficult and often overwhelming. As a result, her social circle even back then had been small and continued to be that way well into her adult life.

The third reason was more basic: Jane was a confidant, which was something Veronica lacked because she didn't have a mother growing up. Veronica could speak to her dad about many things, but because they worked so closely together, there were aspects of her life that she wasn't comfortable sharing.

Peter Shade was a kind, loving man. But he wasn't much for affection, of outward signs of love. Veronica knew that he loved her, there was no doubt about that, but he was old school. His main method of showing he cared was to protect her. Early on, that had meant guiding her away from anything police related. But she was drawn to it. Maybe it was the video that Dr. Bernard had shown her that pushed Veronica into law enforcement, or maybe it was because she grew up to be exceptional at telling if someone was lying. Perhaps if her father had been a banker, Veronica would be in a boardroom somewhere, offering advice to executives regarding whether or not the person trying to sell their company had fudged their EBITDA numbers.

When it became clear that she was going to be a cop, no matter what, Peter kept her close. And when Veronica had been promoted to detective, he'd teamed her up with Freddie Furlow.

Peter Shade wasn't big on kisses, or I love yous, but he made sure she was safe.

"Hi," Dr. Jane Bernard said, clearly startled. "I-I didn't think we had a session until Friday."

The woman had aged well over the years, but never had a face that would turn heads. A plain, bob of a haircut, a Parisian nose upon which sat a pair of unremarkable glasses. Jane wasn't ugly, but was no stunning beauty, either.

Veronica often thought that if you could design a psychiatrist in a lab, Dr. Jane Bernard would be pretty close to optimal. Too ugly and patients would be repulsed. Too pretty and they'd be intimidated, or worse, attracted. Jane ran the literal middle of the spectrum when it came to looks.

"We weren't supposed to," Veronica admitted. "But I think we need to talk. Can you can fit me in?"

Jane smiled.

"I've got a half hour. Come on in."

# Chapter 17

"IT'S... IT'S DIFFERENT THIS TIME." Veronica sighed. "You'd think it would be easy to explain this after all these years, but it's not. It's just... it's the intensity of the feelings. I'm telling you, Jane, this time it was *powerful*. Almost knocked me on my ass. Not only that, but I heard the music, saw the colors, and smelled gas. It was intense, to say the least."

"And has this happened with the other suicides you've investigated?"

Veronica thought back to when they'd pulled the tech millionaire, Collin McLachlan, out of the Casnet River. She'd felt something then, no doubt about it. But it hadn't been the same. Even before she'd seen the recording of the man willingly filling his pants with stones and walking into the water, her synesthesia had been muted, less visceral. She'd seen some flashes of orange and red, but even these were difficult to distinguish from the setting sun.

"No. That's the thing, Jane, this one is different. *Very* different."

Dr. Bernard scribbled something down on a sheet of paper.

"Let's, for a moment, try to ignore your synesthesia. Let's pretend that you didn't have any auditory or visual hallucinations. From a pure detective perspective, how would you view this case? What would your conclusion be?"

Veronica made a face. This was a technique that Dr. Bernard had attempted to employ on several occasions, but it never worked.

"I can't do that—this is... this is a part of me. I can't *not* feel it. If you put your hand on a burning stove and I said try not to *feel* it, would you be able to?"

"I'm sorry, I didn't mean to upset you. And I do realize that it's an unfair question, but I'm just trying to get you to look at this from another perspective."

Veronica looked down at her hands and was surprised to see that they were balled into fists.

*So quick to react, so quick to anger.*

She forced her hands open, stretching her fingers dramatically.

"Everyone thinks it's a suicide. There are some strange elements to this case, sure, but not enough to suggest that it was a murder."

"Let me put it this way: other than the intense feelings you felt, what about this case is different from the others that you've been a part of?"

The speed of Veronica's reply surprised even her.

"She was an attractive woman, about my age."

The three suicides that Veronica had investigated, two as a cop and one as a detective, had all been men. There was Collin McLachlan, of course, and Renaldo Tapia, an elderly Mexican man who had overdosed shortly after receiving a stage four colon cancer diagnosis. During her first month as a detective, Freddie and Veronica had been called in following the death of Emmett Edon, who had been shot in the face with a 45. Emmett hadn't died right away. Instead, he'd crawled all over the house, leaving a trail of blood everywhere he went. The crime scene suggested extreme violence, but Veronica hadn't experienced anything near what she'd felt in Sheriff Burns' barn. And, after a week of painstaking work, CSU managed to retrace all of Emmett's movements following the moment the bullet entered his mouth. It quickly became clear to everyone that this was a suicide, despite the trail of carnage and the prolonged time to death.

"I used to see a lot of cops," Dr. Bernard began, speaking slowly. She always recounted stories the same way—slow and deliberate—especially if they involved other clients. Veronica wondered if this was because the doctor was worried about revealing confidential information, or if she was trying to get the phrasing just right. Either way, it was an endearing quality, and Veronica enjoyed Jane's stories. They put perspective on an otherwise abstract discipline. Unfortunately, this particular tale Veronica had heard before. Several times, in fact. "Not so much anymore, but I used to. Anyways, one of the common themes I saw is that when accidents took place, especially when children were involved, is that it was psychologically difficult to chalk it up to just that: an accident. I once treated a police officer whose son was playing and fell down the stairs. It was just like any other number of a dozen falls kids have growing up, but he must have hit his head strangely because the poor child broke his neck and died. The father, the cop, went through every inch of his house, combing it for evidence. He was convinced that someone had broken in and killed his son. It didn't make sense—it was the middle of the day, and the nanny was home, and nothing was stolen. He took his investigation so far that, eventually, he was relieved of duty and forced to seek psychiatric counseling. Even after weeks of working with him, I'm not sure he ever really accepted the idea that this was an accident."

The first thing that popped into Veronica's head was, *What if it wasn't in an accident?*

She banished the thought.

"My point," Jane continued after a short pause, "is that sometimes, bad things just happen. Lightning strikes, if you know what I mean. Perhaps, you saw a young woman about your age, who had done something incomprehensible. She'd committed suicide. You might have put yourself in her shoes, decided that nothing could ever make you do what she'd done, and therefore concluded that something else must have happened."

Veronica made a face. If it hadn't been for what she'd seen, smelled, and heard, she might be inclined to agree.

"The last thing I want to do is tell you, especially you, Veronica, not to trust your instincts. But there's no shame in admitting that you've been wrong before."

Veronica flinched and discarded the memory before it surfaced.

"We both know that your synesthesia, as helpful as it is, is not infallible. How's your state of mind been, lately?"

"Before this? Fine. After? I seem to blow up at everything. It's not like me. It's only been... I dunno, less than a day, but I don't like what I'm seeing from myself."

Jane nodded.

"Your synesthesia can be affected by your state of mind. It's best not to forget that."

Veronica soaked this all in. Dr. Bernard was a master of common sense, but this still wasn't sitting right with Veronica.

"What about your personal life?"

Veronica scoffed.

"Personal life? What personal life?" When Jane didn't laugh, she continued, "I work, and I go home and watch TV. Sundays, I have dinner with my dad—every Sunday. Is that personal enough?"

"Not really," Jane said. "I know you love your work, Veronica. And you're a good detective. But you need more balance in your life."

Veronica fell silent and Jane leaned forward.

"Are you open to trying something?"

"That's a pretty broad question."

"It'll be fair, I promise. Fair and reasonable."

Veronica shrugged. This was new and she was intrigued.

"I want you to go out."

Veronica was disappointed.

"Go out?"

"Don't be obtuse—you're smarter than that. I don't mean go to the grocery store or Starbucks. I want you to go out, socially, once this week. It can be with a friend, someone you meet online, or just by yourself. Have a drink, or three, take your mind off things."

"I'm not good with crowds."

"I know. But I still think it's worth it."

Veronica couldn't help but feel like she did earlier when her father was making her work with Officer Cameron specifically because they didn't get along.

"I don't know."

"I think that if you're willing to do this, not only would it pay dividends personally, but it will also help you professionally."

"How so?"

"To put some distance between you and your work. As I said earlier, perspective is important. You know what it's like, Veronica. We, as humans, can become so invested in one thing, a singular idea, that we get tunnel vision, can't see the forest for the trees and all that."

Veronica exhaled loudly and stared at the woman whom she'd known for nearly twenty years. The idea of going out— where? With whom? What will I say? What will I do? What happens if I can't handle all the people?—gave her instant anxiety. But she trusted Jane. Trusted her like she trusted no one else. And Veronica had been telling the truth when she'd said she didn't like the way she'd acted today. If going out could help her with that, then it might be worth it.

"I'll do it." Veronica sighed, then immediately backpedaled. "Once. I'll try it *once*."

Jane smiled.

"That's all I'm asking for—for you to try it. And I want to hear all about it... next week, during our regular scheduled meeting, okay? No more breaking down my door unless it's a real emergency."

Veronica, who had been grinning along with Dr. Bernard, suddenly didn't feel so upbeat.

If a woman committing suicide, or had been murdered, didn't qualify as an emergency, what did?

# Chapter 18

CHLOE DOLAN WASN'T EXACTLY THE way that Dylan Hall had described her. She was definitely on the heavier side, but she was closer to two hundred than three hundred pounds. And while her teeth were a prominent feature, 'horsey' was a bit of an exaggeration.

She was also skittish and frightened. It wasn't Chloe who came to the door, however, but the girl's father, Randy Dolan.

"Did you find that prick who is harassing my daughter?" Randy asked. He was the spitting image of his daughter, only instead of blonde hair, he had very thin brown hair and wore glasses. "And where's that other cop?"

After Veronica's impromptu psych session, it had been Freddie who suggested going to visit the Dolan house. This is what Veronica wanted to do in the first place, so she wasn't about to argue. As a bonus, it would piss Ken off and there was nothing he could do about it. Captain Shade might ream Veronica out, but he wouldn't do the same to Freddie—and it had technically been his idea.

"Mr. Dolan," Freddie said, taking the lead. The man was unassuming and congenial, and it made sense for him to speak with Chloe's parents. Veronica, being young and a little more sprightly, and less likely to take shit from pretty much anybody, was more suited to speak to the younger generation. And, when the opportunity presented itself, these were the roles that they naturally fell into. "We are doing everything we can to..."

Veronica spotted Chloe behind her father, almost crouched, using him as a shield.

"Hey, can I talk to you?" Veronica asked as Freddie and Randy Dolan spoke. Chloe was reluctant but a smile and wave were all it took to convince her. The high school senior slipped by her father, a formidable task, given their collective girth, and met Veronica halfway down the impressive walkway. "Chloe, my name is Veronica, Veronica Shade. I'm a detective with the City of Greenham."

Chloe nodded but stayed silent.

"I'm helping Officer Ken Cameron with your case. He told me that you think you saw someone outside your home? When the, *uhh*, incident occurred?"

Veronica expected an enthusiastic response, a definitive identification of Dylan Hall, but that never came.

"I didn't see who threw the, you know," Chloe crinkled her nose and now she did look like a horse. "Or who left the notes."

Veronica tried not to let the surprise she felt show on her face.

"Officer Cameron said that you identified a man, tall, bald, with—"

"A crow tattoo on his forearm. Yeah, Dylan. I know who he is. I *did* see him outside my place, but not that night." Chloe looked down, and what she said next caused Veronica to inhale sharply. "At least, I don't think it was that night. I'm—I'm so sure anymore."

Gas. She smelled gas.

Veronica was confused. Why was Chloe lying all of a sudden? Could it be that Officer Cameron, with his inexplicable hate for Dylan, had turned a maybe identification into a positive? That didn't make sense, though, given how difficult it would be to mistake Dylan Hall for someone else.

"You're telling me that you're not sure if you saw Dylan?"

Just a nod, but even this subtle gesture seemed to reinforce the gasoline smell.

"Chloe, I want you to be very clear about this. Was Dylan hanging around when you got the letters or when someone threw the prophylactic at your window?"

"I don't know—I'm not sure. These past few weeks... I'm just so tired."

This was true, but Veronica wasn't sure if the girl's lack of sleep was the only reason that she looked increasingly uncomfortable.

Chloe suddenly cleared her throat and straightened.

"You know what? It was probably someone who is just angry, angry at the world, angry at me for living in this big house, someone that ..." Chloe let her sentence trail off, but Veronica didn't let her off that easily.

"That, what, Chloe?"

Chloe shrugged.

"I don't know."

The girl was trying to downplay events, but Veronica wasn't having it. There was a clear escalation to her stalker's behavior, clear and extremely fast.

"Why are you lying?" Veronica said, changing her tone to authoritative. "This is serious, Chloe."

Chloe shrugged again and refused to meet Veronica's eyes.

"Chloe, I don't think I need to tell you this, but things will continue, and they'll probably get worse. I'm not saying this to scare you, I want you to be aware of—"

"Detective Shade?" Freddie was approaching with a stern-looking Randy Dolan in tow. Detective Shade, said like that, in that voice, was one of the very few codewords they had.

They needed to leave, now.

But Veronica wasn't done.

"You wanna know what I think?" she said, just loud enough for Chloe, and only Chloe, to hear. "I think you told Officer

Cameron that Dylan was the one who threw the condom and left the notes because you wanted him off your back. You wanted him to leave you alone so that you didn't have to pay him for the drugs he gave you?"

The girl's eyes went wide, but it was feigned shock.

"You did buy drugs from Dylan, didn't you?" Veronica continued to press. "You and your friends, you wanted to party, right?"

"No, no, of course not. I would never—"

The stench of gasoline was so strong that Veronica felt her stomach lurch.

"Chloe? Are you okay?"

Veronica turned and smiled.

"I think we're done here," she said. "Mr. Dolan, we are going to do everything we can to find out who is sending these disgusting things to your daughter." She cast a condescending look over her shoulder at Chloe. "In the meantime, I think you should limit the amount of time she goes out unattended."

"What?" Chloe gasped. "No, I'm not —"

"I'm not suggesting that you stay locked up in your home, of course," Veronica clarified. "Just, maybe, limit the extracurricular activities. Anything where you might be alone, or out after dark, that sort of thing. Like a curfew."

Chloe started to complain again but Randy Dolan was having none of it.

"I think that's a great idea."

"I think that's a good idea, too," Freddie said, backing up his partner. "At least until we have this guy in custody."

"Sooner rather than later," Randy Dolan warned. He held out his hand and Freddie shook it. There was no invitation for Veronica to do the same, which was fine by her.

Back in the car, Freddie stared at her.

"Well, that didn't go as planned."

"Randy Dolan wasn't happy with the progress?" Veronica inquired.

"No, ma'am. Quite the contrary. How about you? You get anything from Chloe? Looked like y'all were pretty heated."

"Not really—heated, I mean. She was lying, though."

"About what?"

"About Dylan Hall." Veronica tried not to smile but couldn't help it. "Suddenly, Chloe changed her tune. She said she saw Dylan, but not at the same time as the notes or the condom incident."

"But Ken said—"

"I know what Ken said."

"You think he was lying, too?"

As much as Veronica wanted that to be the case, she didn't think so.

"Naw, the way Chloe was behaving? I think she just changed her mind. I think she told Ken that Dylan was the guy because she was scared of him."

Freddie pulled away from the Dolan house.

"Why'd she change her mind now?"

"Oh, I just have one of those faces you can't lie to, I guess," Veronica joked. Freddie didn't crack a smile and she dropped the act. "Probably Googled stalker and realized that someone who sends you notes and then throws a condom at your window? They're only just getting started. We both know that they won't stop until they have Chloe."

"Yeah, but why her?"

Veronica had no answer. It could be a myriad of reasons: a perceived slight, an unrequited advance, something completely obscure. There was no way of knowing until they caught the person responsible. And even then, their reasons may only make sense to their own warped mind.

"At least we confirmed one thing: Dylan isn't our guy."

Freddie's features tightened.

"What? You still think he might be behind this?"

"No," Freddie said flatly. "I never really thought he was. Only went on what Ken was saying."

"Then why do you look like you just farted, gambled, and lost?"

Still no smile out of her partner.

"Because Dylan trying to scare Chloe is one thing. But if it's not him? Then there is one truly sick bastard out there. And it's not a matter of if he's going to escalate, but when."

# Chapter 19

"**WHAT DO YOU THINK ABOUT** putting an officer outside of Chloe's house?" Freddie asked when they were back at their desks. Thankfully, Officer Cameron was nowhere to be seen.

"Even if we had the manpower, which we don't, and even if the captain would approve it, which he won't, would you be doing this if Randy Dolan wasn't a city councilor?"

"Would I eat a bag of chips if it was healthy?"

"What?" Veronica said, genuinely confused by the remark. "I'll tell you what, why don't we get Ken to sit outside the Dolan house? Hell, he'll probably love clocking all that overtime."

"So long as he's not here, around you, is what you mean."

"Would I eat kale if it wasn't good for me?"

"You don't eat kale."

"Good point. Where is Ken, anyway?"

"Out looking for Dylan Hall, I guess. What we should be doing." Freddie shrugged.

This made Veronica uncomfortable. Dylan was by no means an upstanding citizen, and they had their personal issues to contend with, but the man had lived, and continued to live, a very tough life. That couldn't be overlooked. It wasn't an excuse, but knowing his history the way she did, Veronica could at least understand the man.

She also understood people like Ken Cameron. Veronica had pushed him, and he'd responded by doubling down on his assertion that Dylan was stalking Chloe. Barring video evidence to the contrary, and even that might not be enough, the stubborn officer wouldn't back down. Neither would Dylan, as evidenced by yesterday's chase and impromptu parkour session. Veronica didn't want to think about what would happen if those two powder kegs came together.

Fueled by this knowledge, Veronica turned her attention to finding out who was behind the stalking. It took her all of thirty seconds to find Chloe Dolan on Facebook, and she was pleased to see that, unlike Maggie Cernak, her profile was public.

Veronica, who didn't spend much time on social media, but admittedly had both a Facebook and Instagram profile, both of which were private, didn't understand why someone would want their account to be public. Especially a high school senior—it was just a recipe for disaster. What good could come out of it? A brand deal? Was Chloe hoping to be discovered?

If there was a theme to Chloe Dolan's account it was good times, which supported Dylan Hall's claim of her and her friends wanting to 'party'. Nearly every shot showed her in a nightclub or bar, which was curious given that she was underage. But the girl had been smart, never appearing with any beverage in her hand and you could never really tell exactly what drinking establishment she was in. Veronica imagined this was for the sake of plausible deniability.

If her father ever challenged Chloe on these photos, Veronica imagined the conversation would go a little like this:

*"Chloe, this looks like a nightclub. How did you get in there?"*

*"Oh, Dad, don't be silly. I'm underage. I could never get in."*

*"But those lights, they—"*

*"It's a filter, dad. Geez, get with the times."*

But it wasn't Chloe's drinking that Veronica was interested in—it was the people she was with. In addition to partying, another recurring theme was the presence of two other girls who appeared to be close to Chloe's age: a tall, lanky brunette with sloped shoulders and wide-set eyes, and a light-skinned black girl with perfect teeth and cornrows. It didn't take any time at all to find out who these girls were, either. Even though the brunette, Monica Tremblay, had her profile set to private, she was tagged directly in almost all the photos. The other girl, like Chloe, had a public profile.

Her name was Laura Knox.

"No such thing as privacy on the Internet," Veronica mumbled. Within minutes, she had not only been able to figure out the girls' names but had acquired their addresses.

Then she stood and looked at her partner.

"Chloe might not have said much, but what do you think about asking her friends a few questions? Maybe they know someone who might have it in for Chloe."

Freddie checked his watch.

"I've got about a half hour before lunch."

"Good, because I suspect that we have about that much time before Ken brings Dylan in."

*And this time, I don't think I'll be able to let him go.*

\*\*\*

The two detectives split up, with Veronica visiting Monica Tremblay and Freddie going to Laura Knox's house. Unlike Chloe, Monica's parents weren't home.

"Monica, my name is Detective Veronica Shade. I'm —"

"Trying to figure out who's messing with Chloe," Monica offered. She crossed her arms over her narrow chest and straightened. The girl was much taller than Veronica, and she fought the urge to try and measure up.

"That's right. I'm investigating the disturbing deliveries that your friend Chloe Dolan has received."

"Disgusting, more like it."

"Agreed. I'm —"

"It's that Dylan guy. Didn't Chloe tell you?"

Monica's assertiveness surprised Veronica.

"Dylan?" she asked, feigning ignorance.

This had the intended result: Monica's staunch confidence faltered.

"Y-yeah. Really tall bald guy." She looked down for a brief second. "Chloe didn't—she didn't tell you?"

"She didn't mention anything about a Dylan." Veronica lied. "Do you mean Dylan Hall? Very tall, skinny, crow tattoo on his right forearm?"

Monica wasn't just uncomfortable now, but she'd started to sweat. Veronica didn't need to see the blue aura to notice this; the girl's substantial forehead had beads on it, and she licked the moisture off her upper lip. This encouraged Veronica to keep up the charade.

"Doesn't—doesn't Dylan Hall deal MDMA, amongst other things? Ecstasy?"

"I don't know. All I know is that Chloe told me she saw the guy there."

"A guy she just happened to know by name?"

Monica shrugged.

"I don't know. It's just what she said. A tall guy—I don't know anything else." Desperation had crept into the girl's voice at an alarming rate.

"I think maybe you know more than you're saying. I think you know Dylan's name because you and Laura and Chloe decided that one time at the club you wanted to do something other than just drink. You wanted to *party*, am I right? Maybe you heard his name being used at school, so you reached out. But then when it came time to pay..."

Veronica examined Monica's face—the girl was close to breaking.

"I—I don't want anyone to get into trouble. All I want—"

*Shit.*

A car pulled into the driveway and the spell that Veronica had put on Monica was broken. When she looked back at the girl, her arms were over her chest again and her posture adroit.

"I don't know what you're talking about," Monica proclaimed, her voice full of confidence.

Veronica frowned and produced a business card. She held it out and refused to take it back. Eventually, if for no other reason than to alleviate some of the awkwardness, Monica took it.

"Monica, if it isn't Dylan? It's somebody else. And I promise you, this isn't going to stop with nasty letters or used condoms. Whoever's behind this won't stop until they get Chloe. Yeah, *get*, as in take. So, if you care about your friend, you'll stop lying and give me a call."

Without waiting for a reply, Veronica turned and smiled at Monica's parents who were getting out of their car.

"Is everything okay here?" Mr. Tremblay asked.

Veronica flashed her badge.

"Detective Shade. Your daughter is not in trouble in any way," she said, making sure to speak loud enough for Monica to overhear. "I was just asking a few questions about one of her friends. Have a nice day."

Veronica ignored matching confused expressions on Monica's parents' faces and got into her car. She'd planted the seed with Monica, one that she hoped would grow —sooner, rather than later, as Randy Dolan had said. Whether the girl could only exonerate Dylan or if she had insight into who the real stalker was, was yet to be seen.

As she started to drive away, Veronica checked her phone. There was one message waiting for her. One that caused her to smile.

"I knew it." She nodded vigorously. "I *knew* it."

And then Veronica forgot all about Monica, Dylan, and Chloe and drove back to the scene of the suicide.

Back to Sheriff Steve Burns' house.

# Chapter 20

IT LOOKED STAGED. TO VERONICA, the entire scene appeared like something out of a cheesy rom-com. Sheriff Burns was washing his car, shirtless, of course. The only thing that kept Veronica from truly thinking that she had been duped into a hidden camera show — *Detectives seeking Love*, produced by the same people who brought you The First 48 — was the fact that the text she'd received was originally sent yesterday, but had only been forwarded to her today.

It was from Freddie.

*"Sorry —forgot to mention this. Sheriff Burns texted me yesterday, wanted to talk to you about the suicide. Stop by whenever you can."*

Sheriff Burns didn't notice her until she was parked. Only then did the man turn. Veronica's father had once told her that the uniform added ten years, and this was the case here. The sheriff was lean but not without muscle. He didn't have a chiseled, Instagram body, but he possessed a well-developed chest and maybe the top two of a six-pack. The sheriff no longer looked to be in his mid-forties, but more like in his mid-thirties or perhaps even a little younger.

Embarrassed, the sheriff waved then reached into his car, pulled a T-shirt out, and slipped it on.

*"Welllll,* this is awkward," the man said, scratching the back of his head.

"You mean washing your car shirtless when it's fifty degrees out?"

The sheriff looked skyward. The sun was shining brightly.

"More like sixty-five," he countered. "But really, I just didn't want to get my shirt wet."

Veronica looked at the sheriff's shirt. It was white and as generic as they came.

"I see."

The sheriff started to blush, and Veronica couldn't help but think of what Freddie had said, that the man got nervous and all jittery around her.

She cleared her throat and made an effort to exude profes-sionalism.

"You wanted to see me? Something about the suicide?"

"*Uhh*, kind of," he stammered.

Veronica's eyes narrowed.

"What do you mean, *kind of*? I told you that I didn't think Maggie Cernak committed suicide. I told you that the second I walked in, and if you changed your mind —"

"No." The sheriff showed his palms. "I still think she com-mitted suicide. And — wait, I thought you and your partner came to the same conclusion. If you're having second thoughts…"

*What is going on here?* Veronica wondered.

And now it was her turn to stammer.

"I-I-I thought that's why you asked me to come by."

The sheriff's face turned an even brighter shade of red.

"Great, this is starting out great," he muttered. "I think something was lost in translation here. Your partner… I told him it wasn't important. I just told him that I wanted to apolo-gize to you."

Veronica shook her head and her thoughts once again turned to Freddie.

"Yeah, I'm not so sure that this was an accident."

The sheriff waited for her to explain, but Veronica didn't bother.

"Okay, well, I'm here. What did you want to see me about, Sheriff Burns?"

"Steve, please, I'm off duty."

"I'm not, and I'm quite busy. Why don't you—"

"I lied to you," the man said flatly. "I'm sorry."

He thought that she would be surprised by this, but, of course, Veronica wasn't.

"You knew Maggie Cernak."

Sheriff Burns' face screwed up.

"No, I mean, yes, I knew her, but not very well. Met her only once or twice."

Unlike the nature of his admission, this was unexpected.

"Let me explain," the sheriff continued. "I lied about not being a regular at the library. The truth is, I love to read. And while I've been to the library dozens of times, I usually only ever go during the day. Maggie works the evening shift while—"

"—Gina works during the day," Veronica finished for him.

Sheriff Burns raised one eyebrow.

"Yeah, that's right. You've been?"

Veronica shrugged.

"It doesn't matter. Listen, Sheriff Burns, I'm a little confused as to why you wanted me to come out here."

"To apologize. I lied to you, and I feel bad about it."

"Why did you lie?"

The sheriff grew uncomfortable, and he started digging his toe in the dirt. It was disarming and charming at the same time. Sheriff Burns was no longer thirty-five years old, but fifteen, nervous and uncomfortable as he tried to work up the courage to ask his crush to the prom.

"I don't know," he said sheepishly. "Who even reads anymore? I guess I was just... I don't know."

"*Rrrright.* You called me all the way out here to the outskirts of Matheson to tell me that you are sorry for lying about *not* being a Colleen Hoover superfan."

The sheriff recoiled.

"Colleen Hoover? No way! I prefer Dan Padovana, Lisa Regan, L.T. Vargus, and Jeff Menapace." Veronica just stared. "Okay, well, that's not the *only* reason." More toe digging, and she knew exactly what was coming next. "I also wanted to ask you out."

A weight seemed to lift off the man's shoulders and he exhaled loud enough for Veronica to hear, even though she was at least fifteen feet from the sheriff.

*Goddamn you, Freddie.*

This wasn't the first time that Veronica thought maybe Freddie had his own sort of synesthesia.

He probably did, only he called it by a different name: experience.

"Yeah, I chalked this," the sheriff said before Veronica had a chance to answer. "I didn't know you were working on a Saturday, and this whole—"

"One drink," Veronica blurted.

*Blurting.* Who blurted? The word alone sounded like a mouth fart. But that's all she seemed to do lately. Blurt shit out of her mouth.

*What happened to your filter, V?*

It was Freddie, setting this up. It was Jane, with her stupid 'try one thing for me', go out, meet people, try to be normal for once.

Veronica almost took the offer back—would have, too, if it weren't for the sheriff's face. He was fifteen and giddy with excitement.

"But I'm working now. Tonight, maybe?"

*Of course tonight*, she scolded herself.

The sheriff beamed.

"Amazing. I'll—" there was a loud burst of static from inside the car, audible even though the window was closed, and the sheriff's smile faded. "I'm sorry, that's work."

"Go ahead."

*One drink, that's all. No harm, no foul. I'll tell Jane that I tried her little experiment and that it failed miserably.*

The sheriff opened the door and grabbed the receiver.

"Sheriff Burns."

"Sheriff, it's Deputy McVeigh. I'm in Sullivan, doing a drive-through like you suggested. You—you gotta come out here. Over."

Veronica didn't mean to eavesdrop, but you couldn't just turn off being a detective because listening in on someone else's conversation was deemed 'rude' in some circles.

"It's my day off, Martin. Are you sure this isn't something you can handle on your own? Over." The little boy was gone now; the man was all business.

"I know, I know. But I think you need to see this. It's… it's another suicide. A woman, twenty-six years old with no history of psychiatric disease just put a gun in her mouth and blew her head off."

# PART TWO:
# A SCENT

## Chapter 21

VERONICA WAS PREPARED THIS TIME. With Maggie Cernak, she'd been taken by surprise, overwhelmed by her hallucinations, and had embarrassed herself.

Not this time.

The door to the large house with a wraparound porch was open, but the view of the interior was blocked by Bear County Deputies. Following just a step behind Sheriff Burns, Veronica heard the song before even seeing the crime scene.

It was low, barely audible, but it was haunting, nevertheless. *La, la, la, la, laaaaa, laaa.*

One of the deputies leaned into the home as they approached, and a second later Deputy McVeigh squeezed his way onto the porch.

"Sheriff," the stern-faced man offered his superior a nod. McVeigh did his best to mask his surprise at Veronica's presence, but it manifested in a slight hesitation before he added, "Detective Shade."

Gone was the deputy's snarky, *maybe you should wait outside* attitude. McVeigh was all business now, which further served to prepare Veronica for what to expect inside the modern home.

The sheriff said nothing to justify her presence, he just continued moving forward.

"What do we have?"

McVeigh fell into stride beside them, and they walked, three abreast, up to the open doorway.

"Two hours ago, a neighbor on the left heard a loud bang. Said it sounded like a gunshot and called it in. Deputy Carlson was first on the scene, tried the door, and found it locked. Saw what looked like a body through the window so made the executive decision to kick the door in. Found her in the kitchen."

The deputies who had been on the porch cleared out of their way to allow them passage. As the shadow of the house blotted out some of the sun, Veronica thought about what the sheriff had said earlier, justifying his shirtless car washing. It *was* a beautiful day. Why would someone choose today to commit suicide? Didn't all suicides need to take place on dreary, rainy days?

Veronica would have continued on this inane train of thought, but the singing suddenly got louder. It was as if there was a small child, a boy, probably, although at that age voice pitch was nearly indistinguishable between genders, standing beside her, holding her hand, and singing.

*La, la, la, la, laaaaa, laaa.*

"Who's the victim?"

This pulled Veronica out of her head. *Victim.* She thought it a curious, but apt choice of words.

"Her name is Sarah Sawyer. Twenty-six years old," Deputy McVeigh informed them. "Lives alone."

"Occupation?"

"Don't know yet. Still looking into it."

The trio entered the kitchen, slipping below the yellow tape that CSU, who had beaten them to the scene, had put up. The victim was on her back, her hands over her head, a chair beneath her. The force of the gunshot had apparently been sufficient to knock the poor woman backward and onto the floor.

Someone, probably CSU, had put a plastic sheet over the woman's face, but some gore, mostly blood, was visible around the edges.

"No signs of forced entry. All doors were locked."

Veronica was barely able to hear the man now — the song was so loud. What had been calm, albeit annoying singing, was now a deafening cacophony. This was exacerbated by the fiery hues that seemed to be coming off the body like heat waves. They weren't as intense as they'd been with Maggie Cernak, but they were there, no doubt about it. A ground fire without the smoke or destruction.

It was difficult to swallow, but Veronica did her best to remain calm. The last thing she wanted was to turn and grab Sheriff Burns and claim that Sarah had been murdered like some sort of estranged mental patient. Even though the colors weren't actually there, black dots began to pepper Veronica's vision as if she'd been staring at the sun for too long. She raised her gaze from the body and spotted two yellow placards, real, actual placards, a few feet above Sarah's head. The first had been placed in front of the gun that had killed her. The second, a single bullet casing.

"Detective Shade?" someone close to her said, but Veronica couldn't reply. It took all of her effort *not* to look at the corpse.

Even though the cause of death was very different — hanging versus gunshot wound — the similarities between Maggie and Sarah were not to be overlooked. Both were young women of similar socioeconomic status.

And both had been murdered — that's what the colors told her.

"Veronica?"

It was Sheriff Burns, and she blinked, hard, and was finally able to turn her head toward the speaker.

The man looked concerned, and Veronica thought that he was going to ask her the dreaded 'are you okay?'. He didn't, however. Eyes partially squinted, he gestured to his right.

The first person who had called her name hadn't been the sheriff. It had been the CSU Tech, Holland Toler. Like Sheriff Burns, the tech also had a queer expression on his face, but Veronica thought it more likely that this was due to what he held in his hand than on account of her strange behavior.

An evidence bag containing a small, roughly torn piece of paper with a drop of blood on the lower left-hand corner.

Veronica's difficulty swallowing extended to breathing now, as well. Holland's hand obscured the text, but she didn't need to see the note to know what it said.

"It was on the table," Deputy McVeigh informed them. "Face up, near the woman's chair."

The tech pinched the plastic bag by the corner and then held it up for everyone to see.

No one was surprised by what was written in all caps on the scrap of paper: *MEENIE*.

# Chapter 22

"CHLOE, A DETECTIVE CAME TO visit me today. A *detective*," Monica hissed into her cell phone.

"What was her name?" Chloe asked, her voice strong and clear.

"I can't remember. Detective something. But she—"

"Brown eyes with little flecks of gold in them? Stares at you like she knows when you're lying?"

"Yes," Monica said desperately. "She *knows* I'm lying."

"Dammit, how did she find you?" Now Chloe lowered her voice until she was in her room with the door closed. She sat on her bed and tried to think.

"I don't know, but I'm scared, Chloe."

Chloe frowned. Monica was always scared. Every time they went out, she was terrified that the drink some cute guy bought her was going to be laced with something. Chloe didn't have the heart to tell her that if anyone was getting a roofied drink it was Laura, not her. Maybe not even Chloe. And yet, it was Chloe who had received the letters and the condom.

"What did you tell her?" Chloe asked.

"What you said—it was the Dylan guy. But she didn't believe me. She knows I'm lying, *Chlo*. What are we going to do?"

"She doesn't know anything," Chloe replied, but this was a lie. The truth was, she shared her friend's concern. It was as if Detective Shade could see right through her lies. And Chloe had cracked, too. "This is just a cop trick—my dad told me they do this all the time. They pretend they know things, and they lie to get people to turn against each other. Then they just wait, stress you out, get you to second guess everything."

"Yeah, but-but she said that things with you... that they're going to get worse. That whoever's doing this isn't going to stop. That they might even... *take* you."

"She said that?" Chloe couldn't control the trepidation that leaked into her voice.

"Yes! She didn't say if, either, but that it *would* happen. That things would—I dunno, *escalate*. And if she's out there wasting her time on Dylan when we know he didn't—"

"We don't know he's *not* the one behind it," Chloe said a little too loudly. She muted her phone for a second to see if she could hear her parents stirring down below. There was no sound from downstairs. "The fact is, we don't know who's behind it. It could be Dylan."

"I don't know, Chloe. Like, we shoulda just paid him. I don't want someone to kidnap you, *Chlo*. Like, c'mon."

Chloe rolled her eyes.

*Kidnap—gimme a break.*

"It could be him," she insisted. "He's pissed because we didn't pay him. This could be his way of getting at us back."

"*You* didn't pay him," Monica corrected her.

"Whatever—that stuff he gave us was bunk anyway."

"You remember at Christmas? That guy who came up to us in the snow? That guy was weird. It could be him. He could be the one sending you all that gross stuff."

Chloe clenched her jaw. The truth was, she didn't remember much about that night and would have forgotten it completely, if it weren't for Monica.

When Chloe had received the first letter, she'd passed it off as a joke. She didn't even mention it. But then there had been the second and the third... after the third note, she'd told Monica and Laura about them. And Monica, who had a picture-perfect memory when it came to faces but clearly not names—she couldn't remember Detective Shade who had visited her earlier that day—had instantly brought up the encounter from late December. Chloe had been so drunk that it was all new to her, but Monica was steadfast in her recollection.

They were coming home from a party, trudging through the snow, when a drunk man approached them. He'd hit on Laura first, but she'd already puked that night and could barely stand. He'd moved on to Chloe next. Chloe, who didn't want to leave the party but was forced to take Laura home, was pissed. Suffice it to say, she wasn't receptive to his advances.

The man hadn't bothered with Monica. He'd just let out a string of obscenities and disparaging comments that had made Monica cringe and squirm.

"I told you, I was wasted. What did he say?"

"I mean, I was drunk too, Chloe. I don't remember exactly what he said." To this day, Monica had staunchly refused to tell her the man's exact words. "But it was like those notes. Those disgusting notes that you got. Why don't we just tell the cops about him?"

"Because Monica. If the cops think it's Dylan, they'll bring him in. Then he'll stop bothering us for the stupid money. He'll leave us alone."

"But he wasn't really—"

"My dad is a city councilor, Monica. He'll find out."

"But wouldn't getting Dylan arrested just make him *more* likely to talk about the drugs he sold us?"

Chloe closed her eyes.

"He knows who I am, now. If we pay him, he'll keep coming back for more. I've seen this before. And now that we lied to the cops? My dad... Monica, he'll *kill* me. Like, seriously."

"The detective said she wasn't going to tell anyone. She just wants to make sure you're safe."

"Oh, yeah, right. My dad knows everything that happens in town. And what do you think is going to happen to him if people start thinking his daughter is a drug addict?"

Monica sighed, long and loud.

"I don't know what to do," she admitted.

Chloe made a face. This was happening to her, not Monica, and yet her friend was acting like she was the one with everything to lose.

"Just relax. Don't do anything. Like I said, it could be—no, it's probably Dylan. They're going to arrest him, and this will all be over. And don't worry about me, nothing is going to happen. Alright?" When there was no reply, she repeated, "*Alright?*"

"Yeah, fine. Just be safe, okay?"

But after she hung up the phone, Chloe continued to just sit on her bed, staring into space.

This was just a prank, right? It had to be.

# Chapter 23

"IT'S THE SAME WRITING," VERONICA said, her eyes locked on the ominous word.

"Looks similar," CSU tech Holland Toler agreed.

Veronica pulled out her phone and scrolled to the picture she'd taken of the note found on Maggie Cernak's body. She looked at it, then showed it to McVeigh, Burns, and Toler.

"Yeah, it's the same," Sheriff Burns turned to Deputy McVeigh. "I want the coroner out here as soon as possible. I don't care if she has a trial, postpone it if you have to."

Deputy McVeigh nodded and reached for his radio.

"I didn't see any evidence of an intruder or anything like that," CSU Toler remarked.

"Right. Well, I want the entire kitchen dusted. If there are any dirty dishes, bag 'em and tag 'em. You never know." Sheriff Burns indicated the note with his chin. "Any fingerprints on the other note?"

"Yes—but all of them belonged to Maggie."

"Shit, okay. Well, I want you to double-check."

"Aye, aye."

Veronica waited for the tech with the strange black hair, which she was beginning to think was a toupee, to leave before addressing the sheriff.

"What do you think? This has to be related to Maggie's death."

"Yeah, definitely. They might know one another. Could be a coordinated thing." The sheriff sounded tired. "McVeigh, can you look into a possible connection between the two suicides?"

"Will do." The deputy stood there for several seconds, just staring at the sheriff before he realized that this was his cue to leave. "I'll keep you in the loop."

"Thanks."

It was just the two of them now, Veronica and Sheriff Burns. And the corpse. Veronica inadvertently looked down at the body. The colors were still there, and the song was still playing softly in her head, which made her inhale sharply.

To distract from her visceral reaction, one that was likely going to inspire questions she couldn't or wouldn't answer, Veronica said the first thing that popped into her head.

"Are you going to reopen Maggie's case?"

Not the best thing to say or do: challenging the sheriff at his own crime scene? A crime scene that, quite frankly, she had no business being at?

Veronica wanted to be on this case. *Needed* to be involved. But when she looked at the sheriff, he wasn't scowling. In fact, he actually had a small smirk on his lips.

"What?"

"I didn't—I didn't close it just yet."

Veronica's eyes narrowed.

*He's flirting*, she thought. And it was cute. Only, it would be a lot cuter if there wasn't a body on the ground not ten feet from them. Sheriff Burns must have realized this fact as well as he quickly cleared his throat.

"I didn't think there was a need to rush things. The coroner hasn't been able to locate next of kin yet."

"It could be a coincidence." Veronica realized that she was arguing against herself here, but she was also musing out loud and helping the sheriff save face.

*Why are you acting like this? First, the lack of filter and now all strangely giddy? Get control, V.*

"Two suicides in two days? I did a little research last night. Do you know the last time someone committed suicide in Matheson?"

Veronica shrugged. Unfortunately, suicide in Greenham wasn't all that uncommon an event. If you considered that some of the deaths marked as accidental overdoses were intentional, the actual number would be considerably higher.

"No idea."

"Me neither. Couldn't find a single case going back twenty years."

"Really?"

"Yeah. But the notes..."

"Right. No coincidence," Veronica agreed.

*Eenie, Meenie, Miney, Mo.*

A child's song, a hundred-year-old counting rhyme.

Veronica was no expert, and while she knew that some versions of the rhyme included racial slurs, she didn't think that any of them made even a passing or obscure reference to suicide.

Or murder.

What the hell is the connection here?

"I want... I want to be kept in the loop," Veronica said.

The sheriff was back to being forty-five and all business.

"I think that's a good idea. The suicides have already taken place in two different cities. Maybe Greenham is —" the sheriff stopped himself mid-sentence.

It was too late.

*Eenie, Meenie, Miney, Mo.*

Veronica knew what Steve was about to say.

*Maybe Greenham is next.*

The rhyme... *Eenie, Meenie, Miney, Mo.*

They'd found Eenie yesterday and Meenie today. As disturbing as the thought was, they had to be prepared for two more bodies.

Veronica's phone started to ring, and she excused herself. She walked outside, grateful to be away from the colors and the song.

"Yeah?"

"Veronica? It's Fred. The sheriff... he didn't kidnap you, did he?"

*Oh, shit.*

She'd completely forgotten about Freddie.

Then she remembered that her partner had essentially set her up with the sheriff.

"Yeah, actually. Turns out he's a *bona fide* psycho."

"*Riiight.* Okay. Did you manage to speak to Monica?"

"Yeah. She's lying, too. Everyone's just fucking lying," Veronica spat.

Freddie paused.

"I didn't get much from Laura, either. I think we should go to the school, speak to the teachers. Maybe someone else was harassed before Chloe."

That was a stretch and they both knew it. Stalkers didn't just get bored and choose a new target. They didn't stop until...

Her eyes drifted back to Sarah Sawyer's house.

She didn't even want to think about it.

"Maybe." Veronica was tempted to tell Freddie about Sarah but at the last second, she bit her tongue. She wasn't sure why and it felt wrong but wasn't compelled to change her mind. "Think you can handle the school by yourself?"

"A bunch of teenagers fat-shaming me and making donut jokes? Piece of cake."

Veronica laughed.

"Thanks."

"Wait—why can't you swing by?"

"Oh, gotta get ready."

"…for?"

"A big date. Catch you later, Freddie."

Veronica hung up before her partner could get another word in.

"Big date?"

Her face turned bright red, and she wanted to run. Instead, she turned and looked at the sheriff.

"No—I said, *crazy eight.*" Veronica lied. "Inside joke."

Her face felt like she'd spent hours on a beach in Mexico with zero sunblock.

"Speaking of eight, how about I pick you up then?"

Veronica said nothing. Steve was standing in front of the open doorway, and behind him, she saw the faintest swirl of color.

"We're still on for drinks, right?" the sheriff asked hesitantly.

Veronica almost told him, no, of course not. Her thoughts were on Sarah Sawyer and how the young woman would never go out for drinks again. And then she thought about Lucy the cat and she wondered if Sarah had a cat. Then Veronica wondered how many cats she could keep in her small home.

"If you don't want to, I'll—"

"Eight sounds good. But no need to pick me up. I'll meet you there."

# Chapter 24

*WHY THE HELL ARE YOU so nervous?*

The answer came quickly and it was harsh.

Veronica honestly couldn't remember the last time she'd been on a date. The last time she'd been asked out was more memorable: Officer Ken Cameron after the Christmas party. She had dated in college, but nothing really serious. Her synesthesia went on the fritz when she drank, and that, mixed with the fact that crowds also affected her condition, ensured that Veronica spent most of her life in either small groups or alone. Not the most conducive to developing romantic ties in a world of volume-based dating.

Her longest boyfriend had been a TA by the name of Conrad Newton. He'd been a nice kid, and handsome. But they had different aspirations—he was starting a Masters in biochemistry, and she was doing whatever she could to finish her undergrad as quickly as possible and enter the police force like her father.

Veronica's lack of dating experience showed which only enhanced her already frayed nerves. She was sitting in the back of an Uber, staring at her phone, trying to slow her heartbeat down. It felt like it was pounding against her rib cage.

Choosing what to wear had been an adventure, to say the least. As a detective for the City of Greenham, she didn't have a uniform, *per se*. Veronica typically wore slacks and a blouse of some sort. Plain, nondescript. Wearing anything too flashy gave an impression as did clothes that were frumpy and ill-fitting. She settled on neutral. And that's what she'd first tried on in preparation for her date with the sheriff. She swapped out the slacks for a pair of dark jeans but kept a work-used blouse on top.

When she looked at herself in the mirror, she saw work Veronica. And that was okay because she was meeting Sheriff Burns... from work.

Only, it wasn't okay because this was a date.

Veronica quickly changed out of her modified work gear and opted for something completely different, which took her too far the other way. She looked like a bridesmaid.

Frustrated, the thought of canceling was at the forefront of her mind. Veronica wasn't even sure why she'd agreed to the date in the first place. But as she rooted through her closet, with Lucy sitting on her bed watching and judging, she found something she didn't remember buying: a navy jumper with small white polka dots. It fit perfectly, and she cinched the waist with a thin, white belt. The jumper ended in shorts, revealing long legs that hadn't seen the sun in, oh, a decade or two. Veronica wanted to apply some tanning lotion, but she'd wasted so much time selecting her outfit that she needed to focus on her makeup. This proved a much easier task. A little eyeliner and just a tad of smoky eyeshadow to accentuate her best feature. Then some pale color on her lips. That was it, that was all she needed.

Next, came her hair. She'd straightened it, and now it fell just below her shoulders.

*I should've made it wavy. Everyone says my hair looks best when it's natural.* Veronica cocked her head. *Who says that? Freddie? No.*

"This is it—we're here."

Veronica slipped her phone into her clutch, thanked the driver, then got out.

Sheriff Burns had picked the place: *Escondite,* a Mexican restaurant and drinkerie. The front facade was nearly all glass, giving Veronica a clear view of the inside. It was busy—packed.

Colorful, too, with Mexican flags and banners above the bar, in addition to a giant neon sign on the back wall that read: *Mescal now, worry later.*

For a person with synesthesia, it was an absolute nightmare.

*Can I go home?*

The Uber hadn't even left yet—the driver was using his phone, probably trying to arrange his next pickup.

Then she spotted him. It wasn't difficult—Sheriff Burns definitely stood out. For one, he was older than most, if not all of the other patrons. Two, he looked as nervous as Veronica felt. This brought a smile to her face. The man was moving the salt and pepper shakers, and the three bottles of craft hot sauce, around the table as if he were playing chess with an invisible opponent.

She couldn't leave him hanging.

The maître d', a sixteen-year-old girl wearing a Mexican outfit that was probably offensive, didn't look up from the mounted iPad when Veronica approached.

"Reservations under Sher—" she stopped herself. "Burns? Steve Burns?"

"Right, the old guy." Veronica raised an eyebrow at this, and the maître d' blushed. She flicked her finger across the iPad screen, and it went dark. "I'm sorry, please come with me."

As she was led through a maze of tightly packed tables, Veronica tried her best to keep her eyes focused straight ahead. It helped... a little. She still saw blue plumes in her periphery — other first daters were also sweating. *Escondite* was awash with odors—seared meat, sweet tequila, and smoky mescal—pleasant, all of them. Underneath, though, Veronica smelled gasoline.

*This was a bad idea,* she thought. But when the sheriff looked at her, Veronica smiled.

The man almost seemed surprised that she'd shown up. He got to his feet as she approached, a grin on his face.

He was wearing a light V-neck sweater, with the sleeves pulled halfway up his forearms. His hair was styled, but not overly so—just a little volume to his medium-length dark brown hair.

"You look great," he said a little awkwardly.

Veronica thanked him and sat down.

"Your server will be with you in a moment."

The maître d' left, and Veronica was aware of her pounding heart again.

"Have you been here before?" Veronica asked.

Steve cringed.

"It's a bit young, isn't it?"

Veronica laughed.

"What?"

"You wanna know what the maître d' said when I asked for your table?"

"Judging by your laugh, I'm not sure I do."

Veronica told him anyway.

"Jesus, I'm not that old," he protested, a smile on his face.

"Can you be more specific? Exactly how old are you?" Veronica teased.

"What is this? A job interview?"

"You can't ask that on a job interview."

"Good point," Steve said, a perpetual grin on his face. "For the record? I'm thirty-four years young."

"Well, you don't look a day over forty."

The sheriff was about to say something when their server appeared. It seemed impossible, but she looked even younger than the maître d'.

"Can I start you guys off with some drinks?"

"You sure can," Veronica looked at the menu. It was over-whelming. Not only did she not recognize any of the drink names, but they all appeared to have a minimum of two ounces of alcohol — tequila or mescal, pick your poison — and most had three plus.

Sensing that she needed more time, Sheriff Burns said, "Actually, I forgot my reading spectacles. Perhaps you could recommend one of your favorite cocktails?"

Veronica chuckled.

"I suggest the tequila Manhattan."

"And for me?" Veronica asked, eyes still on the menu.

"For you, the twisted agave martini."

Veronica smiled and handed the child her menu.

"How old do you think she is?" Steve asked under his breath when the server was out of earshot.

"Nine," Veronica joked.

"What do you think about me pulling out my Sheriff's badge and shutting this place down for child labor?"

"Nice flex."

Steve laughed, a pleasant, full-bodied sound.

"You fit right in with lingo like that."

Veronica shrugged.

"Heard it on Tik Tok."

They chatted a little about nothing specific, and then their underage server returned with their drinks. Veronica took one sip, then licked the salt from the rim of her glass. It had a kick, but it was delicious.

When she looked up, she noticed the sheriff staring at her.

"What?"

Steve shook his head.

"Nothing." He quickly gulped some of his own drink. It was evidently tart because his cheeks sucked in.

"No, not nothing. What?"

Steve took another sip of his drink, which, unlike her, he wasn't enjoying.

"I-I-I'm not really used to this dating thing. I'm not sure what I'm allowed to say, to be honest."

"Me neither, but you of all people should know the old saying, honesty is the best policy."

Despite Steve's comment, Veronica was surprised at how smooth their conversation was going, how natural it was to speak with the man.

"Good point. I was just wondering—what made you get into law enforcement? To become a cop?"

This wasn't exactly what he was going to say, Veronica knew. It wasn't that he was lying, that much she would have picked up on instantly, but there was a hint of another comment. And it was flattering.

*What's a pretty girl like you doing in law enforcement?*

"To be honest? It was my dad's influence—Captain Peter Shade?"

Steve didn't appear to know the name, and she reminded herself that he was new to Bear County.

"Nice flex," he said.

"Ha—touché. Anyways, he's my boss, technically, and also the reason I became a cop. I completed an undergrad degree in criminal psychology, and then immediately joined the force."

"Criminal psychology?"

Veronica nodded and took another sip of her drink. She didn't mind talking about herself, not when she felt that Steve was genuinely interested in her answers.

"Yeah, at one point I wanted to go into the FBI, but my dad convinced me to stay close to home."

They ordered another drink and then it was her turn to query Steve.

"I was actually born in Toronto, but I moved to the States when I was young. My dad was a Professor at the University of Toronto before taking a job at the University of Nevada, Las Vegas."

"UNLV?" Veronica asked, sipping her drink. "That's a long way from here. And from Toronto."

"Yeah, my dad…" Steve took a deep breath, and Veronica sensed that the tone of the conversation was about to change.

"I'm sorry, if you don't—"

He offered a weak smile.

"It's okay, you were honest with me and—" the music suddenly got louder. It was a cross between EDM and Mexican folk, and it didn't fit the mood at all. "One day a disgruntled student came into his office, shot my dad, then killed himself."

"Jesus—I'm so sorry."

"It was a long time ago. But that's the reason why I became a cop. Then a sheriff."

Veronica was tempted to ask why he'd gone from being in the State Police to a sheriff but felt like she prodded enough for now.

They finished their drinks, and another round magically appeared.

Veronica hadn't eaten dinner. She didn't expect to eat—Steve had invited her for drinks at eight—but she'd spent too much time getting ready to prepare anything. Truthfully, she thought that this was going to be a quick date, a courtesy date to make sure that the sheriff kept her on the case. It felt weird pimping herself out for work, but that was the honest truth.

And now, who knows how many ounces of tequila deep, Veronica was feeling the alcohol.

"What kind of professor was your father?" she asked. The music was so loud now that she was forced to nearly shout.

"Literature."

"Ah, hence your love of books," Veronica remarked. "Did he—did your father ever write anything?"

"A couple of things, essays, short stories, but no novels." When Steve spoke about his dad, the man had a far-off look in his eyes, something that Veronica was familiar with having spoken to many people who had lost loved ones. "But that doesn't matter. Every time I read a book, I'm reminded of him, even though we had very different tastes when it came to genres. "

It was sweet, and Veronica found herself smiling without even thinking about it.

They chatted for a little while longer, but for some reason whoever was in charge of the music had their thumb on the volume and every few minutes, they increased the level of the obnoxious beat.

"I'm going to get a headache," Steve said. "You want to get out of here?"

Veronica nodded. She was reaching the point of no return. If she stayed, she was likely to become very, very drunk.

"Kinda sucks, doesn't it?"

"Too young for me," Steve replied with a laugh.

They left Escondite, and Steve surprised her by slipping his hand into hers. She thought this might be awkward, but it wasn't, it was cute.

"I don't think I can drive," he admitted. "Too many cocktails."

"I took an Uber." Her words were slurred but she didn't think Steve noticed.

"Maybe you could teach an old guy how to do that?"

Veronica turned her eyes up at the man whose hand she was holding. He was handsome, there was no denying that. She knew that he was good-looking when she saw him washing his car with his shirt off. What she hadn't realized was that he was also sweet. And kind.

"I have a better idea: how about we just share one?"

# Chapter 25

THE MAN LAY IN WAIT. He didn't move, he just watched.

The girl's parents left first, dressed in their Sunday best as if they were headed to the theater. And maybe they were. They also made sure to lock the front door behind them like the responsible parents that they were. Their fancy Mercedes drove right by him, but he went unnoticed, seated in his car wearing all black from the hood of the sweatshirt that was pulled over his head to the wool gloves.

They weren't the type of people who looked. Looking made them think and thinking made them feel bad.

Fifteen minutes passed, then twenty. Just before the half-hour mark, the front door opened again. To her credit, the beefy girl who peered out glanced up and down the street. He wasn't sure what she was searching for because her eyes didn't linger on his car.

She obviously suffered from the same condition as her parents. But that was okay because she'd see him soon.

Not now, but soon.

The girl ducked back inside her home for a second, then came out onto the front porch. He watched her, watched the way she moved, the way her lips —

A car pulled up to the curb, blocking his view. The girl got in, and then she, like her parents, was gone.

Patience was his only virtue. Five more minutes and then he finally got out of the car. He didn't see if the girl had locked the front door after she left, but he didn't check. That wasn't his way in.

Keeping his head down and staying in the long shadows of the house, the man moved quickly, but not hurriedly, down the side of the impressive home. The gate wasn't locked, but the side door was. That's why he brought his tools. It wasn't hard to pick a lock, especially if you had experience. And the older the lock, the easier it was. The new digital ones? Impossible, at least for a man with a torsion wrench, ball pick, and short and medium hooks for tools.

He made quick work of the pedestrian lock and then dipped inside. With the door closed behind him, the man finally relaxed. He had time and he intended to use all of it.

This was his first foray inside her home, and he took his time familiarizing himself with the main floor layout. He was patient, but even he had his limits. He wanted to go upstairs, *needed* to go to her room, and before long, he found himself there.

She was nineteen, a little old for his taste. But the sight of her room made the front of his black sweatpants suddenly seem two sizes too small. It was a child's room. The walls were painted a pale pink and there were posters — pop bands? Movies? — covering two of them. The bed... the bed had four large wooden posts that stretched nearly to the ceiling. A sheer mesh hung down in a canopy, cinched to each of the posts.

Licking his lips, the man desperately wanted to take off his gloves. He wanted to grab her pillow, squeeze it, *feel* it but knew that that would be a mistake. To distract himself, to quell his urges, he went to the dresser and yanked the top drawer open. The first pair of panties he saw were the ones he took: a lacy pink pair. They were clean, but he smelled them anyway, picturing her wearing them.

After tucking the underwear into his pocket, he left a pair of boxers hanging just a little bit out of the drawer as he closed it. Then he placed the note that he'd brought with him on the girl's pillow, making sure it was perfectly centered.

There was a bathroom attached to the bedroom, and he headed there next.

To his displeasure, it had a modern shower made entirely of glass tiles. The only saving grace was that the tiles themselves were black. There was a cut-out in the wall that housed a myriad of shampoos, soaps, and conditioners. It wasn't the best spot to put the camera, but there wasn't another option. His only hope was that when the girl was showering, the water would be in her eyes and the last thing she'd be looking for was a button-sized camera mounted on the top of the shelf. Eventually, it would be found. They almost always were. But not before he had dozens, if not hundreds, of photos.

And so what if they found it? It was completely anonymous, untraceable. Even the destination that the pictures were wirelessly delivered to was masked by two different VPNs.

The man put his hand into his pocket and massaged the panties as he went downstairs. He took one final look around and then left the way he'd come, locking the door behind him. When he was back in his car, he finally took his gloves off. Then he felt the underwear by rubbing the fabric between his thumb and forefinger.

This was the first time he'd gone inside her house. But it wouldn't be the last. And next time, he'd make sure she was home when he stopped by.

# Chapter 26

"**I HAD A NICE TIME** tonight," Steve said as the Uber pulled up to Veronica's house. "I didn't expect that."

"You didn't expect to have a good time with me?"

"No, I mean, it's just—"

Veronica laughed. Sheriff Steve Burns was thirty-four going on thirteen.

"Yeah, you're new at this. Me too," she said. "Do you wanna come in for a drink? I can't make you a mescal old-fashioned, but I have beer."

Steve practically jumped out of the car.

"Anything to get this godawful sour taste out of my mouth."

Veronica laughed again and unlocked the front door. A tinkling sound coming from inside made her freeze, but she thawed upon seeing Lucy approaching.

"Oh, you're a cat lady, I see," Steve joked as he entered her home.

"Only recently."

Lucy purred and Veronica opened a fresh can of cat food and put it on the plate she'd been using to feed the animal.

"There you go, sweetie."

Veronica grabbed two beers next, popped the tops, and turned. She was surprised to discover that Steve had followed her into the kitchen. He was looking at the cat, and Veronica, worried that maybe he would see the name tag and recognize it as Maggie's, thrust the beer in his direction. The man hadn't been kidding about the taste in his mouth, given the way he chugged a third of the beer in one swig.

"So much better than—"

Veronica didn't let him finish the sentence. With the beer in her right hand, she snaked her left behind his head, then pulled him toward her. She kissed him full on the lips.

Steve was shocked at first but quickly got over his surprise. For however childish he'd been in the cab, and even occasionally at the restaurant, his kisses were mature and tender. Veronica drew him closer still, holding the kiss. Steve hadn't liked the sour taste of his drinks, but they'd made his tongue vibrant and almost effervescent.

Soon, his hands were on her, starting at the small of her back before moving further south. He squeezed her ass gently then his hands slid to her front. Steve's fingers massaged her through the thin material of her jumper, and she moaned softly, disengaging her lips, and throwing her head back as she did.

Now he was kissing the corner of her jaw and her neck, and Veronica could feel his hardness through his jeans.

Her eyes opened and for some reason, the first thing her gaze fell on was Lucy.

And the cat was staring back.

"Not here."

Veronica was suddenly uncomfortable and she led him by the hand to the bedroom.

Sheriff Burns may have been new to the whole dating scene, but he was well experienced in the bedroom. Veronica came twice. The second time, colors exploded across her vision. Not the angry reds and yellows, or the blushing blues that she was used to. But gold—flecks of gold like the specks in her irises.

It was the best sex Veronica had ever had, and when it was over, she collapsed onto Steve's sweaty chest.

Exhausted, both from the recent activity and the long day, Veronica fell asleep almost immediately.

But as enjoyable as the evening had been, the nightmares she experienced soured her mood like one bad apple ruining an entire orchard.

Nightmares that prominently featured Maggie Cernak and Sarah Sawyer. Maggie was still hanging in the sheriff's barn, the plastic rope creaking as the winds of death made her tormented soul twist ever so slightly. Then, somehow, even with her thick tongue lolling from her mouth, the woman spoke in a dry, hoarse voice.

"Help me, Veronica. Help me."

Cut to Sarah. She was lying on the ground, her arms outstretched above her head, the courtesy sheet removed from her face. The mess below her chin was a nearly unrecognizable mass of blood, tissue, and bone. She spoke too, her voice similar to Maggie's but thicker and wetter.

"Help us," she begged. "Veronica, help *ussssss*."

Then came another voice, one that belonged to no one at all. Rather than rendering it less frightening, the disembodied nature made it even more harrowing than either Maggie's or Sarah's.

*Eenie, meenie, miney, mo.*

# Chapter 27

WHEN VERONICA FINALLY AWOKE, IT was later than her usual hour, and Steve was gone. She checked the bathroom and the kitchen, but any romantic idea of him making her breakfast in bed vanished.

And she was glad. Not only was such a thing cliched, but there was an inevitable awkwardness to one-night stands that even scrambled eggs and bacon couldn't alleviate.

*One-night stand... was it a one-night stand?*

Veronica shook her head only to immediately regret the decision.

Her head was pounding, she felt seven feet tall, and her mouth... god, something awful had crawled into her mouth and died overnight.

Another reason to be glad that Steve wasn't around.

But would you care about morning breath following a one-night stand?

A second head shake, double the regret.

Normally, Veronica's Saturday nights involved watching TV by herself and having a glass of wine or two. Rarely would she drink more than half a bottle. It felt like last night she'd drunk an entire agave field worth of tequila.

After brushing her teeth and washing her face, Veronica built up the courage to look at herself in the mirror.

Not bad, all things considered.

"I guess I fulfilled my part of the bargain, Dr. Jane Bernard," she whispered. Veronica pushed the hair back from her temples with hands wet from cold water.

It felt good—*great*.

The only saving grace was that it was Sunday, the one day of the week she had off. Running around looking for Dylan Hall with a hangover wasn't high on her bucket list. It was bad enough sober.

But not working didn't mean not *working*. It just meant not having to get dressed and dealing with pricks like Officer Ken Cameron.

She had what was left of the morning and the afternoon to do her research. The evening was off-limits, already booked. For the past two and a half or three years, Veronica had been going over to her father's house for dinner on Sunday. Every Sunday. Even Super Bowl Sunday—*especially* Super Bowl Sunday.

It didn't hurt that Captain Peter Shade was an incredible cook. But today, in her present state, the idea of food was nauseating.

Still, Veronica forced herself to eat—something she hadn't done since yesterday morning—washing everything down with an entire pot of hot coffee. It helped. And after an hour, she chased the piece of buttered toast with a fried egg and stale muffin.

Then Veronica got behind her computer. Her first search was for Sarah Sawyer, which reminded her of the nightmares. She persevered and quickly found the recently deceased. Sarah was—*had been, she* had *been*—a sales rep for a pharmaceutical company with a regional office in Portland but was based out of Boston. According to some of the photographs from the annual company gatherings that she was able to pull up, Veronica ascertained that Sarah did quite well for herself. The woman appeared in many prominent photos with Directors and VPs alike. As far as she could tell, there was no connection, real or virtual, between Sarah and Maggie.

And that's where the trail started and ended.

Like Maggie, Sarah had no kids, no husband, and minimal, if any, friends. Veronica was able to determine that Sarah had received a business degree from Washington State University. But before that? Elementary school? High school? Place of birth?

Nada.

The lack of breadcrumbs was eerily similar to Maggie Cernak's past, but Veronica wasn't about to give up yet. Moving from public search engines to her secure police database, she held out hope that Sarah had a record, unlikely as that might be. But Sarah wouldn't be the first professional to have an arrest for coke or drunken disorderedly in their past.

Unfortunately, Veronica had no such luck—Sarah wasn't in the system.

Frustrated, she took a break. She needed to get out. Even though the simple thought of going for a run made her quads seize and stomach flip, she donned her running gear and stepped outside. Her goal was five miles but after one and a half, she turned back. Every joint hurt.

But she did it. She ran.

*Small victories, V. Small victories.*

And after a cold shower, she felt better. Not one hundred percent, but closer than before her run.

Dinner plans with her father weren't for at least another hour, so Veronica, with a clearer albeit still moderately fuzzy head, got back to her research, this time with a different approach.

Social media had drummed up nothing. Likewise for criminal searches. But as a City of Greenham detective, Veronica also had easy access to court records.

If she couldn't find Sarah Sawyer or Maggie Cernak any-where online before the age of eighteen—give or take a few—then perhaps it was because they didn't exist.

Five minutes later, Veronica was grinning from ear to ear.

"Bingo."

Maggie remained a mystery, but she found a court docu-ment with Sarah Sawyer's name from when she was seventeen years old. The date matched, and the location—the document had been filed in Portland—made the probability of this being *the* Sarah Sawyer almost a certainty.

The official court document was a request for a name change. This wasn't something that Veronica had dealt with be-fore—in fact, she'd never even seen this form during her tenure as a cop or detective, and it took a few minutes for her to famil-iarize herself with it. There were plenty of boxes and options for written answers, all of which were of interest to Veronica: the reason for the name change, parents' names, list of siblings, and the like. Unfortunately, she quickly got the impression that these were optional, considering that the vast majority had been left blank. In most states, you didn't need to have a valid reason to change your name. Just not liking the way it rolled off your tongue was sufficient.

What wasn't optional, was indicating your *current* name—the birth name that you wanted to change. In this case, Sarah Sawyer's old name was...

Veronica frowned.

"What the hell?"

... blacked out. Sarah Sawyer's birth name was redacted.

But why? Not only were name changes part of the public record, but she was a detective. Veronica tried several back door approaches, but every version of the form that she found was the same.

*Redacted* changed her name to Sarah Sawyer.

Veronica gave up her online sleuthing and shifted her tactics to a more conventional approach. Being a Sunday, however, she got the court records office's answering machine. Part of her wanted to hang up—this wasn't her case, and Captain Shade had already indicated that her priority was finding Dylan Hall. But she'd already gone so far down the rabbit hole that it was faster to dig through to the other side than climb out. At least, that was how she justified continuing to keep the phone pressed to her ear. Just to play it safe, Veronica left a concise message that only included three details, all of which were numbers: the name change case filing, her badge ID, and her cell.

Even after hanging up, the entire endeavor felt incomplete and she considered, however briefly, reaching out to Freddie. He was a journeyman detective, and he had connections everywhere. And if anyone could get the records office open on a Sunday, it was—

Her phone started to ring, and Veronica was so startled that she dropped it. It tumbled onto the couch, bounced once, and she caught it before it fell to the floor.

"Hello?" she asked desperately, almost certain that it was someone, a janitor, overnight clerk, anyone, from records who could help her out.

"V, think you can do me a favor before you head over?"

Her heart sank. It wasn't the records office; it was her father.

"V?"

"Yeah, sure. What do you need?"

"Beer—I need beer for dinner. Ran out. Think you can pick something up? And I'm not talking about that swill made with corn syrup that you usually drink."

Veronica smirked and closed her eyes, her thoughts turning to the shitty generic beer that she and Steve had started last night.

Started, but never finished.

"Sure thing, Dad."

"Awesome. You better get moving because we're eating in forty minutes. Sharp. Don't be late, kiddo."

# Chapter 28

SHERIFF STEVE BURNS HAD MADE a mistake.

The moment he'd seen the enigmatic detective Veronica Shade step out of the Sebring, he'd been instantly attracted to her. She was pretty in an understated way, but it was her eyes that drew him in. Hazel with flecks of gold throughout. There was also something less tangible that he saw in her. It was the way she looked at things as if she could see layers that were invisible to others.

And yet, ironically, she seemed oblivious to his stares, while her obese partner Detective Furlow definitely noticed.

While Veronica had been pretty when he first met her outside his barn, and again when they'd driven together to the Sarah Sawyer crime scene, it was on their date that she'd blown him away—she looked absolutely stunning.

Aside from the unpalatable drinks, the night with Veronica had gone exceedingly well, and ever the gentleman, he'd tried to go home afterwards. Was it his fault that he'd "forgotten" that he had Uber installed on his phone? Maybe. Or maybe that was just the alcohol.

Regardless of how they'd gotten to her house, Veronica was the one who had invited him in and the one who had made the first move.

And Steve wasn't complaining. He had intended to stay until morning and he'd fallen asleep with Veronica on his chest. But sometime around midnight, a sound had awoken him. When he didn't hear anything for several minutes afterward, he assumed that it was the cat. But then Veronica sighed and began to mumble.

"No, please... don't make me do it."

The pain in her voice, accentuated by sleep, was haunting. Steve was about to wake her when she suddenly wrenched her body into a quasi-upright position.

"Veronica?"

Her eyes were open, but blank.

"I don't want to do it."

"You don't—" Steve stopped when he realized that she was still asleep. He reached out, but the second his hand touched her bare shoulder, she recoiled.

At a loss for what to do, he just stared at her. And then Veronica smiled, turned her back to him, and lay back down. Confused, and more than a little frightened, the sheriff didn't do anything. Even when her breathing regulated and the nightmare seemed to have passed, he kept his eyes locked on her. Sleep returned for Veronica, but it remained a stranger to Steve.

He silently got out of bed and dressed. Then he left, enjoying the cool night air on his skin. Having only indulged in a few of the sour drinks, and having sweated at least one of them out, sobering up happened well before he finished the four-mile trek back to Escondite to retrieve his car.

Maggie had been discovered hanging in his barn three days ago and Steve had slept a grand total of nine hours since. He was no stranger to violence but seeing her there, with her tongue hanging out, so close to where he went to sleep?

*I shouldn't have left*, Steve thought as he pulled up in front of the barn and let his car idle. *I should have just stayed at Veronica's.*

*Depcest*, the cute abbreviation for departmental incest, was frowned upon for many reasons. And even though he and Veronica weren't even in the same law enforcement branch, it still felt... complicated. Especially because he intended, even if she hadn't requested it, to keep Veronica in the loop.

Maybe that was why he left. Or maybe it was because he was afraid that she would wake up to one of his nightmares, and he'd say something that would send her packing.

"Shit," he sighed.

Going inside was out of the question, but he needed to sleep. Steve could function fairly close to the status quo with five and a half to six hours of sleep, but anything less and his mental acuity declined quickly.

The last time he'd gone this long with so little actual, restorative sleep bad things had happened. Bad things that had resulted in him being forced to accept a paltry severance in return for him resigning. And now, here he was, relocated halfway across the state, shifting from State duties to County duties.

*This was all a big mistake.*

Sheriff Burns shut off the car and lowered his seat as far as it would go. His mistake had been going for drinks with Veronica Shade.

It had nothing to do with her—it was all about him.

He felt strong feelings for the woman, and that was the problem.

Because Steve had felt this before.

And last time, it had ended in bloodshed.

# Chapter 29

THERE WAS ONLY ONE RULE for the Shade father-daughter Sunday night dinner: no work talk. Typically, this didn't pose a problem, as both Peter and Veronica relished the break from their everyday.

Not tonight, however.

Veronica had so many questions rattling around in her brain that the prospect of not asking them seemed nearly impossible. But her father hadn't become captain of the City of Greenham PD by breaking rules. And the fact that the 'no work' mandate was one of his own, rendered it even more unyielding.

But she was determined to find a way to finagle her questions in. It was just a matter of time.

"Hi, sweetie," her dad said as soon as she opened the door. Veronica gave him a hug, and he hugged her back, awkwardly, because he was holding a large set of tongs in one hand and didn't want to dirty her shirt with his apron.

After they hugged, Peter's eyes immediately went to the beer in her hand. As per his request, she'd gone one-hundred percent craft brews: four New England IPAs and two Stouts.

"Very nice." He gave her an approving grin. "Pop one of those for me, and I'll meet you in the kitchen."

Peter Shade lived a routine-driven life. His house was small, a bungalow with two bedrooms, two baths, and a family room that featured the same couch that had always been there since Veronica could remember. The only noteworthy upgrade since she was a child was the TV, but even that had been years ago. It was a pre-app model, which meant that he would have to use a dongle to watch Netflix or any of the other streaming services, but Veronica wasn't convinced that the man ever used the thing.

Unless, of course, his beloved Seahawks were playing.

The kitchen was the only room in the house that didn't follow this pattern. It was also the only room that her father seemed to care about. It had undergone multiple upgrades over time. First, had been swapping out the electric stove for a gas one, then another upgrade after complaining that four burners weren't enough, despite the fact the man lived alone. His most recent, and also most prized purchase was his sous vide machine. Not much of a cook herself, Veronica wasn't exactly sure how it worked. But, as per her father's lengthy explanation, and her own taste experiences, it essentially cooked meat perfectly, with no chance of over or undercooking. If you wanted a steak medium rare, you vacuum sealed the meat, set the water temp to 131°, and dropped it in. A couple of hours later, your steak will be perfectly cooked.

Veronica could see the device on the counter now, making a whirring sound as the wand heated and circulated the water. Despite her still recovering stomach, her mouth watered at the thought of eating one of her father's perfect steaks.

She cracked two beers, the NEIPAs, and handed one to Peter. He took a gulp before inspecting the label.

"Not bad," he murmured, mostly to himself. "Not bad at all."

Veronica sipped from her own bottle. She wasn't a huge IPA fan, but the cool liquid on her lips did wonders for treating the last vestiges of her hangover. Her first gulp was quickly chased by a second.

"Yeah, not bad," she agreed. "What's for dinner?"

Peter Shade, a man not known to smile at work or elsewhere, grinned from ear to ear.

"You're in for a treat, V. Got a new toy a while back, but I've been hiding it."

Veronica searched the kitchen for the toy and thought she found it near the far wall. Sitting on the counter, roughly the size of a mini fridge, the college dorm room variety, was a metal box with a glass front. There were no IPAs visible inside, but instead, a giant slab of gray/brown meat. The prime rib, at least, what Veronica thought was a prime rib, looked a little shrunken and a lot unappetizing.

Catching her gaze, her father said, "That's my dry ager. I got it about three months ago, and that prime rib in there? Been tenderizing for fifty whole days. I cut two beauties off, big steaks, and they're in the sous vide now. You're gonna love it."

Veronica did not doubt her father's words for an instant. He was an outstanding cook, and while she loved his food, it was his passion that she was drawn to. The man could speak for hours about everything from the virtues of properly seasoning meat to the fallacy that was marinades. She didn't share his interest, not with near the same vigor, but seeing him happy like this was more than enough to lend a patient ear.

"Can I see?" Veronica asked, leaning toward the sous vide.

Her father slid in front of her.

"No way. You don't get to see anything until it's on your plate."

"Okay, okay." Veronica finished her beer. It had gone down way too smoothly and way too quickly. "I'll get out of your hair, then."

"Please do. Ten minutes, tops."

Veronica grabbed another beer, promised herself that she would nurse this one, and then headed to the dining area, adjacent to the living room. Having never been married, and after Veronica moved out had only ever lived alone, her father had no need for a big, banquet-style table. Their Sunday dinners took place at a simple, round, wooden table with four chairs.

Peter always sat in the chair against the back wall. He joked that this was the king's throne, something that Veronica had taken to heart when she'd been a kid. Now, with her experience in law enforcement, she knew differently. Peter took that chair because it had the best view of the front door.

Safety first.

Behind the king's throne stood a bookshelf. Unlike Sheriff Burns, Peter wasn't much of a reader, unless you considered cookbooks literature. The shelf was littered with various medals, crosses, and stars, accolades from a long career in the police force. In addition to a paucity of books, there were also very few photographs on the shelf. There were a handful of black and white images of Peter from various newspaper articles over the years, but three full-color photographs were prominently displayed: the first from years ago, taken the day that Peter Shade graduated from the academy. The image had faded over time, but this only served to accentuate its charm. The man with his arm around Peter, with an equally large smile on his face, was Grant Sutcliffe, Peter's longtime mentor. The other framed photo was similar. Only Grant was replaced by Veronica and Peter had his arm around her shoulders. This was the day that she graduated from the academy.

The third photo wasn't like the others. For one, it had been placed at eye level, whereas the academy photos were on the top shelf. Some Sundays, after a particularly busy week, Veronica saw a thin layer of dust on most of the items on the shelf, including the graduation photos.

But never this one. Never. It was as if the very first thing her father did upon entering the house was to grab a cloth and wipe it clean.

Standing outside the Portland courthouse steps were two people: Peter, with a smile on his face that made the one in the graduation photo look like a grimace, and a cute, brown-haired, golden-eyed five-year-old girl.

The picture had been taken on the day that Peter's adoption of Veronica had gone through.

"Still as pretty now as you were back then," a voice said from behind her. Veronica, her nerves still a little threadbare from all the alcohol, jumped.

"Maybe not today," she said softly, and then looked at her father. He stared back for a few seconds, but when she didn't say anything, the man grew uncomfortable and thrust a plate in her direction.

"C'mon, V, let's eat before it gets cold."

# Chapter 30

VERONICA DIDN'T UNDERSTAND HOW DRY aging a steak changed it, or how it didn't just start to rot, but whatever happened inside that sixteen-ounce slab of marbled muscle was probably illegal.

It was the best steak she'd ever eaten. Not only was it cooked perfectly—thank you sous vide—but her father had seared it in beef tallow on the cast iron, which had created a beautiful crust. Yet, these two techniques were some of Peter Shade's favorites, and Veronica had eaten many of the man's steaks over the years. The only difference tonight was the dry aging. The process had made the meat even more tender, if that was possible, and the beef tasted... *beefier*. That was the only way she knew how to describe it.

Peter never skimped on the sides—tonight's fare included scalloped potatoes, crispy Brussels sprouts finished with bacon, and a Caesar salad with homemade dressing—but these were, by definition, supplementary. The real star was the steak.

Perhaps it was the heightened emotions of the last few days, culminating with the fantastic sex with Steve, but whatever it was, the meal was almost transcendental. And Veronica enjoyed every last morsel.

"That was incredible." Veronica licked her lips. She picked at what was left of her Caesar salad, but she was already full.

"Just wait till next time," her dad said with a smile. "You think fifty days are good? Wait until one-hundred and twenty."

Veronica couldn't imagine what that would taste like, but she relished the opportunity to try.

They were both tired and full and did only a perfunctory job of cleaning the dishes, before taking up residence on the back porch. As usual, her father sat in the chair on the left, while she was on the right. Peter's chair was considerably more weathered than her own, and Veronica pictured her dad sitting here every night, watching the sky go by, thinking about crimes and criminals.

They were done with the IPAs and had moved on to the stouts, which were a little sweeter and a good palate cleanser.

Work talk was banned during Sunday dinners, but work thought was impossible to stop. And Veronica couldn't stop thinking about Sarah Sawyer.

*Why was her birth name redacted? Was she in witness protection? But if that was the case, wouldn't both names be hidden?*

Veronica wasn't sure, but she assumed that people in witness protection didn't have their name changes filed in the county courthouse.

*Was it because of domestic abuse?*

She sighed. This didn't make much sense either, for the same reasons that it made *witpro* unlikely.

"You okay, V?"

Veronica looked up from her beer, not realizing that she'd been twisting the neck of the bottle.

"Yeah, I'm fine."

"You look tired."

*Yeah, Dad, I'm tired because you're forcing me to work this stalker case and I'm moonlighting as a Deputy for Bear County trying to track down a killer.*

"You'd be proud of me—I went out last night."

Peter stared at her suspiciously.

"Out *out*?"

Veronica laughed.

"Yeah, out out."

"With who?"

"A girl never tells."

"Oh, c'mon, who did you go out with?"

Veronica knew that she should be offended by her father's incredulity, but she wasn't.

"No work talk, Dad."

"What are you talking about?" Peter's brow furrowed. "This isn't work talk."

"I dunno. This seems like an interrogation to me, which is technically work," Veronica countered.

"Since when was general chitchat with my daughter considered an 'interrogation'."

"I'll make you a deal, Dad. I'll tell you who I went out with last night if you answer me a question."

Peter frowned and took a deep haul of his beer.

"I shoulda known this was a setup. Some cop I am."

Veronica, grinning now, desperately wanted to know why Sarah's name was redacted. This, however, was something she just couldn't ask. Not only was it a direct violation of the 'no work' talk mandate, but then he would know that she was spending her time on something other than Ken Cameron's stalker case.

And she'd been warned.

"Well, do we have a deal?"

"Maybe. As long as it's not about the past. The past is —"

"—boring, the future is far more interesting." Veronica finished her father's favorite saying with an eyeroll. "I'm not going to promise that. But if you answer my question, I'll tell you who I went out with. That cool?"

Her father pressed his lips together in a thin line.

"Ask your question, and we'll see."

It was a lawyer's answer and not a police officer's, but Veronica knew that this was the best she was going to get out of the man. She looked down at her beer, and the sight of it, albeit a stout instead of a lager, reminded her of last night with Sheriff Burns. Freddie had told her that before Steve had come to Bear County, he'd been a State Trooper—a Statie who had been high up in the chain of command. This was similar to her father's professional journey, something he never really talked about—Grant, his mentor, had been grooming Peter to become the next head honcho in Portland PD, but Peter suddenly up and left.

"Why would a cop leave a higher position in a larger market to come to a small town to work?"

Generic, ill-phrased, but it got Veronica's point across, and now it was Peter's turn to sigh.

"Could be any number of reasons."

"That's not an answer."

"*Hmm*. Okay, well, sometimes a big city can be overwhelming. Big city problems, you know? A change of scenery can help."

That didn't explain why they'd moved around so many times before eventually coming back to where they'd started, but it did offer some insight.

"So, it's not just one case in particular, but the additive effect of many?"

Peter's eyes locked on hers and, for a moment, she didn't think he was going to answer.

"No," he said flatly, "it wasn't just one case."

If Peter Shade had uttered this answer to anyone else, they would've believed him. Although a couple of years removed from field duty, the captain was an expert negotiator and was almost as good as Veronica at spotting a lie. And the better you were at identifying lies, the better you were at lying.

But Veronica wasn't like anyone else. She could literally smell a lie, and right now the reek of gasoline was almost palpable.

"You sure it wasn't one case in particular?" Veronica asked, forgoing all subtlety now, giving her father one last chance to tell the truth.

"I'm sure," the man said. "Why this interest in departmental changes all of a sudden?"

"No reason," Veronica snapped.

She expected her father to press, but he didn't.

"Well, I'm getting tired. Why don't—"

"Why would someone's birth name be redacted on a name change form?"

Earlier, Veronica had been worried about the repercussions of asking this question. Now, fueled by her anger at being lied to, the words just flowed unabated out of her mouth.

"*What?*"

"You heard me."

"I don't know what the hell you're talking about." The man's reaction was visceral and unwarranted, breaking the rules or not.

"I just want—"

"No work questions." This tone Veronica recognized as being reserved for only the most serious versions of her father.

*Why the hell is he so angry?* Veronica wondered. *Was it because of the previous question?*

"Sorry. Just a question."

They sat in silence and finished their beers. When both bottles were empty, Veronica said she had to go, and her father offered to walk her out.

"You aren't going to ask me who I went out with last night?" Veronica said as she made her way to the car. It was an olive branch, an attempt to smooth things over.

"No." At first, she thought that he was still mad at her but then Peter broke into a smile. "Because I already know. Goodnight, V."

"Goodnight, Dad."

Veronica sat in the car with the window open after her father had closed his front door. A few minutes later, she heard the flick of the man's favorite Zippo, the one that Grant had given him, as Peter Shade lit up a cigarette.

*Looks like I'm not the only one who broke a rule tonight.*

But as she drove home, alone this time, Veronica wasn't thinking about her dad's disgusting habit. She was thinking about how angry he'd gotten at a simple question. Peter Shade, a man who rarely ever raised his voice, even at work, but seldom at home, had gotten pissed off by a simple, generic query.

And overreactions to generic questions were almost always the result of very specific answers. And in this case, the answer was something that Veronica was going to stop at nothing to find out.

# Chapter 31

"DO YOU KNOW WHY INFORMATION would be redacted from a name change application? A *successful* application?" Veronica asked as she sat in her chair.

"Well, good morning to you too, Veronica," Freddie replied. Veronica noticed the coffee on her desk, and she looked over at Freddie. There was an identical cup on her partner's desk, along with two foil-wrapped sandwiches that she'd bet her life weren't the healthy alternatives that she'd introduced him to a few weeks back.

"Thanks for the coffee. I've just been racking my brain over this thing... other than *witpro*, why would the birth name on a name change document, which is public information, be redacted?"

Instead of answering, Freddie began to unwrap one of his sandwiches. Veronica could see the cheese and bacon squeezing out the sides of the English muffin.

"Gimme a second — I must not be thinking straight, not without my greasy breakfast." He took a big bite of the sandwich. "Nope, that didn't help. What in the world are you talking about?"

Veronica looked around. It was early, and they were the first two on their floor.

"Sarah Sawyer — I was doing some research and I found out that she changed her name six or seven years ago. But on the form? Her birth name is redacted."

She stared at Freddie, hoping that he would provide some insight, but the man looked as glassy eyed as the inside of the foil wrapper. He took another bite of his sandwich, and Veronica waited patiently for him to finish chewing.

"Sarah...?"

And then it clicked.

"Oh, shit, I didn't tell you, did I? Right, so yesterday I was with Sheriff Burns, and he got another call — there was another suicide, in Sullivan, this time. A woman about the same age named Sarah Sawyer." Veronica hesitated when Freddie's expression soured a little as if something in his breakfast sandwich had gone off. "No, it's not like that. He brought me to the scene. Anyways, Sarah had a note on her: *MEENIE.* Same paper, same writing, same everything."

"Slow down, Veronica. Slow down. You said you were with the sheriff?"

Veronica wasn't sure if the man had forgotten or was just teasing her; she was with Sheriff Burns because he had set them up... *sorta.*

"Yeah. He didn't close the Maggie case, not yet anyway. It can't be a coincidence. So far as I can tell, they didn't know each other. Then I discovered that Sarah changed her name and that her birth name was redacted. Why would that be?"

Freddie went back to eating his first of two breakfast sandwiches, this time not as a distraction, but because he was thinking.

"I don't know about *witpro.* Those aren't filed in regular court. Domestic violence, maybe? Abuse?"

"That's what I was thinking, as well, but if I was an angry husband and I was searching the database for name changes around the time my wife went missing? This redacted text would be a dead giveaway. Besides, wouldn't it make more sense to black out the new name and not the old one?"

"Yeah, that's bizarre. Maybe it was a mistake. You try calling them?"

Veronica, who had checked her phone at least a dozen times that morning already, nodded.

"Left a message. Think maybe you could give them a call?"

Freddie wiped his greasy fingers on a napkin and then checked his phone.

"They don't open for another hour, but yeah, I can give them a call. Aren't you going to ask me how my day on Saturday was?"

Now, Veronica blinked, confused.

"I went to the school, remember?"

*The school...?*

"Ah, yeah, to see if anyone else had been harassed lately. How did that go?"

"Terribly. I mean, they were nice and all—they thought I was Ken at first. He was there about a month ago doing some sort of safety thing. Bet he was a real hit. Anyway, the principal said that they hadn't had any reports of serious harassment, just high school stuff. They're going to be on the lookout, though."

The door to the third-floor offices suddenly banged open and Veronica whipped around.

"Speak of the devil," she muttered under her breath.

"I hope you're happy!" Officer Ken Cameron shouted. His face was red, and he was wagging a plastic evidence bag in one hand.

"What are you talking about?" Veronica asked, eyes narrowing.

"What am I talking about?" Ken took two aggressive steps toward her and then tossed the evidence bag at her. It landed on her desk. "This is your fault."

Veronica refused to look at the sheet of paper. Freddie grabbed it instead.

"Just missed you," he read out loud.

"Yep—that was on Chloe Dolan's pillow. Her *pillow*."

Veronica felt her blood run cold. This was exactly what she feared—that Chloe's stalker would continue to get closer and closer to his prize.

"He even stole some of her underwear."

"Don't put this on us," Freddie said.

Ken didn't even glance at the man.

"I'm not—I'm putting this on *her*. She let him go—she let that prick Dylan Hall go and now he broke into their house."

"Did anyone see him break in?" Freddie asked.

Ken ignored the question, which was answer enough.

"Do the Dolans have any sort of security cameras in their home?" Freddie continued.

"They have some, but they aren't set up yet."

Only now did Veronica look at the note. It was the same writing as the lewd ones found in the girl's locker.

"It's not him," Veronica muttered. Two days ago, she'd been so certain that Dylan Hall was innocent that she'd let him go. But that had been when the crime had been just notes and a used condom. Breaking into someone's house and boasting about it? That was serious. And her proclamation had become a muted statement. "It's not Dylan."

"She fucking saw him!" Ken nearly shouted. "Chloe saw him!"

"Calm down." Even though Freddie was mostly made of Crisco, he was still a big man and he had experience to back him up. "We'll find Dylan."

"You better hurry because Randy Dolan isn't happy *at all*."

Freddie, frowning, grabbed his second sandwich off the desk and looked at Veronica.

"Let's go," he said.

"Where are we going?"

It was a stupid question, but Veronica was just vying for time. Time she didn't have.

Time Chloe Dolan didn't have.

"To find Dylan Hall," Freddie said.

"Yeah," Ken spat, finding his voice again. "And when you bring him in, this time he's not leaving this *fucking* precinct!"

# Chapter 32

VERONICA KNEW THAT FINDING DYLAN Hall wouldn't be the issue. She was familiar with the man's haunts, his routines, and people like Dylan didn't like to stray too far from their *fiending* grounds. The real question was, did she *want* to bring him in?

Nothing that had happened over the past two days had changed her mind about the man's innocence... at least when it came to Chloe Dolan. And if Veronica dragged Dylan back to the station, the search for the real culprit would slow to a crawl. Depending on how loud Officer Cameron could get, it might even stop completely.

But Randy Dolan and his position as a city councilor complicated things. Captain Shade was no politician, but he was hardly an anarchist. Veronica was hard-pressed to believe that anyone, even someone as decorated and respected as her father, could become a police captain without patting at least a handful of backs along the way.

Freddie lowered the phone from his ear.

"Veronica?"

"Yeah?" She was still mostly in her head and hadn't even realized that her partner was talking on the phone.

"That was records."

He had her full attention now.

"And? Did you find out Sarah's birth name?"

The look on Freddie's face was answer enough.

"They... they wouldn't tell me."

Veronica's eyes narrowed.

"They didn't know, or they wouldn't say?"

Freddie shrugged.

"Both—at least that's the impression I got."

"Why?"

Another shrug.

"This makes no sense. Is there anyone else you can call?"

Freddie moved his head in a circle.

"Maybe. But we really need—"

"To focus on this case, yeah, I know," Veronica said with a pout. She let the air out of her lungs in a huff. "Fine, okay. What if Dylan isn't behind this?"

"Oh god, not another *What if.*"

"No, I'm being serious. What if I'm right and Dylan Hall has nothing to do with this?"

Freddie didn't want to play along, but he was compelled.

"Then the real stalker is getting free reign to... well, do whatever it is he's doing with Chloe Dolan's undies."

"Right." Veronica was about to say something, something about how the unsub was also planning his next move—an even bolder move—when a thought occurred to her. "You know what? I've got an idea."

"You always have ideas."

"Don't worry, this doesn't involve you running."

Veronica briefly outlined her plan and then got out of the car before Freddie could protest. It took her three tries, and multiple dead ends, but she eventually found Dylan's blue tarp. Instead of approaching right away, she hung back and out of sight. A minute passed, then two, and Freddie's internal GPS kicked in and she saw his car at the opposite end of the alley. As before, he wedged the Sebring in the T-intersection, but instead of trying to get out, which was likely physically impossible given his girth, the man leaned on the horn.

With the sound echoing up and down the alley, Veronica drew her weapon and approached, crouching down to look below the haphazardly restrung tarp. Even though she wasn't in the mood, she was prepared to run, if she had to.

All it took was a single glance and Veronica knew that running wouldn't be necessary. Blue was everywhere. It was as if someone had poured blue paint on the tarp and by some unknown magic, when it seeped through, it became a vapor, an odorless effluvium that filled the area beneath with every conceivable hue, from cobalt to cerulean. It was so thick in some places, that Veronica, even though she knew that this was all just a projection, was tempted to wave her hand in front of her face.

She missed Dylan—probably would have stepped on him if her toe hadn't struck something hard.

On the ground, wrapped in two or maybe even three sleeping bags, was the outline of a human form.

"Dylan?" Veronica asked, keeping her gun at the ready. "Dylan Hall?"

The shape didn't react to her voice, and if it hadn't been for the fact that she detected a slight tremble, Veronica would have thought that the figure either wasn't a person or that they were dead.

"Shit." Veronica dropped down and started to peel back the layers of fabric that covered the man's head. They became considerably wetter the deeper she went. "Talk to me, Dylan."

She rolled the man onto his back and saw that his eyes were closed, and his jaw clenched.

"So c-c-cold," Dylan stammered. "I'm s-so c-c-c-cold."

It wasn't an overdose, Veronica realized immediately—Dylan was in full detox mode. She placed the palm of her hand on the man's forehead, which was soaked with sweat. He wasn't cold, he was burning up.

"I'll be right back," she said. Veronica carefully stepped over the man, then exited from beneath the tarp. Freddie, still in his car, stared at her with concern on his face as she hurried over.

"He there?"

"Yeah, he's there. I think he's detoxing. He's a mess, Freddie. Pass me a water bottle, please."

They always kept a case of water in the trunk, but it was a pain in the ass to get to it with Freddie's parking. Thankfully, Veronica spotted two in the backseat. She reached through the open window and grabbed both of them.

"Is he going to be all right?"

"He's in rough shape."

Dylan was in the same position when Veronica returned to his side.

She cracked open the first bottle and put it to his lips.

"Drink."

Veronica tilted the bottle and while most of the liquid spilled down the man's chin, some of it got into his mouth. She started to pull back, but his lips desperately sought more. She obliged. When Dylan had consumed the better part of half the bottle, she made him stop.

"Just wait, wait a second."

The man, eyes still closed, waited a good thirty seconds before he extended his lips again, like a suckling pig seeking a teat. As the man drank, Veronica mentally considered the timeline. When she'd brought him in three days ago, he'd been high. If Dylan hadn't used since then, it meant he was a good thirty to thirty-six hours into his detox.

If he made it through the next few hours, he'd probably be home free.

Dylan moaned and sputtered, inspiring another thought.

Someone had broken into Chloe's house *last* night. They'd left a note and stolen some of her underwear.

Veronica looked down at Dylan's pale, slick face.

There was zero chance that he'd left his feral camping ground, let alone made his way across the city, broke into the Dolan house, left a note, stole some panties, and ran off undetected.

Not in this condition.

No *fucking* way.

As Dylan's breathing began to regulate, Veronica stood and clutched the back of her head, unsure of what to do next.

If she called an ambulance, got the man help, then Ken wouldn't be far behind. And Officer Cameron was on a rampage. Alternatively, if she did nothing and just left him here, there was the real possibility that Dylan would slip into a coma from which he might never wake.

There was a third option.

Sighing, she left the bottle with Dylan, hoping that he wouldn't make himself sick while she was gone.

"I'll be right back."

Freddie looked miserable trapped in his car.

"What's going on? I can't—I can't get out of here. Does he need an ambulance?"

*He does,* Veronica thought. She wasn't a doctor, paramedic, nothing of the sort. But she had some experience with addicts. When she'd been a beat cop, Veronica had nursed several people back to health. No one in as bad a shape as Dylan, however.

"Veronica? You can't let him die. You—"

"He's not going to die." She straightened. "And it would take too long for an ambulance to work its way in here. You — you know your way around. Can you get him something? Some ice? An electrolyte drink, I don't know, Gatorade or something, and some food, maybe? Something greasy? A burger?"

Freddie just peered at her for a moment, and Veronica knew better than to push. She was asking a lot of her partner. The captain had told her, both of them, that Ken was in charge of this case, and they were to simply act as support staff. And Ken had made it abundantly clear, on several occasions now, that their main goal was to drag Dylan Hall back to the precinct and throw him in a cell. Then there was the fact that Freddie was technically her superior and all Veronica seemed to be doing lately is bossing the man around. If Freddie had even the smallest of egos, the detective would have already put her in her place.

But he had no ego. And, above all else, Freddie was one thing: loyal.

"Shit. Okay. You stay with him, I'll get supplies. And Veronica?"

"Yeah?"

"Whatever you do, don't let him die. If Dylan dies, we're going to be the ones needing a blue tarp to live under."

# Chapter 33

TWO GATORADES, HALF A CHEESEBURGER, a handful of fries, and twenty minutes later, Dylan Hall's condition had improved dramatically. He was still sweating and shivering, paradoxically so, but he was more or less lucid.

After retrieving the supplies they needed for his recovery, Veronica insisted that Freddie go for a drive. Her partner had predictably refused, citing that he should be there in case Dylan got violent or had thoughts of sexually assaulting her as he had before. But all it took was one glance at the defeated man, all bone and sinew, and he agreed that Dylan posed no risk. And even though he hadn't said so, at least not since finding him on the verge of death beneath the blue tarp, it was clear that he didn't think Dylan was behind Chloe Dolan's stalking, either.

"Just give me an hour, that's all I need," Veronica pleaded. She wanted to speak to Dylan alone—*needed* to. Very few things amongst partners were as important as trust, especially in law enforcement. But that pendulum swung both ways, and Veronica realized that she had to give Freddie *something*. "Look, we both know it's not him. But he makes a living on the street. Dylan might know who the real stalker is. He—he likes me. If you're here…" She let her sentence trail off.

"He likes your ass," Freddie corrected humorlessly.

"Well, it's a nice ass. C'mon, Freddie. Let me just talk to him alone."

Freddie was wavering, but still on the fence, and he pulled out his cell phone and wagged it in her direction.

"I'm keeping this in my hand," he said, and Veronica knew she'd broken him down. "If he does anything just call me. And you have thirty minutes, not an hour."

"Thank you. I owe you one."

"One?"

"Right. I owe you big time."

Freddie reluctantly walked to his car. Behind the wheel, Veronica saw him reach over to the passenger seat and grab a handful of fries. There was no way that Detective Furlow could go to a drive-thru and get something for Dylan without a little *je ne sais quoi* for himself.

After her partner was gone, Veronica force-fed Dylan some more water.

"Thank you," he said, his voice brittle like dried seaweed. The last thing Veronica wanted to do was pity the man. When he'd been running from her, he'd been high, aggressive. In jail, he'd just been scared.

But now, Veronica recognized Dylan for what he was. He was a human being—a torrid mix of mostly incomprehensible emotions. He was an addict who had grown up in the system, someone who needed help for a long time, and either never had access to the right resources or hadn't taken advantage of them. It was sad. It was pathetic. It was life.

Veronica didn't go as far as to justify the man's decisions, nor absolve him of blame. But to ignore everything else that preceded this moment—Dylan Hall wrapped in a sleeping bag, drenched in sweat, coming back from the brink—was akin to observing a waterfall and thinking that it had just appeared, that the water hadn't come from a predictable location and wasn't going to end in a lake or river somewhere down the road. Life wasn't a photograph; it was a video.

"Thank you," Dylan repeated, this time raising his bloodshot eyes to look at her.

Veronica acknowledged this with a nod.

"I want you to tell me about Chloe Dolan." Veronica kept her tone even. "If you lie to me, even once, I'll call Officer Cameron. And the only snacks he'll let you have is whatever you can squeeze into your prison wallet."

Dylan nodded vigorously, an action that was exacerbated by his delirium tremens.

There were rumors about Officer Ken Cameron. Rumors about 'accidents' happening to perps who ran their mouths. And someone like Dylan Hall? Who had been arrested more times than the Montreal Canadiens had won the Stanley Cup? He'd had his share of run-ins with the disgruntled officer.

"Good. First, let's get the obvious out of the way. Were you at Chloe's house last night?"

Dylan's eyes widened in surprise.

"Answer the question."

"No." The word came out as a breathy whisper. Veronica, who had since become accustomed to the scent hanging in the air beneath the makeshift overhang—a mix of body odor and urine—inhaled deeply.

She didn't expect to smell gasoline and wasn't disappointed. In her experience, detoxing addicts were so vulnerable that they almost always told the truth—it was the fastest way to reconciliation. They were also prone to random outbursts, which Veronica was keen to remember.

"Did you ever send her any notes? Flowers? A used condom?"

"No."

"And have you ever sold drugs to Chloe Dolan or her friends?"

"Yes." No hesitation, no smell.

"How many times?"

"Once. I told you, they came to me around Christmas, wanted to party. I gave it to them, but they refused to pay. That's why I was outside Chloe Dolan's house. But I was there once, that's it."

It was the same story, although the language used was less colorful now that Dylan was sober.

"Someone is stalking the girl. Have you heard anything on the street?"

Dylan shook his head and grabbed some fries. Grease dribbled down his chin and mixed with his sweat but went unnoticed.

"You know of anybody just recently released? Anyone with a past history of sexual assault?"

The man scoffed and a half-chewed piece of fry landed near Veronica's left foot.

"Pretty much half the homeless people in the area have a sexual rap. Mostly trumped-up charges, pissing in the playground, shit like that. Officer Ken Cameron shit."

Veronica was surprised. Not by the allegation—she knew that some cops used indecent exposure as a way to get homeless people off the street when business owners started to complain. Where were they supposed to go? If you were homeless and had to take a piss, where do you relieve yourself? No stores will let you in to use their facilities. It was a catch-22. What was unexpected, however, was Dylan's use of Ken's full name. Clearly, they had a history, and Veronica made a mental note to look into this a little deeper when she was back at the station.

"I'm not talking about that. I'm talking about a real scumbag, someone with a history of stalking. Someone who has taken things way too far."

Dylan considered this.

"There's a new guy in Greenham. Goes by Percy. Gives off bad vibes. Someone said he bragged about raping a girl in East Argham —a young girl."

Veronica raised an eyebrow.

"Percy?"

Dylan nodded.

"That's it? No last name?"

"No."

Veronica bit her lip. If he stayed sober, Dylan Hall could be a very useful asset.

"Let me ask you something, Dylan?"

"I thought that's what you were doing." Dylan reached for the bottle in a surprisingly coordinated movement.

He was recovering quickly.

"How come you're not using? How come as soon as you got out, you didn't get high?"

"Because—" Dylan hesitated, and a scowl appeared on his face. "No money. Don't got no money."

And that was the first lie that had come out of his mouth.

Veronica decided to give him a pass.

"You have a phone?"

It was a stupid question and they both knew it.

"There's a pay phone over on Waverly, by the iHOP? I'm going to give you my card, and if you hear anything about Percy or anything else that might help, you call me, okay? Collect?"

She produced her card and laid it on the ground beside Dylan's sleeping bag. He made no move to pick it up.

"What's in it for me?"

Veronica indicated the empty bottles, the fast-food bag.

"I think I've given you enough already." Dylan squinted at her. "Okay, how about this? If I can find you, Officer Cameron can, too."

The card promptly disappeared, and Veronica stood, groaning at her sore legs and back. She considered her options for a moment, and what Dylan had told her about not getting high because he had no money.

Deciding that that had been a lie, Veronica pulled a twenty out of her wallet and placed it where she had the business card moments ago.

Then she turned and left, walking briskly away from the cloying smell. She was halfway down the alley when she heard Dylan's voice call after her.

"Thank you."

Veronica's next step was a little lighter, her back just a bit straighter.

# Chapter 34

"I CAN'T FIND ANY 'PERCY' in the system. No one that was recently released, anyway," Veronica said dejectedly as they drove back to the station. Freddie's rarely used police-issued laptop was open on her lap. With it, they had access to most police databases, including conviction and release records. All of which contained a section for distinguishing marks, scars, tattoos, and, most importantly, nicknames. But Veronica came up empty. "There's a Darnell *Dercy*, but he was just released after shooting another gang banger. No history of sexual assault—doesn't fit the profile."

"Have you considered that maybe Dylan lied to you?"

"No."

Freddie sighed.

"Right, because you just *'know'* when someone's lying, right?"

Veronica looked over at her partner, surprised by his attitude. She'd been so locked in trying to find the mysterious 'Percy' that she hadn't realized that Freddie was sour about being made to leave her alone with Dylan. Veronica supposed that it wasn't just that, however; now that she thought about it, the last two days must have been particularly trying for a man who, as per his reputation and her own experience with him, liked to stick to the rules, to follow protocol.

Traditionally, so did Veronica, which made for a fairly copacetic partnership. But that was before seeing Maggie Cernak and having the... *reaction*. There was something about this case, about both cases that seemed somehow personal. One of the very first rules that they taught you—no, not taught, but ingrained in you—in the academy was to not take things personally. The irony was that she could forgive and forget Dylan's transgressions, including the fact that he'd copped a feel while high, but couldn't leave an apparent suicide alone.

"I'm sorry for being an asshole lately, Freddie. There's just something about this case..."

"This case?" Freddie said. "Or do you mean the Bear County suicide case?"

Veronica closed the laptop and focused all of her attention on her partner.

"What do you want me to say, Freddie? Maggie didn't commit suicide, and neither did Sarah. No way—I didn't think that when I first saw them, and I definitely don't think that now after finding those notes. And Dylan Hall? You really think he broke into Chloe's home in the state he's in? No shot. Let me ask you something—what do you think will happen if we bring him in? No, wait, I'll answer that: in his state? Detoxing the way he is? Once Ken is done with him, I'd be surprised if Dylan *didn't* admit to everything. But hey, if you want me to walk into the captain's office and tell him what *I* did? I will. I'll tell the captain that I let Dylan go... again."

Freddie gripped the steering wheel tightly.

"Don't be so dramatic—*sheesh*. I'm just worried about you, Veronica. I get that these two cases are personal—I have no idea why, but this is the first time I've seen you like this. And take it from me, take it from a man who literally eats his emotions, a man who has been doing this job for practically longer than you've been alive: you start taking things personally, and you'll end up in worse shape than Dylan Hall."

Veronica remained silent. Freddie was right but being right didn't magically make her feelings go away, just like putting a name to her condition didn't make the smell of gas and the colors disappear.

They just *were*.

In the end, Freddie was wrong about one thing, however: it wasn't Veronica who was being dramatic.

It was Officer Ken Cameron.

And her father.

Ken was waiting for her, and the second she stepped onto the third floor of the precinct, he approached.

"You saw him," the man hissed through clenched teeth.

"I don't have time for this, Ken," Veronica said, but the officer wasn't backing down. Even with Freddie at her side, her partner's shadow engulfing the other man, he was beyond reproach.

"You don't have time for this? Really? *You* don't have time for this?" In addition to flying off the handle, Ken also had the annoying habit of repeating his own questions. "But you had time to meet with Dylan. Dylan fucking Hall. And you had time to let him go."

Veronica froze and Ken's sneer transitioned into a smirk. She was about to call bullshit, but the jig was up. He'd caught her—she didn't know how, but he had.

Captain Shade's office door suddenly flew open.

"What's going on out here?" The man's booming voice filled the entire third floor. He seemed as angry as he'd been after their botched Sunday night dinner. "I'm on the phone trying to convince Randy Dolan not to fire all your asses, and you guys are out here bickering?"

Veronica glared at Ken, silently urging him to keep his mouth shut, that they would deal with this in private, but that just wasn't the man's way.

And there was nothing she could do to stop him.

"My CI told me that he saw Detective Shade with Dylan Hall this afternoon. And where is Dylan Hall, you ask? Not here, not in hold-up, either. Because she let him go. *Again.*"

Peter Shade's eyes were hard as ice as he glared at Veronica, but despite this glare, he allowed her to have her say. And Veronica could have denied Ken's claims. She could've said that Ken's CI was full of shit, and Freddie would've no doubt backed her up. But there was a difference between her partner looking the other way and out and out lying to their captain.

She couldn't do that to Freddie, couldn't put him in that spot. Nor did she want to lie to her father.

"It's not him, Captain. I'd bet everything on it."

"I don't gamble. Now give me your badge, Detective Shade," the captain ordered.

"*What?*"

"Your badge. *Now.* I warned you what would happen. This was Officer Cameron's case, and he was in the lead. You can't seem to follow orders, so until you get that under check, you're suspended."

Veronica couldn't believe her ears.

"Suspended?"

"We'll start with two days. Then we'll reevaluate your ability to follow orders and go from there."

Veronica was speechless. She'd never been suspended before. Hell, she'd only ever had a soft reprimand from a superior. And in a day and age when nearly every cop experienced multiple civilian complaints, her record was clean. But now, her own father, suspending her? For what? For not listening to that douchebag Ken Cameron?

"Two days," the captain repeated and Veronica, working on autopilot now, gave him her badge.

There was nothing for her to say or do; her father was a stubborn man and he'd made up his mind. Veronica just ducked her head and started to walk away.

As she passed Ken, Veronica looked up, which proved to be a mistake. The man's smirk nearly put her over the edge. She was within a hair of lashing out and slapping him. If she hadn't been reeling from shock, there was a high probability that Veronica would have done just that.

"It'll be all right," Freddie whispered as she passed him.

But for the second time that day, Veronica thought her partner was wrong: things wouldn't be all right. These two cases were all kinds of fucked up.

And the notion that it might just be her fault refused to go away.

# Chapter 35

IT TOOK VERONICA A GOOD twenty minutes of driving around to cool down. She was furious. Furious at her father, furious at Ken, furious at Freddie, at Dylan, Maggie, Sarah, and even Steve.

Jane, too, of course.

Because it had been Dr. Bernard's idea to go out—her orders. And did Veronica need a personal life, when her professional one was in such shambles?

"Dammit," Veronica whispered, her leather steering wheel creaking beneath her palms. Unlike Freddy, she didn't drive an aging Sebring—her car was a two-year-old Audi S5. It was times like these, as she whipped around residential neighborhoods, that Veronica wished she had a less capable vehicle.

The fact that she'd handed in her badge was a formality. There was no chance she was going to stop working. But it wasn't until she regained her composure that Veronica came up with an idea of what to do next.

"Kristin isn't in at the moment," the secretary manning the entrance of the Bear County medical arts building informed her. "But," she continued, seeing the disappointment on Veronica's face, "the CSU tech, Mr. Toler is finishing up some work if you'd like to head down to the morgue."

She wanted to speak to Kristin Newberry, but the tech in the toupee would have to do.

"Sure."

"I'll take you down there."

The woman started to lift her substantial frame out of her chair.

"That's all right, I know the way. Thanks."

When she finally made it through the bowels of the building to the dungeon, Veronica was so lost in thought that she opened the door without knocking.

CSU tech Holland Toler was seated with his back to her, his eyes in a microscope, when she burst through the door. The man was so startled that he nearly knocked over the entire table of equipment.

"Shit, I'm sorry," Veronica said. "I didn't mean to scare you."

Holland had a queer expression on his face. Not quite frightened but not totally comfortable, either. Veronica chalked this up to the man's profession. In her experience, nobody who spent all day with dead bodies was normal.

"Detective Shade. What can I do for you?" The man subtly adjusted his toupee, which had shifted from moving so quickly.

Veronica didn't answer right away, instead taking a moment to reorient herself in the confined space. Two bodies were on gurneys, completely covered in white sheets.

*EENIE and MEENIE.*

The thought horrified Veronica, as did the next. Her eyes naturally drifted to the single folded gurney pressed against the wall.

*They only have enough room for MINEY... where will they put MO?*

"Are you okay? You look like you've seen a ghost from your past."

Veronica forced the lurid ideas from her mind.

"Fine, just tired." Her gaze fell to the microscope and saw that Holland had been inspecting the note from Sarah's pocket. She could make out the word 'MEENIE' even from several feet away.

"Anything on the paper?"

Holland shook his head.

"No fingerprints, no hairs, unlikely to draw any DNA."

Continuing along this line of thought, Veronica asked, "And the bodies? Anything on those?"

Holland shrugged.

"Kristin was in earlier, wrote up a preliminary report if you'd like to see it?"

"Sure."

The man continued to speak while he rooted through a stack of papers.

"Pretty much came to the same conclusion as with Maggie. Suicide—gunshot wound, self-inflicted. As I said, Kristin had to leave early, but I was free—it's my day off."

He smiled and handed her Sarah Sawyer's report.

"What exactly are you looking for, Detective Shade?"

Veronica honestly didn't know. DNA? Fingerprints? What evidence could they possibly find, outside of an eyewitness or video recording, that these suicides were staged? What evidence could possibly exist that would validate her synesthesia?

Oh, and while they were at it, a link between Maggie and Sarah would be nice.

"I don't know." She was unable to hide the dejection in her voice. "I really don't know."

Veronica scanned the sheet of paper in her hand. Just as the tech had said, Kristin's conclusion was the same—manner of death: suicide. No forced entry, no evidence of theft or disturbance of any kind.

There was nothing else of note, except...

There, near the bottom, under "Additional Information" Kristin had listed Sarah's employer, Verdant Pharma, as well as the address. Veronica tapped the paper against her palm and committed the address to memory.

Then she handed the report back.

"Thanks. Please, keep me updated if you find anything."

"Sheriff's orders," Holland said with a mock salute. "Be safe."

A curious comment from a curious man. Veronica had other things on her mind, however: cats. She was planning to visit Sarah's employer, but she also thought about the woman's home.

And how she might swing by there, too, just in case, like Maggie, Sarah had a cat.

*Maybe that's the link,* Veronica thought dismally. *They both had cats.*

It was a stretch, but at least it was something.

\*\*\*

On the long drive to Verdant Pharma, Veronica discovered another potential link between the two victims, one that was slightly more reasonable than possessed felines.

Although the company that Sarah Sawyer used to work for dabbled in several products, their number one seller appeared to be an HbA1c lowering drug. Verdant claimed that this product reduced the risk of both heart disease as well as developing diabetes. Unsurprisingly, one of the potential side effects was suicidal thoughts and tendencies.

Could both Maggie and Sarah be taking the drug?

Unlikely, considering that both women were in their mid-twenties and in good shape. It was possible, however, and Veronica made a mental note to ask Holland or Kristin if they could check for metabolites in their systems.

What else could a high-powered pharmaceutical rep and a librarian have in common?

Other than a past shrouded in mystery, that is.

As she pulled into the Verdant parking lot, she recalled what Freddie had said before the whole Dylan Hall thing had blown up in her face.

That court records wouldn't release the redacted name to him, a respected City of Greenham detective.

*Why?*

Verdant's entrance was impressive, if a little sterile and aseptic. Having never been in a pharmaceutical company's regional head office before, she expected more of a lab coat and goggle kind of vibe. What she got, was pure business. Off to the right was an elaborate coffee bar where three people in suits were chatting in hushed tones. Toward the back, a polished wall of elevators. And front and center, a large marble desk manned by a caricature with spiky blond hair and a chinstrap goatee.

Veronica put on her best smile and approached the desk.

"Hi."

The man mirrored her expression.

"Hello, what can I do for you today?"

Veronica hesitated. Her intention in coming here was to speak to one of Sarah's colleagues, preferably someone who was also her friend, to get a better idea of who she was before she'd died. Her ultimate goal was to link Maggie and Sarah — that was the key. Veronica was certain that when she discovered that connection, the pieces would fall into place.

But once again, she'd failed to think things through. Sheriff Burns had called Kristin in on an emergency basis to Sarah Sawyer's house, and when Veronica had visited the morgue, Holland had told her that the coroner had to leave early. It was Kristin's job to visit the deceased's next of kin. What were the chances that she'd had time to inform the woman's employer?

"Ma'am?"

Veronica cleared her throat.

"I'm sorry. My name is Detective Veronica Shade." Out of habit, she reached for the badge that was normally hanging from her belt.

But it wasn't there.

*You really didn't think this through, did you, Veronica? Maybe Freddie's right, maybe you are taking this way too personally.*

The man lowered his voice and his eyebrows at the same time.

"Is this about Ms. Sawyer?"

Veronica acquired a more professional posture.

Well, that was one positive, at least; word had gotten around about Sarah.

"Yes, did you know Sarah?"

The secretary nodded solemnly.

"She was a very nice woman. Very nice."

"So I've heard," Veronica said, trying to keep the conversation going. "But, to be honest, that's pretty much all I know about her. She seemed like a private person. Were you guys close?"

The man started to answer, but then he grew suspicious.

"You're a detective?"

Veronica nodded.

"Detective Shade with the City of Greenham."

"Do you have a badge?"

*Not on me.*

"I'm just trying to learn about Sarah."

The man with the goatee straight out of 1994 crossed his arms over his chest.

"Legal has informed us that we aren't to speak to reporters about Sarah or any other employees."

"I'm not a reporter," Veronica protested. "My name is Detective—"

"Yes, sure. Well, Detective, if you would like to inquire about Ms. Sawyer, you'll have to do so through Verdant's quite substantial legal department. If you'd like, I can call a representative and have them meet you—"

"That won't be necessary."

The man gave her a knowing look.

"*Mmm, hmm.*"

"I'm very sorry for your loss."

The secretary didn't reply, and Veronica left Verdant Pharma.

To her credit, she made it all the way back to her car before eliciting a string of curses that would've made a sailor blush.

# Chapter 36

"YOU LOOK TIRED, SHERIFF," DAPHNE remarked as she re-filled his coffee.

"Thanks for the boost of confidence."

Daphne Hawkins, the proprietor of Bear County's favorite eponymous coffee shop, was in her late sixties with pencil-thin eyebrows and a gray bun pulled back tightly to help smooth some of her wrinkles.

"Honey, if you need me to boost your confidence, then you're barking up the wrong tree." She hesitated, topped his coffee right to the brim, then added with a grin, "Tired, but still handsome."

"Thanks."

Daphne turned her back on the sheriff and was on her way to fill another fatigued patron's mug, when she asked, "You want a bite to eat? A couple of eggs?"

Steve looked down at his cup of coffee, and the steam moistened his face.

"I think I'm good."

Veronica saw and heard all of this as she slowly walked from her car to the coffee shop. She was opening the door when she overheard Daphne say to the sheriff, "You've got a guest," and then head out of sight.

"A guest?" The sheriff turned, and their eyes met.

Veronica had hoped that Steve would be happy to see her, but she was disappointed. At best, the man was surprised and apprehensive. Was it nerves? Or was she just putting too much stock in a one-night stand?

After the day she had, Veronica needed someone to talk to — or maybe just to vent. Her father was out of the question, as was

Freddie who had probably spent the afternoon trying to convince the captain to reinstate her. That left Jane, but when Veronica had called her psychiatrist, it went right to voicemail, and it didn't seem right to show up uninvited so soon after last time.

The only person left was Steve.

Fearing that she'd made another mistake, her one-hundredth of the day, Veronica preemptively tried to save face.

"I was driving by, saw your car," she lied. The truth was, Veronica remembered the conversation she'd overheard between Kristin and Holland while she was inside Maggie Cernak's house. One of them had remarked that the sheriff had an evening coffee ritual at Daphne's. "I could do a coffee. If that's alright."

*If that's alright? Really? It's a coffee shop, Veronica. A coffee shop.*

"S-s-sure," Steve said, looking even more awkward now.

"Why don't you guys take a booth?" Daphne suggested, appearing from the ether. She passed the sheriff two menus. "Here. Grab something to eat, too." The woman looked at Veronica. "And you just wanted a coffee, sweetie?"

Veronica wasn't sure if it was just a happy accident or a deliberate act, but Daphne leaned to one side before she could answer and revealed a series of beer taps behind her.

"You know what? I think I'll have a beer, instead."

Daphne's smile grew.

"Sure, I'll be right over."

Sheriff Burns led the way to the booth and Veronica failed to suppress a sigh as she sat down. Neither of them spoke until Daphne arrived with not one beer, but two.

"Thanks," the sheriff said.

Daphne just smiled.

The beer was the type that her father hated, but sometimes cold and crisp was all you needed. And this was one of those times.

Veronica took one sip, then quickly followed that with another. She kept expecting Steve to say something, to ask a question, anything, but he just sat there. In her frazzled state, Veronica wasn't sure if this was an admirable trait or just plain annoying. She was sure that she felt dumb being here. She didn't know the man across from her, not really. And now, struggling with work, Veronica had sought Steve out like a desperate housewife.

Veronica decided that the only way to get out of this with a shred of dignity intact was to flip the script. Pretend like everything was perfectly normal, as if she wasn't suspended and on the verge of some sort of breakdown.

*So, sheriff, I was driving by and, uhh, I wanted to ask you a question about our case, you know? Oh, right,* your *case, sure.*

"I had some downtime and was doing a little research into Sarah Sawyer. Apparently, one of the side effects of her company's most popular drug was suicide."

It sounded real, convincing—at least to her ears.

"Really?"

"Yep."

"What does the drug do?"

"That's the thing. It's for heart disease and diabetes."

There was an awkwardness to the conversation as both of them seemed to be aware of the elephant in the room, but they were content with ignoring its trunk and tail.

"Yeah, I know, no smoking gun." *Cringe.* "But I also—"

"Have you guys decided on food?" Daphne asked.

"No, not yet. Thanks," Veronica said. The timing of the interruption was perfect, diffusing the inappropriately used idiom. When she looked back at Steve, he was staring at her expectantly.

"You also...?"

"Right. Well, you know how we couldn't find out anything about Maggie before she was in her twenties?"

"Yeah."

"Same thing for Sarah. But, get this, I found out she changed her name when she was seventeen."

For the first time since beginning this conversation, Steve appeared fully involved.

"What was her name before?"

"That's the thing—I have no idea. Sarah Sawyer's birth name was redacted."

"Really? Is she in witness protection or something?"

"That's what I thought, but no—doesn't make sense. So, I called the courthouse, but they wouldn't release the name to me or my partner."

Steve sipped his beer and pulled out his phone.

"You have the file number?"

"Yeah," Veronica replied hesitantly. Steve expected her to provide him with this information but when she didn't, he prompted her for it.

"Back when I was a Statie, I used to do some work for missing persons. I might still have a connection or two that can help."

This wasn't a full-blown lie, but Veronica detected a hint of gas in the air. She put her nose in her beer to drown it out and then passed the information along.

Then she watched in awe.

"Right, thanks," the sheriff said after inquiring about the file. "One more thing, do you know why this information was re- dacted? No? Can you tell me who ordered it, then? Awesome. Owe you one." Sheriff Steve Burns hung up the phone and looked across the table at her. Was he showing off? Maybe. But he'd just done in thirty seconds what she and Freddie hadn't been able to in two days—boasting was probably warranted. "Before she was Sarah Sawyer, the victim's name was Amy Davenport."

Veronica's eyes went wide.

"How did you—"

"I told you, I did some work with missing persons in the past. Anyways, my source doesn't know why the name was blacked out, but he knows who ordered it."

"Who?" Veronica asked. Her throat was suddenly parched, and no amount of beer seemed to help.

"A retired detective from Portland PD. Grant Sutcliffe."

Veronica Shade suddenly went pale as a sheet.

"What's wrong? You know him?"

She reached for her beer and finished the rest of the glass. For a woman who, by her own admission, didn't drink much, Veronica sure seemed to put them down when she was around Steve.

"Yeah, I know him." Veronica raised a finger in the air and the ever-smiling Daphne came over. "I think I'll have a burger and fries. We might be here a while. How about you, Steve?"

# Chapter 37

VERONICA NEEDED FOOD.

Fatigue, beer, and this new information had combined to render her lightheaded.

Grant Sutcliffe. Retired Portland PD Captain Grant Sutcliffe. It was a total mind meld. Her father's old mentor and boss had requested Sarah Sawyer's birth name—Amy Davenport—to be redacted.

It put some context to her father's reaction when she'd asked about it after dinner. It didn't explain it, not exactly, but it hinted at something.

While they waited for their food, Veronica put a call into Portland PD. She asked for Grant but was informed of what she already knew: the man was retired. When she requested a cell number, she was denied. The secretary did promise to pass on her details, however.

The next thing Veronica did was retrieve the police laptop from her car, which, admittedly, had been used even fewer times than Freddie's. When she came back inside Daphne's, her food was waiting, and she ate hungrily while trying to remember her password. During this entire bizarre scene, Steve kept quiet. He just stared at her as if she'd gone insane. Veronica owned it.

One of her favorite sayings was, if the shoe fits, wear it.

In this case, the shoes were high tops, and Veronica laced both of them all the way to the top.

Eventually, she remembered her password and smiled when she gained access to the system. If she'd actually been suspended, then all of Veronica's accounts would have been locked. The fact that they weren't indicated that her father hadn't *officially* suspended her. This also meant that her permanent record remained clean.

Her smile was short-lived. Entering Amy Davenport and her date of birth into the system opened Pandora's box. If Veronica had been alone, what was left of the food in her mouth would have fallen onto her plate.

"What is it? What did you find?"

Veronica couldn't speak and Steve, having finally reached the end of his patience, moved from the booth across her to beside her. She tilted the laptop so he could get a better view and his reaction was immediate.

"Jesus."

The singular word brought Veronica back to her senses.

There was one report involving an Amy Davenport from more than twenty years ago. Twenty-two, to be exact, and almost to the day. Veronica had no doubt that this was the correct Amy.

She was the youngest of two children—her brother Derek was four years older—and she lived with him and her mother and father, Alfred and Sophia.

According to the report, two people were seen entering the Davenport house late at night—why the police were not called at this point remains a mystery—their motive unclear. Robbery was suspected, but nothing was definitively determined to have been stolen. In the morning, a neighbor—the same one who had seen the intruders the night before?—was walking their dog when they spotted Amy sitting on the porch. She refused to speak, so the neighbor took the liberty of looking inside the Davenport home.

They were greeted by a scene of pure horror.

Alfred and Sophia had been bound at the wrists and ankles with duct tape. They'd both been shot in the head and DOA.

Little Derek, not even nine years old, had also been shot and while he was alive when the paramedics arrived, he died on the way to the hospital.

It was appalling, disturbing, but also eye-opening.

"Someone came back to finish the job." Steve exhaled. "More than twenty years later."

Veronica glanced at the sheriff. That had been her thought as well, but the way Steve had said it sounded so… innocent, somehow. Childish, even.

"No." She scrolled to the bottom of the report. "Can't be — the case is closed. Trent Alberts, convicted on six counts of first-degree murder. He's rotting on death row."

"Six?"

Veronica saved the report, then searched for Trent Alberts. A surreal feeling passed over her then. Even though this was what she'd been looking for, there was no moment of vindication. There was just a knot in her stomach that refused to go away.

If Dylan Hall had a long rap sheet, his was but a single line in T.S. Eliot's The Wasteland compared to Trent Alberts. Trent started at a young age, expelled from school at eleven for 'continual aggressive and disruptive behavior' and things just escalated from there. Violence begot violence and culminated in murder.

"It couldn't have been him, but maybe a known associate?" Steve suggested.

Once again, they were on the same page. The problem was that Trent's rap sheet was so extensive that the number of criminals he'd fraternized with over the years resembled the character list from War and Peace.

"I guess that explains why her name was blacked out," Steve said.

Veronica pictured the woman lying on her back, a sheet over her mangled face.

"They still found her. Listen, I'm not going to be able to go through this list. We gotta speak to someone involved in the case."

"Or Trent himself," Steve suggested. He pointed at something on the screen. "He's being held on death row at Oregon State Penn—shit, look at that. His execution is scheduled for two weeks from now—maybe he'll talk."

"When's the last time the State of Oregon executed someone?"

"I have no idea."

Veronica chewed the inside of her cheek.

That made a lot of sense. Go directly to the source.

"Why six though?" she said, repeating Steve's question from a moment ago. A quick scroll, a short search, and Veronica led the way down another rabbit hole.

The crime she uncovered was remarkably similar, from a high-level perspective, at least. A family of four, including two young children, one male and one female. Their names were unfamiliar, but as soon as they saw the cause of death, both Steve and Veronica inhaled sharply: hanging.

Bound by duct tape, mother, father, and son were found hanging from the rafters. The young girl, five-and-a-half-year-old Tracy Hesch, was discovered sitting on the floor, unbound, uninjured, and unwilling to speak about what had transpired. Like with the Davenport massacre, nothing appeared to be stolen and the motive was listed as unknown.

"Tracy Hesch…" Veronica said hauntingly, "that has to be Maggie Cernak."

She didn't want to rush to conclusions, but deep down she knew this was true. Just like she knew that whoever was working with Trent had come back to finish the job.

*Two figures were seen entering the Davenport house.*

It was very overwhelming.

And tragic.

Veronica sighed and grabbed her forehead. She was torn between regretting having drunk three beers already and drinking half a dozen more. Steve put his hand around her shoulder, and she leaned into him.

Veronica was a detective, and before that a cop, and she'd witnessed some pretty horrific crimes. But this... this was too much. Freddie had warned her about taking things personally, but how could she do anything other than put herself in little Amy's and Tracy's shoes? A normal person would be brought to their knees just thinking about the psychological trauma of witnessing your family being murdered in front of you. Someone who felt things the way Veronica did?

"Shit," she moaned.

Neither of them moved for several minutes and Veronica could tell by the irregular breathing pattern that Steve was also affected by what they'd read.

This was reassuring. In the public eye, law enforcement was viewed as a completely apathetic institution. The problem with this idea is that it was entirely composed of living, breathing, and feeling human beings. While it's no secret that exposure makes you numb, that threshold varies for everyone.

And it was a threshold that Veronica never wanted to achieve.

Eventually, Steve reached forward and closed her laptop. Then he raised his hand and took care of the bill.

Most of their food remained untouched.

When they left Daphne's, the sun had started to set, rendering the sky a deep orange. Veronica was struck by how very much it looked like the watercolors she experienced when sensing extreme violence.

And she wondered whether it was real or not.

Steve was leading the way to his car, and Veronica stopped him.

"I have my car," she said softly. "I'll be all right."

Steve shook his head.

"You shouldn't be alone tonight. And I don't want to be alone, either."

Veronica handed over her keys and got into the passenger seat. Once home, she fed Lucy, had a glass of water, and crawled into bed. Steve got in beside her, but they didn't have sex this time.

They didn't do anything but lay there until sleep finally washed away the orange and replaced it with deep inky black.

# Chapter 38

THIS TIME, IT WAS SHERIFF Steve Burns who was shaking.

Veronica awoke from a dreamless slumber to Steve trembling and moaning beside her. She wasn't sure what to do and, in the end, did nothing.

Steve's episode passed after a few minutes, but the damage had been done. Veronica was awake now and the prospect of falling back asleep tonight bordered on zero.

Careful not to disturb Steve, who was growing calmer by the minute, Veronica got out of bed. The beer had made its way through her system, and she was relieving herself when she heard a sound. The hackles on her neck stood on end, but Veronica quickly recognized the noise as Lucy's bell.

The cat was waiting for her on her comfy chair when she finished. When Veronica took a seat, Lucy crawled onto her lap, and she scratched beneath the cat's chin.

Veronica knew that if she wanted any chance of sleeping again tonight, she should ignore her laptop, which Steve had graciously brought in from her car and rested on the table beside the chair.

Maybe it was Lucy's presence, or just the fact that there were two other potential victims out there—*MINEY* and *MO*—but sleeping felt wrong.

With a sigh loud enough that Steve rolled over, Veronica grabbed her laptop and opened it.

Instead of wading through regulated forms and reports from police databases, Veronica searched media sites instead. If nothing else, the media were experts at summarizing. Sometimes, more often than not, they were too good at it, omitting vital information depending on which political party the owners supported. But in this case, Veronica found just the right amount of detail. Mass murderers generally pissed off both the blue and the red equally.

*Convicted on six counts of first-degree murder, Trent Alberts still claims innocence.*

Trent Alberts' reign of terror ended in a stolen Lexus with a dead accomplice at his side. Police were alerted of the stolen vehicle in East Argham around three in the morning. The vehicle was spotted running a red light at Winchester and Cork Rd and refused to stop when on-duty Officer Jarvis attempted to pull them over. A chase ensued, which eventually ended sixteen miles later after Jarvis performed a successful PIT maneuver. Shots were fired from the Lexus, and Jarvis, now accompanied by several officers, returned fire. The driver of the Lexus, Herb Thornton, was hit six times and died immediately. Trent, who had been in the backseat at the time, was unscathed and arrested without further incident. DNA from both suspects was obtained and matched to samples found at the Davenport and Hesch massacres...

The article went on to describe the details of these murders, and Veronica, having already read the reports, skipped over this part.

Toward the end of the feature, the reporter had taken some liberties and speculated that Trent and Herb might be responsible for more than the two sets of crimes that the former was eventually convicted of.

Most of these were unfounded rumors, but one case in particular caught Veronica's eye. It didn't have the exact same MO as the others but exhibited enough similarities to make her wonder. The Wilkes family was comprised of three, not four members: mom, dad, and a young boy. Like with Amy and Tracy, the parents were DOA, and the only survivor was five-year-old Anthony. He was in shock, but he did say that he saw two people—shadows, he called them shadows—take his parents away. The official manner of death was a heroin overdose, but the curious thing was that neither parent had any history, either recorded or physical signs, of ever having used before. There was also a brief mention of crime scene contamination, which led to little evidence being admissible.

When it came time for trial, the DA had elected to stick with the Davenport and Hesch slayings, as they had clear DNA evidence of Trent's involvement. From what she could gather, no one else had ever been charged for the Wilkes' murders and the investigations had been marked as 'inactive'.

"Veronica?"

The sound made her jump, and Veronica instinctively closed her laptop. With the light from the screen gone, it took her eyes a few seconds to adjust to the darkness. Steve was sitting up in bed, the comforter pooled around his waist. He looked even younger in the early morning daylight that spilled in through the window than he had washing his car.

"Have you been up all night?"

Veronica stretched her jaw and then rubbed her eyes.

"No, not all night. Just—you were having a bad dream."

A statement, not a question but Steve refuted it anyway.

"No—I mean, if I was, I don't remember."

Veronica sighed, which he interpreted as a sign of fatigue but was actually because she knew he was lying.

And she was too tired for deception.

"Find anything?"

Veronica debated for several seconds before replying. If it hadn't been for the fact that this was technically the sheriff's case, despite her having done the majority of work on it, she might have followed his lie with one of her own.

But the sheriff, while he lacked Veronica's particular talent, wasn't stupid. And even though Maggie's and Sarah's deaths weren't his number one priority—he was, after all, in charge of the largest county in Oregon—Steve would soon discover what she had.

"I think so," Veronica admitted, rising to her feet, and shaking some of the stiffness out of her legs. "There might be other victims and at least one more survivor to look into."

*To look into and to save before whoever got to Amy and Tracy finds and kills them, too.*

# Chapter 39

FINDING ANTHONY WILKES PROVED EASY. He was six feet underground and had been for nearly five years.

And his overdose, unlike that of his parents' years prior, was undeniably self-inflicted. In many ways, Anthony Wilkes' life story mimicked Dylan Hall's: in and out of foster care, never finding a real home. He had run-ins with the law, but they were all non-violent drug offenses.

His body had been discovered three days after his seventeenth birthday, which was listed as his official date of death. Cause of death was accidental overdose, manner of death, hot shot of heroin.

Yet, despite these unrefuted facts, Veronica had to see the crime scene for herself.

East Argham, the smallest incorporated city in Bear County, bordered the Casnet River to the east and Sullivan to the west. It was, for lack of a more endearing term, a ghost town. Every boom cycle, an investor or two came roaring in with delusions and illusions of grandeur, ideas to 'revitalize' or, in the case of East Argham, simply 'vitalize' the city. Building frames went up, but the interiors were never completed. The City of Greenham might hold the title of most crimes per capita in Oregon, but that was only because what happened in EA went unreported.

"You think we're going to find someone who knew Anthony?" Steve asked.

Veronica pursed her lips. The answer was no, of course. EA was populated by transients and the likelihood of anyone knowing, let alone willing to speak about just another addict who'd OD'd years ago was unrealistic, to say the least.

"I just... I just need to see it. I need to see where he died."

Morbid but true.

They fell into silence, with Veronica paying close attention to the street names as she drove by them. She was unfamiliar with EA, and she ended up missing the turn twice.

"I think... I think this is it."

Veronica slowed and eventually stopped in front of the shell of a building that someone might have envisioned becoming a luxury condominium. But not all dreams were meant to come to fruition. Otherwise, they'd be called certainties.

Veronica sensed the sheriff's apprehension as she got out of the car. Not a vision, no swirls of color or a particular scent, but just the way he was carrying himself. A slightly stooped posture, a truncated gait.

"I just want to see," she repeated, for equal measure Steve's benefit as her own.

From the police report, they knew that Anthony's body had been found on the third floor. The building had no doors and no windows—it was essentially just a drab gray, concrete outline. Veronica stepped over the threshold first and through an open archway. Graffiti marred nearly every surface on the ground floor and bottles littered the corners, both intact and smashed, the latter pasting a kaleidoscope of scattered daylight on the walls.

The second floor wasn't much different. Most of the plumbing, as rudimentary as it must have been given the immature state of the building, had been torn out and sold for pennies on the dollar.

When Veronica reached the third floor, the peculiar sensation of being watched fell over her.

*It's just your mind playing tricks on you.*

She must have slowed because Veronica felt a hand on the small of her back, guiding her onward. This was a very different reaction than she was used to. Freddie would have stepped in front of her, asked if she was okay, whereas Steve encouraged her forward progression.

The problem was the police report had only specified that Anthony Wilkes had been found on the third floor of the building. Either they lacked landmarks to be more specific or, more likely, deemed it unnecessary.

Just another addict doing what addicts did until they couldn't anymore.

The first 'room' that Veronica entered was empty. The second, inexplicably, had a bag of diapers against the wall, unopened, as well as what looked like an entire set of Tupperware, cleaned and stacked, sitting in the middle of the room.

Steve was distracted and in the process of commenting on this oddity while Veronica was already onto the third divided space.

She took one step across the threshold and froze.

Tucked in the corner of the room was a mattress. It may have once been cream-colored or even white, but now it was littered with stains — dark maroon, black, and brown.

But Veronica only saw yellow, orange, and red.

*This is where Anthony died.*

Veronica's world started to spin but Freddie grabbed her before she went down.

No, not Freddie — Steve.

"It's okay," the sheriff was saying, but his voice sounded as if it was coming from the other end of a sewer pipe. "It's okay."

But it wasn't okay.

Nothing about this was okay. Nothing was okay about the song, the smell, the colors. Nothing was okay about making a child watch their family being murdered in front of them.

Nothing was okay about Grant Sutcliffe redacting information from Sarah Sawyer's file.

And nothing was okay about *EENIE, MEENIE, MINEY, MO*.

Veronica turned and looked up at the sheriff to gain a momentary reprieve from the swirling colors that obscured the mattress.

But the man's attention was suddenly elsewhere.

"Look," he nearly gasped.

Veronica followed his finger, and she felt a pang in her chest.

There, on the interior wall above the door was one piece of graffiti that stood out amongst the others. It was darker, fresher than the rest, and also clearer.

A single word, written in familiar all caps: *MINEY*.

Veronica pulled away from Steve.

"There's one more," she whispered. "We need to find *MO* before this happens to them."

# PART THREE:
# A SHADE

## Chapter 40

"CAPTAIN STEVE BURNS, HOW LONG has it been?" the lean man in the gray suit said with a lopsided smile. He was older than Steve, older by ten years at least, and this had nothing to do with a uniform. Veronica put the man in his mid-forties, but it was clear by the way his dress shirt hung off him that he looked after himself. He had short blond hair, brushed to one side, and dark blue eyes.

Veronica watched the two men embrace, old friends reuniting after a long time apart.

"It's Sheriff Burns now."

"Really?" The man in the suit raised an inquisitive eyebrow. "What happened to—"

Steve gestured toward Veronica and the man turned to her. He smiled, revealing teeth that were slightly too crowded for his mouth.

"Sorry, got carried away with the bro hug. I'm Special Agent Jake Keller with the BAU."

Jake extended his hand and Veronica shook it.

"Detective Veronica Shade—City of Greenham."

Jake's grip was solid, but not overbearing. He wasn't showing off like some men were inclined to do, as if a strong grip or big hand translated into anything but.

"Greenham, huh? You a townie, Detective Shade?"

Townie was the term that everyone used to describe some-one born and raised in Greenham and the fact that Jake was familiar with this indicated that he was from the area.

"Kind of." Veronica shrugged.

"Well, this is a different beast than Greenham City Jail, I'll tell you that much."

This wasn't a flex or even a warning; Jake simply stated this as a fact. And as he said this, all three of them looked up at the maximum-security penitentiary. Oregon State Penn was an im-pressive sight. A pale-yellow building that stretched for as far as they could see, surrounded by a nearly eight-foot-high wall. Hard men with automatic weapons patrolled the wall.

"So, you want to see Trent Alberts, huh?" Agent Keller mused as he led them to the first gate. They passed through with only a nod—Keller must have pre-cleared them with the Warden. "Don't get me wrong, I don't mind you coming in here, but I wouldn't get your hopes up. I've been visiting Trent on pretty much a monthly basis for the past five years. Not much of a talker, that one. Especially not after the incident."

They passed through a series of metal detectors, and all three of them left their belongings with security. On the phone, Steve had mentioned to Agent Keller that Veronica didn't have her badge, and he assured them that this wouldn't be a problem. He did, however, suggest that she leave her service weapon in the car. Veronica obliged.

The security guards all referred to Keller by his surname, adding credence to the Agent's claim that he'd spent a lot of time here over the years.

"Incident?" Veronica inquired.

"Yeah, let's just say that Mr. Alberts isn't popular here. Or, maybe he's *really* popular—depends how you look at it."

They walked down a narrow hallway to another checkpoint, this one requiring them to sign in. Keller filled out the form for all of them, then passed it first to Steve before requesting Veronica's John Hancock. She was bemused to see that there was no 'Detective' before her name. Instead, her profession was listed as 'psychiatrist'.

Veronica understood Steve's smirk and she thought of Jane. Then she smiled, too.

"Weren't you just here a couple of weeks ago, Keller?" the obese man who took the signed forms asked.

Agent Keller slapped the man's hand as they were buzzed through a massive iron gate.

"Brought some friends with me this time. We're going to try to psychoanalyze the pincushion."

The big man chuckled.

"Good luck."

Agent Keller started walking backward so that he could face them as he talked.

"Back in 2020, the Governor thought it was a good idea to shut down Death Row. Most of the tenants got private cells, but not our friend Trent—overcrowding, you know? Anyways, he was in gen pop when someone took offense to what he'd done and decided to express their displeasure with a shank. Trent lost nearly half his blood, but he managed to survive. Ever since then, the man has this strange proclivity for, well, poking himself with things."

"Hence the name pincushion," Steve Burns remarked as if this was necessary.

"Yeah, about Death Row—how is Trent scheduled for execution in less than two weeks? I mean, didn't the Governor declare a moratorium on capital punishment?" Veronica asked, recalling her reading from the night prior.

Keller shrugged as if this was no big deal.

"Exceptions will be made... seriously, though, the DA managed to exploit some loophole." The man raised his arms and indicated the walls that seemed to get narrower with every passageway they traversed. "The betting line is about 50/50 now. Everyone in here has money on whether or not Trent will get the needle."

It was morbid, the idea of betting on whether a man would be executed, but Veronica wasn't about to feel bad for 'Pincushion'.

"Not much else to do around here—as I said, I spend a lot of time in the beautiful Oregon State Penn," Keller, a born storyteller, quickly fell back into the groove as if her interruption had never happened. "Five years... shit, has it been that long? Anyway, five whole years ago, the FBI was desperate to capture a child predator who was terrorizing the Pacific Northwest. BAU thought that Trent Alberts might be able to help. Spoiler alert, he couldn't. But I'm still here, poking the Pincushion on a monthly basis."

They made it to the final level of security, and Agent Keller's demeanor quickly changed. There was no joking around now, not with the pale man in the dark blue uniform —no back slaps, no handshakes, no 'bros' with this one.

"Trent is in Room Two," the guard informed them. "He's chained to both the table and the floor. One final reminder: at no point are you to touch the prisoner and at no point are you to pass any objects to the prisoner. If I see either of these things, the interview will be over, *immediately*."

All parties agreed to this, and they were led through a door that was unlocked first remotely and then with an old-fashioned key attached to the guard's belt.

Keller's playfulness returned.

"So, you guys think that maybe there was someone else? Like, with Trent and Herb? Someone who's killing the survivors? Someone... I dunno, inspired by his upcoming execution?"

This sounded strange coming from a third party, but Keller had pretty much summed up Steve and Veronica's conversation on the long drive to the penitentiary.

"Not sure," Steve admitted. "All I know is that Amy Davenport and Tracy Hesch were both found dead from apparent suicides, two weeks before Trent's execution. They both changed their names a while back, had decent jobs... one hell of a coincidence if you ask me."

Veronica was glad that Steve decided to keep the creepy notes—EENIE, MEENIE, MINEY—that they'd found to themselves.

"And you're sure that this has nothing to do with —"

"Sure," Steve said quickly.

*To do with what?* Veronica wondered. She looked at Steve, but the man refused to meet her gaze. This was the second time that she'd got the impression the sheriff was keeping something from her, but Death Row didn't seem like the appropriate place to prod.

"As I told you on the phone, Steve, I've been tits deep in this case for years. They only ever found DNA from Trent and Herb at the murder scenes. No evidence of a third party." Keller shrugged. "It could be a fan, a copycat thing. Lord knows, Trent gets all kinds of fan mail."

They were nearing the door to Room Two but before Veronica looked through the window embedded in the thick metal, she reached out and touched Agent Keller's arm.

"What about Anthony? What about the Wilkes family massacre?"

Keller looked impressed.

"I see you've done your homework, Detective Shade."

"Detective?" she joked. "I'm sorry, you've got the wrong person. My name is Ms. Shade—I'm a psychiatrist."

The man laughed.

"Well, the Wilkes thing? That one's a bit messy, as you probably know. At that time, FBI, State Police, County Sheriff—shit, pretty much every law enforcement agency was searching for who was behind the Davenport and Hesch murders. And you have to remember, this was more than twenty years ago. You know how different agencies can't play nice together now? *Pshh,* back then when there were no national databases? It was a shit show. What made it worse, was that everyone wanted to get the notoriety for catching these guys, so when the Wilkes tragedy was discovered, everyone came in to have a look. Not a good thing for crime scene preservation, let me tell you. Local cops took some evidence from the Wilkes house, the FBI has some... well, in the end, it was the opposite of Humpty Dumpty—nobody could put the pieces back together. The DA didn't want to fuck with it, and why would he? They already had Trent dead to rights on six counts. But I'll tell you this: they found heroin in the stolen Lexus. So, if you're asking me if *I* think Trent and Herb were behind the Wilkes slayings? Yeah, they fucking did it. No doubt about it."

Keller's voice had become dry, and Veronica decided not to mention Anthony's fate. She told herself that the man probably already knew—he was, after all, 'tits deep' in this case—but she also didn't want to say anything to upset him, anything that might jeopardize their interrogation of Trent Alberts.

"Well," Agent Keller clearly wanted to change the subject and move things forward, "I'll let you lead. *Paul?*"

They all glanced skyward and a second later there was a loud buzz and the door to Room Two opened a few inches.

Keller waved his hand toward the entrance and Veronica instinctively looked to Steve, but the sheriff made no move toward the door.

He expected her to go first.

Because Steve knew.

She had to do this — *she*. Not him, not Keller, but her.

Veronica swallowed hard and tried her best to prepare herself, even though she knew that this was impossible.

How could someone with her condition prepare themselves for the sights and smells that would accompany meeting a sadistic serial killer?

# Chapter 41

VERONICA SHADE DIDN'T BELIEVE IN pure evil. She believed in mental illness, she believed in the power of nurture, the implication of nature, circumstance, opportunity, and capacity. Veronica also believed in the *possibility* of rehabilitation.

But Trent Alberts came pretty damn close to an incarnation of evil. It was one thing to derive pleasure from taking another person's life. The motivation for such a heinous act was something that Veronica could almost understand; it was the ultimate expression of power and control. Once, in the Academy, over many beers, Veronica and her colleagues had discussed what would be the worst way to go out. Prolonged torture was the clear winner, even with the concession that over time the body might adapt and become more or less numb. If it didn't, the body would eventually shut down and death would be a welcomed reprieve.

What Trent Alberts and Herb Thornton had done hadn't even been considered by Veronica and her colleagues: holding an entire family hostage and making a child watch their parents and sibling be murdered in front of them. And then simply letting them go. This level of sadism, of forethought, was up there with the likes of Dahmer and Gacy. The method of murder might be less savage, but the aftermath was more prolonged. The survivor had to relive their family's tragedy every time they closed their eyes.

Anthony Wilkes couldn't handle it. Anthony had exploited chemical means to forget, which had eventually taken his life.

Amy Davenport and Tracy Hesch had somehow managed to move on, at least for a while.

But your past was like a shadow and while you might not always see it, it was perpetual.

Room Two was hot, loud, and bright. So overwhelming were these sensations that, at first, Veronica didn't notice Trent Alberts.

Although she hadn't realized it, Veronica presumed that the song had started in her head the moment she entered the prison. But now, the booming, taunting paradigm in her skull was impossible to ignore.

*La, la, la, la, laaaaa, laaa.*

Veronica closed her eyes and puffed air into her ears, the way one might try to equalize the pressure while sitting in the cabin of a descending 747. It didn't work—the song didn't go away.

When she opened her eyes, she saw the colors. They were even more vibrant than they'd been in Sheriff Burns' barn. It was like holding a burning sheet of paper inches from your face and forcing yourself to stare, without blinking, for minutes at a time.

A familiar hand came down on her shoulder, rooting her in the present. The colors and song promptly faded, but not enough for Veronica to ignore them completely.

Trent Alberts slowly came into focus. The man was smaller in real life, although, to be fair, she'd only ever seen him from the waist up and in mugshots. It wasn't uncommon to exaggerate both the psychological and physical characteristics of criminals; after all, people like Trent Alberts were called monsters for good reason.

But this was just a stereotype.

Trent was maybe five-five, with short gray hair and sallow cheeks. His skin was mottled and appeared paper thin. Veronica couldn't get a good look at his eyes; the man was staring at his hands, the nails of which were but stubs and caked with dried blood.

A friendly squeeze on her shoulder inspired speech.

"My name is Ms. Shade, and I'm a psychiatrist. This is Bear County Sheriff Burns, and you already know Agent Keller," Veronica said, surprised at how naturally the words came.

Trent, eyes still downcast, began to pick at his fingers, and the dark maroon scabs slowly started to turn a bright red.

"I want to ask you a few questions," Veronica continued. "Questions about you and Herb."

She wasn't sure if it was the mention of the man's partner in crime or simply that the Pincushion had started to come around. Whatever the reason, Trent chose this moment to look up. The man's eyes were dark, like melted chocolate, and when they fell on Veronica's hazel irises, flecked with gold, they did not waver. The stillness of the stare made her incredibly uncomfortable, but Veronica refused to empower the man by looking away first.

Then Trent changed. It wasn't a subtle, 'now I'm going to play the bad guy card', or a 'here is my chance to scare someone new', change. It was immediate and violent. Trent Alberts' eyes hardened, his jaw set, and his brow lifted. He looked like a completely different man.

The temptation to avert her gaze was almost overwhelming, but not because it was uncomfortable—Veronica wanted to know if Steve or Keller had seen this, too.

"Who was with you?" Veronica asked, deciding that the best approach was to get straight to the point. "Who was with you when you and Herb murdered the Davenports and the Heschs?"

No response—just that eerie stare.

"What about when you killed the Wilkes'?" Veronica hoped that this would shock the man into answering but, again, Trent failed to react.

"Come on, Trent," Steve chimed in. "We know that you two weren't alone. Tell us who was with you."

"Hey, Trent, you've heard of the last meal, right? Sometimes called the 'special meal'?" Agent Keller said from the back of the room. "They did away with it a number of years back after some asshole in Texas ordered hundreds of dollars' worth of food but then decided he wasn't hungry. But I *might* be able to hook something up. If you're nice to my friends here and answer their questions."

Again, no response from the convicted serial killer.

"Just tell us who else was there," Veronica asked again.

"Just tell us. What do you have to lose?" Steve insisted.

Veronica didn't expect a response, so when it came, it startled her.

"Y'all know who was there, little one." Trent's voice had the telltale signs of disuse—hoarse with an almost staccato cadence.

"What?" Veronica balked.

"If we knew who was there, we wouldn't have driven across the county to visit you," Steve argued. "But we know it wasn't just you and Herb. Don't you want to get this off your chest? Don't you want absolution? Atonement? Forgiveness?"

Veronica could see in Trent's eyes that Steve's words were falling on deaf ears. This man did not want salvation. He wanted people to *hurt*.

She blinked, and in the fraction of a second that her eyes were closed, Veronica saw Amy, sitting on the ground, her family hanging above her.

"How did you pick which one survived? Was it the kid who cried the most? The one who cried the least?" The words came out of Veronica's mouth in a rush. "Or was it just a stupid random game? Eenie, meenie, miney, mo. How did you choose, Trent? *How did you choose?"*

Trent started to smile, revealing crooked brown teeth. His incisors were missing.

"I never chose, little one." Gruff, sandpaper on aluminum.

"Yeah, you made Herb pick, right? You coward." Veronica leaned forward. "That's all you are, a coward."

"Veroni —"

Trent's hands shot forward, cutting Steve's warning off. Later, Veronica would consider that the man was probably reaching for her throat, only to be stopped short by the chain. Trent did manage to grab the front of her shirt and he was strong enough to drag her in so close that she could smell his fetid breath.

"Veronica!" Steve yelled.

"Paul! *Paul!"*

This interaction lasted but a few seconds before the guard rushed in and put Trent in a rear-naked choke while, at the same time, Steve brought the blade of his hand down on the man's wrists, breaking his hold on her shirt.

But it was long enough for Trent Alberts to whisper three words.

"Eenie, meenie, miney."

There was a fourth, of course, but this wasn't whispered. It was shouted directly into Veronica's face.

*"Mo!"*

# Chapter 42

"**I'M REALLY SORRY ABOUT THAT,**" Agent Keller said once they were outside the walls of the prison. This didn't appear to be lip service—the man looked genuinely upset at what Veronica had been through. "Trent is a piece of work, but I've never seen him lash out like this."

"It's my fault," Veronica admitted. "Shouldn't have gotten close." She shook her head. "Should have controlled my emotions. Shit, I'm sorry."

Steve grabbed her around the waist, letting her know that it was okay.

"Well, you can bill the FBI for your dry cleaning, if you want." Keller was trying to be funny, to add some levity to the stressful situation. But when Veronica looked down and saw what the FBI Agent was referring to, she felt sick to her stomach.

There were multiple smears of blood from Trent's fingers on the lower half of her shirt.

"What did he say to you anyway?" Agent Keller asked, one eyebrow raised.

This confused Veronica because what Trent had shouted had been crystal clear to her.

*Eenie, Meenie, Miney, Mo!*

"You didn't—you didn't hear?"

Agent Keller shook his head and looked at Steve.

"Just sounded like screaming to me," the sheriff said.

Veronica expected to smell gas—surely, the man had heard, but was lying—only, she didn't.

"I don't know—my ears are still ringing," Veronica said, pulling her right earlobe for effect.

Now, she smelled gas.

"Listen, I don't know if you guys are busy but there is a coffee shop just up the road, walking distance. Wanna get a cup? I could use a pick-me-up after that."

Veronica, desperately wanting to change her shirt, was about to say no when Steve spoke up and she remembered the man's evening Daphne ritual.

"Good idea. No, *great* idea."

\*\*\*

"I tried to warn you," Agent Keller said as he sipped his coffee. Unlike Steve and Veronica, who liked their coffees black, Keller preferred three creams and three sugars. It was so thick that he almost had to slurp it to get it down. "Trent's a piece of work. Most of the time Pincushion just hurts himself." His eyes drifted to Veronica's shirt again. "If I thought there was any chance he would be violent, I would never have—"

"It's fine." Veronica was annoyed at being treated with kid gloves. "Let me ask you something, Agent Keller—"

"Just Keller."

"Okay, sure, Keller. Can Trent send outgoing mail?"

"Like snail mail?"

"Yeah."

Keller took another sip of coffee.

"Yes... and no. They can reply to mail, but they can't just, like, spam people—write unsolicited letters. And there are all these rules, and everything is screened."

Veronica shot Steve a glance. The man knew what she was getting at—they'd both seen what got Trent off. In a final act before execution, it wouldn't be beyond Trent to want to torture his victims by sending them letters—*EENIE, MEENIE, MINEY, MO.* Hell, it might have been part of his plan all along.

Except...

"Did Amy or Tracy ever write Trent? They might have gone by their new names—Maggie Cernak and Sarah Sawyer?"

Keller thought about this.

"No."

"You sure?" Veronica asked.

"Yeah, sure. As part of my work with Trent, I reviewed every piece of incoming mail. Some pretty sick fucking people out there—excuse my French—women trying to date him, that kind of thing. But no Maggie or Sarah... or Amy or Tracy. Mostly hyphenated names—Mary-Sue, Jo-Beth, go figure."

*There goes that idea*, Veronica thought.

It didn't make that much sense in the first place. After all, Trent would have needed someone on the outside to write *MINEY* on the wall where Anthony had died. But it was worth a shot.

"What do you think the chances are that there was a third person in on this?" Steve asked. "Trent, Herb, and someone else?"

Keller shrugged.

"I've been over the files hundreds of times. Never any evidence it was anyone but the two of them."

"Right."

"And the two survivors, they committed suicide?" Keller asked. He may have known everything there was about the Trent Alberts case, but because of the name changes, it was clear that this was news to him. And he appeared discomforted by this fact.

*No, not suicide.*

"We think," Steve said quickly.

Unbelievably, Keller added *another* packet of sugar to his coffee.

"Well, it could be survivor guilt, you know? The media has been low-key on Trent's upcoming execution, what with the 'moratorium', but it's out there. If they saw it, maybe it brought back memories."

This made sense. If Veronica could ignore her synesthesia that told her differently, she might even buy this reasoning.

But then there were the notes. Veronica had seen Maggie's writing on her fridge, and it wasn't the same as the note in her pocket. She hadn't seen Sarah's handwriting, but she'd bet her life savings, paltry as they were, on it not being her writing, either.

They finished their coffees, and Veronica thanked Keller for getting them in to see Trent, no matter how unproductive their visit had been. She got into Steve's car and watched the two men hug and say a few words.

When Steve got behind the wheel, he was smiling.

"You guys go way back, don't you?" Veronica asked.

"Yeah, I've known Keller for a long time." He sighed.

"What is it?"

"I dunno... it's just if there was a third person involved? Keller would be all over it."

Now Veronica sighed.

"Yeah, but you saw the notes. What if... what if someone else reached out to Trent, one of the hyphenated ladies. Trent could have convinced them to taunt Amy or Tracy."

"Except they don't go by Amy or Tracy—their names were Maggie and Sarah. You know how hard it was for us to find out their real names. How the hell could someone like Trent do it?"

Veronica leaned back in her chair and closed her eyes.

*This case... this damn case...*

"Veronica?"

She opened her eyes and was surprised to see that they'd arrived at her house.

"I must have fallen asleep."

"Sure did."

"Did I snore?"

"Noooo..."

Veronica punched him playfully on the shoulder.

"Liar."

She waited for Steve to say goodbye so that she could get out of the car, but he didn't. He was focused on the steering wheel as if suddenly interested in the embossed logo.

"Steve?"

"Yeah?"

"You wanna come inside?"

"Yeah, I do."

The first thing Veronica did was remove her soiled shirt. That went directly into the trash. When she turned around, she caught Steve staring at her. Veronica went to him without hesitation, and they made love. It wasn't as passionate as their first time, but it was good.

So good that Steve passed out immediately afterward.

But Veronica, despite not having gotten more than a few hours of sleep, including the time she'd passed out in the car, just couldn't turn off her brain.

It was another long, sleepless night for Detective Veronica Shade.

# Chapter 43

VERONICA LAY IN BED FOR some time, thinking about the case. When this made her mind run in circles, she got out of bed and then found herself in the exact same position as yesterday: sitting in the chair in her room, laptop open, Steve sleeping a handful of feet away.

Nothing popped up on any searches, so Veronica decided to change her focus. On the round table that she'd purchased with the intent to DIY into a makeup stand, but had never gotten around to it, she taped four sheets of paper in a large rectangle.

Then she crudely drew a map of everything east of Portland, starting with the City of Greenham and ending with the Hilltona Forest.

She put a black 'X' on the outskirts of Matheson, the approximate location of the sheriff's barn. She put another in Sullivan, where they'd found Sarah Sawyer, and a third in East Argham representing Anthony Wilkes.

Figuring that they must be missing something, that the clue as to who the fourth and final victim — Mo — was had to be here. They just… skipped over it, somehow. Given her condition, Veronica often relied on feelings and less tangible evidence to solve crimes. And this had worked well for her to date, had helped her rise up to be the youngest detective in the City of Greenham PD. But now that she'd hit such a dead end, Veronica mused that a different approach was necessary; a detail-oriented approach. She decided then that there was only one way to find out where they'd made the mistake: start again, from the very beginning. Go over *everything*. If there was a detail there, a hint, a clue, she'd find it. And when she did, Veronica would find the final victim before someone took them out like they had Amy and Tracy.

She started by jotting down information from the original crimes near the 'Xs', and then added another column for the information from the 'suicides'.

Amy/Maggie was first.

**Original murders: hanging, three victims. One survivor. Two suspects.**

Veronica jotted down the date of the offense, then the address.

Next, she moved over to the suicide from roughly a week ago.

**Recent murder: Hanging, one victim.**

When she got to the date, Veronica paused; it was close to the original date—within a few days. But the address? When Veronica read the address, the marker slipped from her hand.

*What the hell?*

Her eyes went to Steve, who was still sleeping soundly in the bed; no night terrors this time, it seemed.

*No, it can't be.*

Veronica double-checked the address and then confirmed it a third time.

They were the same.

She wasn't sure how either herself or Steve had overlooked this, but Amy Davenport's family had been murdered in Sheriff Burns' barn, and, twenty-two years later, Amy, now Maggie Cernak, committed suicide in the same exact location.

Veronica exhaled and she once again focused her attention on the sheriff.

Steve told her he was thirty-four years old. If she believed that, then he would have been fourteen when Amy's family was killed.

She swallowed hard.

*No, this isn't right.*

An Internet search had yielded no insight into the present case, but how about... *nothing.* Steve Burns either didn't exist, or he'd managed to stay off the Internet almost entirely.

*What the fuck is going on here?*

Veronica expanded her search, with a focus on finding a record of Steve as a State Trooper.

Still nothing.

*How is this possible?*

Her heart started to race, and she felt a tightness, now an all too familiar sensation, in her lower abdomen.

A thought occurred to Veronica. A terrible thought.

Steve Burns came out of nowhere. He wasn't a local but somehow charmed his way into becoming the sheriff of Bear County. The timing was suspect—him arriving just a few months before Trent's planned execution.

A few months before the suicides.

"McVeigh..."

The name entered her mind and refused to exit.

*McVeigh... what about Deputy McVeigh?*

Veronica recalled something and her eyes widened.

When she'd been at the sheriff's house, the day he'd been washing his car, Deputy McVeigh had called him, saying he'd discovered Sarah's body. That, in and of itself, wasn't disturbing. It was *what* the man said that added fuel to the fire.

*"Sheriff, it's Deputy McVeigh. I'm in Sullivan, doing a drive-through like you suggested. You—you gotta come out here. Over."*

A drive-through like *you* suggested.

Why would the sheriff suggest that McVeigh drive through Sullivan when Maggie Cernak had been found in Matheson?

There was only one reason that Veronica could think of: the sheriff knew that Sarah was dead, and he wanted her to be found.

Wanted *MEENIE* to be discovered.

Which meant that Steve had either planned her death, staged it, or killed her.

Veronica shook her head.

*No, this is stupid. Sheriff Steve Burns killed Maggie and Sarah? Why?*

The answer to that came quickly—maybe *too* quickly.

*What if Steve was Trent's son? What if he, like Trent's and Herb's victims, had changed his name and that's why I can't find anything about him?*

It was… possible.

Trent and Herb could have had a teenager tag along with them, help with the crimes. Maybe they used him to get into the homes. And then, he slipped away, and the FBI, State Police, and local PD had their heads so far up their asses that they didn't even notice.

Veronica tried to slow her runaway thoughts, but there were no brakes to an exhausted mind.

If Steve was Trent's son, then that would explain why the man never gave him up. And now that Trent was about to be executed, Steve wanted to finish what his father had started. As sheriff, he had full access to both Maggie and Sarah. And he knew Maggie, probably better than he said—Steve had lied about her, after all.

She grabbed her forehead.

No, this is… this is stupid.

But the more that Veronica thought about it, the more it made sense.

When they'd visited Trent on Death Row, Steve had wanted Veronica to go into the room first. She'd thought that this was because he was being courteous, knowing how emotionally invested in the case she was. An equally likely reason might be that Steve didn't want his father to blurt something out upon seeing him, and wanted Trent to know that others were present, that they were listening. And then, there was the first time that Trent had spoken—it had been in response to something that Steve had said, not her, or Keller.

*"Y'all know who was there."*

Could it be that Trent was talking directly to Steve? Was he saying that *you* were there, as in Steve himself?

Somewhere in the back of her mind, Veronica acknowledged that these could all be coincidences. But it wasn't just Maggie, Sarah, and Trent, it was Anthony, too. Steve had seen the word—*MINEY*—and had pointed it out. If he hadn't, Veronica probably would have missed it, what with the bombardment of colors coming off the soiled mattress in waves.

She took a step back, then another, and bumped into the chair. She caught her laptop before it smashed to the floor, an impressive feat with her eyes locked on Steve the entire time.

He was the link, the connection between all cases.

And she'd slept with him.

*Twice.*

But even if her insane theory was correct, it didn't answer the most important question: who was the fourth victim? Who was *MO*?

There was only one way to find out—keep Steve close. Keep an eye on him and catch him before he kills again.

# Chapter 44

VERONICA HAD BEEN TRYING SO hard to be quiet, to not wake up Steve, that when she unlocked her front door and stepped outside, she somehow didn't see the massive form blocking her path. She bumped into the man, and then bounced backward, letting out a tiny squeak as she did.

"Good morning to you, too," a familiar voice said.

Veronica, her heart thudding in her chest, looked up at Detective Freddie Furlow. He was beaming.

"Shit, you scared me," she whispered.

She started to close the door behind her, when Freddie said, "It's early, aren't you going to invite me in for a coffee?"

Veronica knew that it was early and had been hoping to get to the precinct before everyone else. But somehow, time had gotten away from her, and it was closer to eight now than seven.

"We'll grab one on the way." She tried to close the door without allowing her partner to see inside. He did, though; Freddie was a detective, and Veronica didn't doubt that he'd spotted the pair of male shoes in the entrance. She wasn't sure if he'd recognize them as the sheriff's, but either way, he wasn't going to say anything.

"Oh, I've got something for you," Freddie said as he sucked his gut in to fit behind the steering wheel. With a heavy grunt, he pulled something from his pocket and tossed it to her.

Veronica caught her badge, opened it, and ran her thumb over the gold-embossed shield.

"Welcome back, Detective Shade," Freddie said in a baritone voice. "Your presence has been missed by one and all."

"Ha." Veronica's mind went to Officer Ken Cameron. "I doubt by *all*. But thank you." She hesitated, debating whether or not she should tell her partner about what she'd done during her two-day suspension, about her visit to death row and everything that went along with that—including her suspicions of Sheriff Steve Barnes.

*Are you going to tell him that you fucked him, too?*

Veronica ultimately decided that she was going to keep everything to herself for now. It was better for Freddie. Plausible deniability and all that.

"Speaking of our friend Officer Cameron," Veronica continued, not wanting to allow the silence to be construed as an invitation for Freddie to start asking questions, "Any update on his manhunt for Dylan Hall?"

Freddie pulled out of her driveway and Veronica's eyes drifted to the window above the garage, the one that looked out from her bedroom. For a second, she thought she saw the curtain move just a fraction of an inch.

*Now, you're just being silly. Veronica, get your shit together.*

"He's got pretty much everyone in the entire station out looking for the man."

Veronica rolled her eyes.

Of course, he did. Wasting the whole department's time, while the real stalker was planning their next move.

"The one good thing is that Ken finally put an officer outside of Chloe's house." Freddie cleared his throat, then gave his best Ken Cameron impression. "Just in case that tall bald pervert comes around."

Veronica laughed again.

"Are we still on the case?"

"Are we ever. Officer Cameron loves to tell me what to do," Freddie said.

"Why are we heading in then? Why don't we just grab a coffee and hit the streets and 'look' for Dylan Hall."

"I thought maybe you want to see people in the office."

"What? Why in the world would I want to do that?"

Freddie smirked and he took an immediate left.

"Okay, sounds good to me. But you're—" Freddie sneezed, "—buying the coffee. When did you get a cat, by the way?"

"Adopted one. Love animals."

Veronica grabbed two coffees, black—an extra-large for herself and a medium for her partner.

"What are we going to do if we find him?" Freddie asked. "Because if Ken's CI—"

"Fuck Ken," Veronica snapped.

She didn't swear often, just like she didn't usually say whatever just happened to pop into her mind.

Didn't *use* to, anyway.

But this was the new her: irrational, emotional, untethered.

What a fucking cliche.

"I'm here for you, Veronica. I am—you know that," Freddie said, becoming unexpectedly serene.

"Why do I get the impression a lecture is coming?"

With great effort, Freddie turned his entire body and faced her.

"No, not a lecture. I just—I'm having a hard time understanding. I don't think Dylan is stalking Chloe any more than you do. But why this intense hatred for Ken? What happened between you two?"

"It's him," Veronica protested. "I rejected him, and he went and just lost it. You see how he treats me."

Freddie bit his bottom lip.

"If you don't want to share, I get that. But it would go a long way to helping me understand why he has it in for you."

Veronica closed her eyes and thought back to the night in question. Not only had it been the Greenham PD's annual

Christmas party, but it was also a celebration of her promotion, of Veronica becoming a detective. She spoke the scene that replayed in her mind—being as tired as she was, it sounded like a B-movie more than real life. But she didn't have to worry about Freddie judging her. As he'd said, the man was there for her. Always had been, probably always would be.

*"I think I'm going to take off," Veronica said, her words muddy. Her father looked at her. Unlike pretty much everyone else at the party, Captain Peter Shade had abstained from alcohol. He hadn't even tried some of the special craft IPAs that she'd brought specifically for him. "Tired."*

*Peter nodded.*

*"Want me to take you home?"*

*She shook her head.*

*"I'll get a cab. Thank you for tonight, Dad."*

*The man smiled and sucked her into a large embrace. Even though there was no explicit rule about it, neither Peter nor Veronica liked to show any sort of affection toward each other while at work. Today, after hours at their annual Christmas party, and following the news that the city council had agreed to promote Veronica to detective, exceptions were made.*

*"I'm proud of you, V."*

*Veronica had started her rounds, saying goodbye to people, waving to friends and colleagues, when she spotted Freddie.*

*The big man's cheeks were red, and he was smiling broadly.*

*"See you on Monday, partner."*

*Veronica froze.*

*"Partner?"*

*"Ah, shit, I wasn't supposed to say anything, was I?"*

*"No, you weren't," Captain Shade said.*

*Veronica was grinning from ear to ear.*

*"Seriously? Partners?"*

Captain Shade, sporting a rare grin of his own, nodded.

Veronica loved Freddie—he was like an older brother she never had. She hugged him, or at least tried to—his waist was so large that she could only get halfway around.

"See you Monday, partner," she said. Then she hollered to the crowd, "Night everyone!"

Amidst a chorus of congratulations and other drunken cheers, Veronica grabbed her coat and stepped into the cold.

"Hey, mind if I walk with you? It's so hot in there."

Veronica turned and saw Officer Ken Cameron who must have slipped out behind her. Like Freddie, he was red-faced, and his eyes were glassy.

She shrugged.

"Sure, I'm just gonna walk for a little bit, probably up to Marco's Groceries and catch a cab from there."

"Sounds good to me."

Ken was right, it was warm in the precinct and the cold air outside felt good on her cheeks. Veronica walked briskly, enjoying the sound her boots made as they crunched the fresh snow.

"Congrats on being promoted," Ken said. This was at least the third time that the man had congratulated her directly, and Veronica was starting to feel uncomfortable. There was something disingenuous about Ken's words. Alcohol tended to mess with her synesthesia, but Veronica didn't think he was lying outright. His approach was just a little... off.

"Thanks."

"I just wanted to tell you I think you deserved it." Ken's hand grazed the back of her arm and she stopped.

"I worked hard."

Now Ken grabbed her arm, not aggressively, but enough to make her turn.

"I think you're pretty... really pretty."

*Veronica cringed. But Ken, drunk as he was, mistook her reaction as flattery. His hand moved from her arm to her back, and he pulled her in close. Veronica was also under the influence, which slowed her reaction time. Before she could do anything, his lips were on hers, and his tongue was probing into her mouth.*

*Veronica came to her senses and pushed him away.*

*"What?" he asked, as she wiped her mouth with the back of her hand.*

*"I'm sorry if I gave you the wrong impression, but I want to keep things professional."*

*Embarrassment turned Ken's face even redder.*

*"What?"*

*Veronica took a step backward.*

*"I don't want to mix work and pleasure."*

*This was not a phrase she used often, if ever. It also was a poor choice of words staring down a drunk and horny police officer.*

*"Oh, but you admit it was pleasure." A lascivious grin appeared on Ken's face and Veronica quickly shook her head.*

*"Ken, please. I'm not interested."*

*"Your tongue said different." Ken's words were no longer slurred, and Veronica considered that being drunk might have just been an act.*

*Ken reached for her again, more aggressively this time and despite the distance that Veronica had put between them, he managed to grab her.*

*"Stop."*

*Ken didn't stop. He kissed her hard. It took a good three seconds for Veronica to twist free and even then, Ken's wet lips made track marks all the way to her ear. Enraged, she shoved the man who, until today had been a colleague, with both hands. Ken's feet slipped in the snow, and he fell on his ass, sending a tuft of white into the air.*

*"Bitch," Ken spat as he scrambled to his feet and wiped the snow off the seat of his pants. "Fucking bitch."*

*"I told you; I'm not interested. Stay the fuck away from me, Ken,"*
*Veronica warned.*

*"The fuck you aren't. You wanted it—you led me on."*

*"No, I don't, and no I didn't."*

*"You think you're so fucking special, don't you?"*

*Veronica was having a hard time believing that this was the Ken*
*she knew and had worked beside for the better part of two years. They'd*
*never been partners, never even had a ride-along together, but they*
*worked on the same floor. Veronica had always thought of Ken as the*
*frat boy type, a little boisterous but generally harmless. But now*
*scorned, she saw a real potential for violence in his eyes.*

*"I don't. I'm just not interested."*

*Ken didn't hear her.*

*"Big fucking detective, huh? You would never have gotten the job*
*if it wasn't for your daddy."*

*This assertion came as no surprise to Veronica. She knew that no*
*matter how hard she worked—logging more hours than anyone else*
*in the precinct last year—and no matter what her close rate was—the*
*best in all of Greenham—her father's shadow would loom large.*

*But Captain Peter Shade was no fool. He hadn't promoted Veron-*
*ica. The city council had after a blinded independent arbitrator decreed*
*that she was the best candidate for the job.*

*"Think whatever you want, Ken. Just leave me alone. And if you*
*try any of that shit again? I'll report your ass to IA."*

The imagery was so vivid, the feelings so visceral, that Veronica spilled her coffee on the front of her pants.

"Shit," she cursed, swiping at the scalding fluid.

"Veronica, why didn't you say anything?" Freddie asked.

"What was I supposed to say?" Veronica replied. "That my
first act as a detective is to put in a formal complaint against an
officer in my precinct?"

"No, but—"

"He was drunk and so was I."

"That doesn't excuse anything."

"No, it doesn't, just like being high doesn't excuse Dylan for grabbing my ass."

Freddie looked like he wanted to say more, almost as if he wanted to apologize, which Veronica would not have appreciated, but he bit his tongue.

It took about ten minutes for Veronica to realize that Freddie was just driving in a big circle.

"Where are we going?" she asked.

"I don't—I don't know."

Veronica chuckled, which broke the tension.

"Where *should* I go?"

"Wherever Percy is."

Freddie raised an eyebrow.

"Percy? Ah, yeah, the one who Dylan said was behind the stalking."

"Not exactly what he said, but, yeah."

"And where do we find him?"

Veronica racked her brain, trying to recall what Dylan had told her. Something about Percy bragging about raping a woman in… Sullivan? Or was it East Argham?

For the life of her, she couldn't recall.

"EA," she said at last, her eyes closed. Veronica was only 50/50 on whether this was the right town. But she was sure that if this Percy lead was a bust, at least she'd be closer to where Trent and Herb's stolen Lexus shootout had taken place.

And closer to where Sheriff Burns might be seeking his fourth and final victim.

# Chapter 45

"VERONICA?" STEVE CALLED OUT. WHEN there was no answer, he repeated her name a little louder. "Veronica?"

Concerned, Steve got out of bed and made his way to the window. Veronica's car was still in the driveway, and his was on the street. There was a third vehicle, one he didn't recognize, just pulling onto the road.

Behind the wheel, Steve saw Veronica's partner, the giant of a man she called Freddie but whom everyone else respectfully referred to as Detective Furlow. Veronica was in the passenger seat, a queer expression, an almost emptiness, on her face.

For some reason, Steve was inclined to knock on the glass but resisted.

*Why did she leave without waking me?* he wondered. Steve wasn't delusional, he knew that last night was mostly fueled by intense emotions and those weren't always the best recipe for a long-lasting relationship.

He shook his head.

*Long-lasting relationship? Steve, you can't. You know what happens when you get emotionally involved.*

A long sigh exited his mouth, and Steve let the curtain fall back into place.

He relieved himself and was on his way back to the side of the bed where he'd tossed his clothes last night when he spotted something.

A map.

Veronica had drawn a map across four pieces of paper and left it on the round table near the *en suite*. It was impossible not to look at it, what with her notes written in thick black marker.

Veronica was nothing if not thorough, having retraced Trent's and Herb's reign of terror across Bear County twenty years ago. This surprised Steve; he was the analytical one, while Veronica struck him as intuitive. But this—this *map*? It was something that he would do, not her.

As he traced his fingers over the letters on the sheets of paper, Steve got the impression that there might be more to Veronica Shade than he'd first thought.

What was it about her that had him —

*Shit.*

Steve's finger stopped moving across Veronica's words.

*The address—she found the address.*

Something happened when you desperately wanted a fact to remain hidden. You tucked it deep into the folded gray matter of your brain as if keeping it near the surface would somehow make it more discoverable by others. And then, over time, you forgot all about it. But it didn't go away.

Of course, Veronica had found out that Maggie's, aka Amy's, family had been murdered in *his* barn. What kind of detective would she be if she hadn't figured this out? In truth, Steve was surprised it had taken her this long.

"Shit," he cursed again. "Fuck."

He glanced around the room and saw Veronica's computer lying on the floor beside the pastel blue chair.

*Don't do it, Steve. Don't do it.*

He scratched the stubble on his chin.

"Fuck it."

He had to do it—he *had* to know what she knew.

Steve grabbed Veronica's computer and opened it. It was password protected but he'd seen her log-in and remembered her details. That had been incidental. This, on the other hand, was not.

As he'd suspected, Veronica had searched his name. Steve carefully reviewed her history, looking at each page, combing over what little details she'd uncovered.

With every passing moment, his anxiety began to ease. If Veronica had discovered anything, it wasn't online—not with this laptop, anyway. She might have left without waking him because she was confused and feeling deceived, but it wasn't on account of finding out about him.

That was buried.

Steve heard a muted buzzing sound and glanced around the room again. It was his cell phone, still in his pants bundled beside the bed. Setting the laptop aside, he retrieved it.

He hoped it was Veronica.

It wasn't.

"Yeah?"

"Sheriff Burns, it's Deputy McVeigh. How are ya?"

Steve's gaze drifted to the map that Veronica had drawn.

"Fine. It's actually a good thing you called. I was hoping you could cover for me today. There's something I need to take care of."

"Yeah," the man grumbled, "I would, but we have the Rockford Real Estate cookout today."

Steve made a face.

"The *what*?"

"The annual Rockford Real Estate cookout," the deputy repeated. Steve still had no idea what the man was talking about. "Bunch of fat agents with fat pockets, chowing down on hot dogs and—"

"What about it, McVeigh?"

"Well," the man continued, sounding increasingly uncomfortable. "The sheriff usually gives a speech at this event. I was thinking—"

"Have someone else give the speech this year," he snapped. The idea of going to a cookout after visiting Trent Alberts was asinine. No, not asinine, but insulting. It was insulting to Maggie, to Sarah, to Anthony, and to Veronica. "In fact, why don't you take care of it, Deputy McVeigh?"

"Yes, sir."

"Is there anything else?"

"No, I don't think so.

"Okay, take care."

Sheriff Burns hung up and immediately called Veronica.

There was no answer, so he tried again. And again.

He went to slam his phone down but stopped himself at the very last second.

*You screwed up, Steve, you screwed up* again.

He felt like crawling back into bed and might have done just that if it had been *his* bed. But it wasn't—Steve couldn't even fathom the idea of going home let alone sleeping in his house.

For a long time, he just sat in the upholstered chair staring off into space. His vision alternated between blurring and coming into focus, but his eyes were always pointed in the general direction of Veronica's map. Without thinking, he rose to his feet and picked up the marker that Veronica had left on the table. It was almost as if he was working on autopilot, his mind completely shut off.

*Who's the analytical one now?*

Steve drew a line connecting all of the 'Xs' that Veronica had made, starting in Matheson, moving through Sullivan, and finally to East Argham. When he was done, he took a step backward and observed his handiwork.

Biting his lip, he noticed that there appeared to be a gap in the timeline. Based on the dates of the earlier crimes, Trent and Herb had started in the west and headed east. Anthony's family had been murdered in East Argham and the shootout in the stolen Lexus had occurred near the border of the Casnet River to the east. EA, as underpopulated as it was, covered a large area, close to sixty square miles. And there was a three-month gap between these final two events. Three months... about the same amount of time the duo had waited between terrorizing the Davenports and the Heschs.

Steve drew a small dot approximately halfway between the Wilkes' home and the Lexus shootout.

"There—it has to be *there.*"

Armed with this bizarre certainty, Steve went back to Veronica's computer. After searching for less than five minutes, his skin went cold, and he leaned back.

"This is it."

Back when he'd first met Veronica Shade outside his barn, she'd acted strangely. Her eyes had gone cloudy, and the gold flecks in her irises that he would later come to think of as a sort of trademark nearly disappeared completely.

*"This was no suicide—it was murder."*

Her words had been haunting.

The closest mirror was in the bathroom, but Steve was confident that at that moment, he looked the way she did then.

And when he wrote the details of the final massacre—MO, the missing piece—on the map, he did so with a phantom hand.

# Chapter 46

"**ARE YOU GOING TO ANSWER** that? Because it's driving me nuts," Freddie said.

Veronica switched off her phone.

"What do you know about the sheriff?" Asking about Steve after ignoring four of his calls pretty much negated the effort she'd made to angle her phone to hide his caller ID, but she didn't care.

Freddie had seen Steve's shoes at her house, and if not his shoes, then definitely his car.

"Are you guys—" Freddie shook his head. "Never mind. I already told you what I know, which, admittedly, isn't much. The sheriff used to be a state trooper—no, not trooper, captain, I think. Or maybe it was lieutenant."

"And do you think that's strange? I mean, he's not from Bear County. I don't think, anyway. Yet, he leaves a good position to come here, and gets elected as sheriff?"

Freddie shrugged.

"I'm not too familiar with County politics."

"Right, me neither, but it seems odd."

"I wouldn't disagree with you."

Veronica paused, trying to think of the best way to phrase her ask. Freddie, noticing her discomfort, pre-emptively avoided any awkwardness.

"I can do a little digging, on the down low. Only if you want me to."

Veronica smiled.

"You're the best."

"Good. Then you can treat me to lunch. And no, I'm not eating—"

"Slow down, slow down," Veronica interrupted.

She'd spotted two men with their backs to their car, partially obscured by a building reminiscent of the one that Anthony had died in. They were hunched, their shoulders rolled in a way that Veronica recognized as trying to block the wind when lighting something up. Something on a piece of foil. Thick black smoke wisped upward from between them.

"Let's get lunch after we chat with these guys, shall we?"

"As long as they don't run," Freddie grumbled, as he stopped the car.

Veronica was already out and hurrying toward the junkies. They saw her coming and the foil, a clear pipe, and a lighter all fell to the ground. Then they began backpedaling in preparation to run.

Veronica gripped the butt of her gun, which remained holstered.

"Don't run. My partner," she gestured over her shoulder with her free hand, "he doesn't like to run."

"What you want?" one of the men asked. He had a long, mangy beard and oversized ears. As he spoke, he moved his foot ever so subtly in front of the crack pipe.

"I don't care about what you're smoking." Veronica continued forward. The two men still look poised to run, but they hadn't bolted yet, which was a good sign. "I'm looking for somebody."

"Aren't we all? I'm looking for Amy Adams. Who you looking for, Bobby?" It was the second man who spoke this time. He had teeth that made Trent Alberts' grill look like those belonging to the son of an orthodontist.

"That bitch from Black Swan. That's who I'm looking for," Bobby replied.

"Mila Kunis or Natalie Portman?" Freddie huffed, finally catching up to Veronica.

"What?" Mangled Teeth asked.

"Nothing."

"Well, I'm not looking for any actress. I'm looking for a man who goes by the name *Percy*."

"I don't know no Percy," Mangled Teeth said. Veronica took a few steps forward and inhaled deeply. She could smell the man's reek, even the residual crack in the air, but no gas.

Mostly just piss.

"What about you? You ever heard about a man named Percy? New to the area, likes to rape young girls?" It was Freddie who asked the question, and while the two junkies were distracted, Veronica moved even closer to them. She was within eight feet of the man with the beard, and she thought that if they decided to run now, Freddie might even be able to catch them.

*No, probably not*, she decided. *But I will.*

"Never heard of him."

This was an absolute lie. The man's breath smelled like a gas station.

"You sure?" Veronica prodded.

The man moistened his filthy beard with his tongue.

"I-I don't know nobody."

Both men started to run at nearly the exact same time. It was as if they'd exchanged some silent junkie signal that told them when to move. It was such a strangely coordinated act that Veronica, even though she'd been expecting it, was taken by surprise.

She let Mangled Teeth go but grabbed the one called Bobby by the back of his tattered trench coat.

"I didn't do nothing!" the man shouted.

He continued to try to run even with Veronica holding him, but he stopped when Freddie's meaty hands gripped him by the shoulders.

"Who's Percy?" Veronica demanded, moving in front of him so that she could stare into his dilated pupils.

"I ain't no rat."

"No, what you are is a man who's going to be booked for possession of a controlled substance." Veronica toed the paraphernalia that the men had dropped when she'd approached. "I'm just gonna hazard a guess here, and say that this wouldn't be your first arrest? Which means, you might not be a rat, but you will be in a cage for... I dunno, two years? Maybe three?"

Freddie nodded.

"Two to five sounds about right."

The sneer on Bobby's face was evident even through his beard.

"But the thing is, Bobby—can I call you Bobby?" No reply. "If I'm given information about Percy and go look for him, I might be too busy to book you. Understand?"

The man pouted.

"Something wrong with that guy anyway," Bobby said under his breath, justifying what came next. "He say his name is Percy, but that don't make no sense. I know someone who was on the inside wit' him. His real name is Frank Donovan. Short, fat, fucking guy, weird-ass eyes and shit."

"Frank Donovan? You sure?" Veronica asked.

Bobby nodded.

"Maybe you didn't hear my partner." Freddie gripped the man's shoulders more tightly. "We're looking for a man named Percy. Not Frank."

"I know," he protested. "I know, that's why I remember it. He just fucking made up the name Percy. Trust me, my man was inside wit' him."

Veronica's thoughts went to Amy and Tracy and how they'd also changed their names in an attempt to start over. Completely different context, but still... "You sure?" she asked.

"I'm sure."

"Where does this Percy or Frank or whatever his name is like to hang out?" Veronica said.

"He used to be here in EA, but now he stay up in Sully."

Freddie loosened his grip just a little.

"Where in Sullivan?" the big man asked.

"I don't—shit, that hurts," Bobby complained when Freddie squeezed again. "I heard he got like a camp at Pine and Courier Street. Around there, anyway. That's all I know."

Freddie looked at Veronica for approval, and she gave it to him in the form of a nod. He let go, and Bobby brushed himself off, trying to save face.

"Bobby, thanks for your help." Veronica kicked the foil, scattering its contents across the gravel ground.

"Well, looks like Percy made a name for himself," Freddie said when they were back in the car.

"Very funny. Let's—" Veronica was interrupted by the radio on the dash crackling to life.

"Detective Furlow and Shade, come in. Over."

Veronica felt her body tense in response to Officer Cameron's voice.

Freddie picked up the receiver.

"Detective Furlow here. Over."

"I got him. I got Dylan Hall. And you're not gonna believe this: the sick fuck had a naked picture of Chloe Dolan on him."

Veronica's eyes narrowed.

*No, that can't be right.*

"Yeah, and it was taken while she was in the shower. Over," Officer Cameron continued.

Freddie looked at Veronica, his eyes wide, hers reduced to slits.

"I want everybody on this case back to the station for a debrief. Over."

*A debrief? Who does this guy think he is?*

"Understood. Over and out."

Freddie replaced the radio.

"What the hell, Freddie? A picture of Chloe in the shower?"

The man blinked.

"What about Percy? What about this Frank Donovan guy?"

Freddie still said nothing.

"What the hell is going on?" When her partner elected to remain quiet, Veronica threw up her hands. "Fine. Take me back to the fucking station, then. Let's see what kind of shit Ken Cameron has cooked up this time."

# Chapter 47

SHERIFF STEVE BURNS HAD JUST finished writing on Veronica's map when he heard something from downstairs.

"Veronica?"

He didn't expect a reply as he hadn't heard either a car pull up or the front door open.

The sound recurred. A soft patting, like someone tiptoeing on carpet.

Steve's cop instincts took over and he silently moved to the side of the bed where he'd dropped his clothes. His holster was there, and he pulled his gun free.

Ears perked, he stepped into the hallway and peered down the stairs.

There was no one there and he had a view of the front door, which was closed. Unlocked, but closed.

Steve made his way onto the first step when the cat appeared at the bottom of the staircase.

He lowered the gun.

"Nice, Steve. Almost splattered Veronica's cat."

Cat... cat...

The animal purred and Steve was reminded of when he'd taken the coroner, Kristin Newberry, and the CSU tech, Holland Toler to Maggie's house. They'd gone inside and Kristin, or maybe it was Holland, remarked that there was a bowl for a cat, and a litter box, but they couldn't find the animal anywhere.

The cat purred again.

It could be that Veronica just had a cat as a pet, of course. Lots of people had cats.

Steve slapped his thigh and the cat bounded up the stairs at him. He laughed when it practically leaped into his arms.

"Okay, okay."

He scratched beneath its chin which the cat presented to him, and then flipped over the silver nametag hanging from the collar.

Sure, Veronica could have had the cat for a long time. But a cat with the same name—*Lucy*—as printed on the side of the empty dish at Maggie Cernak's house? And they couldn't find Maggie's cat anywhere?

"What the hell is going on here?"

He heard his phone buzzing from the bedroom and, with the cat in his arm and the gun in his hand, he went to retrieve it, thinking that he might just ask Veronica about her pet.

"Sheriff?"

It was Deputy McVeigh again.

"Yeah?" he said, unable to suppress his annoyance.

"Again, I'm sorry to bother you. And I know you said that I should take over your spot at the cookout—"

"That's what I said."

"Yeah, I know. And I really didn't want to call you again—"

*Oh, for fuck's sake, just get to the point.*

"—but the Kleinmans are here. They're here, and they're asking about you. Like, specifically for you."

Steve looked skyward and put Lucy down.

Of course, the Kleinmans were there. Why wouldn't they be? It was the Rockford Real Estate cookout, after all. And they owned pretty much all the real estate east of Greenham.

If it had been anyone else, the sheriff would've told Deputy McVeigh to just take care of it. But he owed the Kleinmans. To go from a captain in the State Police to sheriff of a county he'd barely ever passed through? That required some serious fire-power. Steve had been forced to call in the one favor he had left, and they, in turn, had reached out to the Kleinmans. It wasn't that the election was rigged in his favor, unless you considered investing ten times the sums of the other candidates, including the incumbent, into his campaign, but he'd won the election.

By a landslide.

If the Kleinmans were asking about him, they wanted him to be there. And how did the old idiom go?

*He who giveth can taketh away.*

Something like that.

"All right," Steve said softly. "Gimme fifteen."

"Sorry? It's a little loud here, I can't hear you."

"I'm on my way. Let the Kleinmans know I'm coming."

Steve hung up the phone.

Most, if not all of his deputies would be at the fundraiser, codeword 'cookout' —the ones he trusted, anyway. And he desperately wanted to get someone out to the address that he'd added to Veronica's map.

It would be best for him to go—with Veronica—but she wasn't answering his calls and he had to deal with the Kleinmans.

The coroner was one option, but he'd already dragged Kristin out of one of her court proceedings once.

There was only one other possibility he could think of.

It took Steve a few minutes to find the man's number, but when he dialed, his call was answered on the first ring.

"Mr. Toler, it's Sheriff Burns," he said, trying to sound upbeat.

"Sheriff," the man shot back. Unlike Steve's, Holland Toler's cheerful demeanor sounded genuine. "I was meaning to call you. Finally finished up with Sarah Sawyer, had some other stuff that I needed to get done first. Anyway, I didn't manage to pull any foreign DNA from her, except for yours, of course. Oh, and I looked into that drug?"

"The drug?"

"Yeah, you asked about checking for an anti-diabetes drug in the girls' system?"

"Ah, yes," Steve said, recalling that he'd passed along Veronica's request to test for metabolites of the Verdant Pharma HbA1c lowering drug.

"Well, I've got some good news and some bad news. Which would—"

"Just tell me, please."

Holland cleared his throat.

"I can do the test for the metabolites like you asked, but it will take at least a week and it will cost the county close to five grand for both Amy and Tracy. But—here's the good news, I looked at a couple of biomarkers for both early heart disease and diabetes—they were left over from a previous case—and they were negative for both. I mean, for both *for both*, if you get what I'm saying. I don't think they'd be taking any anti-diabetes or anti-heart disease drugs. They were in good health."

"Okay, okay, thanks. I was wondering... are you busy?"

"Busy? Not really, pretty slow until the next suicide."

Steve grimaced, thinking that calling the tech might have been a mistake. But he'd gone this far already, and he had no one else.

"Mr. Toler, can you do me a favor?"

"Of course. What do you need, Sheriff?"

"I need you to head out to an old crime scene..."

# Chapter 48

ON THE DRIVE FROM EAST Argham back to Greenham PD, Veronica pulled up Frank—actually Franklin—Donovan's criminal record on Freddie's computer. If you were to create a man responsible for stalking a nineteen-year-old girl, for a book or a movie, all you would have to do is cut-and-paste Franklin Donovan. He had been arrested for indecent exposure, showing pornographic material to a minor, sexual assault, battery, and on and on. His most recent crime was sexual assault on someone who was unconscious. According to the report, Frank was caught massaging the breasts of a college girl who had passed out outside of a bar. The girl's friends had tried to grab him, but the slippery bastard had gotten away. He was caught just an hour later, trying to break into a video store.

Frank served three years for both crimes and had been released just over six weeks ago, which coincided fairly closely with the onset of Chloe's harassment.

Veronica relayed all of this to Freddie, who was nodding so continuously that he looked like the bobblehead he'd once had on the dash—before Veronica told him it made her queasy and he'd taken it down.

"That sounds like our guy," Veronica said. "Doesn't it? Not Dylan Hall."

"No kidding. But if Dylan had naked pictures of Chloe on him…"

It didn't make sense—none of it made sense. She'd spoken with Dylan and had asked him directly if he was behind Chloe's harassment. He'd said no.

Veronica believed him.

The scene inside the station was pretty much what Veronica expected: Officer Cameron prancing around as if he'd just brought down Osama Bin Laden.

And the reason why the man had wanted everyone on the case to come in? Why, to pat him on the back, of course. While Ken's enthusiasm wasn't reflected in the other officers, there was a general lift in the atmosphere. Veronica hadn't realized until it was gone just how tense everyone had been due to the pressure that Randy Dolan was applying.

Captain Shade, however, seemed unaffected by Ken's conquest.

"Please keep the cheering to a minimum." His mouth was a flat line. "This isn't a football game."

Ken's smile faltered a little, but as soon as the captain closed his office door, it returned in full force.

"I told you it was that fucking creep Dylan," he said almost scornfully. He was holding a plastic bag out and thrust it in her direction. Veronica refused to take it, but she couldn't avoid seeing the image inside.

"Jesus, she's a nineteen-year-old kid. Stop waving that around. What's wrong with you?"

"Relax," Ken said, lowering the photograph. "She's covered in this one."

"In *this* one?" Freddie said.

"Oh, yes," Ken said. "Your pal Dylan had plenty of these. And she wasn't covered in all of them, let me tell you."

"What's wrong with you?" Veronica demanded. "Where's Dylan? I want to talk to him."

Officer Cameron stopped grinning.

"No way. No way you're going to see him. Not after last time. You let him go, and he did *this*."

Ken held the photograph close to Veronica's face and she slapped it away. This didn't anger him; rather, it seemed to excite Ken. He had that look in his eyes, the one from the snowy night after the Christmas party. Then, Veronica had been frightened—a little, anyway—but not now. Not even after she saw the first wisps of orange tendrils coming off his head like steam.

"I just want to talk to him," Veronica insisted. "That's it."

"That's not going to happen."

"Stop me."

Veronica spun, intent on walking down to holding and having another conversation with Dylan Hall.

"Don't," Ken hissed through clenched teeth. He grabbed her shoulder, holding her in place.

"Hey," Freddie suddenly shouted.

Ken instantly let go and raised his hand. Usually, this was when Freddie would back off. But not this time. This time, Veronica thought that he was going to get violent.

And it was because of the story, she knew. The story about what Ken Cameron had done that night in the snow.

"It's okay, Freddie," she said, trying to calm the big man. "It's okay."

"No, it's not okay," Ken snapped. "I'm in charge here. You heard the captain. *I'm* in charge. And I don't want her going anywhere near my prisoner."

"Everything good out here?"

It was Captain Shade again, leaning out of his office.

"Fine," Ken replied, suddenly calm. "I was just saying how I don't want anybody speaking to Dylan Hall for the next, oh, I don't know, six hours or so. I want to make him sweat and then he's gonna tell me how he got these photographs."

Captain Shade's gaze drifted from Ken to Veronica, where it stayed.

Veronica frowned and threw up her hands.

"Okay, you got your guy. Congrats. I guess I'm off the case, then." She squinted at her father. "I think I'm going to go for a walk. Clear my head a little, you know?"

# Chapter 49

"WE NEED TO STOP MEETING like this." Dr. Jane Bernard removed her glasses and cleaned them on her shirt. "But I can see that you're agitated. I can spare a few minutes if you'd like to chat?"

Agitated? Veronica wasn't *agitated*. She was incensed.

She didn't know what made Ken happier, the fact that he'd gotten Dylan, the man he claimed was stalking Chloe Dolan, or the fact that he got to rub it in Veronica's face. She prided herself on her ability to separate emotion from her detective work, which is, in her estimation, one of the reasons why she was so successful.

Until today. Or this week. Or this month. Since seeing Maggie Cernak hanging in the sheriff's barn.

The bottom line was that Veronica knew that Dylan, pictures or no pictures, wasn't stalking Chloe. Even if she completely ignored her synesthesia, as Dr. Bernard had suggested at their last meeting, Veronica would have come to the same conclusion. That was detective work. The fact that she didn't want it to be Dylan? That she wanted Ken to be wrong? That was emotion.

"Thank you, Jane. Sorry. It's just... things are getting worse."

Jane led her into her office and Veronica took her regular seat.

"What's getting worse, Veronica?"

"*I* am." She closed her eyes. "My mind, it's racing all the time, I can't sleep, haven't eaten much at all. I don't know—I'm getting confused. Saying shit I normally keep inside my head without thinking."

"What happened?"

What happened? What happened is that these two fucking cases are messing with my brain. What happened is that I can't even move without being overwhelmed by songs, smells, and colors. What happened is that a sadistic bastard grabbed me, shouted in my face, and smeared blood on my shirt.

That's what she wanted to say, but for some reason, Veronica held back. This didn't make sense considering that Dr. Jane Bernard's office was the one place where she could speak openly.

"Things are getting more intense. I used to go days, sometimes even a week without smelling the gas, seeing colors, or hearing the song." She shook her head. "But now, it's happening almost all the time."

Jane nodded.

"You said last time that you were getting emotional about these cases."

Veronica smirked.

"That's an understatement."

"Well, I did a little more research." Jane leaned forward. "There is some evidence to suggest that during emotional or stressful times, synesthetic events can increase in both frequency and intensity."

This was new to Veronica. But she'd been stressed before; hell, she was a detective, she was almost always stressed, and not once had she felt like this.

What was so different about these two cases? What made them special? An innocent man being accused of something he didn't do? Been there, done that. Two murders mistaken for suicide? New, but not wholly unique.

For some reason, they just felt... *personal.*

"Makes sense," Veronica said absently. She raised her eyes to look at Jane. "I mean, that emotions would cause my brain to go on the fritz."

"I'm assuming that this is affecting your professional life?" Veronica scoffed.

"Sure is."

"What about your personal life?"

"It's a hot mess." She paused briefly. "But I took your advice and went out last week."

"You did?" Jane seemed surprised. "How did that go?"

"It went—" Veronica sucked in a breath. It went incredibly well. I met a handsome, smart, and compassionate man. I slept with him, twice, and he seems to really care about me. The only problem is, he may be involved in these murders that have been set up to look like suicides. He may also be the son of a convicted serial killer and possibly helped his father murder at least eight people. "Let's just say, with my synesthesia as intense as it is? Crowds aren't my favorite places."

Jane stared at her, expecting more, but Veronica remained quiet.

"Veronica, the reason I suggested you go out is that your entire life is focused on your career. For short periods of time, this can be very effective for advancement. But the longer you stay entrenched in your work, without any personal life to speak of, the more difficult it can become to distinguish between the two. You start to take everything at work personally because there is no separation. This might be okay for a computer programmer, but as a detective, you can see how this can be very dangerous."

Veronica's phone started to ring, and Jane rested her palms on her desk.

"I know, I know," Veronica said. "But I have to take this. I'm sorry."

Jane looked displeased, but Veronica went ahead and answered her phone anyway.

"Hello?" The caller ID wasn't programmed into her phone, and it wasn't a number she recognized.

"Yes, is this Detective Veronica Shade?" a female asked.

"Yes, and who's this?"

"My name is Meadow and I'm Grant Sutcliffe's nurse. I received a message from Portland PD that you are interested in speaking with Grant?"

*Grant's nurse?*

"Yes, yes, that's right."

"Well, Grant would love to speak to you."

"Great. You're a nurse—is he okay? Is he in the hospital or something?"

"No, he's at home," the nurse replied hesitantly. "I think—Ms. Shade, if you would like to speak to Grant, I suggest you come as soon as you can."

The urgency in the woman's voice made Veronica hear 'immediately' and not 'soon'.

"Yeah, sure, just give me the address."

The nurse relayed the information and Veronica thanked her before hanging up.

"Business or pleasure?" Jane asked.

Veronica grimaced.

"…both?"

# Chapter 50

"I DON'T WANT TO ALARM you, Detective Shade, but Grant isn't in the best of shape. And I didn't feel comfortable discussing his health over the phone," Meadow said. She was young and reminded Veronica a little of the maître d' at the restaurant that she and Steve had gone to. Minus the snark, and with a healthy dose of compassion.

"Please, just call me Veronica. What's… what's wrong with Grant?"

Meadow's eyes started to water, and Veronica suddenly felt for her. Young or not, she must have been Grant's nurse for some time to have such an emotional reaction to what she said next.

"I-I don't usually speak so plainly, but because you guys go so far back, I might as well just come out and say it." It sounded as if Meadow was trying to convince herself. "He—Grant doesn't have much time left. The cancer it-it's spread to his brain."

"The cancer?"

They were sitting in the kitchen with Veronica drinking a coffee while Meadow was sipping on a glass of orange juice.

"Yeah—lung cancer. I'm very surprised that your father didn't tell you."

Veronica cocked her head to one side.

"You know my father?"

Meadow made a strange face.

"Of course. He visits Grant every Sunday."

Veronica sputtered on her coffee and then wiped her lips.

"I'm sorry—every Sunday?"

Meadow nodded.

"Every Sunday."

This came as a shock. Every Sunday... they had their father and daughter dinner every Sunday.

*He came here first? Or did Dad come here after we ate?*

Veronica suddenly felt for both the man upstairs and her dad. No wonder Peter insisted on their family dinners — he was holding on to what little family he had left. His real mom and dad had died a long time ago, and Grant had been like a father to him — *was* like a father to him.

And now...

*He doesn't have much time left.*

Veronica felt her eyes water and forced the sensation away.

"I'm glad you came. He mentioned you, you know?"

"He did?"

Veronica fought back more tears.

"Yes," Meadow said, a sad smile on her face. "Grant gets confused sometimes, and at first, I thought he was talking about his granddaughter. Only, he doesn't have any grand-daughters. It wasn't until I overheard him speaking to your dad that I realized Grant was actually referring to you. Did he — did he ever call you *Lou*?"

"Lou? No. My dad calls me V, but..." Veronica thought back to her time with Grant. She had fond memories of playing in the backyard with him and her dad when she was young. But they'd moved around a lot and Grant was a busy man. The memories, as pleasant as they were, were few and far between.

"No, I don't think so."

Meadow smiled again. This time the sadness reached her eyes.

"Like I told you earlier, he gets confused sometimes."

"I understand. Do you think I can go see him now?"

Meadow nodded.

"Yes, but..." She let her sentence trail off.

"But what?"

"Well," Meadow continued, eyes downcast. "It's just, you called Portland PD to get in touch with Grant and I—I assume this is about your work?"

"Sort of," Veronica conceded. It was about *someone's* work — Sheriff Burns' work—not necessarily *her* work.

"He'll be happy to see you, but he's not in any shape to be discussing intense cases, you know?"

Meadow cared about Grant, Veronica realized. She wondered if he was a surrogate father to her, the way he was for her dad.

"I understand. I'll keep it light."

Veronica followed Meadow upstairs, and even though the nurse had done her best, she was not prepared for the scene that unraveled before her.

It was hard to believe that the shell of a human lying in bed with oxygen tubes up his nose was the same man that Veronica remembered from her childhood.

Grant had always been thin—almost crane-like. He was tall with dark brown horseshoe hair that he kept short on the sides and back. He always wore round spectacles, which made him look more like a professor than a member of law enforcement. Now, it was like everything about him had become exaggerated. Thin became emaciated, small eyes became pinheads. Grant was completely bald and the skin on his face was so tight that it glistened on the bony protuberances that were the man's cheekbones.

And then there was the smell.

The room, filled with more machinery than a Chinese widget factory, reeked of death. A pale orange glow also seemed to permeate the space—a color that Veronica didn't think had anything to do with her synesthesia.

"It's okay," Meadow urged. "You can enter."

It wasn't okay.

And it wasn't just Grant that made Veronica's breath catch. It was her father, too.

Grant and Peter used to share cigarettes all the time—between cases, during cases, on off hours.

That was another memory that stuck in her mind.

*No more joking with Dad to quit smoking. He needs to stop,* now.

Veronica took one step into the room, then another. A machine seemed to hiss in time with her steps, masking her presence. And when she made it to Grant's bedside, his eyes were still closed.

She glanced over her shoulder at Meadow who had respectfully remained in the doorway. The nurse made a gesture that suggested it was okay to wake the man.

Veronica slid her hand into Grant's then fought the urge to gasp. Not only were his fingers ice cold, but it was like grasping a handful of chopsticks.

When she looked up from his bony digits, she was surprised that Grant's eyes had opened. For one fearful moment, Veronica thought that there was nothing behind them, that he was empty inside, that the cancer had hollowed him out like a swarm of overzealous carpenter ants.

But then he started to smile, only a little, revealing teeth that seemed bigger than she recalled.

"Hi, Grant," she said softly.

"Hi, Lou." Or it could have been 'hello'. Grant's voice was acid on peach skin.

Veronica was tempted to fill the ensuing silence with small talk, but Grant deserved more than that.

They stared at each other for several seconds before Grant spoke again.

"I knew you'd be a good cop," he said. "I told your dad you'd make a *great* cop. You were always calling me out when I would tease you, tell you little lies, you know? Harmless things, but you always seemed to just know. Do you remember that time when the three of us—me, you, and Peter—were on a walk and we witnessed that car accident? It happened right in front of us—you were maybe ten or eleven at the time?"

Veronica shrugged. She didn't remember any car accident.

"Peter never told you about it?"

"You know Dad." She imitated his voice. "The past is boring—it's already happened. The future is—"

"—far more interesting," they finished together.

They both laughed, but it didn't last long. Grant soon degenerated into a wheezing and coughing fit.

Meadow stepped into the room and Veronica moved aside. The nurse fiddled first with the oxygen tank and then some of the medical equipment.

After thirty seconds, the fit passed, and Meadow left them alone again.

"It's not contagious," Grant joked.

"Sorry," Veronica said, sidling close.

"What was I—oh, right, the car accident. The three of us had just finished lunch, hot dogs, I think, when two cars collided right in front of us. I was chatting with you at the time and Peter was closest to the accident. Of course, he ran over to make sure everyone was okay. The car with the majority of damage was driven by a middle-aged woman. She was bleeding from her forehead and her leg was pinched beneath the steering wheel. The driver of the other car, a man, got out and began waving his arms around and shouting that it was an accident. Peter called it in, and I tried to keep you distracted. But I couldn't hold you back—you were curious, always so curious. Well, you took one look at the man and — I'll never forget this — you turned to me and said, 'He's lying'. It was so strange. I mean, nobody had asked you, and yet you answered so calmly and so... so *decisively*. When the cops came, they agreed with the man; it was an accident. But there was something about the way you said that — *he's lying* — that made me think. I asked the supervisor to hold off on the determination of the crash and did a little digging. It turned out, you were right. It was no accident. The man had deliberately struck the woman. Something to do with a date gone wrong. The thing is, the woman didn't even recognize him."

The man was rambling, but his words triggered something inside Veronica. She didn't remember the event, not exactly, but listening to Grant evoked a familiar set of emotions.

"That's when — even though you were only ten years old — I knew you'd make a fantastic cop. An even better detective."

"Thank you." Grant's eyes slowly started to close. He seemed tired from talking, and she knew that it was now or never. She took a deep breath. "Speaking of the past, I'm investigating a case of a woman that died of... suspicious circumstances. Her name was Sarah Sawyer." Veronica watched Grant's face closely as she said the name. She thought she saw his cheek twitch. "But she wasn't born Sarah Sawyer," Veronica continued. "She was born Tracy Hesch. She changed her name to forget her past."

Grant closed his eyes.

"Peter's right, the past is boring."

An image of the woman lying on her back, arms out, sheet over her head, flashed in Veronica's mind.

"It wasn't boring to Sarah."

Grant's eyes opened but he wasn't looking at Veronica. He was looking past her, to Meadow.

The nurse had reappeared and entered the room once more. "Grant's tired."

"I know, I know," Veronica replied. "Just one more thing." She addressed Grant. "It wasn't easy finding out Sarah Sawyer's birth name, however. It was redacted. Imagine my surprise when I discovered that you were the one who asked for the information to be blacked out. I just want to know why."

Grant struggled to draw a full breath.

"I'm not going to lie to you, Lou. I mean, I *can't* lie to you. I redacted the name because your father asked me to."

And that was the truth—Veronica knew it instantly.

"My dad?"

Grant nodded again and then started coughing. It was a deep, rumbling sound that seemed to originate from the depths of his stomach.

"Why? Why would he do that?"

But Grant was unable to answer the question. This was no act. He was on the verge of death.

Teary-eyed, Veronica kissed his hand, then let Meadow do her thing.

She'd come to Grant Sutcliffe for answers, but the only thing she'd gotten was more questions.

*Why the hell would Dad ask for Sarah Sawyer's birth name to be redacted?*

# Chapter 51

THIS WAS THE PART OF the job that Sheriff Steve Burns loathed. As a captain in the State Police, the only schmoozing he'd had to do was with his superiors. But even then, it was more sniffing around than pure brownnosing. But the sheriff was an elected position. And Ruth and Dick Kleinman were the ones responsible for getting him elected.

That, in and of itself, was a godsend—considering all the bridges that he'd burned in State, this was the only job he could get. Not just in Oregon, but perhaps in all of the Pacific Northwest.

"First off, I wanted to thank Ruth for putting this fantastic event together," Steve peered down the stage at the crowd as he spoke into the microphone. There were the typical groups that attended these sorts of things, all of which were easily identifiable. You had the moms, the ones who went to every parent-teacher interview, ran the council, gossiped, and huddled. Then there are the Kleinmans, business people with a vested interest in the decisions that the sheriff's department made. People who wanted to be seen and for others to know that they were watching. Finally, there were those with more simplistic desires: free food.

He focused on the latter next, as they were the least offensive of the groups.

"And thank everyone for taking the time out of their day to share some good food and sunshine." Steve looked skyward. It was a beautiful day, and the sun was shining brightly above their heads. "Now, I'm not going to stand up here and pretend that I'm an expert in all things Sullivan—sorry, *Sully*—or Matheson, or even East Argham. But over the past few months,

I've gotten to know the people more than the places." He nodded at Bob, owner of Sullivan's Bob's Hardware, and DJ, the cashier at Marco's Groceries in Greenham who seemed to work twenty-four hours a day and seven days a week. "And I look forward to meeting more of you over the coming weeks."

"And fixing the traffic light at Chester and Main!" someone shouted.

This brought laughter and the sheriff joined in.

"That'll be the first item on this month's city council meeting, Adam! Anyways, please, enjoy the food, the company, and don't be shy! Come say hi!"

The crowd of roughly two dozen started to clap and Steve offered them a friendly wave. Then he leaned over and spoke into Deputy McVeigh's ear.

"That good enough?" It was a genuine question. Deputy McVeigh had grown up in Sullivan and even though he'd only been a deputy for a few years, Steve had no doubt that he had attended more than his fair share of these cookouts growing up.

"Fine job." McVeigh nodded. "Don't forget, in addition to the Kleinmans, you also need to speak to Bruce."

Steve led the deputy down the fountain steps.

"Bruce?"

"Yeah, Bruce Holloway. He owns pretty much every barbershop East of Matheson."

This rang no bells.

"His wife is Barbara? As in, Bruce and Barbara? And she loves to talk."

"And why—"

The gossip moms approached, and Steve smiled.

"Ladies, it's great to see you here."

He knew them all by name and made sure to use each one as he shook their hands. It was a necessary evil.

"It's great that you could make it here, Sheriff, what with... well, you know."

The sheriff didn't know, didn't want to know, and didn't inquire. But the woman who had spoken, Wendy, did so with the intent of elaborating.

"It's a horrible, horrible thing that happened to Maggie. I used to see her every Friday, right before book club. Did you ever find out why she walked all the way to your place?"

Steve was aghast.

"Excuse me?"

Wendy looked to her friends, and then lowered her voice.

"The suicide. Do you know why Maggie chose your place? I mean, we all know how you like to read—"

Not just gossip moms, but Gossip Queens.

"Wendy, I'm very sorry but this is an ongoing investigation. I can't—I can't discuss it."

"Right."

"But, hey, speaking of books? Any recommendations for new releases?"

"Oh, yes," Wendy replied, beaming now as if they weren't, seconds ago, discussing Maggie Cernak's death. "Have you read L.T. Vargus' new one?"

"I haven't had a chance."

"It's one of her best."

"I'll be sure to check it out." Steve shook Wendy's hand again. "Thanks for coming."

He politely excused themselves and then glared at Deputy McVeigh.

"You told them?" he hissed. "You fucking told them?"

McVeigh shook his round head.

"I didn't tell them—I didn't tell anybody."

Steve set his jaw and looked around the cookout, his eyes darting from deputy to deputy. They were all schmoozing, eating burgers.

"This is Bear County—everyone talks here, Sheriff. *Everyone.* That's why you need to talk to Bruce."

"What?"

"Bruce the barber."

"Right, you said that already. Why the hell do I need to talk to him?"

"The rumor going around is that he's considering throwing his hat in the ring for the next election."

The sheriff blinked.

"What?"

The deputy put his hands out and moved his head around, wiggling it a little.

"Yeah, I don't know, I thought maybe if you spoke to him, reached out, maybe—"

"McVeigh, I appreciate what you're trying to do here, but I really don't have time for this shit."

"I'm just—"

The sheriff waved him off and turned his back.

If Wendy knew about Maggie, then McVeigh was probably right: everyone in the county did. They might know about Sarah Sawyer, too, and if the Gossip Queens were on it, they would find out the connection between them, if they hadn't already.

This would eventually lead them to Anthony, and then the fourth crime.

The fourth victim.

Steve took out his cell phone and dialed an old friend.

"I need another favor," he said.

"Let me guess, another redacted name?"

Steve thought about the case report he'd discovered using Veronica's laptop, the one he was convinced was Trent's and Herb's final murders. It wasn't exactly the same as the others, but it was close enough. And the fact that victims' names were also redacted when he tried to search for them? That was proof enough for him.

"Yeah—I need names. As soon as you can." Steve relayed the police case number that he'd committed to memory. "Think you can help me out?"

"Yep, I can look into that for you. I just want to warn you though, the more times we look, the more chance someone looks into you, if you know what I mean."

"Yeah, I know, I know. But this is important. Just give me a call when you—"

"Just hold on a second, I'm in the office now. Just wait— okay... the case, this is the one with the fire, right?"

The sheriff moved even further from the crowd and plugged one ear with his finger.

"Yeah. That's the one. The file is... thin. I don't get it— there's barely anything in there. It did say that there was one survivor though."

"Right, I see that. A boy, seven years old. A lot of this... it's all redacted. There's so much shit that's just blacked out. I don't think I've seen a case with this much—"

"I'm kind of busy right now. Can you—"

"Jesus, Steve, hold the fuck on. Okay, I... yeah, so the boy, his name is Benjamin, Benjamin Davis. I see here... he was shipped off to Renaissance Home."

"Renaissance Home? What the hell is that?"

"Orphanage."

"Ah. Can you find him in the system now?"

Steve waited patiently and heard furious typing.

"That's weird. Can't find anything. Nothing with the DMV, or IRS. No criminal record."

For some reason, Steve wasn't surprised.

"What about a name change?"

"No, no... I don't think so."

He shook his head. He was hoping for more. So much more.

"Thanks."

"You want me to keep looking into all this other redacted shit? There's at least a page full of blacked-out material."

"Yeah, please. Gimme a call if you find anything. And thanks."

"No prob. Talk soon."

Steve hung up the phone and tapped it against his palm.

Benjamin Davis survived a massacre and was shipped off to an orphanage. And then... poof. Gone. Just like Amy and Tracy. He had to go to the scene that the tragedy had taken place. There were clues there—there had to be. Just like where Anthony had died.

But first, he called Veronica, but when that went to voicemail, he dialed another number.

"Detective Fred Furlow," a man's smooth voice said after the third ring.

"Detective, it's Sheriff Burns."

"Hey, sheriff, what can I do for you?"

"Are you with Veron—Detective Shade?"

"Not at the moment."

There was an awkward silence.

"Listen, you know that case I asked you to help out with last week? The suicide?"

"Sure. We signed off on it. What about it?"

*Shit. I should have known that Veronica was keeping this from her partner.*

Steve sighed.

"Well, I was doing some research and I might have found a similar case. I just wanted to keep you and Vero—shit, Detective Shade apprised." He paused, and then just came out with it, and told Detective Furlow about the fire and about Benjamin Davis surviving.

When he was done, Freddie was silent.

"You still there?"

"Yeah," Freddie's voice had a rough edge to it now. "Wait— you said that he was shipped off to Renaissance Home?"

"Yeah."

"Benjamin wouldn't happen to be insanely tall, would he?"

"What do you mean?"

"Was he really tall as a boy?"

Steve wasn't sure what the detective was getting at.

"I don't know anything about him. That's the thing. He went to Renaissance and then just kinda disappeared."

"Sheriff, I'm going to have to call you back."

"Everything okay?"

"Yeah," Freddie said. "But I'll tell you what: I think I know exactly who Benjamin Davis is."

# Chapter 52

FREDDIE TRIED VERONICA, BUT HE didn't expect her to answer and wasn't disappointed.

After his partner had left the station, the party had simmered down. Apparently, Ken's shenanigans had been mostly for Veronica's benefit. Then Officer Cameron had left and the crowd on the third floor had promptly dispersed.

With Dylan in holding, Freddie Furlow didn't have much to do. But now, after the disturbing call from Sheriff Burns, he felt obligated to accomplish one more task before heading home.

As the big man waddled down to holding, his anger at Veronica wavered. The feeling that he'd been deceived, however, did not. He trusted Veronica and he respected her. Freddie had thought that this was mutual. But over the past week or so, he'd seen a change in her. Veronica had always been different—as a cop and a detective, she did things her own way.

And Freddie liked that about her. After so many years in the system and seeing everyone who passed through the institution being molded into the same type of cop? Her approach was refreshing. Which was why, when Veronica had been promoted and Peter had asked him to be her partner, he'd said yes, without hesitation.

And this was how she repaid him? By going behind his back?

He wasn't stupid. Freddie knew that Veronica was involved with the sheriff—he didn't care about that. He did care about her working on a case without him. This wasn't about his ego, either. It was about a promise he'd made to Peter and to himself.

The reality was, he couldn't keep an eye on her if she was off on her own. Freddie gave Veronica plenty of latitude with other cases—she needed it to do her job her way.

But this was different. This case, the suicide case, was somehow personal to her.

The real question was, *why*? Why was this different from all the other cases they'd worked on together? Keyword, *together*.

"Detective Furlow?"

Freddie looked up and saw Officer Furnelli standing in his path.

"Officer Cameron said that no one was—" he stopped speaking when he saw Freddie's face. Then he bowed his head and stepped aside.

Freddie continued down the hall and stopped in front of the last cell on the right.

"Dylan?"

The tall man was sitting on the concrete bench, his elbows resting on his thighs. Dylan had a surprising amount of color in his face and looked healthier than Freddie had ever seen him. There was a welt below his left eye, but other than that, he looked good.

Maybe he was staying sober.

"Well, if it isn't the Stay-Puft Marshmallow Man."

Dylan squinted through the bars at Freddie.

"That's me. And you're Dylan, right?"

Dylan sneered.

"Last time I checked. What is this? Is pretending not to know who I am some sort of good cop, bad cop thing?" He stood and walked right up to the bars, making sure that his face was clearly visible in the dull yellow light. Then he glanced dramatically up and down the hallway. "I don't see any good cops. In

fact, I don't think there's a good fucking cop in this entire station. Least of all that piece of shit Officer Cameron."

Freddie tried to ignore the man's spite, to see what Veronica
saw in the foul-mouthed convict.

"You went to Renaissance, didn't you?"

"What the fuck is this? Twenty questions? Maybe I should
ask for my lawyer... *again*."

"Look," Freddie said staunchly. "I'm trying to help you, all
right? I don't think you were the one stalking Chloe Dolan."

Dylan snarled.

"Then what the fuck am I doing in here?"

"Let me remind you that you had naked pictures of Chloe
Dolan on you—"

"On me? I didn't have those pictures *on* me. Officer Cameron
said he found them in my tent. I ain't never seen them before."

A common refrain.

"I'm not here about that," Freddie remarked, trying to get
back to the reason he'd broken a sweat by coming down here.

"Well, I sure as hell am," Dylan protested, squeezing the
bars in his hands. "I'm in this eight by ten because your colleague Officer Cameron has a fucking hard-on for me."

"I just want to ask you about your time in Renaissance,
Dylan. Or should I call you Benjamin? You went by Benjamin
back then, didn't you?"

Dylan pulled back, confusion plastered all over his face.

"Has cholesterol gone to your brain or something? 'Cuz
you're making zero sense."

Freddie wasn't buying it. He thought about Anthony
Wilkes, about how similar his story was to Dylan's. Anthony
was *MINEY* and Freddie was determined to make sure that
Dylan didn't become *MO*.

But he needed proof.

"I understand why you'd want to put your past behind you," Freddie said, trying to come off as compassionate. "If I saw my family—well, let's just say if I went through the trauma you went through, I'd change my name and get away. Try to start over."

"Am I high again? No, really—am I high?" he paused. "Are *you* high? I thought you were coming down here and getting me to write another nasty letter for your Penthouse Stories and then you'd let me out."

"So, you're telling me your name, the name you were born with, isn't Benjamin Davis?"

"No. My name is Dylan Hall."

Freddie didn't have Veronica's truth-seeing ability, but he didn't need it. Dylan was being honest. It wasn't even what the man said or how he acted, it was because this was something Freddie already knew. Dylan Hall was Dylan Hall—Freddie had seen his rap sheet multiple times. His first arrest had been as a young boy.

Freddie had just been so eager to get involved in the case, maybe to spite Veronica or maybe to team up with her again, that he'd just jumped to a conclusion.

A very wrong conclusion.

"I'm sorry."

Freddie started to turn, and his mind, as if it often did, was already onto something else.

A familiar topic: food.

"Hey, where you going?" There was desperation in the man's voice.

Freddie looked at Dylan for one last time and even though the lighting was the same, he saw someone different.

No longer was Dylan Hall a foul-mouthed junkie who had once grabbed Veronica's ass. He'd been reduced to a scared and lonely man.

*Is this what Veronica sees in him?* Freddie wondered. *Is this why she keeps giving him a pass?*

"Did you say, Benjamin Davis?"

Freddie decided to entertain this, for Veronica's sake.

"Yeah."

"I–I–I knew a Benjamin. In Renaissance." Freddie was never any good at hiding his emotions and this time was no different.

"I'm serious," Dylan protested. "Everyone called him Benny. He had this fucked up burn scar on the back of his neck that went up to his hair."

This gave Freddie pause.

"Did you say, *burn scar?*"

Dylan nodded enthusiastically.

"Yeah, he was burnt all the way up his back to his head." Dylan scratched his own bald head. "That was when he was young, though. When I saw him years later, he was completely bald. I called out to him, 'Yo, Benny', but he didn't answer. Guy changed his name."

This wasn't jumping to conclusions. This was it.

He'd found *MO.*

Freddie licked his lips.

"What was his name?"

"It was—" Dylan tilted his head. "You know what? I don't think I remember."

"What?" Freddie balked.

"Naw, I forget. He was named after a country or some shit, but that's all I recall."

"You're lying. Tell me—"

"Detective Furlow!" The shout startled Freddie. "*Detective Furlow!*"

He turned and saw Officer Furnelli running toward him. "You gotta come quick. Fuck, you gotta hurry." Freddie's thoughts immediately went to Veronica. "What? What happened? Is she okay?" Officer Furnelli struggled to catch his breath. "Court! Is Veronica okay?" This made the man lift his head.

"Veronica? No, it's Chloe." The young officer's eyes darted to Dylan behind bars. "Someone took her. Someone broke into her house and dragged her away."

# Chapter 53

VERONICA WAS DESPERATE TO SEE her father. He *knew*. He was the one who had told Grant to redact the names from the case files.

The real question, as it had been from the beginning, was *why?*

But no matter how badly she needed to speak to him — to *interrogate* him — Veronica had to stop at home first. Her jeans were still damp from where she'd spilled her coffee, and the hastiness that she'd felt this morning to get out before Steve had awoken had left her a hot mess.

If her partner had been anyone else, anyone other than Detective Fred Furlow, they would have, at the very least, given her a strange look. Her hair, pulled up in a loose pony, was messy, and she'd applied zero makeup this morning. Typically not one to cake it on, Veronica at least made an effort to put on a little mascara and some colored lip gloss.

Not today.

Today she felt as dirty as she looked.

Traffic in Matheson slowed to a halt. There was some sort of celebration or ceremony happening in the town center, and Veronica cursed her decision not to take the back roads.

A sign indicated that the event was the 'Rockford Annual Real Estate Cookout', but she knew differently. This was the 'Annual Appreciate the Donor who got me into Power Affair'. Which meant...

Sheriff Steve Burns was standing on the steps in front of a giant fountain, leaning into a microphone. He was smiling and this set Veronica off.

How *can* he be smiling?

She'd softened on the idea that Steve was behind what she was now mentally referring to as the nursery rhyme murders — *EENIE, MEENIE, MINEY, MO,* who dies next, only the killer will know—but even if he had nothing to do with it, how can he smile?

Trent and Herb had an accomplice, and that person was behind at least two deaths. And yet, the sheriff, the man technically in charge of this case, was grinning and rubbing palms with Eastern Oregon's affluent influencers.

Any man who was capable of such dichotomy, of having sex with her, of schmoozing, and chasing a killer all in the span of a single day?

That said something about them, and what it said wasn't complimentary.

Veronica clenched her jaw and averted her eyes before Steve looked in her direction. Unlike Freddie's car, which is the one they drove while working, hers wasn't equipped with any dashboard lights. Regardless, she pulled onto the shoulder and aggressively circumvented the traffic, ignoring the angry looks and honks from other motorists.

Within thirty minutes of leaving Grant's home, she pulled into her driveway and hopped out of the car.

Veronica was greeted by Lucy, whom she had completely forgotten about, and she prepared some fresh food and water, making a mental note to pick up additional food as the supply she'd taken from Maggie's house had dwindled to a single can.

With Lucy distracted, she hurried upstairs and rifled through her clothes, looking for something clean to wear. The last few days had been such a clusterfuck that the pile of dirty laundry had grown and now exceeded the pile of clean clothes, unfolded, still in the bin. But she found a fresh T-shirt and threw it on. Pants proved more difficult, and Veronica eventually settled on the jeans she'd worn the day prior.

She was about to leave the room when her eyes fell on the map of Oregon she'd drawn. There was something different about it, and it took her a few moments to figure out what the change was.

Someone had added something—Steve, it had to be Steve. Between the Xs that Veronica had placed, indicating Anthony Wilkes' location of death and the Lexus shootout, the sheriff had added another notation: a date and a single word, all in capital letters: DAVIS.

Davis?

Unfamiliar with the name, Veronica's eyes drifted to her laptop, which was closed and lying on her chair.

*Did I put it there?* she wondered.

Veronica wasn't sure. She was positive that her laptop had been open, however.

Her suspicions returned tenfold.

The events of the previous night were hazy, but Veronica was certain that Steve hadn't had his own laptop with him. There was, of course, the possibility that the sheriff had access to police files on his phone but that wouldn't explain the distinctive writing.

Her heart racing, Veronica pulled out her own phone and scrolled through her images. When she reached the photograph of the first note, the one obtained from Maggie Cernak's pocket, she stopped cold.

The writing… it was the same.

DAVIS was written in the same slanted, all-caps text as EENIE.

"No," she moaned. With numb fingers, Veronica was scrolling to the other note—MEENIE—when her phone started to ring.

She was so startled that she actually shouted and pressed answer by accident.

"Hello? Veronica? Thank God I—are you okay? Veronica?" Veronica was breathing heavily, and her vision started to swirl.

"*Veronica?*"

"Y-y-yeah," she managed, although she wasn't sure how. Her vocal cords were taut.

"What's wrong? Are you okay? Where are you?" Freddie's questions came fast and furious.

"Home, Freddie—I'm at home. I think—I think there's—" *something wrong with the sheriff*, she intended to say, but her partner interrupted her before she could finish her sentence.

"Veronica, someone got her. Someone *fucking* grabbed her."

Detective Furlow rarely swore, and his use of the curse word now made Veronica momentarily forget all about Sheriff Burns.

"What? *Who?*"

"Chloe Dolan. Someone walked into her house in the middle of the day and kidnapped her."

"Who?" Veronica repeated. "Who took her?"

"I don't—I don't know. But Dylan's in lock up and—"

"Percy." Much like the word DAVIS, and EENIE, MEENIE, and MINEY, *PERCY* appeared in all caps, in her mind. Veronica cleared her throat and immediately started down the stairs, taking them two at a time. "Franklin 'Percy' Donovan—he's the one who took Chloe, Freddie. And if we don't stop him, he's going to kill her."

# Chapter 54

VERONICA MADE IT AS FAR as her car before her phone rang again.

"Freddie?"

When there was no answer, Veronica pulled the phone away from her face to make sure the call had connected. It was, but Freddie's name wasn't on the display—it had an unknown caller.

"Who is this?"

"M-M-Monica."

"Who?"

Veronica put her car into drive and began speeding toward Sullivan, the location where Dylan had told them 'Percy' had been last seen. If he had the girl, the likelihood that he was heading to a place that he was familiar with was very high.

"Monica—Chloe's friend?"

Veronica's entire attention was on her phone now.

"Have you heard from her? She called?"

"N-no," Monica said. "It's just—she told me not to say anything, but I think... I think—"

"Monica, your friend is missing. If you know *anything* that might help us find her, you have to tell me. I don't care about the drugs. All I want to do is find Chloe."

"I'm just—I'm scared."

Veronica looked up, observing street signs overhanging intersections that she didn't even bother slowing down as she passed through. Time—that was the most important element right now. Not manpower, not technology, or evidence.

Time.

And for Chloe Dolan, it was running out.

Veronica weighed her options. She could go to Sullivan with a high degree of certainty that Percy was there. But Sully was a big place—a big place where someone who didn't want to be found could hide for days, maybe even weeks.

Chloe wouldn't last that long.

"Where are you?" she demanded.

"I-I-I'm at h-home."

"Good. Stay there. Don't move."

Veronica made it to Monica's house in eight minutes. She found the girl sitting outside on the stoop, her elbows on her knees, her face buried in her hands.

Normally, a situation such as this one, with Monica distraught and frightened, would call for a certain degree of tact.

But, time...

"Monica, you need to tell me everything. *Everything.*"

Monica finally looked up, revealing red eyes and soggy cheeks. The girl's lower lip trembled, but no words came out.

"I know you and Chloe bought ecstasy from Dylan. That's why he was outside Chloe's house–you guys didn't pay him."

Monica nodded and bit her lower lip, the only thing that would make it stop quivering.

"The person who took Chloe? It wasn't Dylan Hall."

Monica shook her head.

"No, I don't think so," the girl said softly.

"You need to start talking. This is no joke—if we don't find Chloe soon, we may never find her. I'm serious."

Harsh, but true.

"Okay, okay," Monica relented, eyes wide. "It happened last year, around Christmas. I don't really know if it means anything but, I just—I get things stuck in my head, you know? And this... it was—I just can't forget it."

Veronica squatted so that she was on the same level as the girl.

"What happened?"

"We were at this party, just a kid from school —his parents were out so we raided their liquor cabinet. There were these boys that Chloe was trying to impress? Anyways, we all drank too much and had to leave because Laura puked. Chloe didn't want to go, but she was wasted, too. We left the party and started stumbling through the snow —it was cold, like—"

"Please, Monica."

"Yeah, sorry. Anyways, we were walking home when this creepy guy came up to us. He was hitting on Chloe, but he was old. Like thirty? I dunno, maybe even older. Chloe was pissed for having to leave the party and she wanted nothing to do with him. And she told him that. Chloe... she has a bit of a mean streak, you know? Anyways, she told the guy off, but he didn't get the hint. He just stared at Chloe, like *really* stared. And he had this look on his face... I don't know how to describe it. But I thought... I thought he was going to rape us all, right there in the snow. That's how scared I was."

"What happened next?" As Veronica asked the question, she scrolled to a copy of the police report she'd saved to her cell phone.

"He started saying these things... disgusting things, just like the letters, you know? That's why I think he might have something to do with this."

Veronica showed Monica the image on her cell phone.

"Is this him? Is this the man who came up to you guys?"

Monica leaned in close and squinted. She stared at the photograph for a good five seconds and then slowly shook her head.

"No, that's not him."

"You sure?" Veronica held Frank 'Percy' Donovan's mug-shot up for a moment longer.

"I'm sure. I'm really good with faces. It wasn't him."

It *couldn't* be him, Veronica suddenly realized. It couldn't be Percy because he was still in prison in December.

"Shit," she cursed.

"This guy was better looking, you know? Like a frat boy?"

Frat boy. That struck a nerve with Veronica.

"Do you—do you remember what day it was? You said this happened around Christmas... was it before or after Christmas?"

"The 23rd. It was the 23rd of December."

Veronica's heart rate spiked. And now, like Monica's lip, her hand was trembling. She sifted through more of her camera roll before stopping on an image that she'd taken from her joint promotion and work Christmas party.

Then she turned her cell phone around, hoping, pleading that what she was thinking now wasn't true.

But when Monica's jaw fell open and her face turned a lifeless white, Veronica knew what the girl was going to say.

"That's him," she stated breathlessly. "Yeah—that's the guy."

# Chapter 55

AFTER SPEAKING WITH DETECTIVE FURLOW, Sheriff Burns spent the next fifteen minutes pressing the flesh with the Kleinmans and anyone else who wanted to talk. Nothing deep —just platitudes and anecdotes, which suited him well.

The sheriff's mind was firmly rooted elsewhere. He couldn't get Sarah and Maggie out of his head. Couldn't stop thinking about Trent Alberts, about Anthony Wilkes.

About Veronica Shade.

Having been married before, Steve thought he knew love. And while the idea of love at first sight was just that —an idea, a romantic, lustful construct of hormone-addled teenage minds —he felt something for her, had the moment she'd appeared in front of his barn. Something he hadn't felt in a long time. She was special —Veronica was complicated, different, but *special*.

And he'd fucked it all up.

His phone rang, and the sheriff excused himself from a conversation that was going nowhere and answered. He was hoping it was Detective Furlow with an update about the possible identity of Benjamin Davis.

He was disappointed.

"Sheriff Burns?"

"Yeah —who's this?"

"This is Holland —Holland Toler."

A cheer arose from around the barbecue, and Steve backed further away from the cookout and placed a finger in his ear.

"Did you find the house?"

"I found it, all right. It's mostly just a shell, all boarded up. No one bothered to rebuild it after the fire, I guess. But..." He trailed off.

"But what?"

"It's probably better if you see for yourself."

"Holland, I'm busy here. If you—"

"I think—I think there's someone living here," the CSU tech said hesitantly.

"What do you mean? I thought you said it was all boarded up?"

"Yeah, I can kinda see inside and there's like a sleeping bag and dishes."

"Is there someone there now?" Steve snapped.

"Just me, I think. I mean, I can find a way inside and start to process the scene, if you want. It's been abandoned for twenty-plus years, so I dunno—"

"No," Steve said forcefully. "Just stay outside." He glanced over his shoulder. There were a handful of people still eating burgers, but the crowd had thinned considerably.

*I did my part,* he thought. *Now let me do my job.*

"I'll be there in half an hour. Stay out of sight."

Steve hung up and walked over to Deputy McVeigh.

"I have to go."

McVeigh took one look at his face and knew that this was non-negotiable.

"All right, I'll wrap up here. Need me to—"

"No," Steve said preemptively. "Just take care of things here. Please."

"Sure thing, Sheriff."

Steve watched Deputy Marcus McVeigh turn around, and then smile and wave at Bruce Holloway, the barbershop magnate. Both men laughed at an unspoken joke.

As Steve drove off, heading to meet Holland Toler at the Davis disaster, he couldn't help but think that maybe Bruce wasn't the one he had to worry about taking his job, but that it might very well be his own deputy.

# Chapter 56

IT MADE SENSE, NOW. IN a twisted way, it all made sense.

The man's assertion that it was Dylan who was stalking Chloe Dolan. His anger directed toward Veronica.

That night, in the snow.

Veronica was pissed at herself for not noticing the connections earlier. After all, it was right there. Right in front of her eyes.

At the very bottom of Frank 'Percy' Donovan's last warrant was the name of the arresting officer: Ken Cameron.

"Fuck," she cursed.

Veronica had been so distracted by her budding romance with the sheriff, and the suicides, that she missed a clue that might just have cost Chloe Dolan her life.

"Fuck!" she shouted again, gripping the steering wheel tightly.

When she'd driven from her home to Monica's, she'd been going fast. Now, she was traveling at lightning speed.

She grabbed her phone and dialed her partner's number.

"Freddie? Where are you?"

"Veronica?" Detective Furlow nearly shouted into the phone. "I'm in Matheson. Where the hell are you? It's crazy out here—Captain Shade has everyone in the entire city out looking for Chloe Dolan. He's with Randy Dolan right now, working on a plan. They're trying to trace her cell phone and—"

"Where's Ken? Where's Officer Cameron?" Veronica cut in.

"I—I haven't seen him. But he's gotta be out there looking for Chloe Dolan—everyone is. After that whole thing with—"

"He's in Sully," Veronica said with such conviction that Freddie didn't even argue. "I can't explain now, but there's something I need you to do, Freddie. It has to be you — can't be me. If it's me, he'll know."

"Who will know? What do you need me to do? Veronica, I don't understand —"

"Just listen, Freddie. *Please.*"

Veronica outlined the plan to her partner, then hung up the phone. As she waited for Freddie to call her back, she continued driving to Sullivan, hoping that she wasn't too late.

Praying that all three of them would still be there.

And that Chloe Dolan was still alive.

Her phone rang.

"Yeah? Did you get a location on his car?"

"I did," Freddie replied, citing the address. "You were right — Ken's in Sully. He should be in Matheson with the other cops, but... Veronica, are you going to tell me what's going on?"

"Not until I know for sure. Freddie, meet me in Sullivan but if you get there before me, lay low until I arrive. Please, don't do anything. If I'm wrong about this, and I really hope I am, then it's going to blow up worse than anything I've done before."

"And... and if you're right?"

Veronica bit her lower lip.

"Then we might just save Chloe Dolan's life."

And bring the entire City of Greenham Police Department to its knees in the process.

# Chapter 57

VERONICA HAD BECOME INCREASINGLY MANIC over the past few days, and her actions were more and more irrational.

And Detective Freddie Furlow was starting to blame himself.

*I should have gone to Peter—I should have told him what happened after that very first episode at the barn.*

Instead, Freddie had enabled her. Hell, he'd gone as far as to leave Veronica alone with an addict who had previously sexually assaulted her.

He shook his head. That was the problem with retrospection; it all seemed so *factual*. What happened in the alley? Well, Veronica asked—*begged*—me to leave her alone with Dylan Hall. What did you do? I left.

The details were lost or ignored. Retrospection didn't consider the *way* Veronica had asked him, the look of desperation in her eyes, or the fact that she was just... different.

And now this wild goose chase for Officer Ken Cameron's car?

Freddie was aware that if things went sour here, it might not just be Veronica's job that was in jeopardy. Sure, he had a stellar track record and the benefit of experience on his side, but this might come back to haunt him. After all, how would the headline look? *Greenham's most decorated detective unavailable while city councilor's daughter is raped and murdered.*

Likely, the papers wouldn't be that brash, but his superiors would. And though Captain Peter Shade had his back, even he had limits. And if the leeway that Freddie had afforded Veronica ever came to light? The captain might elect to throw him into holding with Dylan Hall rather than just take his badge and gun.

Sullivan wasn't as nice as Matheson, nor was it nearly as decrepit as most of East Argham. But like every city, irrespective of size, there were pockets of seedy neighborhoods, places like the abandoned apartment structure that Anthony Wilkes had overdosed in.

It was in one of these areas that Detective Fred Furlow found Ken's squad car. It was tucked near the back of a building that had long since been condemned. It was three stories tall, likely a textile mill back in the day, and most if not all of the ground floor windows had been destroyed, only some of which, a paltry few, had been boarded up.

As per Veronica's instructions, he cut his headlights after spotting the officer's car and drove past without slowing. He made two additional turns and angled his Sebring so that it was pointed at one of the larger sections of broken windows.

Oregon dusk came fast in early spring, and the streetlights had already flicked on. But long shadows and diabetic retinopathy were a bad combination. Freddie turned off his car and got out, trying to see inside the building.

It was still too dark.

He crept closer, trying not to slip or make any noise. But the ground was made mostly of rubble, and he was as athletic as an arthritic tortoise.

Freddie got within fifteen feet of the shattered windows when he was forced to stop.

It was a good thing he did, as there was a flicker of movement from inside the abandoned building. Movement that was quickly followed by voices.

*Veronica? Where the hell are you?*

\*\*\*

Veronica noticed Officer Cameron's car immediately. And the location it was parked only reinforced her suspicions.

Approaching from the south, she parked half a block away then continued on foot. Staying light on her toes, she easily traversed the broken terrain, pausing every few seconds to listen.

She heard nothing, which wasn't a good sign. Fueled by the terrible prospect of being too late, Veronica doubled her pace, and when she reached the building, she didn't hesitate to climb through the nearest broken window.

It reeked like sour beer and piss inside and the ground was slick with some sort of grease. Moving was more difficult here, but thankfully, Veronica didn't have to go far before she spotted him.

The muscular man in the police uniform had his back to her, with his hands out in front. It was even darker inside the building than outside, and Veronica was still waiting for her eyes to adjust.

"Fucking *notes*," the man hissed. "You were just supposed to leave *notes*."

Veronica unclasped her holster and drew her gun. Careful not to slip, she took one, then two steps closer.

"Fucking used condom? You sick fuck. I told you to stop."

Veronica moved to her left and the entire scene suddenly opened before her.

Officer Ken Cameron was pointing his service pistol in front of him, aiming it at a man dressed all in black. The latter had an outline of a bowling pin, and even though Veronica couldn't quite see his face, she knew that this was Percy.

Percy mumbled something that Veronica didn't pick up on, but it enraged Ken.

"God dammit! You weren't supposed to touch her! You weren't supposed to go into her house or anywhere near her! *Notes*! I told you to leave notes! That's it! You know who her fucking father is? He's a city councilor, for Christ's sake!" Ken hissed through clenched teeth.

"You told me to scare her." Percy's tone was oddly matter-of-fact. "You told me to—"

Ken stamped his foot.

"I didn't tell you to—fuck, you made me do this." Ken adjusted his posture and extended the arm holding the gun even further. "Come to think of it, this might actually be better. I'll be a fucking hero for killing you."

"B-b-but you were the one who—"

Ken Cameron pulled the trigger and Franklin 'Percy' Donovan's words were swallowed by the echo of a gunshot in the confined space.

# Chapter 58

FREDDIE SAW THE MUZZLE FLASH before he heard the gunshot. And then came the scream. Even though he only saw two males inside the building, the scream was definitely female in nature.

There was no question that the man on the ground was Percy—like Freddie himself, he had a very distinctive shape—and he was the one who'd been shot. Only, he wasn't screaming. He was writhing, grunting, and moaning, but the high-pitched shrill was coming from elsewhere.

He tried to move forward but on his third step, Freddie slipped and fell to one knee. Pain shot up all the way to his hip and he was unable to rise for several seconds.

This hunkered position allowed him a unique perspective of the interior of the building and within moments he spotted the person who had screamed.

Seated on the floor of an adjacent, open-aired room was a gagged and blindfolded Chloe Dolan.

Freddie was now immobilized by confusion as much as he was by the pain in his leg.

Ken Cameron had found Chloe Dolan, and the man who was responsible for taking her: Frank 'Percy' Donovan.

And instead of calling it in, the police officer had shot the unarmed man in the stomach.

*What the fuck is going on?*

Freddie's first instinct was to call Veronica but worried that she was hiding somewhere in the darkness, and not wanting to tip off her position, he decided to call the captain instead.

No answer.

Chloe had stopped screaming now, but Percy's painful wails were more than enough cover for Freddie to leave a message, telling the captain where he was, and that Chloe was there.

"Shut up," Ken shouted at Percy. "Just shut the fuck up!"

And then, for some reason, the convicted sex offender listened and fell silent. This just happened to coincide with Freddie signing off on his message.

Ken whirled around, leading with the gun.

"Who's there? Who the *fuck* is there?" There was a falsetto tremor in the man's voice, which didn't match the sheer fury on his red face. Freddie attempted to duck but there were few places a man of his size could actually hide. He thought about drawing his gun, but by the time he got it out, if Ken was inclined to fire, Freddie would already be riddled with holes.

He had his cell phone in his hand, so Freddie decided on the next best thing, something that ruined perhaps as many lives as bullets: to record a video.

"Who's there?" Ken demanded, moving away from Percy and toward the broken windows. "Who's—"

Another sound, this one not from Percy or Ken or even Chloe.

It was coming from the other side of the building.

It was Detective Veronica Shade, and unlike Freddie, what she held in her hand shot bullets and not video.

"What the hell are you doing, Veronica?" Freddie whispered. "What the hell are you doing?"

*\*\*\**

The interior of the building was suddenly illuminated by swirls of color in the dark. Most of the warm hues were coming off Ken, while the shades of blue were pouring out of Chloe Dolan.

Then there was the red. Only this wasn't a synesthetic projection; it was blood leaking out of the bullet hole in Percy's midsection.

"What the—what the fuck are you doing here?" Ken demanded.

"It was—it was just a hunch," Veronica lied. "But you found her! You found Chloe!"

Veronica, trying her best to pretend as if she hadn't overheard Ken's comments moments ago, hurried to the girl, who was secured to a support structure.

"It's going to be alright, Chloe," she whispered. The girl, still bound and gagged, moved her head spastically. "I'm a cop—you're going to be okay. Just hang in there."

That's when Veronica realized that Chloe also had earplugs jammed in her ears. She was in the process of trying to dig one of them out when Ken spoke.

"How did you know I was here?"

Veronica replied without turning.

"We got a tip that someone named Percy was behind this and figured out that the man's real name is Franklin Donovan. This is one of his favorite hangouts."

When there was no immediate reply, Veronica feared the worst. She stopped fussing and slowly turned as she rose to her feet.

She wasn't surprised to see that Ken was pointing the gun at her now.

"You traced my car, didn't you?"

Veronica did her best to appear shocked.

"No, I didn't even know you were—"

"How long were you standing there, Veronica?"

"I ran in as soon as I heard the shot," she lied. "Put the gun down. Please, Ken, you're scaring me."

Ken said nothing and Veronica gestured to Chloe who was still seated on the concrete floor behind her.

"We gotta get her out of here, Ken. And we need to get help for Percy."

"Fuck Percy," Ken spat. Veronica didn't like the look on his face. It reminded her of that night after the Christmas party. "You're a shitty liar, Veronica. A shitty fucking liar."

"What? What are you talking about? Ken, call for help. Now."

"I don't think so. Drop the gun, Veronica."

"What?"

"I said, drop your gun."

"Ken, whatever happened between us, it's not—"

"Drop the fucking gun or I'll put a bullet in you just like I did Percy!"

Veronica continued to play dumb but was fearful that Ken would actually shoot her. She slowly put the gun on the ground and held both hands out in front of her.

"Okay, just calm down. I don't understand what's going on here?"

"You don't, huh?" Ken mocked. "You don't understand what's going on? Really? When it's all your fault?"

"M-my fault?"

"Yes, your fault!" Ken shouted aggressively. "If you weren't such a bitch—fucking leading me on for months, none of this would have happened."

"Please, just put the gun down and we can talk about it."

Ken didn't appear to hear her.

"You think you're so fucking good, so much better than everyone else—just shaking your tits and ass to make your way to the top. You flirt with me, lead me on, only to reject me? Reject *me?*" Ken pointed at himself with the muzzle of his gun. "I deserve to be detective, not you. *Me*. I worked my ass off but just because my daddy isn't the boss, I'm stuck here, dealing with filth like Percy." Now he pointed at Chloe. "And that cunt? *Phhh*. She's just like you. Too good for me, huh? Well, I guess she regrets that decision, now. What do you think?"

Chloe, who Veronica doubted could hear any more than just mumbling with the plugs jammed so deeply in her ears, moaned softly.

Veronica decided that now was the time to drop the act.

"How did you think this was going to end, Ken?"

"What?"

"You set a deranged sexual predator after Chloe—did you really think he would stop at notes? Are you that fucking stupid?"

Ken's eyes darted to Percy, who was still rolling on the ground.

"Shut up," he warned. But Veronica was on a roll—gun or no gun, she wasn't stopping now.

"I bet you didn't even plan this. I bet you found Percy by accident. Now, what? Let Percy die? Save Chloe? You think that's going to get you the promotion?"

"It's not a bad idea," Ken said, a touch defensively. "And it would have fucking worked, too."

"Yeah, maybe—probably not, but maybe. Except you didn't count on me, did you? I'm going to tell everyone what you've done."

Ken extended his lower jaw and sneered.

"*You*? Who's going to believe *you*? After how crazy you were acting, telling everyone that your boyfriend Dylan Hall isn't our guy. Letting him go, getting suspended... and everyone knows you go see that shrink all the fucking time. They aren't going to believe shit."

"You don't think so?" Veronica challenged, feeling her anger start to rise. "You don't think my dad will at least listen to what I have to say?"

"I-I—" Ken cocked his head and aimed the gun at Veronica's chest. "Maybe you're right. On second thought, maybe it is better if I just got rid of—"

The figure behind Officer Cameron moved, blocking out most of the light coming in through the broken windows.

Ken fell like a stone, his legs buckling beneath him, the gun scattering on the concrete. Veronica, who had seen the big man slowly approaching as she egged Ken on, sprang to action. She kicked the gun aside, then grabbed her own and pointed it at her fallen colleague.

"Ah, you fat fuck," Ken groaned, clutching the back of his head.

Veronica ignored the insult and turned to her partner.

"You have your cuffs?"

Freddie nodded and passed them to her. Veronica was about to cuff Ken when she heard a moan from behind her. She looked at Percy, still bleeding, about ten feet from Officer Cameron.

"Can you drag him over here? Next to Percy?"

Freddie reached down and roughly grabbed Ken by the neck. The man cried out as he was pulled across the concrete to Percy's side.

"You're both filth." Veronica cuffed the men together. When she saw Freddie's expression she added, "They're in this together, so it only makes sense to handcuff them to one another."

Satisfied that neither man was going anywhere, Veronica rushed to Chloe next. She removed the earplugs, then tore off her blindfold and gag.

As the first of what would soon become many sirens pierced the night air, Veronica hugged Chloe Dolan.

"You're safe now," Veronica said, closing her eyes to the swirls of blue surrounding them both. "You're safe now, Chloe."

# Chapter 59

AS A PRECAUTION, CHLOE DOLAN was going to be taken to the hospital, but the EMS could find nothing physically wrong with the girl. The one good thing that Ken had done was get to Percy before he had a chance to have his way with Chloe.

Percy himself was a different story. Shot in the stomach, EMS postulated that there was a high probability of survival. Stomach wounds bled profusely but took a long time to kill. It was suggested that Percy would likely be shitting through a bag for the rest of his life, a life that Veronica hoped was behind bars.

Ken predictably tried to argue that it was all a mistake, a mix-up, but Freddie had video evidence to the contrary. That shut him up pretty quick, for which Veronica was grateful. She never wanted to hear the man's voice again.

Among the first cops to arrive was her father, but Veronica had already started to extricate herself from the scene.

Crowds and synesthesia didn't get along.

Captain Peter Shade found her with her back up against her car. He didn't say anything, at least not at first. He just leaned beside her, making the Audi rock on its axles. There was a cigarette between his lips, but it wasn't lit.

"This is going to be a shit show," Peter said after a minute. "Don't get me wrong, I'm grateful, V. Everyone's grateful, including Randy. But... Ken Cameron? A cop?"

Veronica remained silent.

It was hard for her to believe, too, and she'd seen it in the flesh. Ken Cameron, passed over for a promotion, shoots his shot at Veronica and misses badly. Drunk and scorned, he approaches Chloe and her friends next. Once again, shot down and ridiculed.

Can't get it out of his head. Arrests Percy, comes up with a plan to get them all back, including Dylan Hall who was, in Ken's mind, Veronica's 'boyfriend'.

It was a perfect plan.

It was a terrible plan.

"There's going to be some blowback from this, coming in your direction," Captain Shade informed her.

Veronica wasn't surprised by this. Ken had blamed her and would continue to blame her until the moment his sentence was passed down. There were a lot of people who liked Ken, in the PD, and elsewhere.

Some of them would inevitably follow the man's lead.

"I know," Veronica said softly. "And I don't care."

Peter chuckled. It had been a while since she'd heard her father laugh.

"I figured as much. You manage to get in to see Jane at all?"

"That's personal."

The man chuckled again. A second outburst of emotion was exceedingly rare, and Veronica chalked this up to heightened tensions from the case.

She also thought that this was the man's way of saying thanks.

"Still smoking?" Veronica asked, eyes drifting to the cigarette that dangled from between Peter's lips.

The captain stared straight ahead, likely focusing on Freddie, who was speaking to a handful of Internal Affairs officers. Once again, Veronica was grateful for the man. She wasn't sure if her partner liked to do the things she hated or just did them because Veronica despised them so much.

He'd also saved her life—there was that, too.

Veronica made a mental reminder to grab Freddie some KFC or something equally as unhealthy as a thank you.

*Dad says thank you by laughing, you say thank you by clogging arteries.*

"Good thing I am." Peter pulled the cigarette from his mouth and held it in two fingers.

Veronica raised an eyebrow, wondering how he was going to spin this.

"What do you mean?"

"Well, remember our agreement?"

And then Veronica understood.

"You'd quit smoking if I gave up the Ken Cameron crusade."

"*Uh-huh.* Looks like there's something good that came out of this disgusting habit."

"As long as you admit that it's disgusting. But now that the case is behind us…"

"Last one, promise." Peter patted first his breast pocket then his pants'. "You wouldn't happen to have a light, would you?"

Veronica tapped her pockets like her father.

"Nope. Can't help you there."

Her cell phone was in her left pocket, as were her keys, but she felt a small, unfamiliar bulge in her right. She was in the process of teasing the object out when her dad leaned over and said, "Good work tonight, V. Now, go take some time off. You deserve it."

*Jesus, he must have really been feeling the pressure from this case,* Veronica thought. Before she could say thank you, her dad was gone, walking toward Freddie and the other officers in search of a lighter.

Veronica slid the item out of her pocket. It was a piece of paper, folded in half.

*What the hell is this?*

But part of her, deep down, knew what the note was.

And what it would say.

She opened the torn rectangle and looked down at two letters, written in black ink.

*MO.*

Her heart skipped a beat. In her mind, she pictured the Oregon map she'd drawn back at her house. The one that Sheriff Steve Burns had added to when Veronica had been gone.

It was the same writing—*DAVIS* and *MO.*

Same black pen, same capital letters.

The sheriff was the only one who could have put the note in her pocket.

It was him.

It had been him all along.

Veronica's eyes drifted to her father, who was smoking next to Freddie. She wanted to ask him about Grant, about why the names had been redacted.

But that would have to wait.

Because someone was waiting for her—Sheriff Steve Burns was at the Davis' house, the site of Trent's and Herb's final massacre.

He was going to finally finish his twisted nursery rhyme.

And Veronica was the final piece.

She was *MO.*

# Chapter 60

NIGHT ROLLED IN DURING Veronica's drive from Sullivan to East Argham. By the time she found the Davis' home, she could barely see it. Most of the outer walls were covered in soot and coated in twenty years of neglect. Some of the windows had been broken, but most were boarded up.

Veronica spotted the sheriff's car almost immediately—he wasn't even trying to hide it. It was parked by the side of the road, across the street from the house, and Veronica did two laps around the block just to make sure that she wasn't going to be blindsided.

This was a trap, of course. Unlike Ken Cameron, who was guided by his dick and his pride, Steve was smart. Steve was calculated.

And Steve was a murderer.

The sheriff wanted her here, the final piece to his macabre plan. Veronica had slept with him, fed him information, and compromised the case, all by herself.

It was only fitting that she was here alone.

Veronica parked out of sight and turned off the car. Then she glanced down at the note that she'd found in her pocket.

*MO.*

She balled it up and threw it on the passenger seat. Then Veronica took out her phone, set it to silent, and placed it in the glove box.

Sheriff Steve Burns was smart, but Veronica was smarter. She'd known it was him long before the note.

She'd known it when he'd first lied to her about being familiar with the librarian Maggie Cernak.

For the second time that night, Veronica drew her gun and started toward an abandoned building. The closer she got, the faster her heart raced. What was left of the exterior bricks was marred by black stains, but Veronica soon started to notice yellow, and orange mixed in with the black. It was as if the bricks themselves were bleeding, the mortar acting as veins and arteries that pumped yellow, orange, and red threads. Before long, the bricks were completely engulfed in a splash of fiery watercolors.

Extreme violence had occurred here. Veronica was unfamiliar with the Davis case, but she knew that people had died in this house. She didn't know how many, but she guessed a man, a woman, and a child.

There would be one survivor.

*EENIE, MEENIE, MINEY, MO.*

It ended here. It ended now.

Veronica silently moved to the front of the house and peered in through one of the blown-out windows. It was dark inside but not pitch. She was about to pull back, to go searching for a less obvious place to enter, when she spotted something.

A sleeping bag and a pillow.

Sheriff Burns was sleeping here?

Veronica knew that the man didn't want to stay in the same place that Maggie had hung, but here?

*Only when he wasn't in your bed, Veronica.*

She pulled away from the window, and headed around the back of the house, staying low, quiet, and ready.

The rear facade was in much better shape, suggesting that the fire had started toward the front.

Toward the area that the sheriff now called his bedroom.

There was a gap between the door and frame, the former of which had been long since knocked from true.

*Where are you, you piece of shit?*

By turning her body sideways, Veronica managed to fit through without touching anything. Her cop instincts took over, and she systematically cleared the back rooms, which was fairly easy on account of them being empty. There was further evidence of someone living here—in the kitchen, torn Ramen packages, as well as at least half a dozen empty beer cans, dotted the warped countertop—but the sheriff's tenure didn't appear to be a long-standing one.

Just when Veronica was beginning to think that perhaps he wasn't here, or maybe Steve was outside, watching her, she heard something: a muffled noise like someone breathing heavily into a pillow.

Veronica pressed her back against the nearest wall, protecting her six, as she slowly advanced toward the sound.

She heard it again, louder this time.

It was coming from the front of the house, near the area where she'd spotted the sleeping bag. The kitchen was separated from the front room by an arched doorway, but with her back against the far wall, her angle was off, and she couldn't see much of anything.

The sound, this time not just louder but also more panicked, drove Veronica onward. She lunged into the room, her finger shifting from the trigger guard to the trigger.

And she nearly shot Sheriff Steve Burns in the face.

"Wh—wh-what the fuck?"

Her hand trembled and the gun wavered.

If this had been a trap set by the sheriff, something had gone terribly wrong.

The man was on his knees, sitting on duct-taped ankles, a dirty rag forced into his mouth. His hands were behind him, also duct-taped together.

Blood trickled from above his left eye and ran down his face.

"Steve?"

The man's eyes flicked in her direction, and when Steve saw her, he made that sound again, an attempted shout into the dirty fabric.

It was an incompressible stream of terror.

"*Mmmphhhhfff! Mpppppphhhhhhhfff!*"

It grew louder and the man tried to stand but was unable to. Veronica just stared, unsure of what to do, of what was happening.

Then the sheriff's eyes moved from her face to above her left shoulder.

Veronica started to turn, but she was too late. Something hard and heavy came down the back of her neck and the kaleidoscope of oranges, yellows, and reds decayed into an infinite blackness.

# Chapter 61

DETECTIVE FRED FURLOW SPOTTED VERONICA get into her car. He waved to her, thinking that she just wanted to be away from the crowd.

But she didn't appear to even notice him.

His next thought as he watched his partner drive by, was that this whole Ken Cameron thing had gotten to her, that she felt partially responsible for what had happened to Chloe.

But that didn't seem right either. Veronica looked scared.

"You know why Veronica left?" Freddie asked Captain Shade who was still by his side.

The man exhaled a cloud of blue smoke.

"Not sure. She's earned some time off, though."

Freddie didn't disagree, but Veronica had no understanding of the meaning of time off. No, this was something else.

He could feel it in his chest, like angina after a heavy meal.

"You okay here?" he asked the captain.

The man took another drag of his smoke.

"You've earned some time off, too, Fred."

"Thanks."

Freddie was almost at his car when someone called his name.

"Detective Furlow!"

Not recognizing the voice, he turned in a guarded fashion. It wasn't a fellow detective, officer, or even IA.

It was a Bear County Deputy. He had a round face but a solid body, and while he looked familiar, Freddie was too tired to recall either his name or where they'd met.

"Deputy McVeigh," the man reminded him with a handshake.

Now Freddie remembered.

"We met at the sheriff's barn, right?"

"Yep. Once Bear County heard about Chloe Dolan, we sent every deputy we had out into the field. Glad you found her in one piece. Hey, is it true that Detective Shade saved her? That it was a cop who was stalking the young girl this whole time?"

"Something like that," Freddie confirmed. He'd already gone over the story so many times with his union rep and internal affairs, that he didn't feel like saying it again. He looked past the deputy. "Speaking of the sheriff, is he around?"

Deputy McVeigh shook his head.

"Naw, he was doing some publicity stuff at the park, then he took off."

Freddie's eyes widened.

*That's right. He called me from there, asked me to —*

The conversation with the sheriff came roaring back, but it was the one that Freddie had with Dylan Hall that gave him pause.

"Did he go to the Davis' house?"

The deputy made a face.

"The... Davis' house? I don't know about that. I do know that it had something to do with the suicides. Something about a place in East Argham." The man finished his comment with a shrug.

*Looks like the sheriff is as good at keeping secrets as Veronica.*

"When did he leave?"

"An hour ago? He sent a tech up there earlier in the day to check the place out. I think they might have found something."

Freddie reached out and grabbed both of the man's arms, digging his thick fingers into the deputy's triceps.

"Which tech?"

The deputy made a face and looked down at his arms, but Freddie didn't let go.

"What's the tech's name?"

"I dunno—it's the new guy we used on the two suicide cases."

"What is his fucking name, deputy?"

McVeigh didn't strike Freddie as a man who appreciated being bullied, but the desperation in the detective's voice convinced him to answer.

"Holland. His name is Holland Toler."

All Freddie could think about as he sped toward East Argham, was what Dylan Hall had said when he'd asked him what Benjamin Davis had changed his name to.

*He was named after a country or some shit…*

A country… a country like Holland.

Benjamin Davis was Holland Toler.

# Chapter 62

SINGING. THE FIRST THING VERONICA heard was singing.

*La, la, la, la, laaaaa, laaa.*

She opened her eyes, not sure where she was and why she couldn't move.

A smothered shout cut through the song. Sheriff Steve Burns was beside her, bound and gagged.

"Steve?" she tried to say, but her tongue touched something foul, and she sucked it back into her mouth.

Like the sheriff, she too was gagged.

Instead of speaking, Veronica nudged Steve with her foot. She knew the man felt this, but he refused to look at her.

The singing stopped and Veronica heard a sloshing sound now. This was quickly followed by the stench of gasoline.

There was someone else in the room. A tall, lean man, wearing dark jeans and a light blue T-shirt. Veronica was still rattled from whatever had robbed her of consciousness, and she wasn't sure if what she saw was real or imagined.

The man was bald, and the skin on the back of his head and neck was rumpled, like that of an elephant.

Before Veronica could make sense of this, she saw the red jerry can in the man's hand.

"You don't remember, do you?" the man asked.

Unable to do much more, Veronica shook her head.

"Well, then maybe this will help."

The man swiveled his hips, and the next splash of gas wasn't on the floor or walls but struck Veronica directly in the face.

\*\*\*

*Gas.*

The stench of gasoline was so powerful that Lucy's eyes started to water. The skinnier of the two men was spraying it on the furniture, the floor, the walls, and even on the couch around which Lucy and the rest of her family sat. They'd been arranged in descending size—she was at one end, followed by her brother Benny, then by her mom, and dad.

"Don't look so worried, little one," the bigger man, the one who had grabbed her and hit her father in the head, said. He had horrible, brown teeth. "No one's going to get hurt. We're just playing a game. Trust me."

He was lying.

Lucy knew he was lying. And every breath of the gas that burned first her nose, then her lungs, confirmed this fact.

The big man turned to face his partner.

"We're just playing a game, aren't we, Herb? Ain't no one gonna get hurt."

Herb giggled a high-pitched sound that made Lucy cringe.

"We sure are," he answered after his tittering ceased. "Just playin' a game…"

***

"You remember now?" the man asked.

Veronica, who must have passed out again, felt her head loll and snapped awake.

The man in the blue shirt was still there, still standing with his back to both her and the sheriff. Based on the shadow, the jerry can was nearly empty. Yet, despite the impending danger, Veronica's eyes were locked on the man's shirt. It had been a light blue, was still mostly a light blue, but where he was sweating, the cotton was dotted with patches of dark color. The odd, almost tie-dye characteristic of these stains and their patterns was mesmerizing. And as Veronica's vision waned, it was almost as if the blue extended beyond the borders of the fabric.

\*\*\*

"When I was a kid, I used to play this game all the time," the man with the foul teeth told them. "I used to play it with my dad and brother. And the loser? Well, my dad would put his cigarette out on the loser's—"

Trevor Davis suddenly leaped from the couch. No one suspected this—after he'd been knocked out trying to escape, Lucy hadn't even thought her father had woken up yet. His hands were taped behind his back, so he attacked with his shoulder, driving it forward until it collided with the man's chin. They both went sprawling, and the man's arms flew above his head, revealing dark blue sweat stains in both armpits.

"Run! *Run!*" someone yelled, her mom, probably—but Lucy couldn't run. She could only stare. Tears filled her eyes now, making the sweat stains on the man's blue shirt waver and dance. It almost seemed as if they extended beyond his body like spilled blue ink.

"Run!"

Lucy's father was doing everything he could to give them a chance to escape, and they just watched.

The big man recovered quickly.

He picked Trevor Davis up and threw him onto the couch so hard that Lucy thought it was going to topple. Her father immediately tried to get up, to attack again, but blue shirt was on him.

He delivered a punch to the side of Trevor's face—a heavy blow. Lucy had seen this happen in the movies, and the victim always staggered or stumbled before making a quick recovery.

Not so in real life.

Trevor's eyes rolled back, he elicited a low moan and didn't move again.

When Lucy turned back to face the man who had broken into their home, tears were spilling down her cheeks.

The man's shirt no longer looked sweat-stained, but like a melted blue candle, dripping down her entire field of vision.

\*\*\*

"I looked for you, Veronica. For years, I looked for you *everywhere*. But someone changed your name, and they did their best to hide your identity. Imagine my surprise when you showed up here."

The man stepped forward and Veronica saw that his skin wasn't rumpled but scarred. Burns covered most of his neck and scalp.

"I thought you would recognize me right away. In fact, I thought you did, the way you reacted at the barn. But... no. And I was offended—really, how could you not remember me?"

Veronica's mind was swimming, caught between the past, a memory, a police file, a nursery rhyme, and the present.

*Suicide... murder... gas...*

The man cocked his head and then brought the thumb and forefinger of his right hand to his face. He pinched his eye, pulling a contact lens free and tossing it to the ground. He repeated this with his other eye.

"Still don't remember me, do you?"

Veronica looked away, not wanting to see the man's face.

"No," she moaned through the gag. "No, this isn't... it's not real."

Beside her, she heard the sheriff mumble something incoherent, and shift his weight.

"It's real," the man taunted, somehow having understood her.

Veronica shook her head violently.

"Oh, it's real. Maybe this will remind you."

And then, as tears began to stream down Veronica's cheeks, the man with the burns began to sing.

\*\*\*

"Close your eyes, Benny and Lucy. Don't look at their faces!" Roberta Davis pleaded. "Just—whatever you do, don't look."

The skinny man, the one called Herb, laughed. Lucy hated that sound.

"Ah, don't be shy. Ain't no one gettin' hurt."

Lucy closed her eyes so tightly that she saw flashes of light behind her lids.

"Don't listen to them either, don't listen to their voices," her mom sobbed. When her comment was met with additional laughter, she implored more aggressively. "If you can't identify them, they'll let you go. So, sing, Benny. Sing! Please just sing…"

And then, inexplicably, Benny started to sing. It was a stupid song, the one that he always sang when he was bullying her.

Lucy hated the song. But she hated these men and that laughter even more.

"*La, la, la, la, laaaaa, laaa.*"

More laughter and Benny raised his voice, more shouting now than singing.

At any moment, Lucy expected the big man with the sweat stains to punch her brother as he had her dad, but instead, he sang along with Benny.

She opened her eyes and saw that both men were singing now.

*"La, la, la, la, laaaaa, laaa. La, la, la, la, laaaaa, laaa."*

It kept getting louder and louder until it reached a near-deafening crescendo. It was like the roar of a drumroll during a dramatic movie scene. And then at the very height of its volume, it would stop, in anticipation of a catastrophic event.

Lucy wasn't sure if she wanted it to end. She despised the sound but feared what came next even more.

The man with the brown teeth suddenly looked at her, and only her.

"Oh, don't be sad, little one. It's all just a game," the man said.

*Liar! You're lying! This isn't a game! Look at my dad! He's bleeding! And the gas... there's gas everywhere. I smell it, I can even taste it. It's not a game. Not a game... something bad is going to happen. The music stopped... something really bad is about to happen. Something worse than what you did to daddy.*

"Are you ready, Herb? You ready to play?"

"I'm always ready, Trent. Always ready to play the game."

\*\*\*

Veronica whimpered and she tried to speak, but the gag made it impossible.

The man stepped forward and she cringed, expecting to be struck. The blow never came. Instead, the gag was wrenched from her mouth.

"You recognize me now, don't you, Lucy?"

"You're dead," Veronica managed between sobs. "You're dead. I know you're dead."

"No, little sister, I'm not dead," the man whom Veronica had known as Holland Toler said. And when she looked into his eyes and saw the gold flecks in his irises, so distinct and yet similar to hers, she knew that the only gas she smelled was that which he'd spilled all around them. "I *lived*. You wanted me to die, Lucy, but I didn't. Those idiots Trent Alberts and Herb Thornton? They fucked up. They'd hung the Davenports and shot the Heschs. And with Wilkes? Hell, those poor bastards had been injected with enough heroin to kill ten families. But they fucked up with us—with the Davises. The fire they started burned too hot, too fast. They barely made it out with you in their arms. You wanted me to die, Lucy... but I didn't." Benjamin Davis ran a hand over his rough, burnt scalp. "Sometimes I wish I had, but I didn't."

"I-I didn't—" Veronica broke down. "I didn't want you to die, Benny. I didn't want anyone to die. I didn't have a choice."

Her brother cocked his head. When he spoke next, his voice was deep, his words slow.

"You didn't have a choice? Really? You were the only one who had the choice, Lucy. Maybe I need to jog your memory a little more. How about this: eenie, meenie, miney, *mo*." With 'Mo', Benjamin Davis pointed a finger directly at Veronica's chest.

\*\*\*

"The game's simple." Trent was like a kindergarten teacher outlining the ABCs. "You've probably even played it before."

"Can I do it?" Herb whined. "Please, can I do it?"

Trent looked over his shoulder and nodded.

"Sure. Why not?"

"Yes!" Herb dropped the now empty jerry can to the ground. Then he clapped his hands together and extended a pair of long, wet fingers at Lucy's father, who was still unconscious. "Here we go! Eenie, meenie, miney, mo." He moved his finger to the next person in line with every word. Lucy cringed every time he pointed at her. "Catch a tiger by the toe, if he hollers let him go." Both men were smiling now—grinning madly. "Eenie... meenie... miney... *mo.*"

Lucy cried out when the final word ended with Herb's finger aimed directly at her.

"Oh, don't you worry," Trent said, still smiling. "You're the lucky one. You get to choose."

"Leave her alone," Roberta screamed. "Leave her the *fuck* alone!"

Lucy froze—she had never heard her mother swear before. Not ever.

"We're fair people, Herb and I." Trent said, speaking slowly now. "I just want you to have a chance to play the game like I did with my dad. Only we don't use cigarettes, do we, Herb?"

"No, we don't."

"And you get to pick, little one. Are you going to do what little Amy and Tracy did—are you going to pick yourself? It was different with Anthony. His dad won that game, and of course, he chose his son. Kinda boring and predictable if you ask me—I really wanted him to pick his wife. But, hey, it's your turn, now. Who are you going to pick, Lucy Davis?"

Lucy didn't understand.

"Pick... pick for what?"

Trent's grin grew to impossible proportions.

"Haven't you been paying attention? You get to pick which member of your family survives, little one. *Eenie, meenie, miney, mo,* you get to pick the only person besides me and Herb who gets to leave this house alive."

***

"You remember now," Benny whispered. "I *know* you remember."

And she did. Repressed memories came flooding back in horrible waves. Everything that had happened before she'd been adopted by Peter Shade was front and center in her mind now.

Her dad, Trevor Davis, always goofing around, pranking her. Her mother, Roberta, proper to a fault, caring but strict. And her brother, her annoying, teasing brother, who pretended like he didn't care but always stood up for her when it really mattered.

"I was a kid," Veronica protested. "Just a little fucking kid. What was I supposed to do? If I didn't pick, they would have killed us all. Th-th-they said that."

"The will to survive is ingrained at birth, Lucy. Young or not, you had a choice. And you chose yourself."

Veronica closed her eyes again, unwilling to look at the man whom she'd thought died more than twenty years ago. Her brother, Benjamin Davis, whom she'd sentenced to death when she'd broken down and told Trent Alberts that she wanted to live.

"I'm-I'm so sorry, Benny. I-I didn't... I couldn't..."

Veronica heard the sound of a match sparking to life and her eyes snapped open.

"No, please. Benny, don't make me choose. Not again." The words just flowed out of her.

Benny Davis was holding a match, still attached to the matchbook, in front of his face. The orange flame glowed impossibly brightly between his fingers.

"You already made your choice once, Lucy. You don't get another chance. Now it's my turn. And this time, no one leaves alive. Eenie, meenie, miney, *mo*."

With *Mo*, Benny touched the match to his shirt and Veronica had a moment to think that, unlike with Trent Alberts', the stains on her brother's shirt weren't sweat.

They were gas.

Benny Davis was smiling as he erupted into flames.

# Chapter 63

VERONICA SCREAMED. BESIDE HER, SHERIFF Burns tried to rise, but with his feet taped and having been sitting on his heels for so long, he couldn't manage to get up.

Benny Davis was drenched in fire but somehow, during all of this, he managed to continue to stare at her. The man's gold-speckled eyes were locked on Veronica even as the flames consumed first his clothes, then his flesh.

Steve shook and bucked until the gag fell away from his mouth and slid down his throat.

"You have to get out!" The sheriff spat something foul on the floor. "Veronica, you need to get out!"

Only the idea of Benny's eyes remained now; the blaze had degenerated from a human form to a less distinguishable shape as the walls that still had substance began to ignite. And the smoke... it was becoming thicker and more dense, difficult to see through.

Veronica didn't move. She didn't want to leave.

This was her fate.

This was the origin of her synesthesia, her brain's way of dealing with trauma that her consciousness had all but deleted.

She was going to die in this fire with her mom and dad and brother like she should have all those years ago.

She didn't deserve to live, let alone to choose who died.

*Eenie, meenie, miney, mo, who survives, only little Lucy knows.*

There was a soft thump as what was left of Benny Davis collapsed to the floor, further spreading the fire.

"Veronica! *Veronica!*"

Sheriff Burns was coughing so hard, deep wracking coughs, that he was barely able to shout her name. In her periphery, Veronica saw that Steve, like Benny, had fallen and was now lying face down on the floor. His legs and feet were moving, but for some reason, Steve couldn't roll onto his back and stand.

"Veronica... *Verrrooonicaaa...*"

She was coughing now, too, and the flames were no longer confined to the walls. They had destroyed Benny and now ignited the gasoline that the man had splashed about the room.

A thought—an inexplicable thought—suddenly crossed Veronica's mind.

She'd been wrong.

Her claim that Maggie and Sarah had been murdered was incorrect.

They *had* committed suicide. Holland Toler—Benny, his name is Benjamin Davis—had delivered notes to them, reminding them of what they'd done. Of the choice they'd made.

And Veronica's note? She'd been convinced that Steve had put it in her pocket, that it could have only been the sheriff. But that wasn't true; Veronica had gone to the morgue to visit Kristin Newberry, but the woman hadn't been there. Holland had been, however, and that was when he must have slipped the note into her pocket.

Had he done the same thing with Maggie and Sarah? Was that all it took? A simple reminder of the horrible, devastating choice that they'd been forced to make? Or was it somehow tied to Trent Alberts' upcoming execution?

Both women had gone to great lengths to reinvent themselves, to move on. But based on how Veronica was feeling now, she understood that recalling repressed memories was a disorienting and overwhelming feeling.

And then there was her visit to the despicable Trent Alberts on death row. He wasn't saying that the sheriff knew how the survivors had been chosen, but that she—*Veronica*—knew.

Somewhere far away, Veronica could feel the air in her lungs start to boil. Her mind was racing and incoherent on account of the lack of oxygen.

*I'm sorry, Mom, I'm sorry, Dad.*

*I'm sorry, Benny.*

There was pressure beneath her arms and Veronica felt her limp body being dragged across the floor.

*That's my soul leaving my body. Will I go to Hell for what I did? Or will God understand? Will he forgive me, just a child, for choosing to live and for the rest of my family to die?*

The coarse plywood floor gave way to something softer.

*Grass? Could it be grass?*

Veronica, now sitting up, stared at the house where she'd spent the first few years of her life. It was completely engulfed in dancing red, orange, and yellow flames.

Someone stepped between her and the fire—a young man in a police uniform, thick, strong. He had a serious but somehow also kind face.

"You're going to be okay, sweetie. My name's Peter, Peter Shade, and you're going to be okay."

Lucy leaned to one side, trying to see around the police officer. She was transfixed by the house, the hypnotic, destructive nature of the fire that completely disguised the violence that was trapped therein.

Smothering it, burying it, locking it away.

"Veronica? *Veronica!* Please—please say something."

Big hands shook her shoulders.

"*Please!*"

Veronica tried to speak but opening her mouth caused a cloud of smoke to irritate her throat and she broke into a coughing fit.

"It's okay—an ambulance is on its way."

It wasn't Peter now, but Freddie. He reached beneath her arms and tried to pull her further from the burning house, but Veronica dug her heels in.

"No," she managed to croak between coughs. "Benny's still in there. My brother is still in there!"

# Chapter 64

"CHILDHOOD TRAUMA CAN SHAPE WHO we are, even if we don't remember it."

Veronica looked down at her hands and massaged the burns. Her skin was improving, and the doctors had promised her that after a few months it was unlikely that anyone would be able to tell that she'd been in a fire.

But while her external wounds would heal, the internal ones might not.

Not this time, anyway.

"I just... I just don't understand how I could have forgotten *everything*. I mean, I met my own brother and I-I-I didn't recognize him. Even when I walked into that house, I didn't recognize it. How is that possible?"

Dr. Jane Bernard leaned forward, and Veronica looked up from her hands.

"For a moment, let's ignore the fact that these events took place more than twenty years ago. Veronica, our minds protect us from extreme violence and emotional damage. It's like your hands—the scabbing, the scarring. These processes are designed to protect us, to stop the pain and start the healing. Your mind is no different. It blocks things out, places a wall around memories so they can't continue to hurt us. The drive to survive is incredibly powerful, and if our memories and past trauma put that in jeopardy, well, sometimes we forget."

Veronica chewed the inside of her cheek, trying not to think of Benny who had said something similar right before he set himself alight.

"When I finally remembered what I'd done, the first thing that came to mind was the gas that Herb Thornton was splashing around the room while Trent reassured me that nothing bad was going to happen. Then it was Trent's blue shirt, covered in sweat as he fought with my dad. Then the singing —Benny was singing, trying to transport himself elsewhere. Finally, the fire… the dancing fire. I remember that most of all —sitting on the grass staring at the flames. They were beautiful, in a way, and I liked them because they blocked my view of the horrors inside the house."

Jane nodded.

"Most cases of synesthesia are developmental, but there are reports of trauma-induced cases. PTSD, mostly. And when you saw the girl in your elementary school, the one who later committed suicide? Your brain recognized a pattern of lying and impending violence, based on your earlier experience as a child. But instead of surfacing painful memories, your mind chose to show you more abstract patterns."

Veronica closed her eyes, trying not to think of the girl in the bathroom.

There was a short pause, and then Jane, as deftly as a surgeon replacing an artery, segued into something a little different.

"Have you spoken to your father about what happened?"

"You mean about what happened with Chloe Dolan?"

Jane gave her a curious look and shook her head.

"No, I mean about your past, about what happened after he found you in front of your childhood home."

Veronica, feeling ashamed, averted her eyes.

As usual, Freddie had taken care of most of the paperwork from that night. And he was an expert at including just enough details to satisfy their superiors without invading her privacy.

Her father knew, of course. The nurses told Veronica that he'd visited her in the hospital, but she'd been so drugged up that she didn't remember. He'd tried to call her multiple times since, but Veronica had ignored him.

"I think you should talk to him, Veronica. I think you should hear his side of the story."

"You mean ask Peter why he lied to me for twenty years?"

Jane was unmoved by her sudden anger.

"That's exactly what I mean. Ask him, speak to him."

Veronica considered this for a moment.

"Maybe I will. Maybe I will."

The moment Veronica stepped out of Dr. Jane Bernard's office, Freddie rose to his feet. After the fire, the detective insisted on driving her everywhere, even though she was still on leave and wasn't expected back at work for at least another month and maybe more. Veronica implored that this wasn't necessary, but her partner was having none of it.

"You wanna go for coffee or something? An organic vegan egg white gluten-free wrap?"

Freddie seemed nervous as they walked toward his car.

"What's going on?"

The man stared at his toes.

"I looked into the sheriff like you asked. Steve is a —"

Veronica held out her hand, silencing her partner. If this case, if her life had taught her anything, it was the importance of trust.

"Thanks, but I don't want to know."

"You sure?"

"Yeah."

"Okay, okay," Freddie conceded. He looked pleased by her decision, even though he couldn't possibly understand her motivations. "Well, how about that wrap then? Or maybe we could stop by the precinct? Everyone's been asking about you. I'm not trying to rush your back or anything but—what? Why are you looking at me like that?"

It took Veronica several seconds to realize that she was actually smiling. The expression felt foreign on her face.

"You're freaking me out, Veronica. Why are you smiling?"

Veronica reached out and hugged the big man. Her arms barely made it halfway around his waist.

"I'm smiling because I just realized something," she said.

"What?"

Veronica let go of her friend and partner and looked up at his face.

"I finally found the one thing that you'd run for."

Freddie raised one eyebrow.

"Which is?"

Veronica hugged Freddie a second time, and she felt tears fill her eyes.

"*Me*. You ran for me, Freddie. You ran into the burning house to save *me*."

# Epilogue

"I'M NOT LYING, PETER, THIS steak is ridiculously good," Steve said, dabbing the grease from his lips with a napkin.

"I'm glad you enjoyed it. I wanted to age it for a hundred and twenty days but felt like this was a good enough occasion to pull it early. What do you think, V?"

"It's great, Dad," Veronica replied.

Her father eyed her suspiciously and then turned his attention back to Sheriff Steve Burns.

"How you holding up?"

Steve gently massaged his throat.

"I get these coughing fits every once in a while, but the doc says they'll go away eventually. My back's a mess—damn shirt melted right to my skin. But hey, I guess I earned my namesake now."

This was meant as a joke, Sheriff Burns with the burns, but nobody laughed.

Veronica stood and started to clear her plate.

"Let me give you a hand," Steve said.

Veronica placed her dish on the kitchen counter and then closed her eyes and took a deep breath. Steve came up behind her and put his arm on her shoulder.

"You okay?"

Veronica was about to nod but, at the last second, changed her mind and shook her head instead.

"I think I need a moment with my dad."

Steve nodded.

"Sure. I'll take care of the dishes."

Veronica found her father on the porch, smoking a cigarette.

"I thought you said you were done smoking?"

Peter shrugged and took a drag.

"Stressful time."

"I don't want you to end up like Grant."

Her father stopped smoking and looked at her.

"You went to see Grant?"

Veronica nodded. She'd been thinking of a way to broach the subject on the drive over, and this was the opening she needed. Now that the cat was out of the bag, it was time to let it scratch.

"Yeah, I saw him. He told me that you were the one who wanted Maggie Cernak's birth name redacted. Then, when I looked into the Davis tragedy, I…" Veronica couldn't finish her sentence.

Peter Shade reached into his pocket and pulled out a sheet of paper. He offered it to Veronica, and she took it.

It was the original police report from the Davis case. The only one that Veronica had come across to this point was a heavily redacted one. That report, which Sheriff Burns had given her, indicated that there was one survivor, a young boy who was badly burnt but somehow lived: Benjamin Davis. There was no mention of a second child, of Lucy Davis.

Of *her*.

The report that Peter handed her now was clean of blacked-out text. She read the report as her father smoked and talked.

"I was thirty years old when I found you outside, *V. Thirty*. And you were—God, you were staring at the fire, and you had this look on your face? Even back then I'd seen some pretty horrible things, but I had never seen a look like the one you had." Peter took a deep breath before continuing. "I went to visit you in the hospital, to see how you were doing? They said you were doing so well, that you didn't really remember much, if anything, about what happened in your home. But then they told me that you were going to be put in the system. Even though they said you were doing great, you still had that haunted look in your eyes, you know? So, I broke all the rules. I couldn't let you go into the system, and I decided to adopt you. It was a rash decision made during an emotional time. But once I had my mind made up about it, there was no stopping me, stubborn asshole that I am. I pulled in a few favors to expedite the process. Then, the whole Trent and Herb thing blew up. I knew that they were behind what happened to your family, and I thought that when the media found out, they'd tear you apart like they had with Amy and Tracy. The media would have chewed you up and spat out what was left of you."

Peter sighed and lit another cigarette, giving Veronica a moment to process what her father had told her.

*Pulled in a few favors...*

Grant—Grant had helped him bury her past. Veronica was reminded of the man in his delicate state, referring to her as *'Lou'*. It was the short form of Lucy, of course, but even the mention of her birth name wasn't enough to trigger memories.

Only seeing Benny had done that.

"The last thing I wanted was for you to be forever associated with that horrible crime. I spoke to the DA, and he told me that they had more than enough to put Trent away —maybe even give him the needle. So, I buried some of the information from your case, redacted the rest. Everything was great for years. You had no recollection of your past, and I wanted to keep it that way. But when the incident happened at school with that poor girl when you were ten or eleven? I got scared. I thought you were relapsing or something, and I panicked. Thought you'd find out about your past and everything that we both spent so long building together would collapse like a deck of cards in a strong wind. I reached out to Grant and asked him to retrospectively redact some of the information from Trent's and

Herb's other victims. I thought, what the hell, it might even help them, in case anybody came looking. True crime podcast, that sort of thing. Look, I'm not proud of what I did, *V*, especially about lying to you. But I was young, scared, and thought it was for the best."

Veronica wasn't sure how to react to her father's admissions. On one hand, she was furious at being deceived, but on the other, she understood why he'd acted the way he had.

"What happened to my brother? To Benny?"

Peter huffed. If admitting that lying to her had been difficult, what he was about to say next nearly broke the proud man.

"I didn't even know he was in there—I didn't know *anyone* was inside the house until much later. Your parents —they went quickly. But your brother was a survivor and he held on. It was touch and go for a while, but he made it. I thought about adopting him, too—I really did. But unlike you, he remembered everything. And Benjamin was having a hard time dealing with what happened. He had these fits —I'm sorry, shit, I'm so sorry. I couldn't do it, *V*. I couldn't raise both of you alone."

Veronica wiped the tears from her eyes.

"Did you ever—did you ever look into him?"

"Yeah," Peter admitted. "I did. For a while, I kept tabs on Benjamin. But places like Renaissance Home can be cruel, especially for someone like him, with his scars and no hair. He moved around a lot, and I lost track. I never, *ever* thought that he would come for you, V. I mean, your name had been changed and you lived a completely different life."

Veronica let her gaze drift from her father to the dark horizon. Neither of them said anything for several seconds. Eventually, Peter spoke up.

"They're going through with Trent's execution tonight," he informed her quietly. "Got word that the Governor is going to be indisposed and just let it happen. A sort of better to ask forgiveness than permission situation."

Veronica was about to say something, then shrugged.

She wasn't happy or elated. She felt nothing for Trent Alberts. And, perhaps, that's the way it should be.

"The past is boring—it's already happened," she said without thinking. "The future is far more interesting."

Veronica was speaking about Trent, but she was also talking about herself and her father.

Was this forgiveness for his deceit? Or was this just an olive branch?

She didn't know.

But either way, Veronica hugged her dad. She was surprised to see that he was crying.

"Thank you," she said.

Forgiven or not, the man had saved her and that was worth something.

Peter gave her a sad smile in return.

"Okay, V, let's get back to the sheriff before he breaks something."

After further extolling the virtues of the dinner, they parted, with the sheriff behind the wheel and Veronica in the passenger seat.

Steve was quiet, and Veronica knew that there was a lot going on inside his head. She'd mentally accused him of murder, and he'd nearly been burned alive, for one. And why? Because he had sloppy writing like her brother? What man didn't?

Freddie had asked on several occasions why these cases seemed so personal to her, and she hadn't known—at least not consciously. It frightened Veronica how irrational she had become, how her subconscious had battled and struggled to tell her what it knew, and how the rest of her brain had held strong, and kept her memories locked away like long forgotten prisoners.

What other secrets did her mind hold?

Her eyes drifted to Steve.

He had secrets, too. Veronica could sense that something from the man's past haunted him.

Freddie—Freddie had done his research on the sheriff and had offered it to her. She'd declined, citing trust. Part of her wanted to know—*desperately* wanted to know—but it felt hypocritical to ask after what she'd just told her father.

*The past is boring—it's already happened. The future is far more interesting.*

But even if the past was boring, that didn't mean it wasn't worth remembering.

"I don't want to go home just yet," she said.

"No? You want to stop somewhere for a drink?"

While Veronica could go for another drink, she had something else in mind.

"You think we can go for a drive?"

"Of course. Where to?"

"East Argham."

Veronica saw Steve's hands tighten on the steering wheel.

"No, not the house," she clarified. "Somewhere else."

The roads were empty, and they arrived at the cemetery in East Argham in just under thirty minutes. Steve, having since caught on to what she wanted to do, asked Veronica if she wanted him to come with her.

She thought about it and then nodded.

By the cemetery gates, there was a small outcropping of wild daisies that must have just sprung up with the warm weather. Veronica plucked three of them and then walked down the rows of tombstones until she found the ones she was looking for.

The two grave markings were simple, with names and dates but no inscriptions.

Steve stayed back as she approached the stones and dropped to her haunches. Veronica placed one daisy in front of the tombstone marked Trevor Davis. Then she kissed her hand and touched the rough surface. She did the exact same thing for her mother, Roberta Davis. Veronica was about to stand when her eyes fell on the empty space beside her mother's tombstone. She placed the third flower there and thought about her brother Benny. There was no tombstone for him, and there never would be.

Even though Veronica didn't remember much of Benny as a boy, in time, she thought she might recall more than just a song.

And if she didn't? Maybe she'd make something up.

Veronica slipped her hand into Steve's and squeezed it tightly. Together, they walked out of the cemetery towards his car.

As Veronica left her parents behind, she thought of the last words her brother Benjamin Davis had spoken.

*The will to survive is ingrained at birth, Lucy.*

Haunting, chilling, but undeniably true.

Amidst everything, Veronica Shade was, without a doubt, a survivor.

# END

# Author's Note

I really enjoyed writing in this new world — Veronica's world. Not only is it a departure from my regular cast and crew, but the location — fictional Bear County — is set outside of the major metropolises that I usually entertain. The places in this book are fictional, but it's not hard to locate 'sister' cities in real life. I'm very much drawn to the people and places that populate Veronica Shade's world, and I have great plans to expand them (hopefully with more success and follow through than the developers of East Argham).

Bear County has many more mysteries to unravel and criminals to apprehend, so I hope you come along for the ride.

On a personal note, thank you to everyone who stuck with me over these tumultuous and difficult past two years. I appreciate your support — writing without an audience is like spitting into a void.

It's just not nearly as satisfying.

You keep reading, I'll keep writing.

Best,

Pat
Montreal, 2022

Made in United States
Orlando, FL
19 May 2024

47012184R00211